Tales from The Lake

Volume 4

edited by:
Ben Eads

Let the world know:
#IGotMyCLPBook!

Crystal Lake Publishing
www.CrystalLakePub.com

Copyright 2017 Crystal Lake Publishing
Be sure to sign up for our newsletter and receive
two free eBooks: http://eepurl.com/xfuKP

All Rights Reserved

ISBN: 978-1-64007-469-9

Cover Design:
Ben Baldwin—http://www.benbaldwin.co.uk/

Interior Formatting:
Lori Michelle—http://www.theauthorsalley.com

Proofread by:
Paula Limbaugh
Hasse Chacon

This is a work of fiction. Names, characters, businesses, places, events and incidents are either the products of the authors' imagination or used in a fictitious manner. Any resemblance to actual persons, living or dead, or actual events is purely coincidental.

No part of this publication may be reproduced, stored in a retrieval system, or transmitted in any form or by any means, without the prior permission in writing of the publisher, nor be otherwise circulated in any form of binding or cover than that in which it is published and without a similar condition including this condition being imposed on the subsequent purchaser.

Other Anthologies by Crystal Lake Publishing

Behold! Oddities, Curiosities and Undefinable Wonders edited by Doug Murano

Gutted: Beautiful Horror Stories edited by Doug Murano and D. Alexander Ward

Tales from The Lake Vol.1 edited by Joe Mynhardt

Tales from The Lake Vol.2 edited by Joe Mynhardt, and Emma Audsley

Tales from The Lake Vol.3 edited by Monique Snyman

Fear the Reaper edited by Joe Mynhardt

For the Night is Dark edited by Ross Warren

Or check out other Crystal Lake Publishing books for your Dark Fiction, Horror, Suspense, and Thriller needs, and join our newsletter while you're there.

Copyright Acknowledgements

"The Folding Man" by Joe R. Lansdale was previously published as part of a collection in a deluxe hardcover edition by Subterranean Press, November, 2013, as well as *Drive-in Creature Feature* by Evil Jester Press. Reprinted by permission of the author.

A former version of "Liminality" by Del Howison was published in Biting Dog Press' 2012 e-book "Fresh Blood, Old Bones"—Kasey Lansdale (editor)

Table of Contents

Foreword i
  by Ben Eads

When the Dead Come Home 1
  by Jennifer Loring

The Folding Man 11
  by Joe R. Lansdale

Go Warily After Dark 34
  by Kealan Patrick Burke

To the Hills 48
  by T. E. Grau

Everything Hurts, Until it Doesn't 63
  by Damien Angelica Walters

Drowning in Sorrow 79
  by Sheldon Higdon

Whenever You Exhale, I Inhale 90
  by Max Booth III

The Withering 104
  by Bruce Golden

Grave Secrets 111
  by JG Faherty

End of the Hall 132
  by Hunter Liguore

Snowmen 152
  by David Dunwoody

Pieces of Me 161
  by T.G. Arsenault

Neighborhood Watchers............................173
  by Maria Alexander

The Story of Jessie and Me 196
  by Timothy Johnson

I will be the Reflection Until the End 216
  by Michael Bailey

The Honeymoon's Over 234
  by E.E. King

Song in a Sundress....................................240
  by Darren Speegle

Weighing In 252
  by Cynthia Ward

Reliving the Past 256
  by Michael Haynes

The Long Haul 266
  by Leigh M. Lane

Dust Devils..273
  by Mark Cassell

Liminality 301
  by Del Howison

The Gardener 315
  by Gene O'Neill

Condo by the Lake 333
  by Jeff Cercone

Foreword

I'd hate to get in the way of you enjoying these wonderful stories, so I'll be brief.

When Founder and CEO of Crystal Lake Publishing Joe Mynhardt asked me to edit Volume: 4, I was very excited as well as honored. I wanted to get away from the "urban legends" feel that the previous volumes had. I wanted something more modern that would pluck at the reader's heart strings and resonate with them, leaving them haunted for some time. In a word: *Harrowing*.

We began picking some of the best horror writers to headline the anthology. Once we opened for submissions, I received nearly eight hundred stories, which is a new record for the press. And the talent and quality made it easy short-listing the stories with the most power, whilst keeping it diverse. There's something in here for everyone. I had a blast, and sincerely mean it

The worlds you'll encounter will be dim and cold, like the water beneath your canoe. If you feel a bump underneath, don't turn off your flashlight.

Ben Eads
Orlando, Florida
August 22nd, 2017

When the Dead Come Home

JENNIFER LORING

There were worse things, she told herself, than New Jersey.

Trevor had thought it would be good for her. A smaller house (who needed all those rooms without a child to run through them?), tucked away in the woods where she wouldn't have to see her neighbors and their children and wonder, *Why me?*

There were indeed worse things than New Jersey, she told herself. But nothing worse than a dead child.

On an early summer day, boxes full of little boy's toys lay stacked by the door for Goodwill and all the detritus of their life together heaped into a U-Haul outside. "Why, Trevor?" she had shouted. "Why a swamp in the middle of nowhere?"

"It's not in the middle of nowhere. We're right in town. Once you're on your feet, you can look for a job. Listen. Heather got me a good job with the EMS, and I'm not passing it up. It's better than what I've got here."

Translation: I want you out of the house so I can fuck her in comfort on my lunch break.

Jennifer Loring

"You know they're never gonna give me the promotion with all the political bullshit that goes on here. Besides, you'll have peace and quiet."

"I don't want peace and quiet!" Kate screamed, shattering any illusion Trevor might have had that she was recovering. "I want my baby!"

Two days later, they had moved into a small ranch-style at the edge of the Pine Barrens, and she was on Zoloft within the week.

Trevor tried to cheer her up by annoying her with stories about the Jersey Devil. With an indifferent sigh, she stared out the window at the cedars that bled into the Mullica River and watched fog float on the water like the souls of all the dead things drifting in its depths. She thought about wading into the gentle current and slitting her wrists, then slipping beneath the rust-colored bog where five thousand years from now some alien archaeologist might excavate her. If she cut deep enough to scrape the blade against the bone, they would know what killed her.

"Katie," he said, massaging her shoulders, and she loathed him for it. She loathed him period.

"It's 'Kate,'" she snapped. Trevor's hands abruptly fell away from her.

"You better start dealing with this." His voice had gone cold.

She did not look at him.

***

It was easy for him to detach from the loss. He hadn't carried Aiden around inside of him for almost ten months. He didn't spend every waking moment with him, watching him learn to sit up, then walk, then talk, and finally start potty training.

When the Dead Come Home

"I hate you," she whispered when Trevor wasn't in the room and knew she hated him because life would be different if he'd never gotten her pregnant, if he'd never given her two years to love something she couldn't keep. Logically, she understood it wasn't his fault, but it had to be someone's. Her chubby, jabbering toddler lay in the ground in another state, and Trevor had taken her away from even that much. *For the best,* he'd told her.

Bullshit, she'd spat back. But she hadn't the energy to fight the move or to call a divorce lawyer. Apathy, the cheapest drug of all.

Trevor had taken to sleeping on the couch, and Kate preferred it that way. When he tried to cuddle her at night, she twisted away until he sighed with disgust and rolled over. Alone with her racing thoughts, she stared at the shadows of the pines on the wall and waited for sleep that brought only nightmares.

***

Trevor began working as much overtime as the EMS allowed. Kate grew more convinced of an affair with Heather, whom he had met in college. Although it should have been the final nail in her coffin, she couldn't make herself care. She lay in bed, listening to the eerie, faraway whistles of a train, and imagined she was running with Aiden in her arms, from the darkness. It had a face, and she couldn't run fast enough; Aiden began to cry, and he slipped from her arms and the darkness swallowed him up—

A shrill cry startled her out of her daydream. She strained to hear anything unusual, but there were only birds, the ones that made the high-pitched shrieking sound people mistook for the Jersey Devil.

And something else. Far off, like the train whistle—

Oh God Trevor why near the water you know he drowned you goddamned insensitive idiot—

—a baby was crying.

Kate shook her head. Birds, that was all. Next thing she knew, she'd have a nice padded room in the state hospital. She doubted Trevor would hesitate in having her committed. Especially if he was fucking the First Responder that drove his ambulance.

The front door opened, and Trevor threw his bag down beside it. The crying sound vanished.

"Kate? I brought pizza."

She supposed she could show him some appreciation for that. Kate wrapped herself in a pink terrycloth robe and plodded into the dining room. Trevor flipped open the lid of the pizza box as she slid into a chair.

"What's wrong?" He wrinkled his forehead in a specific way when he was forcing concern, consciously drawing his eyebrows together to create a deep, troubled V between them.

"Nothing."

He rubbed his hands on his uniform pants. "Kate, we really need to talk."

Here it comes. "I'm fucking my co-worker. Also, you're crazy. Should've called that lawyer when you had the chance, Katie."

"I know how hard this has been on you, but you're not . . . healing. Are you even taking the meds? It's really important that you do. I think you need to see another therapist, and—"

"I heard a baby crying," she said, startled by her voice's flat affect. She stared at her thighs. Two years

When the Dead Come Home

and the weight refused to budge, no matter how much cardio and strength training she endured at the local Curves. Trevor said she looked better with the extra weight, but she did not delude herself with the idea that she was some kind of Marilyn Monroe. She didn't need pizza, of all things.

He was doing it on purpose. Fattening her up so he'd have yet another excuse to leave. That bitch in the ambulance probably put him up to it.

"Maybe it was just a bird, or—"

"No. It was a baby." She let out a frustrated snort. "I know what one sounds like."

"You know, when people saw the Mothman, they often reported hearing a baby crying." Trevor fancied himself a cryptozoologist. Kate let him have his illusion. "So maybe it's some kind of weird electromagnetic disturbance, or an auditory hallucination—"

"Great, now I'm hallucinating?" Not that it was impossible by any means. Many animals found the forest hospitable, announcing their presence with various disconcerting vocalizations.

"I didn't say that. I just—"

"I know what I heard." Kate massaged the back of her neck, her head, where a headache began pounding on the walls of her skull like an angry neighbor. Heat rose behind her eyes.

"Okay, okay. Let's just . . . eat."

"I'm not crazy, Trevor," she murmured.

Trevor munched on a slice of pepperoni-with-extra-cheese and didn't say another word.

***

Trevor came home early the next night. He sat in the

kitchen, eating as usual. Leftover pizza. He'd picked up copies of John Keel's books on monsters.

Through the window beside the front door, Kate gazed at the riotous forest beyond the river. The golden, fading summer sunlight created lambent shadows between the trees and on the ground. It would be beautiful, an adjective not commonly paired with New Jersey, under different circumstances.

Yes, there were worse things than New Jersey. Like going crazy.

"Kate?" Trevor called. "What do you think about going to Atlantic City for a weekend?"

That, she knew, was Trevor's last grasp at saving their marriage. What would happen if she lost him, too? At least he was something of Aiden, even if his face bore too much a resemblance to their dead child's, making it too painful to look at him.

She started to answer "Yes" when something in the trees caught her eye. Vague at best, and small, and she could distinguish no real detail in the darkness. *A fox,* she thought.

Until she heard the baby crying.

"Trevor! Trevor, it's out there! Trev—"

Trevor came thumping into the room. "What? What's wrong?"

"Don't you hear it?"

"Hear what?"

Kate listened to water surging down the river. Leaves clinging to their last memories of summer rustled in a wind picking up strength. Nothing else.

"Oh God," she whispered.

Trevor's hands were on her arms, guiding her to

When the Dead Come Home

the couch. "Kate, I think you need to see someone who specializes in depression."

"It's only been three months, Trevor. I don't know why it's so easy for you."

"Why do you think I work all the time? So I don't have to dwell on it. I miss him as much as you do, so don't even think for one second that I don't."

"I'm sorry," she mumbled. Hot tears burned down her cheeks.

"I'll make an appointment for you tomorrow. It'll do you some good to talk to someone."

She nodded and wiped her face with her hands. She tried not to think that First Responder had encouraged him, because having a crazy wife would make the divorce that much easier. But for the first time in weeks, Trevor enclosed her in his arms as he used to, when they had a big house in Philadelphia and a little boy to love.

***

Kate couldn't sleep, not even with Trevor beside her. The Ambien had run out a week ago, and her new psychiatrist refused to extend the prescription for what she believed therapy and antidepressants could solve. That seemed to be the consensus these days.

She crept out of the bedroom and into the living room. Tree shadows striped the walls and ceiling. The room was too white, too plain. Too lifeless. The refrigerator should have been plastered with finger paintings, with pages torn from coloring books. She wanted to scrub Crayola stick people off the walls.

Outside, distant trains blasted their spectral whistles, and a shadowy deer or two galloped into the woods. Kate slumped against the glass. It began to rain, and fog rose in ghostly fingers from the ground.

The baby cried.

Her heart hammered in her chest. This time she would prove—if not to Trevor then to herself—that something was out there. She peered into the forest, waiting, hoping it wasn't a bird. Or the Jersey Devil, just her luck.

Even through the rain, the dark, and the trees, she saw the unsteady, shambling gait and knew it was no animal. It walked on two legs, and while part of her brain told her it could be a large bird, she rejected that immediately. The body was all wrong. Sometimes it fell on the rain-slicked grass but pushed itself up as it continued with great purpose toward the house. Kate shrank back from the window. The creature stretched out its maggot-white arms, opened its purple mouth, and began to shriek. The scream of a terrified two-year-old punctured her eardrums and her heart. She banged a fist against the glass.

"Aiden! It's Mommy!"

The child turned toward the river. Kate's stomach churned.

"No. Not again."

Aiden had been so precocious, sneaking out of his bed and into the bathroom because he loved water, learning how to turn on the faucets—

—floating in four inches of bathtub water, blue and limp and dead—

Kate burst through the front door. Her bare feet provided no traction on the soaked ground, and mud sucked at her ankles. She flailed wildly to keep from

When the Dead Come Home

sliding down the slight grade of their backyard. The child was mere yards from the river.

"Aiden!"

A shout more distant than it should have been met her cry. Her own name, Trevor's voice behind her, as she raced through the yard.

The baby must have gone in. She could still save him.

The water's autumnal chill filled her legs with ice and turned them into numb, useless stumps. Moonlight carved a bloody swathe through what, at night, resembled spilled ink. Kate swished her arms through the water, groping for the baby as mud oozed between her toes. Trevor's shouts were louder now. She trudged farther, waist deep, found nothing.

Kate plunged into the middle. Calmed by the earthy smell of moldering vegetation and wood, of fresh pine needles and wildflowers, she let the river carry her downstream. Fish slipped past her bare legs. She floated with the current, forgetting that she'd never let Trevor teach her how to swim. She did not share his and Aiden's fondness for water.

The cold tired her quickly, convinced her to let go, and she began to sink. She looked back once at the shore, where Trevor stood as impassive as an Eastern Island moai. She'd convinced herself the bruises on Aiden's neck were something else; he had bumped something, or fallen. Children, especially toddlers, did things like that. God, it was so easy, she thought with the terrible clarity of the dying. She was so pliant in her grief. Her entire adult life a deception that, finally, had run its course.

The pain Aiden had felt settled in her chest as

water invaded her lungs, heavy and brutal as a closed fist. In the frigid blackness, her last bubble of air was an apology to him as Trevor's voice faded into a calming burble far above.

The Folding Man
JOE R. LANSDALE

They had come from a Halloween party, having long shed the masks they'd worn. No one but Harold had been drinking, and he wasn't driving, and he wasn't so drunk he was blind. Just drunk enough he couldn't sit up straight and was lying on the back seat, trying, for some unknown reason, to recite The Pledge of Allegiance, which he didn't accurately recall. He was mixing in verses from the Star Spangled Banner and the Boy Scout oath, which he vaguely remembered from his time in the organization before they drove him out for setting fires.

Even though William, who was driving, and Jim, who was riding shotgun, were sober as Baptists claimed to be, they were fired up and happy and yelling and hooting, and Jim pulled down his pants and literally mooned a black bug of a car carrying a load of nuns.

The car wasn't something that looked as if it had come off the lot. Didn't have the look of any car maker Jim could identify. It had a cobbled look. It reminded him of something in old movies, the ones with gangsters who were always squealing their tires around corners. Only it seemed bigger, with broader windows through which he could see the nuns, or at least glimpse them in their habits; it was a regular penguin convention inside that car.

Way it happened, when they came up on the nuns, Jim said to William at the wheel, "Man, move over close, I'm gonna show them some butt."

"They're nuns, man."

"That's what makes it funny," Jim said.

William eased the wheel to the right, and Harold in the back said, "Grand Canyon. Grand Canyon. Show them the Grand Canyon . . . Oh, say can you see . . . "

Jim got his pants down, swiveled on his knees in the seat, twisted so that his ass was against the glass, and just as they passed the nuns, William hit the electric window switch and slid the glass down. Jim's ass jumped out at the night, like a vibrating moon.

"They lookin'?" Jim asked.

"Oh, yeah," William said, "and they are not amused."

Jim jerked his pants up, shifted in the seat, and turned for a look, and sure enough, they were not amused. Then a funny thing happened, one of the nuns shot him the finger, and then others followed. Jim said, "Man, those nuns are rowdy."

And now he got a good look at them, even though it was night, because there was enough light from the headlights as they passed for him to see faces hard as wardens and ugly as death warmed over. The driver was especially homely, face like that could stop a clock and run it backward or make shit crawl up hill.

"Did you see that? They shot me the finger," Jim said.

The Folding Man

"I did see it," William said.

Harold had finally gotten the Star Spangled Banner straight, and he kept singing it over and over.

"For Christ's sake," William said. "Shut up, Harold."

"You know what," Jim said, studying the rearview mirror, "I think they're speeding up. They're trying to catch us. Oh, hell. What if they get the license plate? Maybe they already have. They call the law, my dad will have my mooning ass."

"Well, if they haven't got the plate," William said, "they won't. This baby can get on up and get on out."

He put his foot on the gas. The car hummed as if it had just had an orgasm, and seemed to leap. Harold was flung off the backseat, onto the floorboard. "Hey, goddamnit," he said.

"Put on your seat belt, jackass," Jim said.

William's car was eating up the road. It jumped over a hill and dove down the other side like a porpoise negotiating a wave, and Jim thought: Goodbye, penguins, and then he looked back. At the top of the hill were the lights from the nuns' car, and the car was gaining speed and it moved in a jerky manner, as if it were stealing space between blinks of the eye.

"Damn," William said. "They got some juice in that thing, and the driver has her foot down."

"What kind of car is that?" Jim said.

"Black," William said.

"Ha! Mr. Detroit."

"Then you name it."

Jim couldn't. He turned to look back. The nuns' car had already caught up; the big automotive beast was cruising in tight as a coat of varnish, the headlights making the interior of William's machine bright as a Vegas act.

"What the hell they got under the hood?" William said. "Hyper-drive?"

"These nuns," Jim said, "they mean business."

"I can't believe it, they're riding my bumper."

"Slam on your brakes. That'll show them."

"Not this close," William said. "Do that, what it'll show them is the inside of our butts."

"Do nuns do this?"

"These do."

"Oh," Jim said. "I get it. Halloween. They aren't real nuns."

"Then we give them hell," Harold said, and just as the nuns were passing on the right, he crawled out of the floorboard and onto his seat and rolled the window down. The back window of the nuns' car went down and Jim turned to get a look, and the nun, well, she was ugly all right, but uglier than he had first imagined. She looked like something dead, and the nun's outfit she wore was not actually black and white, but purple and white, or so it appeared in the light from head beams and moonlight. The nun's lips pulled back from her teeth and the teeth were long and brown, as if tobacco stained. One of her eyes looked like a spoiled meatball, and her nostrils flared like a pig's.

Jim said, "That ain't no mask."

Harold leaned way out of the window and flailed his hands and said, "You are so goddamn ugly you have to creep up on your underwear."

Harold kept on with this kind of thing, some of it almost making sense, and then one of the nuns in the

The Folding Man

back, one closest to the window, bent over in the seat and came up and leaned out of the window, a two-by-four in her hands. Jim noted that her arms, where the nun outfit had fallen back to the elbows, were as thin as sticks and white as the underbelly of a fish and the elbows were knotty, and bent in the wrong direction.

"Get back in," Jim said to Harold.

Harold waved his arms and made another crack, and then the nun swung the two-by-four, the oddness of her elbows causing it to arrive at a weird angle, and the board made a crack of its own, or rather Harold's skull did, and he fell forward, the lower half of his body hanging from the window, bouncing against the door, his knuckles losing meat on the highway, his ass hanging inside, one foot on the floor board the other waggling in the air.

"The nun hit him," Jim said. "With a board."

"What?" William said.

"You deaf, she hit him."

Jim snapped loose his seat belt and leaned over and grabbed Harold by the back of the shirt and yanked him inside. Harold's head looked like it had been in a vise. There was blood everywhere. Jim said, "Oh, man, I think he's dead."

BLAM!

The noise made Jim jump. He slid back in his seat and looked toward the nuns. They were riding close enough to slam the two-by-four into William's car; the driver was pressing that black monster toward them.

Another swing of the board and the side mirror shattered.

William tried to gun forward, but the nuns' car was even with him, pushing him to the left. They went across the highway and into a ditch and the car did an acrobatic twist and tumbled down an embankment and rolled into the woods tossing up mud and leaves and pine straw.

***

Jim found himself outside the car, and when he moved, everything seemed to whirl for a moment, then gathered up slowly and became solid. He had been thrown free, and so had William, who was lying nearby. The car was a wreck, lying on its roof, spinning still, steam easing out from under the hood in little cotton-white clouds. Gradually, the car quit spinning, like an old time watch that had wound down. The windshield was gone and three of the four doors lay scattered about.

The nuns were parked up on the road, and the car doors opened and the nuns got out. Four of them. They were unusually tall, and when they walked, like their elbows, their knees bent in the wrong direction. It was impossible to tell this for sure, because of the robes they wore, but it certainly looked that way, and considering the elbows, it fit. There in the moonlight, they were as white and pasty as pot stickers, their jaws seeming to have grown longer than when Jim had last looked at them, their noses witch-like, except for those pig flare nostrils, their backs bent like long bows. One of them still held the two-by-four.

Jim slid over to William who was trying to sit up.

"You okay?" Jim asked.

"I think so," William said, patting his fingers at a blood spot on his forehead. "Just before they hit, I stupidly unsnapped my seat belt. I don't know why. I just wanted out I guess. Brain not working right."

The Folding Man

"Look up there," Jim said.

They both looked up the hill. One of the nuns was moving down from the highway, toward the wrecked car.

"If you can move," Jim said, "I think we oughta."

William worked himself to his feet. Jim grabbed his arm and half pulled him into the woods where they leaned against a tree. William said, "Everything's spinning."

"It stops soon enough," Jim said.

"I got to chill, I'm about to faint."

"A moment," Jim said.

The nun who had gone down by herself, bent down out of sight behind William's car, then they saw her going back up the hill, dragging Harold by his ankle, his body flopping all over as if all the bones in his body had been broken.

"My God, see that?" William said. "We got to help."

"He's dead," Jim said. "They crushed his head with a board."

"Oh, hell, man. That can't be. They're nuns."

"I don't think they are," Jim said. "Least not the kind of nuns you're thinking."

The nun dragged Harold up the hill and dropped his leg when she reached the big black car. Another of the nuns opened the trunk and reached in and got hold of something. It looked like some kind of folded up lawn chair, only more awkward in shape. The nun jerked it out and dropped it on the ground and gave it a swift kick. The folded up thing began to unfold with a clatter and a squeak. A perfectly round head rose up from it, and the head spun on what appeared to be a silver hinge. When it quit whirling, it was upright and in place, though cocked slightly to the left. The eyes and mouth and nostrils were merely holes. Moonlight could be seen through them. The head rose as coat-rack style shoulders pushed it up and a cage of a chest rose under that. The chest looked almost like an old frame on which dresses were placed to be sewn, or perhaps a cage designed to contain something you wouldn't want to get out. With more squeaks and clatters, skeletal hips appeared, and beneath that, long, bony legs with bent back knees and big metal-framed feet. Stick-like arms swung below its knees, clattering against its legs like tree limbs bumping against a window pane. It stood at least seven feet tall. Like the nuns, its knees and elbows fit backwards.

The nun by the car trunk reached inside and pulled out something fairly large that beat its wings against the night air. She held it in one hand by its clawed feet, and its beak snapped wildly, looking for something to peck. Using her free hand, she opened up the folding man's chest by use of a hinge, and when the cage flung open, she put the black, winged thing inside. It fluttered about like a heart shot full of adrenaline. The holes that were the folding man's eyes filled with a red glow and the mouth hole grew wormy lips, and a tongue, long as a garden snake, dark as dirt, licked out at the night, and there was a loud sniff as its nostrils sucked air. One of the nuns reached down and grabbed up a handful of clay, and pressed it against the folding man's arms; the clay spread fast as a lie, went all over, filling the thing with flesh of the earth until the entire folding man's body was covered. The nun who had taken the folding man out of the car picked Harold up by the ankle, and as if he were nothing more than a

The Folding Man

blow-up doll, swung him over her head and slammed him into the darkness of the trunk, shut the lid, and looked out where Jim and William stood recovering by the tree.

The nun said something, a noise between a word and a cough, and the folding man began to move down the hill at a stumble. As he moved his joints made an un-oiled hinge sound, and the rest of him made a clatter like lug bolts being knocked together, accompanied by a noise akin to wire hangers being twisted by strong hands.

"Run," Jim said.

***

Jim began to feel pain and knew he was more banged up than he thought. His neck hurt. His back hurt. One of his legs really hurt. He must have jammed his knee against something. William, who ran alongside him, dodging trees, said, "My ribs. I think they're cracked."

Jim looked back. In the distance, just entering the trees, framed in the moonlight behind him, was the folding man. He moved in strange leaps, as if there were springs inside him, and he was making good time.

Jim said, "We can't stop. It's coming."

***

It was low down in the woods and water had gathered there and the leaves had mucked up with it, and as they ran, they sloshed and splashed, and behind them, they could hear it, the folding man, coming, cracking limbs, squeaking hinges, splashing his way after them. When they had the nerve to look back, they could see him darting between the trees like a bit of the forest itself, and he, or it, was coming quite briskly for a thing its size until it reached the lower down parts of the bottom land. There its big feet slowed it some as they buried deep in the mud and were pulled free again with a sound like the universe sucking wind. Within moments, however, the thing got its stride, its movements becoming more fluid and its pace faster.

Finally Jim and William came to a tree-thickened rise in the land, and were able to get out of the muck, scramble upwards and move more freely, even though there was something of a climb ahead, and they had to use trees growing out from the side of the rise to pull themselves upward. When they reached the top of the climb, they were surprised when they looked back to see they had actually gained some space on the thing. It was some distance away, speckled by the moonlight, negotiating its way through the ever-thickening trees and undergrowth. But, still it came, ever onward, never tiring. Jim and William bent over and put their hands on their knees and took some deep breaths.

"There's an old graveyard on the far side of this stretch," Jim said. "Near the wrecking yard."

"Where you worked last summer."

"Yeah, that's the one. It gets clearer in the graveyard, and we can make good time. Get to the wrecking yard, Old Man Gordon lives there. He always has a gun and he has that dog, Chomps. It knows me. It will eat that thing up."

"What about me?"

"You'll be all right. You're with me. Come on. I kinda of know where we are now. Used to play in the graveyard, and in this end of the woods. Got to move."

***

They moved along more swiftly as Jim became more

The Folding Man

and more familiar with the terrain. It was close to where he had lived when he was a kid, and he had spent a lot of time out here. They came to a place where there was a clearing in the woods, a place where lightning had made a fire. The ground was black, and there were no trees, and in that spot silver moonlight was falling down into it, like mercury filling a cup.

In the center of the clearing they stopped and got their breath again, and William said. "My head feels like it's going to explode . . . Hey, I don't hear it now."

"It's there. Whatever it is, I don't think it gives up."

"Oh, Jesus," William said, and gasped deep once. "I don't know how much I got left in me."

"You got plenty. We got to have plenty."

"What can it be, Jimbo? What in the hell can it be?"

Jim shook his head. "You know that old story about the black car?"

William shook his head.

"My grandmother used to tell me about a black car that roams the highways and the back roads of the South. It isn't in one area all the time, but it's out there somewhere all the time. Halloween is its peak night. It's always after somebody for whatever reason."

"Bullshit."

Jim, hands still on his knees, lifted his head. "You go down there and tell that clatter clap thing it's all bullshit. See where that gets you."

"It just doesn't make sense."

"Grandma said before it was a black car, it was a black buggy, and before that a figure dressed in black on a black horse, and that before that, it was just a shadow that clicked and clacked and squeaked. There's people go missing, she said, and it's the black car, the

Joe R. Lansdale

black buggy, the thing on the horse, or the walkin' shadow that gets them. But, it's all the same thing, just a different appearance."

"The nuns? What about them?"

Jim shook his head, stood up, tested his ability to breathe. "Those weren't nuns. They were like . . . I don't know . . . anti-nuns. This thing, if Grandma was right, can take a lot of different forms. Come on. We can't stay here anymore."

"Just another moment, I'm so tired. And I think we've lost it. I don't hear it anymore."

As if on cue, there came a clanking and a squeaking and cracking of limbs. William glanced at Jim, and without a word, they moved across the lightning-made clearing and into the trees. Jim looked back, and there it was, crossing the clearing, silver-flooded in the moonlight, still coming, not tiring.

They ran. White stones rose up in front of them. Most of the stones were heaved to the side, or completely pushed out of the ground by growing trees and expanding roots. It was the old graveyard, and Jim knew that meant the wrecking yard was nearby, and so was Gordon's shotgun, and so was one mean dog.

Again the land sloped upwards, and this time William fell forward on his hands and knees, throwing up a mess of blackness. "Oh, God. Don't leave me, Jim . . . I'm tuckered . . . can hardly . . . breathe."

Jim had moved slightly ahead of William. He turned back to help. As he grabbed William's arm to pull him up, the folding man squeaked and clattered forward and grabbed William's ankle, jerked him back, out of Jim's grasp.

The folding man swung William around easily,

The Folding Man

slammed his body against a tree, then the thing whirled, and as if William were a bullwhip, snapped him so hard his neck popped and an eyeball flew out of his skull. The folding man brought William whipping down across a standing gravestone. There was a cracking sound, like someone had dropped a glass coffee cup, then the folding man whirled and slung William from one tree to another, hitting the trees so hard bark flew off of them and clothes and meat flew off William.

Jim bolted. He ran faster than he had ever ran, finally he broke free of the woods and came to a stretch of ground that was rough with gravel. Behind him, breaking free of the woods, was the folding man, making good time with great strides, dragging William's much-abused body behind it by the ankle.

***

Jim could dimly see the wrecking yard from where he was, and he thought he could make it. Still, there was the aluminum fence all the way around the yard, seven feet high. No little barrier. Then he remembered the sycamore tree on the edge of the fence, on the right side. Old Man Gordon was always talking about cutting it because he thought someone could use it to climb over and into the yard, steal one of his precious car parts, though if they did, they had Gordon's shotgun waiting along with the sizeable teeth of his dog. It had been six months since he had seen the old man, and he hoped he hadn't gotten ambitious, that the tree was still there.

Running closer, Jim could see the sycamore tree remained, tight against the long run of shiny wrecking yard fence. Looking over his shoulder, Jim saw the

Joe R. Lansdale

folding man was springing forward, like some kind of electronic rabbit, William's body being pulled along by the ankle, bouncing on the ground as the thing came ever onward. At this rate, it would be only a few seconds before the thing caught up with him.

Jim felt a pain like a knife in his side, and it seemed as if his heart was going to explode. He reached down deep for everything he had, hoping like hell he didn't stumble.

He made the fence and the tree, went up it like a squirrel, dropped over on the roof of an old car, sprang off of that and ran toward a dim light shining in the small window of a wood and aluminum shack nestled in the midst of old cars and piles of junk.

As he neared the shack, Chomps, part pit bull, part just plain big ole dog, came loping out toward him, growling. It was a hard thing to do, but Jim forced himself to stop, bent down, stuck out his hand, and called the dog's name.

"Chomps. Hey, buddy. It's me."

The dog slowed and lowered its head and wagged its tail.

"That's right. Your pal, Jim."

The dog came close and Jim gave it a pat. "Good, boy."

Jim looked over his shoulder. Nothing.

"Come on, Chomps."

Jim moved quickly toward the shack and hammered on the door. A moment later the door flew open, and standing there in overalls, one strap dangling from a naked arm, was Mr. Gordon. He was old and near toothless, squat and greasy as the insides of the cars in the yard.

The Folding Man

"Jim? What the hell you doing in here? You look like hell."

"Something's after me."

"Something?"

"It's outside the fence. It killed two of my friends..."

"What?"

"It killed two of my friends."

"It? Some kind of animal?"

"No... It."

"We'll call some law."

Jim shook his head. "No use calling the law now, time they arrive it'll be too late."

Gordon leaned inside the shack and pulled a twelve gauge into view, pumped it once. He stepped outside and looked around.

"You sure?"

"Oh, yeah. Yes, sir. I'm sure."

"Then I guess you and me and Pump Twelve will check it out." Gordon moved out into the yard, looking left and right. Jim stayed close to Gordon's left elbow. Chomps trotted nearby. They walked about a bit. They stopped between a row of wrecked cars, looked around. Other than the moon-shimmering fence at either end of the row where they stood, there was nothing to see.

"Maybe whatever, or whoever it is, is gone," Gordon said. "Otherwise, Chomps would be all over it."

"I don't think it smells like humans or animals."

"Are you joshin' an old man? Is this a Halloween prank?"

"No, sir. Two of my friends are dead. This thing killed them. It's real."

Joe R. Lansdale

"What the hell is it then?"

As if in answer, there was the sound like a huge can opener going to work, and then the long, thin arm of the folding man poked through the fence and there was more ripping as the arm slid upwards, tearing at the metal. A big chunk of the fence was torn away, revealing the thing, bathed in moonlight, still holding what was left of William's ragged body by the ankle.

Jim and Gordon both stood locked in amazement.

"Sonofabitch," Gordon said.

Chomps growled, ran toward it.

"Chomps will fix him," Gordon said.

The folding man dropped William's ankle and bent forward, and just as the dog leaped, caught it and twisted it and ran its long arm down the snapping dog's throat, and began to pull its insides out. It flung the dog's parts in all directions, like someone pulling confetti from a sack. Then it turned the dog inside out.

When the sack was empty, the folding man bent down and fastened the dead, deflated dog to a hook on the back of what passed for its ankle.

"My God," Gordon said.

The thing picked up William by the ankle, stepped forward a step, and paused.

Gordon lifted the shotgun. "Come and get you some, asshole."

The thing cocked its head as if to consider the suggestion, and then it began to lope toward them, bringing along its clanks and squeaks, the dead dog flopping at the folding man's heel. For the first time, its mouth, which had been nothing but a hole with wormy lips, twisted into the shape of a smile.

Gordon said, "You run, boy. I got this."

The Folding Man

Jim didn't hesitate. He turned and darted between a row of cars and found a gap between a couple of Fords with grass grown up around their flattened tires, ducked down behind one, and hid. He lay down on his belly to see if he could see anything. There was a little bit of space down there, and he could look under the car, and under several others, and he could see Gordon's feet. They had shifted into a firm stance, and Jim could imagine the old man pulling the shotgun to his shoulder.

And even as he imagined, the gun boomed, and then it boomed again. Silence, followed by a noise like someone ripping a piece of thick cardboard in half, and then there were screams and more rips. Jim felt lightheaded and realized he hadn't been breathing. He gasped for air, feared that he had gasped too loudly.

Oh, my God, he thought. I ran and left it to Mr. Gordon, and now . . . He was uncertain. Maybe the screams had come from . . . It, the folding man? But so far it hadn't so much as made breathing sounds, let alone anything that might be thought of as a vocalization.

Crawling like a soldier under fire, Jim worked his way to the edge of the car, and took a look. Stalking down the row between the cars was the folding man, and he was dragging behind him by one ankle what was left of William's body. In his other hand, if you could call it a hand, he had Mr. Gordon, who looked thin now because so much had been pulled out of him. Chomps' body was still fastened to the wire hook at the back of the thing's foot. As the folding man came forward, Chomps dragged in the dirt.

Jim pushed back between the cars, and kept

pushing, crawling backwards. When he was far enough back, he raised to a squat and started between narrower rows that he thought would be harder for the folding man to navigate; they were just spaces really, not rows, and if he could go where it couldn't go, then—

There was a large creaking sound, and Jim, still at a squat, turned to discover its source. The folding man was looking at him. It had grabbed an old car and lifted it up by the front and was holding it so that the back end rested on the ground. Being as close as he was now, Jim realized the folding man was bigger than he had thought, and he saw too that just below where the monster's thick torso ended there were springs, huge springs, silver in the moonlight, vibrating. He had stretched to accommodate the lifting of the car, and where his knees bent backwards, springs could be seen as well; he was a garage sale collection of parts and pieces.

For a moment, Jim froze. The folding man opened his mouth wide, wider than Jim had seen before, and inside he could glimpse a turning of gears and a smattering of sparks. Jim broke suddenly, running between cars, leaping on hoods, scrambling across roofs, and behind him came the folding man, picking up cars and flipping them aside as easily as if they had been toys.

Jim could see the fence at the back, and he made for that, and when he got close to it, he thought he had it figured. He could see a Chevy parked next to the fence, and he felt certain he could climb onto the roof, spring off of it, grab the top of the fence, and scramble over. That wouldn't stop the thing behind him, but it

The Folding Man

would perhaps give him a few moments to gain ground.

The squeaking and clanking behind him was growing louder.

There was a row of cars ahead, he had to leap onto the hood of the first, then spring from hood to hood, drop off, turn slightly right, and go for the Chevy by the fence.

He was knocked forward, hard, and his breath leaped out of him.

He was hit again, painfully in the chest.

It took a moment to process, but he was lying between two cars, and there, standing above him, was the folding man, snapping at him with the two dead bodies like they were wet towels. That's what had hit him, the bodies, used like whips.

Jim found strength he didn't know he had, made it to his feet as Mr. Gordon's body slammed the ground near him. Then, as William's body snapped by his ear, just missing him, he was once more at a run.

The Chevy loomed before him. He made its hood by scrambling up on hands and knees, and then he jumped to the roof. He felt something tug at him, but he jerked loose, didn't stop moving. He sprang off the car top, grabbed at the fence, latching his arms over it. The fence cut into the undersides of his arms, but he couldn't let that stop him, so he kept pulling himself forward, and the next thing he knew, he was over the fence, dropping to the ground.

It seemed as if a bullet had gone up through his right foot, which he now realized was bare, and that the tug he had felt was the folding man grabbing at his foot, only to come away with a shoe. But of more

Joe R. Lansdale

immediate concern was his foot, the pain. There hadn't been any bullet. He had landed crooked coming over the fence, and his foot had broken. It felt like hell, but he moved on it anyway, and within a few steps he had a limp, a bad limp.

He could see the highway ahead, and he could hear the fence coming down behind him, and he knew it was over, all over, because he was out of gas and had blown a tire and his engine was about to blow too. His breath came in chops and blood was pounding in his skull like a thug wanting out.

He saw lights. They were moving very quickly down the highway. A big truck, a Mack, was balling the jack in his direction. If he could get it to stop, maybe there would be help, maybe.

Jim stumbled to the middle of the highway, directly into the lights, waved his arms, glanced to his left—

—and there it was. The folding man. It was only six feet away.

The truck was only a little farther away, but moving faster, and then the folding man was reaching for him, and the truck was a sure hit, and Jim, pushing off his good foot, leaped sideways and there was a sound like a box of dishes falling downstairs.

***

Jim felt the wind from the truck, but he had moved just in time. The folding man had not. As Jim had leaped aside, his body turned, through no plan of his own, and he saw the folding man take the hit.

Wood and springs and hinges went everywhere.

The truck bumped right over the folding man and started sliding as the driver tried to put on brakes that

The Folding Man

weren't designed for fast stops. Tires smoked, brakes squealed, the truck fishtailed.

Jim fell to the side of the highway, got up and limped into the brush there, and tripped on something and went down. He rolled on his back. His butt was in a ditch and his back was against one side of it, and he could see above it on the other side, and through some little bushes that grew there. The highway had a few lights on either side of it, so it was lit up good, and Jim could see the folding man lying in the highway, or rather he could see parts of it everywhere. It looked like a dirty hardware store had come to pieces. William, Gordon, and Chomps lay in the middle of the highway.

The folding man's big torso, which had somehow survived the impact of the truck, vibrated and burst open, and Jim saw the bird-like thing rise up with a squawk. It snatched up the body of Mr. Gordon and William, one in either claw, used its beak to nab the dog, and ignoring the fact that its size was not enough to lift all that weight, it did just that, took hold of them and went up into the night sky, abruptly became one with the dark.

Jim turned his head. He could see down the highway, could see the driver of the truck getting out, walking briskly toward the scene of the accident. He walked faster as he got closer, and when he arrived, he bent over the pieces of the folding man. He picked up a spring, examined it, tossed it aside. He looked out where Jim lay in the ditch, but Jim figured, lying as he was, brush in front of him, he couldn't be seen.

He was about to call out to the driver when the truck driver yelled, "You nearly got me killed. You

Joe R. Lansdale

nearly got you killed. Maybe you are killed. I catch you, might as well be, you stupid shit. I'll beat the hell out of you."

Jim didn't move.

"Come on out so I can finish you off."

Great, Jim thought, first the folding man, and now a truck driver wants to kill me. To hell with him, to hell with everything, and he laid his head back against the ditch and closed his eyes and went to sleep.

***

The truck driver didn't come out and find him, and when he awoke the truck was gone and the sky was starting to lighten. His ankle hurt like hell. He bent over and looked at it. He couldn't tell much in the dark, but it looked as big as a sewer pipe. He thought when he got some strength back, he might be able to limp, or crawl out to the edge of the highway, flag down some help. Surely, someone would stop. But for the moment, he was too weak. He laid back again, and was about to close his eyes, when he heard a humming sound.

Looking out at the highway, he saw lights coming from the direction the trucker had come from. Fear crawled up his back like a spider. It was the black car.

The car pulled to the side of the road and stopped. The nuns got out. They sniffed and extended long tongues and licked at the fading night. With speed and agility that seemed impossible, they gathered up the parts of the folding man and put them in a sack they placed in the middle of the highway.

When the sack was full of parts, one nun stuck a long leg into the sack and stomped about, then jerked her leg out, pulled the sack together at the top and

The Folding Man

swung it over her head and slammed it on the road a few times, then she dropped the sack and moved back and one of the nuns kicked it. Another nun opened up and reached inside the sack and took out the folding man. Jim lost a breath. It appeared to be put back together. The nun didn't unfold the folding man. She opened the trunk of the car and flung it inside.

And then she turned and looked in his direction, held out one arm and waited. The bird-thing came flapping out of the last of the dark and landed on her arm. The bodies of William and Gordon were still in its talons, the dog in its beak, the three of them hanging as if they were nothing heavier than rags. The nun took hold of the bird's legs and tossed it and what it held into the trunk as well. She closed the lid of the trunk. She looked directly where Jim lay. She looked up at the sky, turned to face the rising sun. She turned quickly back in Jim's direction and stuck out her long arm, the robe folding back from it. She pointed a stick like finger right at him, leaned slightly forward. She held that pose until the others joined her and pointed in Jim's direction.

My God, Jim thought, they know I'm here. They see me. Or smell me. Or sense me. But they know I'm here.

The sky brightened and outlined them like that for a moment and they stopped pointing.

They got quickly in the car. The last of the darkness seemed to seep into the ground and give way to a rising pink; Halloween night had ended. The car gunned and went away fast. Jim watched it go a few feet, and then it wasn't there anymore. It faded like fog. All that was left now was the sunrise and the day turning bright.

Go Warily After Dark
KEALAN PATRICK BURKE

I

The bombs fell just after midnight.

They tell you to prepare for such things. There are drills, kits, leaflets and posters, stern voices instructing you over the radio, but nothing can prepare the human mind for the sound of the world coming down. It is as if the devil has felled God. It is thunder from above and below. It is the very earth sundering. It is a single prolonged moment of chaos and destruction. It is The End. For months, since the retaliatory statements from their chancellor, we had lived in fear that this day would come, but as the days stretched on and the weeks went by, we did what people in fear will do and reached a sort of numb acceptance infused with a vein of hopeful doubt. If they were truly going to attack the city, then where were they? Wouldn't they have struck already? What were they waiting for? Such frail hopes, however, were easily thwarted. The city had become lightless, blacked out so as not to make a target of itself, which seemed a rather pointless exercise when the enemy already

Go Warily After Dark

knew where to strike. People walked blindly through the streets, narrowly avoided the cars and buses with their extinguished headlights, and stumbled on in a daze, confused at this new dark world in which they found themselves marooned.

The soldiers came with their portable shelters, little more than caged tables, cheap and shoddy forms of protection for those of us who did not have yards in which to build proper ones. They gave us gas masks and told us how to use them. Wear them always, they told us, and for a while we did, until our faces grew too hot and too sore, and the smell of the rubber gave us headaches. Mostly we sat around the rabbit hutch table and enjoyed the silence with tension making us as rigid as the chairs. And at night, we dutifully pulled down the black curtains and turned out all but the weakest of lights. In the feeble glow, we huddled together like the refugees we feared we'd one day become at the behest of an enemy to whom we had done nothing, and we listened. When we spoke, it was merely a whisper, as if the threat might not be limited to the skies above, as if night's dark agents might be abroad, faces pressed to the windows, ears attuned to the slightest of sounds.

Sleep became a luxury few could afford. Often, there were sirens, howling up into the night like a stricken animal pleading for mercy. Instantly, we woke from restless slumber, muscles tightening, bodies subconsciously braced for impact, for death. The hair on the body rose; the heart began to race. The children, still sleepy headed, hurried into my arms, as if that could ever be adequate protection. My husband stood guard by the window, peeking through the tiny perforation in the black plastic. And always, there was nothing to report. By the time the sirens fell silent again, sleep had fled. Exhausted, we lay on the floor staring up at the cracks in the ceiling, thinking them nothing less than the blueprint of its destruction.

During the day, my husband worked. He was gone by dawn, drunk by six.

I sent the children to school where I knew they could learn nothing, washed their clothes, tried to keep up the pretense that this was still our home and not a brick prison waiting to collapse. It made my dutiful ministrations seem foolish. Bombs care little for scrubbed floors. To counter the malaise, I played scratched music on the tired Victrola, but found no reprieve in the rapturous heights of those arias. Instead, I was stricken by the profound and long delayed realization that, quite often, those women sung of war and tragedy, grief and loss. Thus, it was not joy I heard in their heavenly voices, but sorrow and anger. I felt no kinship with these strangers. Many of them had already died, the others away where windows did not need to be blackened and voices did not need to be muted. Safe.

For much of the day, I sat in silence and stared at the cracks above my head, the pattern that portended a terrible fate, and waited for my children to come home, my nose filled with the acrid stench of smoke from fires I couldn't see.

II

The night the bombs fell, the children were sleeping. We had moved them down into the basement, a closet

Go Warily After Dark

sized room with a dirt floor and walls of hardened clay, the shoddy joists making it seem more like the gullet of some diseased animal than a sanctuary. It had been presented by the soldiers as a haven, a better bet, in any case, than the exposure of the main floor. Both my husband and I had resisted, and when we spoke of it amongst ourselves, the suggestion was instantly dismissed by the tone used to convey it as a possibility. Without knowing why, we did not want to send our children down there into the dirty dark. We had lived in the house for six years by then, and had ventured into the basement only a handful of times, three of those without clear reason. Once, after falling asleep on the sofa, my husband had woken up to find himself standing in that tiny room in the pitch dark. Blind, he had screamed himself hoarse and clawed at the walls, the tendrils of roots brushing between his fingers, fearing he had somehow been buried alive. That Christmas, I stashed the gifts on the uppermost step of the rickety wooden stairs, knowing the children would never look there, and returned Christmas Eve to find them gone. Rats, my husband said, they'll eat anything. We laid traps, and the traps disappeared, too.

After that miserable Christmas, in which we'd been forced to gift our children cheap consolation prizes, we closed the stolid wooden door and bolted it shut. We did not discuss it. There was simply nothing down in that room we wanted or needed, hence, no cause to venture down there again. Of course, these were the naïve pre-war days. Once the sirens began their wailing on a nightly basis, and there were sounds of percussive strikes on the horizon, we stopped thinking of the unpleasantness of unused rooms, the silly fear of inexplicable things, and began making a rudimentary shelter in the basement. The room did not run the length of our house. It was a design decision that confounded my husband and nulled its usefulness as anything other than a hiding space. Not a basement, but a nook. Perhaps, he said, it had been abandoned before they'd had a chance to finish it. It was the only thing that made sense, and though the wooden braces supporting all four walls suggested the job had been completed to the architect's satisfaction, I did not feel compelled to argue. By then, it hardly mattered.

April 20th, soldiers at the door instructed us to go down into the shelter and stay there. They were ashen faced, their eyes large and glassy, and did not seem possessed of the kind of bravery necessary to emerge victorious from the fray. It hardly instilled hope. Though bound to protect the citizens, many of them seemed more inclined to join them in their shelters, or run far away from the danger. I could hardly blame them. With some blankets to protect against the frigid cold down below, and some bottles of water, a loaf of bread and a wedge of cheese, we hurried into the basement and pulled the door shut behind us, the air sirens already yowling at our backs.

Only this time, they did not stop.

The bombs fell after midnight.

The sound was like all the engines of the world breaking down at once, or as if a locomotive had been dropped from the sky. The human ear is not designed to process such cacophony, and as one we winced, our hands clamped to the sides of our heads.

Go Warily After Dark

The roar made a mockery of my husband's whispered assurances, sucked the life from his words. As if he were an expert in such things, he quickly changed tactics, began to speculate loudly about which part of the town the bombs might have fallen. "That's probably the barracks," he said. "Or maybe the port." Pointing out that those two locations were at opposite ends of the town would have accomplished nothing, so I stayed silent, listened to the drone of the aircraft, the whistling of the bombs, the pounding of the explosions. Vibrations carried through the dirt walls, shuddering our organic unit. The children were wrapped around us, their heads buried in the folds of our clothes, dampening them with their tears. They wept soundlessly. My husband jolted with each explosion, his voice high and reedy. I could smell the whiskey on his breath but did not, as was customary, resent him for it. When the world wants to kill you, a bottle is as good a place to hide as a basement.

"Jesus Christ in Heaven," he said. "We forgot the gas masks. I should go get them."

"You'll do no such thing," I told him, and refrained from adding that if a bomb fell close enough to do us harm, it wasn't likely to be the gas that killed us.

More explosions, thunder through the walls, and dirt rained down from the ceiling. My daughter screamed into my stomach. My son buried his face deeper into my husband's shirt. The dozen or so candles we had set around us in a crude semicircle fluttered, sending shadows carousing around the room.

"They might be getting closer," my husband said. "But we'll be okay. We'll be safe down here."

Kealan Patrick Burke

I looked at him, glad he was here with us, but struck by how unfamiliar he appeared in his fear. Previously I had only ever known him as a strong man, determined, capable but not altogether liberal with his emotions, particularly love. He was a good father and kind, but often I could see when he was too tired or unwilling to handle the demands of the job. Dependent on the light on a given day, I sometimes detected shreds of lost dreams in his eyes, the vestigial traces of squandered ambition and goals unattained. We did not marry for love, but we had found the threads of it over time, mostly through the children that had necessitated our formal union. And now, here, on what might be the end of the world, I found his fear humanized him in a way his love never could, maybe because there was no doubting its legitimacy.

Another violating thrust as another bomb penetrated the city. More dirt rained on our heads. One of the candles went out. The room shook and I held my daughter tighter to my chest. Her fingers were claws, nails drawing blood from my sides. I did not tell her to ease off, would have let her crawl inside me if it meant she'd be safe.

"We'll be okay," my husband said again. "We'll be okay."

I did not believe him. He had ceased his speculation about the location of the strikes, because they were getting closer, the last sounding as if it had hit a few streets away to the east. I looked away from him, the evident fear on his face only exacerbating my own, and straight ahead into the dark beyond the small arc of candles. There, I saw a pale smudge of something illuminated in the guttering flame, like a

Go Warily After Dark

crooked stripe of paint on the opposite wall. Candle-shadow animated it, made it twist in on itself like a dash of milk in water. Perhaps the wall was crumbling. It filled me with dread that instead of the quick mercy of death from a sudden explosion, we might instead slowly die from suffocation as the walls gave way and the ceiling came down, choking us with dirt.

Further movement, this time closer to the floor, nearer the candles. My labored imagination and the poor light told me it was a spider, though I had never seen one quite so large. The splintered nails at the tips of its feet as it approached the flame told me I had been foolish in seeing it as anything other than a gnarled hand. My spine went rigid with shock, even as I reminded myself that now, under the existential stress of potential annihilation, I was likely to see and imagine anything from hands to enemy soldiers materializing from those walls.

"All right now," my husband said, hushing the anguish from our son. "Everything will be—"

The bomb that hit was not direct, as I would discover later. It hit the houses across the street from us, leveling most of that row, but the impact blew out our windows and most of the front wall, turned our furniture to splinters and collapsed the ceiling. Everything on the second floor tumbled down into the first, caving in the rabbit hutch the soldiers had assured would protect us in the event of such a calamity. None of the protective measures would have saved us, and I found myself thinking back to the reaction from one of the soldiers, little more than a boy, who had shaken his head at the mention of us remaining in our homes. "Unless you have an exterior shelter, it's better to leave than take the chance," he'd said. "Otherwise it'll be like trying to stop a tank with an umbrella." But this was our home. We could not afford to leave the city even if we'd had someplace else to go. And always that nagging doubt that the country was overreacting to verbal threats that would yield no physical retaliation. We were stubborn, and we stayed, held in place by some atavistic notion that we were merely caught in a dream from which we would inevitably awake before it could hurt us.

As the house above us fell, a cascade of dirt from the basement ceiling buried us from the waist down. The wall at my back crumbled, not completely, but enough so that I found myself reclined into a hollow, my mouth full of roots. Roots that seemed to move, fumbling like worms against my cheeks and eyes and between my lips, though that was most likely my own frantic attempt to be free of the concavity. Through the fall of dirt, I saw my husband bend over and clutch our son harder, and despite the madness, I felt a swell of love and gratitude for him, made myself a solemn promise to whomever might have the power to grant salvation, that if I survived, I would try to love him more, even if he was not emotionally capable of reciprocity.

I grabbed onto my daughter's frail quivering shoulders and screamed in anguished protest at the war, at the insanity of it all, and tasted coarse dry dirt on my tongue and in my throat. Why? I raged. Why us when we had done nothing to anyone but live our lives in a country that had challenged another? We were not the authority, the instigators. We were not the antagonists, but the spectators, the people in other

Go Warily After Dark

rooms who only heard the mumblings of discontent through the walls. Why should *we* die? A lifetime of struggling, of trying to get by, undone in a heartbeat as a punctuation mark to a disagreement among strangers.

The hail of dirt subsided, the rumbling ceased. Other than the occasional sound of something shifting in the remains of the rooms above, it was quiet. My ears rang. It would be some time before I could hear properly again.

Only a single candle had endured the fall of dirt and dust. It guttered, appeared to die, then returned to cast its meager light through the haze. And in that feeble light, I saw a woman sitting against the opposite wall. I gave an involuntary gasp. She was no more than six feet away, but the light and the dust rendered her indistinct. Her crooked posture suggested injury, her eyes and mouth mere black thumbprints of shadow in the dirty gray egg of her face. I had the impression of an old print dress swaddling an oddly shaped body. She was sitting, her feet pointing toward the stairs. One foot was upside down, the toes buried in the floor. Her head faced in the opposite direction, turned slightly away from us. There were strange folds in the flesh of her neck. The bomb must have twisted her and flung her across the street and down here with us.

Dirty air rushed into the room from the holes in the ceiling.

I alerted my husband. It took him some time to hear me. When he looked at me, I saw that there was a nasty gash running from between his eyes up into his hairline. It was bleeding furiously down onto his shirt. He blinked rapidly and smiled at me with dirt-darkened teeth.

Kealan Patrick Burke

"We're going . . . to be . . . okay," he said, and looked down at our son. The boy, lying half in the dirt, looked up at him, his eyes watery with panic.

I looked back into the dark.

The woman had moved and now her face and upper body were facing the wall. Her lower body had not changed position. Her feet were still pointed toward the stairs. But now her arms were raised, broken hands hanging loosely at shoulder height as if she were attempting some strange interpretation of an Egyptian dance. From the wall around her, more dirt tumbled as other hands began to worm their way through into the basement.

Rescuers? I wondered, and then I was being shaken violently enough to make my teeth clack together. Confused, I looked at my husband. He was very close and snarling at me. He must have gone mad. He was shaking me, then shoving me, then pulling our daughter out of my arms. Her nails dragged more furrows in my flesh. She was not moving. Her mouth was open and full of dirt. Wet warmth trickled from my nose. I brought a hand up to probe it and saw that I was holding the knife I had brought to cut the bread.

I mouthed questions into the darkness. No one answered.

I looked to the lady sitting by the far wall and saw that she had moved again. She was kneeling before me now, weaving slightly, using her weight to force her broken neck to bring her head around to where she needed it. Trying to face me.

My husband screamed in anguish. I dared not look. He was gesticulating wildly above the inert body of our daughter.

Go Warily After Dark

With a grunt, the old lady's head swiveled around to regard me, allowing me to see that her labors had been in vain. Somebody had stitched her eyes shut with black shoelaces. Her mouth too, but not tightly enough to deny her a smile.

My husband lunged at me, his hands hooked into claws. I saw that he was screaming, but heard nothing but the ringing in my own ears and the very faint sound of the old lady's laughter.

Over her shoulder as my husband's hands found my throat, I saw that our son had crawled into the corner away from the chaos. From the dirt wall, a multitude of hands reached for him like plants drawn to the light.

"If you wish to see them, close your eyes," said the old woman.

I did as she requested, imagined what it would feel like to never have to open them again, and felt the old lady's hand guide my own, guide the knife, up and toward my husband's neck.

The next bomb reduced the house to rubble.

III

The shelling continued for three more days.

The basement withstood it all, only coming down at the behest of the rescuers' picks and shovels.

By that time, I had gone quite mad with grief and horror and sorrow. They took me to a mobile hospital and treated my injuries, most of which were superficial. In soothing tones, people—whether doctors, soldiers, or something else, I'll never know—informed me that my husband and two children had yet to be found. They advised me not to give up hope. Quite the contrary, they said. If the bodies were not in the basement, then it was quite likely they'd escaped and would find their way home in due course. But these people know nothing of errant Christmas presents and rat traps, of broken bodied old women with stitched up eyes, and of pale clambering hands bursting from the walls. Despite the authority in their voices, they are quite ignorant indeed.

They released me a week later, and I walked through a metropolis of debris, of fire and smoke, of pain and misery, of fear and confusion, to find my home. I missed it twice and had to backtrack. Home is harder to find when its face has been removed. Once I located the ruin in which I had married and raised my children, some kindly men assisted me in clearing some of the rubble that had fallen since my rescue, exposing for me the now exposed basement. I thanked them, dismissed their advice to stay clear, and clambered my way into the remains of that square of dirt. The walls were gone. Only the floor remained. The candle was there too and I lit it with one of the three items I had taken from the hospital.

In the dirt, I sat and waited until the street and the city fell silent.

The moon rose high above my ruin, casting a patchwork of shadows on my face as the old woman's voice echoed through the feverish chambers of desperate memory.

"If you wish to see them, close your eyes."

From my pocket, I produced the other two items I had brought: a needle and some black thread.

She whispered to me of history, and of the future,

Go Warily After Dark

and of holes blown in the earth by uneducated men, of broken prisons and freedom, and of old ones come again. She whispered to me of pain.

While I worked, and when it was time, the old lady's hand grew like a weed from the bloodied dirt before me, and pinched out the candle flame.

By then, I didn't need the light.

To The Hills
T.E. GRAU

Daddy woke me up that night, and put his finger to my lips so I wouldn't scream, just like he said he would. That's how I knew.

"Is this it?" I whispered.

"Yes it is," he whispered back. I didn't need to hear the confirmation, because his face told me everything.

We'd practiced this before, he and I. He and Brother practiced separate. Mommy and he did too, he'd said, but in a different way, because adults needed to worry about different things.

"Dress rehearsal for the end of the world," he'd called it.

But that night, it was the real thing. Rehearsals were over.

It *was* the end of the world.

***

I got up and got dressed, extra quiet, just like he'd shown me, putting on warm clothes even though it was July. My travel pack was ready, stuffed tight with five pairs of underwear and socks, five T-shirts, two pairs

To The Hills

of jeans, one wool sweater, a knitted scarf and hat, spare boots a size too big, toothpaste and brush, a bottle of shampoo, hair ties, a compass, a hatchet, pocket knife, and a .22 caliber pistol that I'd shot exactly twelve times, hitting four bottles and a tin can. Firing the gun had scared me. I even cried a little, but Daddy said it was important, to build up muscle memory and lay down a new line of instinct. Probably the *most* important.

"You need to know how to use this," he'd said, a frown in his voice. "Against them. You understand?"

"Yes sir," I'd said, looking down at the pistol, feeling how hot it was after I fired it empty.

"And if they get me, if they get me first, you know what to do, right?"

I didn't say anything. I knew what to do, which was why I didn't answer.

***

I pulled the heavy backpack over both shoulders, shrugged it high and tightened the straps, then headed out into the hallway. Daddy was shutting his bedroom door, fastening it behind him with the extra lock none of the other doors had. He'd gotten dressed faster than I did. He'd obviously been practicing more than me.

I stood before him, not moving, hoping it was all a dream and I was still back in my bed. He gave me one last inspection, rifle in one hand, flashlight in the other, full pack slung over his back. He looked about twelve feet tall. A monster killer.

"Let's go," he said.

***

I followed him down the stairs into the living room. The entire house was dark, the silence of the late hour cut weird by the heavy things we carried clinking against each other inside our packs.

"Where's Mommy?" I whispered. "Where's Brother?"

"I sent them on ahead, in the other car," he said, not whispering as well as I was. He didn't have as much practice at that. Not by a long shot. "We're going to need two."

"They're already at the cabin?"

"They're on their way."

I always knew if this day came, I'd be riding up with him. Brother and Mommy were more alike, closer. Daddy and I were the same. I was a daddy's girl and he was a girl's daddy.

"I'll pray for them. To make it there safe."

"Pray for the other ones, too," he said.

I never did.

***

We walked outside. Daddy closed and locked the door behind him, turning the knob to make sure it was secure. He picked up the spare key under the concrete turtle and put it in his pocket.

There wasn't a sound in the neighborhood, nor any lights. It looked abandoned, and might have been, if they got the news before we did. Mommy and Brother were already gone, so why not the neighbors too? Still, you would think a dog would bark, a car would drive by, but nothing.

"Why's it so quiet?"

"Because they're coming," he said. "And everyone's hiding."

***

Daddy stowed our packs in the bed of the pickup,

To The Hills

sliding them close to the front wall to keep them out of the wind. Boxes of canned food and bottled water were already there, as were four blankets wrapped in twine, a tool box, and a plastic tub filled with ammunition.

I climbed into the cab of his truck; the overhead light didn't come on. He must have turned it off sometime before, sensing what was coming, or just because he was prepared. He was always prepared. The food, tools, and bullets in back confirmed it. I asked him once if he was ever in the Boy Scouts and he just laughed.

I slid down onto the floor like he'd shown me while he climbed in behind the wheel, the weight of his body tilting the suspension on his side. I wanted to take a last look at our house, at the window to my room, in case we never came back, or in case they tore the place down before we could come back.

Daddy pushed the top of my head below the sightline of the window, hurting my neck a little.

"Keep your head down," he said. "Remember? You don't know who's watching."

"They have people watching?" I said.

"I don't know. I don't know everything. But just because I don't know, doesn't mean it can't be true."

He started the engine, grimacing at the sound it made as the eight pistons chugged to life. He carefully put the truck in gear, backed out of the driveway, and drove up the street. I never did get to see our house that one last time.

***

I lay on the floor, breathing through my nose, taking in the rubber odor of the floor mats, the paving tar stuck to my daddy's boots, the particular scent of his jeans, which always smelled like him, no matter how many times Mommy washed them.

Mommy and Brother were probably waiting for us by now. I smiled a little bit, despite myself and the situation, imagining them on the same road, nervous too but lighting the way, setting up the cabin for us until the other pair arrived, completing the square, making each angle right. We'd all make it up there, I just knew. Nothing could get to us when we were all together. Not even what my daddy said would come someday, with that day being tonight.

The road hummed just below me, occasionally grinding over rough parts of the cement, the tires sometimes drifting over the raised pavement markers that glowed yellow like an animal's eyes. We were on the highway, which sounded different than the roads.

After several minutes, lulled by the rhythm of motor and movement, I stretched out my legs one by one, and then my arms, because I was young and my bones were growing and couldn't help but fidget. My fingers accidently grazed the radio button and Daddy snatched my wrist tight. His hand was hard and dry and could have snapped my bones like matchsticks. I always thought he was the strongest man in the world, and hoped I'd never have to find out otherwise now that it was the end of the world. I knew he'd be up for the task, the fight, the killing when it came to it, but it was the other stuff that I worried about. The day-to-day things. Decisions. Daddy didn't always make the best decisions.

"What did I tell you about that?" he said, his grip tightening on my wrist. I couldn't see his face, just the

To The Hills

side of his body, and his arm connected to my own, skin to skin. His hand was hurting me. I don't think he knew his own strength sometimes.

"To never touch the radio," I said.

"That's right. You *never* touch the radio. Ever. You hear me?"

"Yes, Daddy."

"What did I tell you? Why don't you ever touch the radio?"

"You don't want me to hear."

"That's right. I don't want you to hear. It won't be good for you to hear. Don't you get that?"

He let go of my wrist, and it ached. I clutched it close to my body, curling my other hand around it as the engine decelerated, the truck turned, and the sound of the highway under me changed as we sped back up. The surface under the tires was softer, smoother. It was asphalt. We were on the roads now, heading to the hills.

***

There wasn't any light out there. No streetlamps, stoplights, no glow from the city behind us. Not even any stars. Not on that night. This was dark country, broken every so often by the pale glow of an overnight security light set high on a pole to mark each farmhouse we passed. As the hours wore on, even those lights disappeared, and then it was just dark.

Daddy lit up a cigarette, leaving the window up. He'd quit seven years ago, and promised my mom he'd never smoke again.

"Why are you doing that, Daddy?" I asked from the floor, watching him, his face reflected in the dim glow of the console lights.

T. E. Grau

He took a deep drag and held it, then blew it out slowly, the smoke billowing from his lungs like castle fog in old scary movies. "What does it matter now?" he said.

I didn't like that answer, and wished that he'd roll down his window. I didn't mind the smell of cigarettes when they were fresh, because it reminded me of something that I couldn't quite remember from my childhood. My early childhood, probably toddler years. But it was a pleasant memory, even vague as it was. But I still wanted him to roll down his window, because the cab was filling up with smoke. Fresh air had collected up under the bench seat, so I put my mouth there, breathing through my lips.

Daddy smoked the whole cigarette, putting it out in the empty ashtray next to the radio, and then never smoked another one the rest of the time.

***

I think I was asleep. I could have been daydreaming, at night, but I was probably asleep when the sound of the truck hitting something in the road jarred me alert. It must have been big, heavy, based on the sound of impact and how high the truck lurched off the ground as it went right over it. And it made a noise, that thing we hit. A sort of groan.

I screamed from the floor of the truck.

"Quiet!" Daddy shouted, realigning the tires on the road.

"What was that?" I leaned up to look out the window. I couldn't see anything beyond the glass. Everything was black. "What did we hit?"

"Nothing you need to worry about."

I expected him to push me down onto the floor again, but he didn't.

To The Hills

"Was it one of them?"

"Who?" he asked quickly, like he always did when a question was more than a question.

"You know." I certainly wasn't going to say it. Not out loud, not even to myself. I held out my hands, doing an impression of a lurching creature from all the horror films and some of the TV shows.

Daddy shrugged a little, finally remembering. "I don't know. Could have been."

My eyes widened. He noticed this.

"But it probably wasn't," he said. "I was going pretty fast. Didn't get a good look at it."

I shrank down in the seat, not touching the door, or any surface. "They're out here." Fear crept into my voice for the first time that night. "They followed us out here."

"No they didn't. They can't. No one knows about it, where we're going. The cabin's not even in my name. You think I'm stupid?"

This seemed like a strange thing to say, as they didn't need to know whose name was on the cabin. They'd come anyway. That's what they did. They just came. I looked at my daddy, who was running something over in his head, jaw muscles working in concert with his thoughts. I turned around and peered out the back window. Nothingness trailed behind us, as if we'd driven off the end of the world while I slept, and were now driving through space.

"So they're not following us?"

"No. Don't you worry. No need to worry, okay?"

"Okay." I then realized that my head was exposed. "You want me to keep my head down?"

He didn't answer right away, squinting out his own

window at the nothingness that was cut shallow by the headlights in front of him, but then quickly smothered after they passed. There were more trees here, and the road was rutted, climbing into the hills. "No, I don't think so."

"Really? Why not?"

"Nothing's going to see you out here. Not tonight."

I sat back in the seat, stretching out my legs that couldn't touch the deep bottom of the passenger side floor. I put my head on my father's shoulder, and looked out the front window, watching the light eat up the road, the trees growing thicker on both sides.

"What do you think Mommy's doing right now?"

"Waiting," Daddy said, rubbing the side of his face like he always did when he was concerned. "She's waiting for us. God willing."

***

We got to the cabin just as the sun was coming up, crawling slowly over the mountain peaks and stealing down into the pines that covered the earth in every direction. It would have been one of those postcard moments you hear about if Mommy and Brother were there, but they weren't. The cabin was dark, and their car wasn't anywhere.

My daddy got out of the truck and looked around the property, first checking the cabin and then the woods behind it, thinking they might have hidden their car after unloading it. He told me to stay in my seat so I did, and watched him walk quickly inside and outside the cabin. He was trying not to run, because he didn't want to scare me. I wasn't scared, because I believed in Mommy, and because I'd prayed.

I'd never seen the cabin before. Daddy bought it

To The Hills

"on the cheap," he'd said proudly a few months before, telling me that it was going to be a surprise for Mommy on her birthday. A vacation home in the mountains. I asked him if I could tell Brother, and he said no, because Brother told Mommy everything, which usually led to arguments. That's why Daddy put the lock on their bedroom door. So they could fight in private, without us getting in to stop it.

I never told Mommy or Brother about the cabin, waiting for Daddy to surprise them with it, but I did write about it in my journal in the meantime. I didn't bring my journal with me to the cabin mostly because it was a secret that not even Daddy knew about, but also because it wasn't on the list. Everything on the list was in the backpack now.

Daddy returned to the truck, sweating and breathing hard.

"They're not here," he said, his mind still working over things.

"They'll be here, Daddy."

He looked at me suddenly. "How do you know?"

"Because I just do."

But I didn't. I didn't know anything.

***

We took our packs into the cabin. It smelled like dust and smoke and dried wood. There were a few pieces of furniture, a gas stove, some boxes against the wall. It was someone else's place, and would stay that way until Mommy came and made it into their home.

"Same rules here as in the truck. No going outside. No looking out the window."

"No playing in the woods?"

"No way."

"Where do we pee?"

He slid a bucket over to me with his foot.

I crossed my arms and pouted. I'd rather have faced death than go in a bucket.

"Just until we figure out our next move."

"And until Mommy and Brother arrive."

"Of course."

***

That night, I curled up on the couch, under one of the old quilts from our closet. Daddy slept on blankets spread across the floor. He said he preferred it, but I knew it was hurting his back. He was generous like that with me, when he wasn't that way with anyone else.

I had a hard time sleeping at first, because it was too quiet, and I kept hearing the sound of that thing we hit in the road. I waited to hear Daddy's breathing even out, then snore a little, like he always slept back at home. That would have helped me sleep. But he breathed hard and fast all night.

***

I woke up with Daddy's finger on my lips, and for a moment, I thought it was starting all over again. That it was a dream that just kept repeating. More frightened than I was the night before, I went with the script, flowing with the *déjà vu*, because to go off course might get a person lost in their dream forever.

"Is this it, Daddy?" I whispered.

"Yes it is," he said in a voice that was too loud to be a whisper.

A jolt of happiness shot through my limbs, and I felt like crying because I had woken up inside a dream by mistake, and everything would be back to normal

To The Hills

once I woke up for real and it wasn't the end of the world. Then Daddy said something that ripped everything in half.

"They're here."

"What? Who? Mommy and Brother?"

"No," he said, again too loud. "Them."

He cocked the hammer on his own pistol, much larger than mine, and got to his feet.

I sat up, and could hear car engines outside the cabin. Slamming doors. Terse voices and radio chatter.

"Who's outside, Daddy?"

"Them. *They're* outside."

The thumping of a helicopter drew close out above the trees. Twirling red and blue lights painted the walls of this stranger's cabin, not yet full of our smells, our ways. Mommy hadn't had a chance to fix it up yet, make it home. Brother hadn't had a chance to dump his dirty laundry in the bathroom. Daddy never smoked in here.

"But that's not who you said," my whisper turning into something else. "That's not how it would be at the end of the world."

"I was wrong, wasn't I?"

I was dumbfounded. He'd never admitted to being wrong a day in his life.

"Cover your ears," he said, taking up a shotgun and loading it with extra shells. "You plug them tight, and don't uncover them no matter what you hear, okay?"

"Okay."

"And remember what I told you. If they get me, you do what I showed you. You remember how, right?" He placed the .22 on the blanket in front of me. "You remember, don't you?"

T. E. Grau

I nodded. Tears pushed up into my eyes, and made it hard to see him, like he was talking to me from inside a rainstorm.

"All right. That's a good girl. Listen to your daddy. Don't let them take you alive, you hear? They'll eat you to the bone."

I nodded my head again, warm wetness spilling down my cheeks. I did hear.

"Good. Now plug your ears."

I did as I was told, shoving my fingers into my ears and bending them down with my thumbs, watching my daddy while the sound of my beating heart and rushing blood and shaking fingers filled my ears with the roar of a hurricane.

He filled his pockets with ammo clips, pumped a round into his shotgun, and went to the door. His mouth moved, spit flying as he pointed at the door, cursing the ones outside who had come. He was furious. He was glorious.

Daddy threw open the door and started firing, shooting two guns at once as he stepped out of the cabin and away from where I could see him, smoking trailing behind him and filling up the empty doorway. He would get a lot of them, I thought, but they'd probably end up overtaking him, dragging him to the ground, then eating him. Pulling out his guts, chewing off his fingers. Then they'd come for me, when they were done with my Daddy, and I would have to do what I was told. I'd hit four bottles and a tin can and now I'd have to hit one more thing, a little bigger, a little softer, with everything I was inside of it. I had to do what Daddy said, before they got through him and got to me.

To The Hills

I lowered my chin and put the pistol to my forehead and waited for my finger to do it. I waited, knowing that eventually it would. I would. It was such a tiny trigger. Made just for the hand of a little girl.

The smoke protecting the open door parted and they came inside, a whole group of them, looking different than what I expected, what I had seen in all of the horror movies and some of the TV shows. They were all wearing the same thing and the same expression. Wide faces and wider brimmed hats. Mostly men, but also a girl. It was the girl who I looked at, because I didn't expect it. I didn't expect any of it, to be honest.

They had their arms out, gesturing, reaching for me. They were making faces, and also noises, which eventually formed into words. They surrounded me and kept talking, the girl most of all, probably thinking that I was a mommy's girl when I was a daddy's girl and he was a girl's daddy. Or used to be, before he ran outside, and before what was outside came inside. She had something in her hand and showed it to me. It was my journal. She'd found it and read it and that's how she knew. That's what brought them out here.

I was furious that she was in my house, in my room, digging through my stuff and finding my secrets. I told her to keep her distance, and she did, talking the whole way, holding out my journal like some sort of cross while watching what I had in my hand and where I was pointing it.

After I heard what she said, about my daddy, about my mommy and brother and what they found behind that locked bedroom door, after she explained to me the real story of the end of the world, I did what my daddy taught me. It didn't even take me that long. Muscle memory, my daddy had said. Instinct. It's the only thing you can count on in the end.

He asked if I remembered how to do it, before he went outside, facing down the end of the world. I did remember, and I did it.

But it wasn't because of memories. It was because of what he never told me.

Everything Hurts, Until it Doesn't

DAMIEN ANGELICA WALTERS

"**No pain, no sorrow**, no anger. Nothing inside you, nothing at all," Leah whispers in my ear before she slides the blade down the inside of my thigh. It's a small cut—I can tell by the sting—but it bleeds a larger pool of warmth, and the sensation of insects creeping beneath my skin abates. Her eyes are sapphires glittering in the half-light, but there's no cruelty in their depths. I touch her arm and smile, even though I miss the way Mom spoke the words, the way she wielded the knife so it almost never hurt, no matter where she chose.

I make a cut just above the crook of Leah's elbow, but I don't say anything. The words don't feel right in my mouth yet. We lie on our backs in the back yard under the early morning sun, side by side, and bleed all the ugliness into the grass.

As much as we can anyway. Some things you're born to. Some things you can't escape.

After the wounds clot, Leah rises, tugging me

along. "We need to get ready and go. We shouldn't be late."

"Mom wouldn't care."

"No, she wouldn't, but Aunt Grace would never let us hear the end of it."

On the way, I grab one of our aunt's blueberry muffins. It's weird how death makes everyone bring food. Our refrigerator is full of lasagna, stuffed shells, and a strange, fluffy salad in a sickly shade of green.

Changed into properly somber black dresses, we take Mom's car—Leah might be the oldest, but I'm a better driver—and head to the church. The sleeves of my dress feel too tight, the skirt too long. Leah's looks better on her, but everything does because she's the pretty one.

Aunt Grace hugs us too long and too tight, sobbing into a handkerchief, her eyes red-rimmed and puffy. I want to say, "Tears can be especially dangerous," which is what Mom always said, but Aunt Grace isn't like us. It's safe for her to feel whatever she wants. Uncle Allen gives one of those hugs that isn't really one at all, but at least it's honest. He and Mom never liked each other; he doesn't think much of me and Leah either. Bryce, our twelve-year old cousin, looks bored, and he keeps tugging at the tie they've made him wear.

The pastor's voice is a helicopter drone. Leah and I ignore him as best we can, though we stand and sit when he tells everyone to so we don't stand out. Our mother didn't want any of this—the funeral home viewing, the service, the mourners—but it's easy to overrule your wishes when you're dead. Unfortunately, Leah's two weeks away from eighteen and I'm six from seventeen, so Aunt Grace was in charge of making the

Everything Hurts Until it Doesn't

decisions and she found religion when she married our uncle, or so Mom said. I guess everyone needs something to believe in.

The coffin's closed here, and I'm glad. We gave Aunt Grace a recent picture of Mom, but the funeral home did what they wanted, because the woman in the box didn't really resemble our mother. She let her curly hair hang any way it wanted to; they brushed it into some weird wavy Hollywood style. And she never wore makeup. Ever. When no one was looking, I tried to wipe off some of the lipstick. The dress Aunt Grace picked covered all her scars, too, and Mom never cared if they showed or not. Besides, most of them are barely visible; we heal pretty well. Still, it's not right that they should do that, turn you into someone else when you're dead.

Everyone was all *she was too young* and *those poor girls* and fake hugs and signatures in the guest book. And they all had a friend or a relative or a coworker who had an aneurysm and it was *horrible* and *tragic*. One of the chairs had a loose staple underneath, and I pressed my thumb against it until it slid in and everything slipped out.

After the church comes the cemetery and Aunt Grace is still crying. I wish I'd worn different shoes because a blister's forming on my heel. After the cemetery comes Aunt Grace's house, all distant cousins and neighbors who barely had two words for Mom when she was alive. They look at my face, at Leah's, our dry eyes, and make their judgments. I feel the words they want to say: cold fish, like their mother. They don't know what we are, but they know we're different. Other. They always have.

Damien Anjelica Walters

We sit in the front room in two chairs—Aunt Grace's idea, not ours—and people bring us drinks we don't want to drink and food we don't want to eat. Bryce vanishes upstairs when his mother's not paying attention, and I wish I had that kind of invisibility.

My skin itches and I can tell by the way she's fidgeting that Leah's does, too. Most days, one pass of the blade is enough, but today isn't most days. I breathe deep until it lessens enough to tolerate, but after a while, I lean close to Leah. "Can we please go home?"

"Not yet, but soon. I promise."

Soon doesn't come fast enough but it does come. People start leaving, a few telling us how sorry they are and to be strong before they do. Unneeded advice; we're always strong. Most of them give all their sympathy to my aunt. By now she's cried off every last trace of makeup and she's carrying around a wad of snotty tissue. It's embarrassing. If she cared so much, why was she always criticizing Mom and everything she did? I know she's older than Mom was, but Leah doesn't treat me that way.

"Now," Leah says close to my ear, after Aunt Grace says goodbye to Uncle Allen's brother and sister-in-law, the last ones at the house, and goes into the kitchen. We get halfway to the door.

"Girls?"

We turn as one, our fingers linking.

"I have the guest room prepared, if you're already tired, and Bryce can help you bring in your things."

"Our things?" Leah says.

"Yes."

"Why? We only live fifteen minutes away."

Everything Hurts Until it Doesn't

"You shouldn't stay alone tonight."

"We've been staying alone. Why should tonight be any different? And we're not alone, we have each other."

"Yes, I know that. I also thought you might need some space to grieve privately, but now that everything's over, we need to talk about getting you settled."

My skin begins to prickle anew.

"Here?" Leah's voice holds laughter.

"Of course here. Where else?"

"We can't stay here. There isn't enough room for all of us. Your house is too small."

Aunt Grace looks as though Leah smacked her in the face. It's the truth, though. They have three bedrooms, which means Leah and I would have to share not only a room, but a bed. I love my sister but she steals the blankets at night. Once in a while is fine, but permanently or even for the two months until she's legally an adult? No thank you.

"But I thought you'd want to stay here with your family," she says, her eyes wet once again.

I bite the inside of my cheek. The itch beneath my skin amplifies. I try to think of puppies and kittens, of anything that will make it stop, but nothing works. I dig my fingernails in my palms, and the pain helps a little.

"Let them go," Uncle Allen says from behind our aunt. "Leah has a point. One guest room isn't enough. Let them go home. She's almost eighteen."

"But Paige is sixteen. What if the neighbors call Child Protective Services? We'll get in trouble."

"Come on, Grace, the neighbors know the girls,

they know us. No one's going to call anyone. We can talk about everything later."

"You two are sure you'll be all right?"

Leah and I both nod.

"Do you promise to call me when you get in the house? And lock the doors tight and the windows, too?"

"We will," Leah says, practically dragging me out. No hugs, no goodbyes, exactly the way Mom always did it.

I'm turning the car out of the driveway when Leah starts laughing.

"Did you see her face? She really thought we'd want to stay there. '*Stay here with your family*,'" she says, her voice pinchy and tight. "They are *so* not our family."

I reach under my dress and scrape off the new scab, sighing as it begins to bleed. "The ants go marching on," I sing, my voice whisper-soft.

"Are you okay?"

"I am now."

"Why didn't you tell me it was so bad?"

"It wasn't. Not until we were getting ready to leave. I could've even waited until we got home," I say, but it's a lie and she knows it.

She's better at holding it in. She's always been better. Half her scars are my fault alone.

"We have to be careful, Paige. They could make us live with them."

"They won't. Didn't you see Uncle Allen's face? He doesn't want us there anymore than we want to be there. And your birthday is in two weeks."

"But not yours. And it doesn't matter what he

Everything Hurts Until it Doesn't

wants. Aunt Grace was too tired to argue, but she wants us with her."

"She doesn't want us. She wants the insurance money," I say.

"Who wouldn't?" Leah says.

Mom had lots of life insurance. She said it was because she was young when her parents died so she knew how hard it could be.

"Well, she can't have it. Mom left it to us. It's *for* us."

"But neither one of us are eighteen so technically we're not in charge of it until then. And you won't be in charge of your half for another year and a half. You heard her last night talking to Mrs. Attman, griping about how expensive the funeral was."

"She didn't need to spend anything," I mutter as I pull into our driveway.

"But she spent it anyway and she's going to want it back somehow. I know she will."

I pull into the garage too fast, slamming on the brakes to keep from plowing into the wall. Leah thumps her palms on the dashboard, but she doesn't reprimand me.

When I get out of the car my thighs are damp and sticky. In the second-floor bathroom, I peel off my dress, drop it on the tile. Blood is still oozing from the scratched-off scab, and my flesh is smeared with ruddy Rorschach blots. I take a razor from the medicine cabinet and open a new wound on the opposite thigh, scrubbing it with a clump of toilet paper so it'll burn more. And I wonder what they did with my mother's blood.

When I wake in the morning I smell bacon. I swing

my legs out of bed, wipe the sleep from my eyes, and my skin is suddenly awash in insects. Crawling, creeping, and I want to tear it off so they can get out. I've never felt this heat, this movement before, and all the air rushes from my lungs and stays there. My ankles tangle and I fall, driving bruises and carpet burns into my knees, and then I hear heavy thumps.

Leah crouches by my side. "What's wrong? Oh my god, Paige, what's wrong?"

But I can't speak, can't do anything but curl my fingers into claws. The ants aren't marching; they're stampeding. For the first time ever I'm scared.

Leah races from the room, returns with a knife. Her gaze meets mine and I blink several times, hoping she'll understand. She yanks up my pajama top and runs the blade across my sternum. I don't feel the pain, I don't feel anything, but the itch the itch the itch. Leah's hand moves again and this time, the sharpness of the pain machetes through the insects. Slowly, slowly, they march away.

When I can find my voice again, I say "What was that? What happened to me? I just woke up. I wasn't thinking about anything. I wasn't feeling anything."

She swallows hard. "I don't know, Paige."

Buried beneath the worry, I see truth in her eyes. "Mom would know," I say, my voice husky.

"Maybe it's because of the funeral and everything."

"Do you ever wonder what would happen if we didn't let it out? Don't you wonder what it would be like to get mad or to cry?"

She shakes her head. "Don't say that."

"But maybe it wouldn't be so bad. I mean, I know that Mom always said it would be and that we might

Everything Hurts Until it Doesn't

hurt ourselves or other people, but she never told us exactly what would happen to us."

"She told us enough."

"Maybe we'd turn into werewolves," I say with a smile.

"Werewolves?"

"You know, big gigantic hairy beasts with big teeth and chompy jaws."

"I know what werewolves are."

"Maybe we'd go nuts and kill everyone in the neighborhood. Howl at the moon. Piss on bushes and trees."

"You're such a goof."

"Or maybe we'd fall asleep and when we woke up, we'd be back a week ago and Mom would still be alive," I say softly.

The smoke alarm goes off, the high-pitched beep loud enough to hurt, and after she runs downstairs, I clean myself up, tracing a fingertip across the marks. I've never needed two before. Neither has Leah. Neither did our mother.

Over the next few days, we're extra careful. I cut my right thigh every morning, Leah, the left every night. When Aunt Grace calls to check on us, Leah answers. We eat the lasagna and stuffed shells, but the green salad sprouts mold and I throw it away, bowl and all. Everything starts to feel, not normal, but kind of close, even though I keep waiting for Mom to come in the room or to call me into another.

Mr. Trent who lives across the street brings us a batch of his homemade vanilla ice cream and I let Leah make her bowl first. I start to make mine, but hear a thump from the living room and drop the scoop on the counter.

Damien Anjelica Walters

Leah's on the floor, her bowl upside down on the rug. Both arms are pulled tight to her chest, all four limbs stiff and quivering, and her cheeks are flushed. I grab a knife from the kitchen and slice her ankle, just above the bone. Her mouth works, but nothing else moves. I make a hasty second slash on her other ankle, and she collapses as if she's suddenly boneless and inhales loudly at the same time. We both burst into tears, and I pull her head into my lap.

"You'll be okay," I say. "Everything will be okay."

Later, when I bring her a warm washcloth and adhesive bandages, I say, "What's happening to us?"

She says, "I don't know, Paige, but I don't think it's anything good."

It takes me a long time to fall asleep that night because I can't stop my thoughts. I think of Mom cold in her bed that morning. I think of what they said killed her. But they didn't know what she had inside her, what we have inside us, so what if they were wrong? What if what happened to Mom is happening to us? And if we don't know what it is, how can we stop it?

If there's even a way.

In the morning, Leah and I don't really talk about anything, but I can tell she didn't sleep a lot either because purple half-moons live under her eyes. We're sitting at the table with bowls of cereal when someone knocks at the front door, making us both jump. Before we can get up, Aunt Grace's voice calls out, "Girls! Open up quick please, my hands are full!"

We barely have the door open when she pushes through, a paper bag under each arm.

"Paige, there are a couple more bags in the car to

Everything Hurts Until it Doesn't

bring in, please. There's blueberry muffins on the passenger seat, too. Leah, can you help me put things away?"

When I come back in with the rest of the bags and the box of muffins, Leah and Aunt Grace are talking in low, tense terms. They both fall silent and give me weird, overly bright smiles.

"Thank you for this," Leah says.

"What kind of person would I be if I didn't make sure my nieces were eating well? I made the muffins this morning, so please eat them in the next couple of days so they don't get stale." She folds her arms across her chest and glances from me to Leah and back again. "What's going on? What's the matter? You both look pale."

"We're fine," Leah says. "Honestly."

"Sit, both of you," she says, ushering us to the kitchen chairs. She takes away the bowls of cereal and replaces them with muffins and glasses of milk.

I start eating, but Leah picks at her napkin until Aunt Grace raps her knuckles on the edge of the table. "Come on now. I can't have either of you wasting away. Speaking of, we want to take you out for your birthday, Leah. Any place you want."

Leah goes very still. That was one of our mom's traditions.

"I was hoping to spend it here with Paige. I don't want to go out this year. Not with anyone."

Aunt Grace nods, but her eyes are wide with hurt. "Okay, I understand."

"I'll think about it, though. Maybe I'll change my mind."

That prompts a smile at least.

Damien Anjelica Walters

After she leaves, Leah throws the rest of her muffin in the trash, but I finish mine. Aunt Grace might be a pain in the ass, but she's a good cook.

"Are you sure you don't want to go out?" I ask, picking at a thread on my jeans.

"No, I really don't."

I trace my finger in muffin crumbs. "I miss Mom."

"Me, too."

After that, we keep quiet. What else is there to say?

In the middle of the night, I wake, unable to breathe or move. The itch is so bad it burns, as though I've been doused with lava or set afire. I try to speak, to shout, but nothing comes out and I know I'm going to die just like Mom. I keep trying and finally let out a strangled sort of cry, but I know it's too low for Leah to hear.

I'm wrong. She runs into my room, flicking on the light, panic high on her cheeks. She keeps her gaze locked on mine and cuts. Once. Twice. Three times.

When the bugs are gone and I feel like me again, I don't want to go back to sleep so we go downstairs.

"How about if I make popcorn and we watch a movie," she says.

While the microwave runs, I take a muffin out of the box, and Leah smacks it out of my hand. It bounces across the floor, shedding crumbs along the way, coming to rest near the refrigerator.

"What did you do that for?"

"You ate one the day of the funeral."

"Uh-huh. So?"

"So, you had one yesterday, too."

"Uh-huh?"

"Think, Paige. Think really hard."

Everything Hurts Until it Doesn't

"No, she wouldn't," I say.

Leah scrubs her cheeks. "How do we know?"

"But you ate one too and nothing happened to you."

"I didn't eat as much as you did, and I threw out the rest."

I fist my hands. "So what do we do?"

"Throw them all out."

"And then we should call the police?"

"We can't. If we do, they'll take us away. Even if they don't take me, they'll take you."

"They wouldn't."

"Yes, they would," she says, picking up the muffin with a paper towel. "You're only sixteen. And I'm still seventeen."

"For less than a week."

"They wouldn't care about that," she says as she walks out of the kitchen.

"Where are you going?"

She doesn't answer, but I hear her retching in the powder room, and she comes out a few minutes later, wiping her mouth. "Just in case."

"Maybe we're wrong. Maybe it's something else. Maybe it's what—"

"If we're gone, she gets all the money. You know that. But as soon as I turn eighteen, I'll call a lawyer and get custody of you so she won't be able to take you away. And I'll make sure she can't get the money, even if something *does* happen to us."

"But—"

"I won't let that happen. Don't worry."

The words hang in the air, and then the microwave bings. We end up throwing out the popcorn, too.

Damien Anjelica Walters

The days keep passing, bringing Leah closer to eighteen. When Aunt Grace calls, we try to act normal. The one time I answer the phone, she says she wants to bring over more muffins on Leah's birthday. I can't exactly say no. If she insists, we'll figure out a way not to eat them. I can always knock over the box or drop it on the floor. We play Scrabble without tallying our scores, we watch movies, we cut and bleed so we're empty. So we're safe.

And then it's her birthday.

I wake first and sneak downstairs to hang the purple streamers I found in the basement. Leah's still asleep when I finish so I start mixing the ingredients for a cake. I know it probably won't be as good as Mom always made but I measure everything twice so at least it won't be awful.

Footsteps tap on the steps and I jump out of the kitchen. "Surprise!"

"I can't believe I didn't hear you do all this," she laughs.

"I'm making a cake, too."

She smiles and holds out her arms. As I lean in to give her a hug I feel a sting on my shoulder blade. I pull back with a yelp and see the knife in her hand, the blade red with my blood.

"You know, you could've let me know first."

She doesn't say anything, just rinses off the knife and pulls a small brown vial from her pocket. My skin prickles.

"What's that?" I say, but my voice comes out distorted and taffy-thick.

I reach out for her but the world starts swimming around me and I fall to my knees. "What did you do?"

Everything Hurts Until it Doesn't

She rinses the knife and dries it. Adds a few drops from the vial to the blade. "I wasn't sure if the same amount I used on Mom would work on you so I did a couple tests. Pretty sure I've got it right now."

She crouches beside me and I try to back away, but I'm tangled in a million knots and can't do anything as she pushes up my nightgown and cuts my inner thigh. "You know, when I was little, all I wanted was to be like the two of you. I thought you were special, but you're not. You're monsters. And I don't want to be stuck here, taking care of you and pretending we're the same. Now I won't have to."

I find my voice in the fog. "You were faking?"

"Of course I was. There's nothing bad in me. Nothing at all. Mom knew it, too, and she cut me anyway."

"No, not true," I manage.

"Yes, true. She admitted it to me." She washes the blade again, tips the vial over it once it's dry.

"She wouldn't. She loved you."

"If she loved me, would she have done this to me?" She holds out her arm. "All these scars? All these years? No, that's not love. I don't know what it is, but it's not love. Trust me, it's better this way. You won't be able to pass this onto anyone else, and no one will ever know," she says, leaning close, her eyes hard as she prepares to open my flesh again.

Whip-fast, I grab the knife and slide it between her breasts. Hands butterflying in the air, she falls to the floor. I sit beside her, brushing her hair back from her cheeks as her mouth opens and closes and opens again without a sound. "No pain, no sorrow, no anger. Nothing inside you, nothing at all." I kiss her forehead.

Damien Anjelica Walters

"I can't believe you did that to me, Leah." I take the vial and let a few drops fall. "Or tried to anyway. It's only water now, not poison.

"I found it the morning after Mom died. I didn't say anything to you. I thought maybe she did it to herself, but when I collapsed the first time, I knew it was you.

"I guess I'm lucky it didn't kill me then. It's funny, I've always suspected you weren't like me and Mom—I could never smell it in you, even when you were bleeding—but I kept thinking maybe you'd change and then, when I knew you wouldn't, I waited for you to tell me the truth. I wanted you to tell me the truth.

"And in spite of it, in spite of what you did, I still love you, Leah," I say. "I'm sorry. I never wanted any of this, but you were right. It's better this way."

She's even prettier when she stops breathing.

When Aunt Grace's car pulls in the driveway, my skin thrums with anticipation. I unlock the front door and wait in the kitchen with knife in hand, going over what I'll tell the police.

Leah attacked Aunt Grace because she thought she was poisoning us, and then she tried to attack me when I defended her. I didn't mean to hurt her. I was trying to protect my aunt, trying to protect myself. No, I don't know why she did it, but she hasn't been coping well since our mom's death.

After it's all over, I'll file for legal emancipation. I don't think Uncle Allen will make much of a fuss. He can't touch the money anyway; Mom made sure of that.

The front door opens with a low creak. "Girls?" Aunt Grace calls out.

"We're in here," I return, smiling as I speak.

I've always been good at faking things, too.

Drowning in Sorrow
SHELDON HIGDON

The writhing worm struggled to slip free from the hook. Its bulbous ends curling, fighting to escape its inevitable end as though it knew what waited in the cold abyss of the Androscoggin River. As the water flowed by, Simon pierced the hook through the worm and then wrapped it over, skewering it once more for good measure. With a crude fishing pole he had made from a long, thick stick, he tossed the fishing line into the river and watched the bobber battle the current as the worm waited out its fate below.

He placed his homemade rod into a y-shaped branch he had plucked from the thicket behind him, shoving it into the ground as a makeshift holder.

Simon wished it was the one his dad had, the one he used to use.

He dug into a brown paper bag and pulled out a sandwich that was jacketed in wax paper. On it a heart had been drawn in green marker with the words, 'I'm sorry, Sweetie. Love you.' printed beneath it. Simon un-wrapped the sandwich his mom had made. No note would make up for what she did.

You ruined our family.

He shook his head and leaned back on his elbows beneath the shady shelter of a poplar tree, and forced the bubbling resentment back down. The grass was lush and green beneath him. He wiggled his toes and smiled as the blades tickled his skin. A cool breeze skimmed across his hair splaying strands across his forehead and with reluctance he bit off a morsel from his butter and grape jelly sandwich.

The sun reflected off the river like thousands of crystals dancing about its surface. Simon shielded his eyes from the gleaming river that sparkled in his face. The bobber went under and popped back up. Simon sat up, dumping his half-eaten sandwich back into the brown bag, and took a hold of his fishing stick. The bobber went under and stayed under. Before he could jerk the line back, it shot straight across the river. Droplets of the Androscoggin dripped from the line as it drew taut to the other side. He yanked his stick back and felt it arc, giving a little but not breaking from the pressure. Simon hoped he hooked whatever had taken the worm into its mouth. He felt the line tug and dart up stream and then shoot directly back across from him to the other side.

He dug his heels into the green grass, readying himself for the fight. His mind flipped through images of salmon or trout he'd caught in this river with his dad throughout his thirteen-year history. But this was bigger, stronger. His dad once had told him how he caught a northern pike in the 'scoggin, but it had snapped his line and got away.

Drowning in Sorrow

Maybe this was that fish.

The thought of his dad brought a memory of when he'd learned to cast his first line when he was nine. Warm and bright like today. He wore his *Clam Diggers Dig Muck* shirt, the one his dad had picked up at the annual clam bake that occurred at the end of October. Simon had stood at the river's edge with his pants rolled up into cuffs, wide-eyed as his dad gripped his large hands over his and guided him, casting the line into the river.

"Remember, Simon," his dad had said, "fishing is not about the catch, but the time we have between casts." He had flashed a movie star smile and ruffled Simon's hair. "We only have so much of it."

The thought faded to last year when he overheard his dad and mom arguing, her voice screaming the words "Get Out," which forever impaled themselves into Simon's consciousness while he sat on his bed with his knees to his chest and arms wrapped up over his head. Tears flowing like the Androscoggin. The man he loved was gone. With him that fishing pole he learned to cast on.

Because of *her* Simon would miss out on future memories such as learning how to drive the truck in the parking lot of Hannaford's grocery store, learning how to throw a solid punch, or how to be a gentleman on his first date.

A *snap!* brought Simon back to his battle but instead of a fight, the fishing line fell into the river. The bobber floated downstream. With a heavy sigh, he pulled in the remaining wet line and tossed the makeshift rod down next to him. He sat wiping his face with the back of his arm and plucked his remaining

Sheldon Higdon

sandwich from the brown paper bag. The shade from the poplar tree had grown in size and now had covered the rest of the bank and spilled down into the river. A cool breeze pricked Simon's skin. He shivered as he ate the remains of his sandwich. He gazed out across the river wondering what he had lost, but no fish came to mind . . . .

We only have so much of it.

Across the river, at its edge, Simon's eyes fell on a spot where bubbles began sprouting to the surface. Even in the river's continuous flow they could be seen distinctly. They were rapid like boiling water. He leaned forward, knitting his brow and cocking his head to the side, trying to figure out what it came from. Up above, the sun slid behind a gray cloud cloaking the river in darkness. Simon lost sight of where the bubbles had been popping and bursting in succession.

A large splash came from the water. He studied the river and waited for another. And just as fast as the sunlight disappeared it returned. Squinting from the now bright light, he scanned down the 'scoggin and saw nothing. No fish leapt into the air. There was nothing—except for a wet boy who stood on the other side of the river, staring directly at him. A sense of sadness entangled Simon like a backlash of fishing line.

He shielded his eyes to get a better view only to see that the young boy had disappeared. He rubbed his eyes. Maybe the glare of the sun reflecting off the river caused him to see something that wasn't there. Maybe the boy jumped into the bushes that lined the river. Maybe it was all in Simon's head. Even though he stood on the other side of the river far from Simon's

Drowning in Sorrow

view, the boy looked familiar in some odd way. And hopelessness. The feeling of hopelessness swathed him when he looked at the boy, but it was one with no reason.

Simon wanted to cry.

He put his head into his hands and drew a deep breath, releasing a sigh. His thoughts crashed around like rapids smashing over jagged rocks. He pictured himself being carried away down the Androscoggin, head slipping below the surface, hands following and disappearing into the cold water.

The voice reeled Simon's thoughts from the river. It was a voice he'd never heard before but yet was somehow familiar. It came from over his shoulder. A drop of cool water splashed on top of Simon's head. He turned around to the wet boy standing before him.

"It's like looking into a mirror, ain't it?" the soddened boy said.

Simon lost his breath, and the feeling of water trickling down his skin gave him a chill that ran deep into his bones, burrowing itself into the marrow.

As Simon slowly stood, the familiarity came into pinpoint focus. The boy looked just like him, except the boy's appearance seemed darker as if covered in constant shade. His hair wasn't blond but an ashen gray. His eyes were like the color of burnt charcoal. Bruises and infected lacerations covered his skin, which was slimy and milky like the bottom of a dead fish floating belly-up down the river.

And the boy's shirt! Just like when Simon wore that shirt the day his dad taught him how to cast his first line. *Clam Diggers Dig Muck!* Even his pants were rolled into cuffs.

Sheldon Higdon

Nauseousness swept over Simon causing his head to swim and his belly to sour.

"Like a twin," the boy said, leaning against the poplar tree and swatting at a fly that circled him.

Simon took several steps back. He forced what little saliva he had down his dry throat.

"Might wanna watch yourself," the boy said, plucking a leaf from the tree. The fly landed on his forehead, and then darted off. "Don't wanna *fall* in, now do we?"

"Wh-who are you? I mean . . . you . . . ?" Simon rubbed his palms into his eyes, trying to clear away what he hoped was the after effect of a bad sandwich.

"You already know," the boy said, taking a step closer and examining the homemade fishing rod that lay on the ground. Simon glanced down and saw that the boy's every step left a brown footprint in its wake—green grass dying. "It's not the same as the one we learned on, but it works."

Simon glanced at his rod.

Fishing is not about the catch.

"Miss him, huh?" the boy asked.

But the time we have between casts.

Simon still wasn't sure if this was a daydream or if he was lying in the shaggy grass, sleeping in the shade of the poplar tree. Tears bubbled in Simon's eyes as his dad's image floated back to him. He swore he felt his dad's hands over his. The confusion and fear he felt earlier now swirled sadness back into the whirlpool of his emotions.

We only have so much of it.

"Yeah," Simon wiped his eyes clear with the back of his arm, "but . . ."

Drowning in Sorrow

The soaked boy smiled, revealing chipped, black teeth, jagged and sharp like the protruding rocks of the river.

"But what?"

Simon sniffled. "But he never came back for me." He thumbed his eyes clear.

The conversation flowed between them as if they had spoken to each other a thousand times before, but it didn't squelch the emptiness Simon felt. The loss.

Or was it lost?

The weather turned again and the blue sky gave way to gray clouds. Thick and dark. Plump. Clouds that looked like they were about to burst into a torrential downpour at any moment.

"Why is that, Simon?" He sat on the ground, the green grass turning brown beneath him. The fly was now on his hair, crawling across it. "Why didn't he come back for us?"

Simon turned and faced the river. The water rushed past. For a moment he ignored the question and thought about the worm he had baited earlier. How it struggled between his fingers, flipping its ends to break free from its demise.

"I don't know," said Simon.

Cold rain began to fall from the laden clouds.

"What about Mom?" the boy said.

"Who cares!" Simon spun toward the boy. "Why didn't *she* leave instead?" Tears fell from his eyes and intermingled with the rain. "She's the reason he left!"

"If she is," the boy stood up and took a step closer to Simon, "then why'd you come here?"

Simon turned back to the river. It was a question he'd thought about a hundred times since his dad left.

Sheldon Higdon

A question he never answered aloud, but one he had an answer for. The rain fell harder now, large drops splashing into the river. The Androscoggin roared, carrying dead branches down its wide throat. Water crept up the side of the grassy bank, licking his toes.

"What would you say if she were dead?" the boy asked from behind him, and then chuckled, piercing Simon's ears as if his words were a crack of thunder.

Simon winced, hunching his shoulders.

"He's never coming back for us, you . . . so who cares, right? She told him to leave, remember? And if she were dead then he'd *have* to come back for us, you."

Simon took a step toward the rushing water and looked down river at the sharp granite rocks sticking out. The water cascaded over them creating a white, angry waterfall.

"I can't."

"I know," said the boy. "What else do you remember?"

"Nothing. Just–"

"How could you! And with her? With that-that . . . GET OUT!"

The rain fell harder. Thunder rolled. Lightening sparked overhead, causing the hairs on his neck to stand. His heart pounded like fists against the door of his chest as more of his mom's words revealed themselves to him.

"Yes, you do!" the boy said. "You blocked it out as you cried in your bed, arms wrapped up over your head. Why do you think they argued?"

Simon's mind raced for more images, another memory, anything to bring back his dad, happiness,

Drowning in Sorrow

but nothing emerged. His dad left that day because . . . because . . .

"Why, Simon? You know!"

Because.

"You heard the screaming!" The boy poked the air at him. "The words!"

Because.

"Why?"

Simon turned back to the boy and said, "Because he loved another lady!"

The boy splashed a grin across his face. His broken teeth glistened in the rain.

"Yeah, that one he worked with." Several flies crawled across the boy's face and he brushed them away. "Marta. The red-headed lady. *He* chose *her* over Mom. Over *you!*"

The dam broke and suppressed memories flooded Simon.

With his dad's large hands over his, guiding him, they had cast the line into the river.

"Remember, Simon, fishing is not about the catch, but the time we have between casts. We only have so much of it."

"Speaking of time," Marta said. She was curvy, and wore red lipstick that matched the color of her bra that peeked out from her loose blouse. Her high heels and tight skirt completed her ensemble. "Let's take that walk we talked about." She leaned against the poplar tree with a blanket over her arm and bottle in her hand. "You sit here and catch whatever's in the water, alright kid?"

Simon balled his hands into fists and pressed his fingernails into his palms at the reverie.

"I'll be back, Simon. Stay here. Maybe you'll catch a big one."
"I know I will."
The red-headed lady had giggled.

He held his hands out and saw crimson half moons carved into his palms. He snatched the homemade fishing rod from the ground and flung it into the river.

And with it he screamed.

With his whole body tensed, muscles corded, he released the memories, the moments, the words.

"I hate you!"

It wasn't directed at the boy, or his dad for that matter, but at himself for refusing to accept what he always knew deep down. At a lost boy who loved his dad so much that he had no love to offer his mother once his dad left. For the first time, Simon accepted the painful truth that was inside him all along.

He let go of his dad.

He let go of himself.

"I couldn't . . . face-face it," said Simon, balling into his hands. "Wouldn't b-believe it."

How can I face mom now? After how I've treated her!

Regret clawed its way up Simon's back and perched itself on his shoulders.

She wasn't the one who gave up.

"You know she won't understand now," said the boy. "Not after what *you* put her through. The anger toward her."

I did.

Simon continued to cry. The Androscoggin competed against him as it howled in the falling rain. The river now splashed around his ankles, cold against

Drowning in Sorrow

his skin. He looked up at his doppelganger and bellowed, "I wish I were . . . "

"I know. It's why you came here. It's why *I* came here. To help you." The boy leaned toward Simon, flies buzzing at his ear. "The damage has been done. You can't go back home."

The boy's words sank down into the pit of Simon's stomach, never having the chance to rise back up into a crying fit of shock and misery, because Simon had taken a step and splashed into the river.

The water was cold. Its current swirled him under and around in its murky depth. He fought to the surface and took a deep breath. The rain poured from the darkened sky, pelting his face. Through blurred vision he saw no boy on the riverbank. Only the poplar tree.

"You made him leave!"

Simon rushed downriver toward the crashing falls. To the jagged rocks. He writhed in the water with his head above the surface, gasping for air, and flailed his arms, grasping at dead branches that drifted along with him.

"I wish you weren't my mom!"

Then like a bobber he went under, and popped back up.

"I-I wish I-were . . . ," he quickly inhaled as much air as he could, swallowing river water as he did so, "d-dead."

He held his breath.

"I know you don't mean that, Sweetie. I love you."

Keeping his mom's words with him, Simon stopped fighting the strong current and exhaled, letting the Androscoggin take him under to where he faced his fate just like the worm.

Whenever You Exhale, I Inhale
MAX BOOTH III

The house was supposed to be empty. It was Friday evening, which meant Michael's mother was down the street at her sewing circle and his father was on his way to Columbus. Michael's grandmother hadn't been too well these days, so his father had made it his routine to drive down to Ohio every week after work and visit her in the hospital. Tom felt bad for Michael's grandmother, but at the same time, he felt grateful that it opened an opportunity for him and Michael to have alone time somewhere besides the quarry. The quarry was special and meant more to him than any other place in the world, but that didn't change the fact that it was very wet and dirty and Tom was growing tired of coming home with sand in his clothes. If not for Tom's seven sisters, they would just go to his house—but privacy did not exist in a house with seven sisters. Now that Michael's grandmother was dying, things had changed. On Friday evenings, Michael's house became their new sanctuary.

Whenever You Exhale, I Inhale

Except today, the house wasn't empty.

Michael's father, Mr. Golden, was sitting in the living room when Michael and Tom entered the house, holding hands. Mr. Golden stared at them from his recliner, slowly sipping a glass of liquor. The man's eyes were contaminated with tears. Tom broke his hand away and shoved it in his pocket, remembering the way Mr. Golden had acted last time he caught them together. Remembering the way he'd chased Michael down and repeatedly slapped him across the face. Remembering how, still on top of his bleeding son, Mr. Golden looked over his shoulder at Tom and told him if he ever caught them together again he wouldn't hesitate to snap his little neck.

Judging by how badly Michael was trembling, he also remembered.

"Da-dad, what are you doing home?"

"Your uncle called today at work, caught me just as I was about to leave. Your grandmother's dead, boy. She's passed on."

"Oh."

Tom backed away, slowly, praying that Mr. Goldman had yet to notice him through his tear-veiled vision. Maybe he could still slip out before being discovered. Before Mr. Goldman turned into the monster Michael had often described him as being.

The man's body trembled in the recliner, devastated. In his short fifteen years on this planet, Tom had only seen another grown man cry once, and that had been a homeless man him and his own father had walked past while heading into a grocery store. The homeless man had been rolling around on a dirty blanket, hugging ghosts only he could see, and begging

God to answer all of his questions. "Why is that man crying?" Tom had asked, then only nine years of age. "It is not our business to know," his father had replied, rushing him inside the grocery store.

But this was different. The homeless man had been a stranger, someone Tom had never seen before nor ever saw afterward. Mr. Golden, on the other hand, was no stranger. Tom'd grown up knowing this man. He was the father of the person Tom loved most in this world. He was also someone Tom immensely despised. He'd grown up fearing this man. Michael had told him enough stories to conjure a storm of nightmares. Mr. Golden was anything but a nice person. Watching him cry in his recliner filled Tom with confusing emotions. At first, silent satisfaction ran through him. Good, he thought, this monster deserves sadness in his life. After what he's done to his own son, this moment was long overdue. But the satisfaction quickly expired after Tom took a few more moments to consider the situation and recollect how violent he had become the last time he caught them together. Mr. Golden had been in a relatively good mood that night. But now? He was an animal on the verge of busting out of its cage.

And Tom needed to get out of this house before he was bitten.

"And where do you think you're going?" Mr. Golden turned his head toward him and Tom froze, two steps away from the front door.

"I need to go home," Tom said. All he had to do was just continue walking. Exit the house and run down the street to his own house. There was no way Michael's old man could rise from his recliner and catch him in time. He was fat and drunk and could only butcher what was laid out for him.

Except Tom couldn't move. If he took another step, his bladder would explode and his pants would dampen. He was far too old to still be the boy who pisses his pants.

Mr. Golden snorted snot back up his nose. "Go home? Shit, kid, you only just got here." He motioned for Tom to come closer. "C'mon, let's have ourselves a talk."

"I . . . I think I gotta go home."

"Bullshit."

"Dad, please, don't," Michael said. "Grandma just died."

Mr. Golden nodded. "Indeed she has. But I suppose we ought to be grateful for these small favors."

"What?"

"I imagine she would've just gone and killed herself anyway the second she found out her only grandson was a goddamn queer."

"Dad. Stop."

Mr. Golden ignored his son and motioned at Tom again. "C'mere, boy."

"I don't want to."

"I don't give a shit. Get over here."

"Why?" Tom found the courage to move his hand closer to the doorknob.

"I wanna have a talk with ya." He leaned forward in the recliner and smiled. "I was curious whether you were fucking my son in the ass or the other way around. What kinda faggot is my boy?"

Tom opened the door and booked it out of the house. Behind him, glass shattered and Michael screamed. Tom paused in the middle of the street, the sun heavy on his face. Oxygen struggled to process through his lungs. Inside that house, Michael was being beaten. He needed somebody to save him. He needed a guardian angel. *He needed Tom.* But here the guardian angel was, fleeing from the scene, allowing him to take another punishment, allowing the horror to continue. Tom considered returning to the house. Everything inside him wanted to be a hero. Yet he couldn't. Some kind of invisible force field prevented him from stepping forward. There was only one way Tom could stop Mr. Golden, and Michael had made him promise never to use the gift on his father.

"No matter what he does to me, he's still my father," Michael had once told him, while tending to a bloodied nose. "We can't hurt him. We just can't."

If not for the fear of how Michael would react, Tom would have just stormed back into the house and fried the bastard. He'd done it enough times with rubber tires. All it took was one hit with enough built-up energy to destroy the target. He could stop Mr. Golden. He could show that fucker that just because he was an adult that didn't make him any more powerful than him. But Tom made a promise to Michael, and if he couldn't keep his word to his soul mate, then what was the use of tongues? Tom turned back around and fled to the quarry. He couldn't go back to his own house. He needed to be alone. The quarry was their special place. There was safety in the quarry. There was warmth. Only good things were allowed. All evil was absolutely forbidden.

He sat on the ground, in the center of The Spot, where the stone had blackened many weeks ago during

Whenever You Exhale, I Inhale

a severe thunderstorm, the same spot Tom and Michael had been holding each other and exchanging their love. *The Spot.* The only place that truly mattered. The origin of love and everything beautiful. The beginning and the end. Tom lay back against the concrete, which was still warm after all this time. Somewhere, Michael was suffering, but it would eventually be over. Then Michael would meet him here, and Tom would explain that they needed to run away together—tonight, forever. With their new powers, nothing could hold them back. They could go anywhere, do anything. This town no longer had anything to offer. They had themselves, and they needed nothing more.

***

Michael knew better than to linger. He fled upstairs to his room and locked the door before his father had a chance to rise from the recliner. From the living room, he could hear, "I don't know where you think you're going, boy. You know damn well the longer you hide, the worse it's gonna be. Now get your ass back down here."

Michael pushed a dresser in front of the door and sat on his bed. Tears rained down his face. This was bad, real bad. The last time he'd been caught with Tom, he didn't think his father would ever stop hitting him. That day he realized his father would rather have a dead son than one who was a homo. Perhaps the man had lived in denial since then. But now he'd caught them again. There was no more hiding. If his father tried to separate them, Michael didn't know what would happen. Michael could do things that'd take his father out of the equation. Powerful, scary things. But doing those things would make Michael a monster. He didn't want to be a monster. He just wanted to be loved.

Who would love a monster?

Downstairs, glass shattered. Wood crashed. His father was on the war path, which would eventually lead to Michael's bedroom. He fled to his window and pulled it up, then looked down. It was a good drop to the grass. Over the years, when it got especially bad, he'd often contemplated diving headfirst out of this very window. But since that special night at the quarry, those thoughts were rare. Now he contemplated leaping for another reason. Instead of an end, he begged for a new beginning. A fist banged against the outside of his bedroom door and his father yelled his name. He stopped thinking and leapt. For a moment, he thought he might just fly away. Then his body crashed into the earth and he rolled down the front yard. His ankle exploded with pain and an immense heat swallowed his body whole. He rolled around on the grass, screaming and trying his damnedest to get up, but it was useless, *he* was useless. He stopped moving and just remained still for a moment, listening to his own heartbeat, grinding his teeth together, trying to tame the pain in his leg and failing miserably. He could have just lay there for the rest of the day, soaking in his agony. Except his father had already burst into the bedroom and was looking at him through the window.

"What do you think you're doing?"

Michael forced himself up and began limping down the street.

"You get your ass back here, boy!" his father yelled.

Whenever You Exhale, I Inhale

"You come take your punishment, boy! You come accept what's comin' to ya!"

The echo of his father's hatred followed Michael as he fled from home.

***

Tom heard Michael before he saw him. They embraced each other and Michael explained what'd happened. His words pained Tom, but the fact that Michael had escaped filled him with relief. Now that he had him again, he would never let him go.

"Do you think it's broken?" Tom asked.

Michael shook his head. "I don't know. Hopefully just sprained."

"Please promise me you're done jumping out of windows."

"I promise."

"I have an idea." Tom closed his eyes and concentrated.

"What?"

"Shh."

Tom focused and listened to Michael's heartbeat. He searched for his love's pain. A sheet of electricity formed over Tom's body. He reached forward and softly grabbed Michael's ankle. He caressed the injured area, felt static emitting from his fingertips and melting into Michael's skin. Michael did not scream. He did not make a sound. Tom refused to let go until the heat grew hot enough to scare him off. When he opened his eyes, he was face-to-face with Michael, who stared at him in shock.

"It's gone," he said. "The pain is gone."

Tom nodded. "This power that we share. It will keep us together."

"Yes."

"It's you and me now."

"Me and you."

They kissed, and electricity flowed through their bodies.

***

Once John Golden finished destroying his son's room, he returned downstairs and opened a new bottle of whiskey. He was numb and the burning sensation of the liquor reminded him that he still existed. Reminded him that he was still pissed.

He was beyond the point of sulking in his recliner. He needed to destroy, needed to release this rage building up inside of him. He wanted to break the whole goddamn world, just crack the planet like an egg and toss the shell in the trash. His mother was dead and his son was a queer. He had utterly failed as a human being. What did he have to show for this miserable life? A fat wife? A job he hated? Shit. What was the point of anything?

John drank until it felt like he was choking, then smashed his foot through the TV, his fist through the wall. It didn't even hurt. He was fucking invincible. He was a god. Rage leaked out of him like nuclear radiation. It fueled him. He had very good reasons to feel this way. Hell, he'd been feeling this way for as long as he could remember. Nothing had ever gone the way he'd wanted. His family constantly disappointed him. Nobody respected him. Nobody gave two goddamn shits about him. He meant nothing to the world and the world meant nothing to him. He drank more. He would drink the whole goddamn ocean and nobody would stop him. Someone might try, but they'd be unsuccessful. This was his house. This was his body. This was his life. He'd do whatever the hell he pleased. So he drank. So he destroyed.

The night grew darker. Eventually, Lucille returned from Betty's house. She took one look at the wrecked living room, and her fuming husband, and said, "Where's Michael?"

"Probably sucking cock, if I had to guess."

"What did you just say?" Lucille stepped forward and glass crunched beneath her feet.

"You heard me, woman. Your son's a goddamn queer." John laughed and hiccupped. "A little faggot boy."

"What did you do to him?" She moved closer to him.

For once in their marriage, she didn't appear to be afraid of him. He didn't like the look in her eyes. It made him feel less in control. "You don't seem too surprised that your son's a faggot. You ought to mourn with me. There's more to drink. More to break."

"*John.* Where's Michael?"

"You gonna tell me you fuckin' knew about this shit?" He tightened his fists, gritted his teeth.

"I am his *mother.* Of course I knew."

His eyes vibrated, scheduled to explode from their sockets. "And *what,* you're *okay* with that?"

"He is my child. I accept him for who he is."

"Well I sure as hell don't."

"There's a reason I didn't care to share this information with you."

"You bitch. I am your *husband.* You do not keep secrets from me. Especially *these* kinds of secrets."

"Tell me where Michael is, John."

Max Booth III

He laughed again. Here he was, trying to have a moment, and she had the gall to bark orders at him. Every day he took endless shit from an incompetent boss just so he could feed this family and keep them under a roof, and this was the thanks he got in return. He was a joke to them. He was nothing.

"John. *Goddamn you*. Where is—"

John swung the bottle of whiskey and it bashed into his wife's face. The bottle was strong and did not break, so he smacked her a couple more times. "You think you can tell me what to do? You think you can talk back to me? Huh? You think I'm a bad person? Well, I got news for you, honey, I'm the only good man you'll ever meet."

When Lucille didn't respond, he brought the bottle down on her face again and again and didn't stop until it shattered.

***

The next morning, they stood in front of Michael's house, too afraid to continue. Tom had insisted they didn't need to return here, that anything Michael might own could be replaced during their travels. Michael argued they wouldn't be traveling anywhere without any money. In his room, he had over two hundred dollars stashed away from various birthdays and Christmases. It was time to finally put it to good use.

"This is a bad idea," Tom said as they stood on the street, frozen. "A really bad idea."

"We don't have any other choice," Michael said. "Just stick close to me. If he tries anything . . . I don't know. I don't want to hurt him. But he isn't hurting us. Not anymore. I'm done."

Whenever You Exhale, I Inhale

He headed into the house. Tom followed close behind, swearing under his breath. Maybe Mr. Golden had left. The house might've been empty. They could just run up to Michael's room, grab the money, pack a few clothes, then leave before anyone even knew they were there.

But the house wasn't empty. Mrs. Golden lay on the floor in the living room, covered in blood. Her head didn't look like a head was supposed to look.

"Oh my God," Tom said.

Michael screamed and collapsed next to his mother. Tom stood in place, unable to move, unable to help. He'd never seen a dead body before and he didn't know what to do. Mrs. Golden wasn't just dead. She was slaughtered.

"Michael, we have to go," Tom whispered. "Now."

But Michael wasn't listening. He hugged his dead mother and sobbed long and hard, and Tom watched and struggled to breathe. This was not real. This wasn't happening.

Footsteps behind him. He spun around just in time to see Mr. Golden raising the hammer, followed by pain, so much pain. Tom's legs disappeared and he felt the floor.

Then: Pain. Screaming. Something wet.

The pain faded. The screaming increased.

The universe darkened.

Michael.

***

Michael heard Tom screaming but refused to accept the sound as reality. Nothing else mattered right now. He was holding his dead mother in his arms and he couldn't concentrate on anything else. He wasn't supposed to see his mother dead. Mothers lived forever. Fathers didn't kill mothers. This was not a horror story. This was real life.

This was real life.

He released his mother and stood. Tom lay on the floor covered in blood. His face was sunken in and sticky with gore. His father sat on top of him, holding a hammer. But this thing wasn't his father. The thing sitting on Michael's love was the devil. His father no longer existed. The devil had killed his father years ago and possessed his corpse for sport. It all made sense now. This was the truth he had to accept.

"Dad," Michael whispered, shaking.

The devil stopped swinging the hammer, noticing Michael for the first time. He snarled at him. "You've made me do this. This is all your fault."

"No." Michael refused to cry in front of him. He wouldn't allow him the satisfaction. "All I wanted was to be happy."

"Happy?" The devil laughed. "Well take a good goddamn look at what *happy* brought you. You *happy* now? Are ya?"

He raised the hammer and attempted to swing it down on Tom's face again.

"STOP."

Michael screamed.

All fear of becoming a monster vanished. Fear itself no longer existed. Just a burning desire to avenge his love. To make the devil ache the way he ached.

Michael raised his hand. A bolt of lightning shot out of his palm and connected with the devil's chest, throwing him off Tom and against the wall. He slid to the floor, into a sitting position. He stared at Michael,

Whenever You Exhale, I Inhale

blood trickling out of his eyes, smoke wafting out of his burnt chest.

"I tried, I really tried," the devil said, then went still.

Michael dropped to the floor and grabbed Tom, screaming his name, begging for him to wake up. But it wasn't going to happen. The devil had ended him just as he'd ended Michael's mother.

"No. Please. No."

He hugged his love tighter and wished he could take it back, take it all back. If only he could restart the day. They'd leave the quarry and skip town and never give it a second thought. Money wasn't important. The only thing he cared about was Tom. He was all he needed. He was his oxygen. He was his everything.

Sobbing, Michael gently laid Tom's body back on the floor. He lay next to him and cuddled, wishing they could trade places, wishing he could make all the pain go away.

Make the pain go away.

Michael closed his eyes and rested his lips against Tom's lips. He thought about all the beautiful moments they'd shared together, and all the beautiful moments that were still destined to happen. His face warmed and electricity flowed. He drowned himself in memories and plans for the future, plans him and Tom had made together. They would be united forever. They were two halves of a perfect being. Broken, they were nothing.

Together, together, together.

Michael breathed.

Then so did Tom.

The Withering
BRUCE GOLDEN

I lay here, as I have lain for so long, like a crumpled fetus, waiting for an end that will not come. I beg for it . . . I pray for it. But even as I wait for a cessation to my terrible existence, I know it is only a seductive fantasy. I imagine release, escape, blissful freedom—for imagination is all I have left. How perversely ironic that the cause of my damnation is now my sole salvation.

The air reeks of disinfectant as it does habitually, and the only sounds I hear are distant murmurings. There's a chill in the air so I clutch futilely at the lone, coarse sheet that covers me, and open my eyes to the same austere wall, the same mocking shadows that greet me in perpetuity.

This time, though, I see a slight variation. Something is there. Something I can barely discern in the feeble light. A tiny, quivering, wiggle of activity. I strain to focus and see a caterpillar laboriously weaving its cocoon. Somehow it has made the herculean trek to where the wall and ceiling intersect, and has attached itself in the crevice there.

The Withering

As I lay here, I wonder what resplendent form will emerge from that cocoon. But even this vision is eventually muted by the despair that possesses my soul. I struggle not to reason, because there is no reason. Guilt or innocence, fact or fiction—they are concepts that no longer matter. All that matters are the gray ruins of my memories—memories that play out across the desolate fields of my mind. I cling to them the way a madman clings to sanity. In truth, I'm but a single, aberrant thought from slipping into the murky, swirling abyss of madness myself. So I try to remember.

I remember the carefree excursions I took to the ocean as a child—the warm sand, the cool water, the waves lapping at my ankles. I remember the university, in the days before reformation. The camaraderie of my fellow students. The give and take of creative discourse. Soaring over the sea cliffs on a crude hang glider built by a classmate. The girl with the bright red hair for whom I secretly longed. I remember many things, but always there is one tenacious, tumultuous recollection that intrudes.

It's always the same. The same thunderous sound of cracking wood as my door bursts open. The same flurry of booted feet violating the sanctum of my thoughts. The same rough hands that assault and bind me.

I remember the looks of hatred and repugnance, the shouted threats of violence from unfamiliar voices. The relentless malice focused upon me was like a living thing. Time and space became a rancorous blur as I stood in the center of an imposing room, still bound, surrounded by more strangers. I was on display, the accused in a courtroom where only the degree of my guilt seemed subject to debate.

Much of what occurred that day is lost in a haze of obscurity, but I clearly remember the prosecutor's embittered summation.

"The facts are incontrovertible, honorable Justice," I recall him stating with restrained assurance. "A routine scan of the accused's personal files disclosed numerous writings, both prosaic and poetical in nature, which can only be described as obscene and disturbingly antisocial. Public decorum prevents me from detailing the improprieties here, though the complete volume of these degradations can be found in the articles of evidence.

"In addition to the *possession* of these heinous works of pornography, the accused fully admits to authoring them. I say he stands guilty of counts both actual and abstract. I request that no leniency be shown by the court, and that he be sentenced under the severest penalties allowed for such crimes."

I distinctly remember the prosecutor, indifferent but confident, returning to his seat as the presiding justice contemplated the charges.

Turning a stern glance toward me, the justice methodically asked, "Does the accused have any statement to make before judgment is passed?"

I remember standing there, befuddled by the ritual of it all, unable to accept the realization that it was *my* fate they were discussing. When it seemed I wouldn't reply, the justice opened his mouth to issue the verdict, and I quickly stammered the only thing I could think of.

"I . . . I admit I wrote things that may be considered

The Withering

inappropriate by some, but they were simply meanderings of a personal nature, never meant for public dissemination. In no sense was I propagating the enforcement of my ideals upon society. They . . . they were simple fantasies, scribblings of an unfettered imagination, nothing more."

"Surely," boomed the justice, "throughout the course of this trial, if not previously, you have been made aware that, under our governing jurisprudence, thought *is* deed."

When I failed to respond, he went on. "If you have nothing further to say in your defense, I rule, by law, your guilt has been determined within reasonable doubt. I hereby sentence you to the withering."

I remember the clamor of hushed voices swelling like a balloon about to burst as the words were repeated throughout the courtroom.

"The withering."

The sound reverberated inside my skull, but terror and denial colored my reality. The withering. It was something spoken of only in whispers. No one I had ever known knew the truth of it. There were only rumors, grisly tales with no substance, yet the power to invoke dismay and horror.

Much of what happened next is a void of innocuous bureaucracy, but I remember the room where it took place. I was still bound, this time by sturdy leather straps that embraced my wrists and ankles. Except for the straps I was naked. Lost in the surreality of the moment, I felt no humiliation at my nakedness, but was overwhelmed by a pervading sense of vulnerability. I remember a chill in the room. There was a draft blowing from somewhere nearby. A single bright light was positioned so that it blinded me with its glare.

Three others were in the room. One I designated the "doctor," and two men who assisted her. They went about their business with systematic efficiency, seeming to ignore my obvious presence.

Then, without really acknowledging me with her eyes, the doctor began explaining the procedure. Paralyzed with fearful anticipation, I failed to absorb much of what she said. I remember only bits and pieces. Something about "hormonal injections" . . . "osteo and rheumatoid mutations" . . . "effects which bypass the brain."

The technical details of her explanation became a mere backdrop when I spied the row of hypodermics. Its length extended beyond absurdity, and when she reached for the first one I braced for the pain to come. However, after a few minor stings, I felt only a pinching sensation as needles were inserted with care into my thighs, my forearms, my neck . . . and on and on until each violation of my body no longer mattered. I must have passed out at some point, because when I awoke I was in another place.

I have no idea how long I was asleep, but as I weaned myself from unconsciousness I felt a stiffness that convinced me I had been lying there for some time. I tried to move but couldn't. I saw no restraints holding me down, so I tried again. I was successful, briefly, if you consider inducing a stabbing pain somewhere in my back a success. The pain convinced me to forego any further attempts at movement. So I shook off the vestiges of slumber and tried to recall with more clarity what had happened.

The Withering

Oh, that it could only have been a horrible dream. But my reality had become a nightmare, one I hadn't yet grasped in its fullness. I know now nothing could have prepared me for what I was about to learn.

After I lay motionless for some time, a white-coated attendant approached me and bent over to engage in some sort of interaction with my bed.

"Where am I?" I asked, my voice cracking with dryness. "What's wrong with me? Why can't I move?"

The attendant made no sign he heard me. Instead he pushed my bed into a corridor that stretched on without end. The wheels churned below me as we passed cubicle after grim cubicle. In the dim light I saw other beds, beds occupied by inert bodies. The shadows and the constant jog of movement prevented me from seeing more until we came to a halt. The attendant departed, leaving me as naked and helpless as the day I was brought into this harsh world.

The alcove where I had been left was much brighter, and it took time for my eyes to adjust. Unable to turn my head without great pain, I could look in only one direction. Facing me was a metallic wall or door of some sort. The metal's sheen was highly reflective, and in its mirrored surface I saw myself.

Rather, I saw what I had become.

I have no idea how long I screamed before my cacophonous lament attracted a swarm of attendants who quickly sedated me. But I'm sure I wasn't the first, or the last, to wail in terror inside those somber halls.

I try not to remember what I saw in that hideous reflection. But I can't forget that my fingers are now gnarled deformities, my arms shrunken and folded against my chest as if my tendons had shriveled. I

Bruce Golden

know the slightest attempt to move my legs will cause indescribable agony that writhes up through my hips and assaults my spinal cord. I can try to forget that my once wavy hair has been shaved to a coarse stubble, but the feeling my lips are dry and cracked is ever-present, and too often my skin is aflame with a devilish itch I cannot scratch.

Warehoused like a spare part that no longer serves any purpose, my days passing into years, I suck sullen gruel through toothless gums and wait for the impersonal touch of an attendant to wipe my body clean. It is a morose whim of fate indeed, that even such routine maintenance is a welcome diversion to an otherwise monotonous subsistence.

Trapped in a useless husk, perched on the precipice of lunacy, I turn inward for deliverance. From a place deep within I rise and soar high above other lands, gliding lazily into other times. They don't know about my journeys. They think I'm a prisoner of this room. They don't know I become other people—bold people, curious people, people who commemorate their adventures in rhyme. I don't tell them about the rhymes or the improper thoughts that creep into my head. I still dare to imagine the unimaginable, but no one knows. They won't find me in here. In here I don't allow myself to dwell on past transgressions. I seek no pity nor submit to reproach. And, no matter how seductive its siren call, in here I resist the longing for sweet death.

Instead, like the caterpillar, I wait to emerge from my cocoon, spread my glorious wings, and fly.

Grave Secrets
JG FAHERTY

The town exuded an air of sullen hostility that seemed as much a part of its natural condition as the clammy mists obscuring the moss-encrusted sign announcing *Welcome To Rocky Point*.

Eric Wagner's pulse sped up and he gripped the wheel of his 1965 Fleetwood tighter, although it wasn't the slippery road that had him anxious.

This is it.

He guided the car down the exit ramp. In the passenger seat, Arthur leaned forward, his brow furrowed as if trying to part the mists through sheer force of will.

Not for the first time since leaving Hoboken, Eric wondered if he'd made the right decision bringing the boy.

He's a young man now, not a boy. Almost twenty-one. I wasn't much older than him when I got married.

Since Annie's death the previous year, Arthur had grown distant, withdrawn, spending most of his time in his room. He'd always been close to his mother. So when he'd insisted on coming along, the thought of them spending time together had been too appealing and Eric eventually gave in, despite his misgivings.

I won't let anything happen to him.

Besides, there'd been no time to discuss things. The urgency to leave had been too great. He just hoped the decision wouldn't come back to haunt him.

He already had one ghost doing that.

A mile of driving brought them to the center of town. Gray vapors leached all the color from the small village, turning it into a faded version of reality. The bright colors of autumn leaves, which had created a spectacular watercolor of vibrant joy during the ride up from New Jersey, were gone, replaced by monochromes of brown. Even the buildings and cars seemed muted, as if God had put the entire town through too many wash cycles.

The few people they saw looked pale and listless as they went about their morning routines, opening shops or getting into cars.

"So where do we go now?" Arthur asked.

"The bungalows." It had been twenty-five years since his parents were notified that Wade's Packard had been found abandoned in the forests north of Rocky Point, but he remembered the name of the tourist court as if he'd heard it yesterday: Andre's Lodge. He'd been overseas, aiding with the administration of war supplies for the Allied troops, when Wade disappeared, so he'd never seen his brother's last known address in person.

Now he intended to stay there, recreate Wade's visit. And in the process, discover why his brother had

Grave Secrets

been so interested in the desolate forests outside of town that he'd given his life to discover their secrets.

Hopefully, that would also end the dreams.

Wandering through a dark landscape, surrounded by towering trees and vast swamps. Cold mist hiding things that lurked in the gloom. Things that spoke in peculiar grunts and clicks. Dread laying heavy across his shoulders, causing his heart to pound and his legs to shake. But he couldn't stop. He had to keep going. Had to help Wade—

Eric bit his lip and forced down the memory of his nightmare. The same one he'd had the past three nights. Each time, he'd woken covered in sweat, hands trembling and heart pounding so badly he'd feared it would burst. Still, he'd never considered visiting Rocky Point until the letter came.

It arrived on October sixth, two days after Wade began plaguing his sleep. No return address, although the blurred postmark indicated it originated in Rocky Point, New York. The sight of that name, after dreaming of his brother, turned his stomach to ice.

The handwritten script on the envelope gave no clues. Jagged, scrawling letters, as if written by a shaking or uneducated hand. A single sheet, neatly folded, sat inside. He removed it, noting several dark smudges on the paper, which smelled vaguely of mildew. Lines of the same rough characters ran across the page in uneven fashion.

Dear Eric,

It's been too long since I last wrote, and for that I apologize. But events here in Rocky

JG Faherty

Point have had me occupied to the point of obsession. However, I believe my work has come to fruition. I've discovered something, a wondrous secret. The library here, it's a treasure trove of lost information. And if what I think is true . . . No, I won't tell you. You'd think me crazy. And perhaps I am. God knows it feels that way sometimes. You must come, see for yourself. Join me, Eric. One last adventure, like old times.

All my best,

Wade

He and Arthur had left the following day.

***

Eric dropped his bag on the bed and sat down. A thin, lumpy mattress greeted him, and he wondered if it was the same one Wade had slept on in 1940. Arthur tested its twin on the other side of the small room and frowned, then headed for the tiny bathroom.

Alone, Eric's thoughts turned to his younger days, when he and Wade had spent weekends and holidays chasing Wade's elusive theories. Those had been good times, helping his older brother search for clues to mysteries most people had never heard of.

And what led you here? Eric stared out the window. The dismal October morning was grudgingly giving way to a dreary October day, the sun struggling to force its rays through the fog that continued to shroud the town. *What theory were you chasing?*

Theories.

Grave Secrets

Wade never lacked one, and they always centered around things decidedly unnatural. Hauntings. Strange lights in the sky. Rumors of creatures lurking in deep woods. Local legends scientists scoffed at.

Over the years, Wade had continued to seek out answers, long after Eric gave it up and joined the family business. He'd kept in touch sporadically, mailing Eric from one remote locale or another, draining his bank account as fast as their father replenished it.

Throughout the thirties, those letters arrived every few months. St. Georges, Bermuda. Sedona, Arizona. Bridgewater, Massachusetts. Lake Champlain.

The final one had arrived several days after Wade's disappearance. October 3, 1940. Decades later, Eric still remembered it word for word.

Eric,

I've arrived in Rocky Point. How I wish you were with me. Not a day goes by that I don't miss having you as a companion on these quests. Your cheerful demeanor would be most welcome here. The people of this gloomy place are like their town, dour and surly. Attempts at conversation are met with guarded answers at best, and downright hostile glares as often as not. Tomorrow I will visit the library. If all goes well, I will find the information I need.

Mysterious, I know, and this may prove to be yet another dead end. I have high hopes, though.

JG Faherty

> *All my best,*
>
> *Wade*

Dour and surly. That certainly described the clerk who'd registered them when they arrived. He'd been a most queer fellow, with a thin, oddly-shaped head and crooked, protruding teeth that hinted strongly at inbreeding. After struggling to count the cash Eric handed over, he'd passed them their key with a glare.

"Don't want no trouble, hear?" he'd muttered, his breath bordering on poisonous. Repelled by the stench, Eric took the key and left.

Dour and surly, indeed. Maybe tomorrow—

A series of three quick knocks interrupted his thought. He crossed the room and opened the door, expecting to see the rodent-faced clerk. Instead, he found an empty parking lot.

And an envelope on the top step, with his name on it and the address of the motor court underneath.

Eric's gut twisted as he recognized the barely legible writing.

Once again, dark smudges tarnished the otherwise clean paper, like blight on healthy fruit. A foul odor wafted up as he pulled the letter free. More of the marks stained the edges.

> *Eric,*
>
> *This place! I believe it's the key to everything I've been searching for. A nexus, if you will. Like the one in Arkham. There are*

Grave Secrets

things there, things that shouldn't exist. I know how this sounds. You must think me crazy. Perhaps I am. But if I'm not, then how to explain the movements in the shadows, the whispers in the night? Voices in empty rooms?

I hope you will join me soon. I want you to witness this. Please hurry. They're waiting for us.

All my best,

Wade

A quick check of the postmark showed it had been mailed on October sixth, the same day he'd received the previous one. And like the other, the year on the postmark was ruined, as if someone had run a thumb across it before the ink dried.

"How did anyone know we'd be here?" Arthur asked, peering over his shoulder.

Eric shook his head, fighting the urge to crumple the letter and throw it across the room. He wanted to believe it was somebody's idea of a sick joke, but who would do such a thing? And why now? Twenty-five years to the week of Wade's disappearance. And then there were the dreams . . .

Eric rubbed his temples, where a dull ache had formed. He needed answers.

And he knew where to start.

***

The Post Office squatted at the end of Main Street, gray stone walls nearly invisible in the fog, a limp, discolored American flag hanging from a pole.

JG Faherty

A grim-faced young woman greeted them with narrowed eyes and a curt, "Yes?" No name tag adorned her uniform; a peculiar decorative pin sat in its place. A brown octopus. Or perhaps a squid. Eric couldn't be sure.

"Someone sent these to me from here." Eric laid the two envelopes down. "I need to find out who."

The woman shook her head. "Can't help you."

"Then tell me who can. I'm not leaving until I get some answers."

"Only person who can help you is Rory Calvert, the regular clerk. And he's dead."

"What?"

"Yep. Murdered. Right there." The woman pointed behind her. For the first time, a hint of animation entered her voice. "Three days ago. I'm just filling in."

"What happened?" Arthur asked.

"It was awful." A vulgar grin showed her true feelings. "They found him all torn up. World's getting to be a crazy place."

Her smile grew wider, almost manic. Seeing it, Eric lost all desire to question her further. They could find out the rest of the details at the library.

"Yes. Well, thank you." He turned toward the door, Arthur already two steps ahead of him.

"You're gonna die out there, just like your brother."

Eric whirled around. The woman was gone.

"Hey!" He ran to the counter and shouted again. When no one answered, he climbed over. A quick search of the sorting area revealed nothing but bags of mail and a back exit, locked from the inside. A dank odor permeated the small space, reminiscent of wet earth and rotting leaves.

Grave Secrets

"Dad, let's go." Arthur tugged his sleeve, his eyes troubled.

Walking to the car, Eric found himself glancing back, unable to shake the feeling of being watched.

***

At two in the afternoon, Eric and Arthur had the second floor of the Rocky Point Public Library to themselves. Weak, flickering lights fought a losing battle against a gloom created by thickening clouds outside and decades of grime on the tall windows.

Eric leaned back and rubbed his eyes, which burned from hours of scanning microfilmed documents. At a nearby table, Arthur made his way through stacks of books on the history of the Hudson Valley in general, and Rocky Point in particular.

Eric's stomach churned as he struggled to make sense of everything he'd learned. Based on Wade's interest in the town, Eric had expected to find something odd when he delved into Rocky Point's past, but nothing like the awful things he'd read.

Since its formation in the 1600s, the town had endured a non-stop series of macabre occurrences that continued to the present time. A leper colony burned to the ground. A mental institution illegally experimenting on patients in the 1940s. Rumors of ghosts haunting the cemetery. Entire families vanishing in the middle of the night. Strange lights in the swamplands to the north of town.

The same area where the police had discovered Wade's car.

Eric clutched his sweater tighter as a chill danced its way through him. Questions swirled in his head like the wind-blown leaves on the sidewalks outside.

JG Faherty

Sudden claustrophobia constricted his chest and made it hard to breath. The room took on an ominous air and he realized it had grown much darker. He glanced at the windows, saw heavy storm clouds looming over the town. A miasma of corrupted flesh and rotten vegetation assaulted his nose. Downstairs, a door closed with a *bang!* that made him jump and turn, half-expecting to see a monstrous creature coming toward him, fangs dripping and claws ready to rend meat from bone.

Get out!

He leaped up and ran for the stairs, took them two at a time, his pounding footsteps echoing off the cinderblock walls. At the bottom, he shouldered the door open and sped past the front desk, where a librarian with a noticeable hump glowered through thick glasses. Only when he stood on the sidewalk, breath steaming in the chill air, did his anxiety fade. By the time Arthur burst through the front doors, Eric had calmed himself to the point where his pulse no longer throbbed in his temples.

"What happened?"

"I'm fine." Eric waved him away.

"You don't look fine."

"I needed to get some air. Clear my head."

"Oh." Arthur's face registered disbelief, but he didn't press the issue. Eric took a deep breath, then glanced up as the first rain drops struck the ground.

Movement in one of the library's upstairs windows caught his eye, an indistinct shadowy form that raised the hairs on his neck. Something about its shape seemed . . . *wrong*.

"We better get back to the room."

Grave Secrets

For the rest of the evening, he couldn't stop thinking about the image in the window.

That, and the postal worker's pin.

***

A queer silence surrounded him, as if the mist had sucked away all sound. Or perhaps all life. Yet somehow he knew he wasn't alone. The sensation of being watched followed him, unseen eyes observing his every move.

Over hills, squeezing between broken mountains of stone, the trail led deeper into the forest. Pockets of slick leaves soaked his shoes and threatened to send him tumbling down rocky slopes.

The stench of sulfurous swamp gas mixed with putrid flesh filled the air. A branch snapped, the sound a gunshot in the preternatural stillness. He turned, caught the merest glimpse of movement among the shadows. An impression of something tall, with too many limbs. A few steps later, a belching croak spun him in the other direction. The feeling of unseen eyes grew stronger. More grunting, deep and low, now from both sides of the path. Someone calling his name. A familiar voice. Wade—

Eric woke with a gasp, the depraved noises fading as his dream dissolved. A final grunt, followed by a muffled thump, turned his gaze toward the windows, where dull, pre-dawn light filtered in through a haze of damp filth. For a moment, it had almost seemed like the noises came from outside . . .

No. He shook his head, as much in negation as to clear the last remnants of sleep.

The path. I know where it is. He could still see it, a map imprinted in his brain. The trail Wade had followed. A new urgency filled him. They had to leave now or they'd lose the window of opportunity.

A part of him insisted he should just get in the car and leave, put Rocky Point and its awful secrets behind him, never return. Except he couldn't. If he did, Wade's fate would forever remain a mystery, a question nagging at him.

So I'll be careful. I know it might be dangerous. I won't take any risks. But I can't delay.

He roused Arthur, told him they were leaving, then opened the door, intending to go warm up the car. Omnipresent mist delivered a damp greeting. The previous day's rains had abated, leaving moist air that reeked of mold and earth. A wet carpet of leaves, pine needles, and acorns covered the ground in somber yellows and browns, a harbinger of November's drab coat.

Returning from the car, he approached the open door and paused at the sight of peculiar marks on the window.

Four vertical lines extending out from wide smudges. In between the two fan-shaped blemishes was a single, circular smear. He put a hand up to one of the larger marks and shivered. Take away his thumb and the pattern looked alarmingly like a hand. One twice the size of his own, with fingers much wider at their tips than their base. And the mark in the middle . . .

He thought about the noises he'd heard earlier and a disturbing picture formed in his head. A wild beast, its feet and nose pressed against the glass, watching them sleep. Darting away when it saw him start to wake.

The grunt. The thump.

Grave Secrets

He turned his gaze downward. Areas of flattened grass under the window. More of them leading toward the parking lot, longer and wider than a human foot. They disappeared when they reached the blacktop. Eric looked across the lot, where the woods and swamplands began, their depths veiled by the mist. A fetid, boggy smell hung in the air, reminiscent of the odor they'd encountered in the post office.

No animal did this. Wild animals don't peer into windows. Or leave letters.

Another shiver made him twitch. For the first time since arriving in Rocky Point, he prayed the fog wouldn't lift.

Some things were better left unseen.

***

Arthur remained silent during the treacherous drive through the winding roads of Harriman State Park, hands gripping his armrests with white-knuckled intensity as they sped through harrowing bends and twists that remained hidden by the mist until the very last second. Anxiety permeated Eric's being as well, but it had nothing to do with the sharp curves or slick surface. Despite the poor visibility, he knew which turns to take, just as he knew when to bring the car to a stop next to a shallow stream that carved through the woods.

His concern stemmed from a growing pressure inside him, a gut sensation that they needed to hurry. *Wade . . . he's out there. Waiting. But not for long.*

"This is it."

Arthur raised an eyebrow but didn't question the statement. Instead, he joined Eric at the front of the car to view a somber, primeval world, as if they'd driven back in time rather than twenty miles from town. Their breath created miniature clouds in the cool air, which quickly melded with the all-encompassing fog. That same fog reduced visibility to a few yards and dampened noise and flesh alike, leaving the trickling water and the metallic *tic-tic* of the engine as the only sounds. Eric stared at the vine-covered trees, their tops lost in the murky vapors, and an image came to him, so real his heart stuttered. A prehistoric beast lumbering out of the forest, its maw filled with jagged teeth—

"Which way?"

"There." Glad to have his thoughts interrupted, Eric pointed at a narrow space between some crimson thorn bushes. Everything was just as he'd dreamt. The gradual uphill slope, the whirling vapors filling the spaces between the trees with cloying moisture, the preternatural silence.

He stepped across the creek into the thick underbrush, ignoring the wet leaves that soaked his pants and the twigs and barbs that snagged his coat. Twenty feet in and the fog swallowed the car. Another ten and he lost the chuckle of water flowing over rocks, leaving nothing but the soft swish of their pants and the muffled scuffing of their shoes against decades of moldering leaves to break the graveyard hush.

For the next hour, the trail twisted between towering trees and boulders the size of houses and took them over several hills before it reached a stretch of flat land bordered on both sides by endless swamp.

"This place gives me the creeps," Arthur said.

Eric looked at Arthur, who was scanning the woods, his eyes narrowed.

Grave Secrets

"It doesn't matter." Eric continued on, doing his best to ignore his own imaginings of bloated nightmare creatures hiding behind trees and rocks. Arthur sighed and followed.

As they moved deeper into the wetlands, the air took on a rank aroma, a heady mix of sulfur and decomposition that turned breathing into an unpleasant chore. From time to time the mists thinned, creating narrow bands of visibility, just enough to reveal glimpses of black waters covered in a repugnant greenish-brown slime. Dead trees jutted from the quagmire, gray spires devoid of branches and tapering to sharp points at the top. Their hollow, decomposing trunks made Eric wonder if the water contained toxic chemicals, a noxious byproduct of the dreadful scum coating everything.

Furtive noises broke the silence. The soft plop of something ducking into the water, the low *chunk-glunk* of clandestine amphibians calling out. Ordinary sounds, yet somehow threatening at the same time. No mundane creatures could survive in such a malevolent environment. Eric's imagination was only too happy to deliver images of deformed, semi-sentient monstrosities, with tentacles for limbs and too many eyes. Mutant guardians announcing the presence of intruders to whatever lay beyond the next set of hills.

The trail curved and bent its way ever deeper into the forest. The stench of corruption grew worse, coating Eric's tongue and filling his nose. He found himself worrying about what contaminants or vile spores he might be breathing in. Still, there could be no turning back.

Wade needs me.

JG Faherty

The noises increased in volume, chirps and bleats and croaks graduating into crocodilian bellows and rumbles.

Splashes in the water drew his attention, but each time he was too slow, left with only glimpses of muddy ripples. Hints of movement along the trail caught his eye, momentary flashes of darker gray that never resolved into distinct shapes.

"Maybe we should turn around."

Eric jumped a little at Arthur's words, the first he'd spoken since they entered the wetlands.

Maybe we should. This place, it's not safe. It's already taken your brother. Why risk losing your son?

"Eric, I need you." Wade's voice. Urgent.

No. I have to go on. I have to know.

"I can't stop now." Without explaining further, he turned and continued walking. Arthur muttered a curse but Eric ignored it. Nothing was going to prevent him from seeing the journey to its end.

Nothing.

After another half hour, the trail sloped upward and mounds of earth and rock replaced the fetid waters. Trees created impenetrable walls on both sides of the path, some with trunks so wide two men couldn't have circled them with their arms. These giants stood sentinel among their smaller relatives, all clothed in offensive molds and lichens that made Eric wary of touching anything, for fear of contagion. As the path grew steeper, dirt and leaves gave way to loose stones interspersed with sections of flat shale made treacherously slick by moisture and slime. Repulsive mushrooms sprouted between the rocks and along the sides of the trail, their bulbous caps brown and leprous.

The movement in the mist grew more pronounced, the vague shapes setting Eric's heart pounding as they darted between trees or behind rocks. Some of the shadowy creatures appeared no larger than foxes, slinking along the ground. Others gave the impression of immense size, with shapes that defiled natural order, blasphemous figures with bizarre protuberances and limbs in places God never intended.

The trail continued to rise and their breathing became labored, adding a steady rhythm to the intimidating sounds of snapping branches and antediluvian grunts emanating from the shrouded depths. Eric forced his legs to work harder, paying no heed to the twin dangers of the steep slope and slippery surface. When they reached the summit, Arthur asked him if he wanted to rest and Eric shook his head.

"No. No time." A wordless voice kept telling him to hurry, to—

Find me. Find me.

"I'm coming, Wade. I'm almost there."

They descended into a fog so dense it created an almost solid wall that made it impossible to see more than two steps ahead. Brown-leafed trees crowded the trail, forcing them to walk single file. The vicious fetor of decay attacked their noses with each brush of flesh against mildewed wood, with each abhorrent fungus crushed underfoot.

Eric's compulsion built to a crescendo and he broke into a run, dashing blindly down the slope. A distant voice called to him but he ignored it, all his attention focused on what lay at the bottom of the rocky path.

Wade. He's there. Waiting. They've brought me to him. That was their purpose, to—

The mist broke, revealing the pit at the base of the hill, a voracious, gaping maw eager for food. He tried to stop but his feet slid on a patch of wet leaves and he fell, arms wind-milling in a desperate, hopeless attempt to catch his balance.

Too late—

Strong hands pulled him away. He hit the ground hard, the impact driving the breath from his lungs. He lay there, gasping for air, his body so close to the edge one arm dangled over the side.

"Are you all right?"

Arthur's face appeared above him, eyes wide with concern. Eric nodded and sat up, wincing at the aches in his hip and ribs.

"Thank you," he whispered. He wanted to say more, but his heaving chest wouldn't allow it.

Arthur moved away and knelt at the edge. Looked down. His face went pale and he bit his lip.

"What is it?" Eric asked. Arthur shook his head.

Eric's body moved of its own volition, even as his brain screamed for it to stop. He had to see. Despite his pain, he knelt on the sodden leaves and peered over the edge. Cold air wafted from the pit, carrying a sweet yet sickening odor, sugar and spice and sun-baked roadkill all rolled into one.

Twenty feet down lay the remains of a body.

Wooden spikes protruded through the corpse's stomach, legs, and shoulders. More jutted from the dirt. Layers of aged, yellowed bones provided evidence this wasn't the first victim the pit had claimed.

I was supposed to be the next.

Grave Secrets

Eric brushed the disquieting thought aside and forced himself to look at the impaled remains.

Mottled strips of decomposed flesh decorated the lich. A skeleton face stared up, jaw open in a madhouse grin. Strings of white hair, long enough to reach the shoulders, created a mop-like effect around the skull. Only a few shreds of clothing remained, identifiable as denim pants and a tan bush shirt. Naked bones protruded from disintegrating hiking boots. Patches of gelatinous brownish-green mold sullied large areas of the body.

One fleshless hand clutched a leather-bound book.

Eric let out a low moan. He recognized that book, knew it as surely as he knew it was Wade lying at the bottom of the pit.

I should be right next to him, skewered and dying the way he did.

Everything he'd experienced—the dreams, the letters, the force compelling him to throw caution to the wind—all of it with one purpose.

To kill me.

But why? Eric stared down at his dead brother and wished he would speak, reveal the secrets he'd kept all these years.

The book.

Hope surged in Eric's chest. Wade's notes. The answers would be in there. The leather strap and metal buckle holding it closed looked intact, despite decades of exposure to the elements.

He leaned farther over the edge. Could he climb down? A closer look . . .

Earth gave way under his hands and knees and he pitched forward. A dozen spikes loomed beneath him, promising a slow, painful death.

Then he was on his back, staring at the same gray sky Wade had contemplated for so many decades.

"Jesus, Dad, what were you thinking?"

"The book. We have to get it." Even as he spoke, he understood he'd been tricked again. Whatever wanted him dead hadn't given up yet. Which only made him need the answers even more.

"It's too dangerous. We can't get down there."

"No." Eric struggled to sit up, pulling free of Arthur's grip. "Wade's secrets, they're in that book. He wants me to have it."

"That's crazy."

"I have to." Eric stood up. The world tilted and Wade's voice whispered, *"Just one more step."*

Arthur stepped in front of him, put his face close. "Dad, listen. It's this place. We have to leave. Now."

Eric saw fear in his son's eyes, a barely-controlled terror that did more to break through his insane need than any pleading words.

What if it wants us both dead?

He couldn't let that happen. Discovering the truths he sought wasn't worth his son's life. Whatever unwholesome things his brother had uncovered would have to remain a mystery.

At least for now.

Eric looked at Arthur and felt like he was seeing him for the first time. His son really had grown into a man.

That man deserved to live.

"You're right," he said, feeling a sense of relief he saw echoed in Arthur's eyes. "Let's go home."

This time Arthur led the way, giving the pit a wide berth. Eric glanced back only once. The dark hole already lay unseen in the deceiving mists, once again waiting to engulf the unwary.

I'll come back for you, Wade. And next time, I'll be prepared. I'll bring you and your secrets home.

Deep in the forest, a primordial bellow challenged his promise.

End of the Hall
HUNTER LIGUORE

An iridescent glow, a mixture of the moon's soft light and the mahogany floors, formed a tunnel from my bed to the window at the end of the hall. As far as I knew the window was nailed shut—a dozen rusted nails—so, how did the woman with red, muddy boots get through?

The house was an old colonial, constructed by Dutch immigrants in the late 1700s when the town of Durham, Connecticut, was just beginning to settle. The town was known for its agriculture, wooded lands, and the occasional visits of George Washington before he became the first president, an honor still recognized every Memorial Day with the George Washington Run, a marathon that followed the original trail forged by Washington. While there are many bronze trail markers scattered around town to mark the trail, one happened to be situated at the end of our property, a fact, my mother said, is the reason Grandma Issy purchased the house.

After Grandma Issy died seven years ago, when I

End of the Hall

was eight, my family moved into the house. My older brother Tad, now a senior in high school, had first dibs on the attic room, while my younger sister Jill, who was just a baby then, got the room at the top of the stairs, down the hall from Mom and Dad's room, and up until two weeks ago I had the largest room on the first floor across from the kitchen.

Mom stopped me at the front door one morning when I was on my way to school.

"Davey, we need to have a little talk."

I could see her reflection in the glass pane. Her hair looked like yellow yarn and was pulled back into a ponytail. Her forehead was sweaty, like she'd been working hard even at that early hour, and she had on Dad's dirty work-gloves. She had been hounding me all week for a talk. I'd avoided her each time assuming it had something to do with progress reports sent out that week and the D+ I was holding in history.

I followed her into the kitchen where Dad was at the table drinking the milk left over from his cereal. He was wearing a Hartford Whaler's T-shirt and jeans.

"Aren't you going to be late for work?" I asked.

"I'm taking a couple days off so me and your mom can do a little redecorating. That's why we wanted to talk to you, buddy." Dad placed his bowl in the sink and pulled out a chair from the table, indicating I should sit. I drank the juice I had hurriedly left behind, hoping in some small way to hide behind it.

"We wanted to talk to you about your room." Mom folded her arms and leaned against the sink.

"I said I'd clean it this weekend. What's one more day?" I reasoned.

Hunter Ligoure

"What your mother is trying to say, Davey, is that we want to make a switch. Your room for ours."

"Huh?"

"We've outgrown our room," Mom began, "there's hardly enough space for our clothes. I've taken over most of the closets in the hall, and your father has been storing things in the basement. Frankly, it's too small for us."

"Take Tad's room." My mind went through a series of excuses why they shouldn't take my room. It wasn't fair, for starters. Just when I was about to say something, Mom pulled out a pink slip of paper.

"This came in the mail yesterday." She placed it in front of me, so I could see the D+ clearly. "We could go easy on you if you agree to make the switch."

"This doesn't mean we won't be checking your homework," Dad began, "or keeping you in after school until the grade goes up. It means we won't ground you which would be a lot worse."

There was nothing worse than being grounded. It amounted to endless rigorous chores like cleaning the radiators, cleaning the supper dishes, or washing the basement walls, and being bored at home to the point that grocery shopping with Mom would be a relief rather than torture. I had no choice but to accept.

Two weeks ago, on a sunny May weekend, the entire family moved all my things into my parent's room. The bathroom was closer, but so was Jill, who could be a pain when she wanted. Her red pigtails bobbed every time she knocked on the doorframe to see if I wanted to play. Having to listen to Tad's music thumping through the ceiling really sucked. And there was the window at the end of the hall.

End of the Hall

When we originally moved in I remember Dad trying to open the window to let in some air. I was carrying boxes up to Tad's room when Mom said, "It's nailed, see? She pointed to each nail. "Why would someone do a thing like that?" he asked. "For a reason," Mom said, nonchalantly, and added, "It's been that way since I was in high school." That's the only time I ever remember them discussing it.

I always considered myself a sound sleeper, even though I had a brief bout of sleepwalking when I was younger, around the time Grandma Issy died. My parents thought it might have been because of losing her. Now, I also rarely woke up in the middle of the night. But that all changed in my new room.

The first night, I awoke to the sound of footsteps on the wood floor, and no ordinary footsteps either, not like Tad's when he comes in late and tries to tiptoe to the attic door. It sounded more like wet mud and a hard heel dragging closer and closer to my room. Light came from a tiny nightlight in the bathroom, allowing me to see down the hall. I called for Jill, but then I could hear her snoring loudly. My heart raced. I turned, placing my pillow in front of me like a shield. The footsteps came nearer and then disappeared altogether. The house was quiet again, all but the clock ticking.

I chocked it up to typical house noises that I wasn't used to. But then each night, for several days, I woke up to the same sound of footsteps—it was like someone was moving down the hall towards me—only when I looked, no one was there. The steps came to the foot of my doorway, and then they would stop.

By the following week I decided to leave a light on

in my room, but Tad made a wisecrack, calling me a baby, so I shut it off. I stayed awake until nearly two o'clock in the morning. Then I heard a creak and thud, and the sound of a window opening—the same window that had been nailed shut for forever!

I sat up, bundling the bed covers around me, as the footsteps neared my room. I tried to call out, but my mouth only hung open, wordless, as fear filled my body. I began to sweat and tremble, hoping the noise would go away. But then a pair of red leather boots, caked in mud appeared out of the darkness. Slowly, the boots came closer. My heart and pulse intensified, until I could hear only my shallow breathing. Something or someone was there, shifting in the hallway moving toward me.

The outline of a figure took shape. One bluish pale arm reached out for me, covered with a torn shirt, wet and entangled twigs and bark, as if it had just risen out of a swamp. I screamed, just as I made eye-contact with the figure's one blue eye—then the other eye, which hung by a blood vessel. The closer it came, I saw it was a woman with matted head of red hair. She wore red-leather boots, and her face was water-logged and gray—on her face was a long, red scar, that cracked open with worms, that had been feeding on her decaying flesh; some fell out of her mouth, onto the floor, as she made a heavy frown.

Fear engulfed me—and disbelief—I shook myself, making sure I was awake, and fell off the bed backwards, the blankets falling on top of me. When I looked back to the hall, the woman was gone.

The house seemed ordinary: the clock tick-tocked on the wall; Jill was still snoring down the hall; Tad's

End of the Hall

bed squeaked under him, as he turned over above me. I crawled into bed, still shaken, still wondering if I really had seen the woman or if it had been a hallucination. I sat, eyes on the hall, unable to go back to sleep.

***

The next day I was in history class, falling asleep through the lesson on the Spartan war. My mind was imprinted with the image of the woman and those eyes staring at me. What did she want? I jumped up in class with a slight shriek, causing everyone to laugh at me.

"Give him a break, will you?" Kristen Avery stood up for me, our eyes meeting as she handed back the papers I'd knocked to the floor. It's the longest I think she ever looked at me, and it made me go numb with butterflies inside.

Mr. Dwight, our Neanderthal-looking professor, who used a pool stick as a pointer in class, was attempting to bring the students to order the Spartan way by slamming the stick on the desk in the front row. Luckily, class was over and I escaped my Spartan enemies by retreating into the hallway.

About halfway down the hall, I heard someone calling my name. It was Kristen. She had my notebook raised over her head. Kristen's eyes had a way of saying *I know you*, even though I had hardly said two words to her all year. I wished we'd said more, but I never had the courage to talk to her. She had long brown hair and always wore some shade of lavender clothing. She was one of only a handful of kids in town with divorced parents, something taboo in Durham, and so, according to the masses she was considered an outcast. She also hung out with the older kids. As freshmen, to

Hunter Ligoure

hang out with older kids meant drugs or alcohol were involved. So, rumors circulated that she was also wild in addition to having a poor upbringing. But none of that mattered. To me she was just Kristen, the pretty girl I wished I had the nerve to talk to in history class.

"You forgot this." Kristen smiled, as she handed me my notebook covered in doodles. "I could give you the notes you missed. Mr. Dwight hinted at giving a pop quiz on Monday."

"That would be cool," I mustered, wiping the sweat from my forehead, hoping she didn't see how nervous I was just talking to her.

"Rough night?" We walked to her locker, where she put her books away for first period lunch.

"Couldn't sleep."

"You should hang out with us this weekend. We're all up late enough. You'll sleep afterward."

Kristen didn't have to explain who the "we" were, it was assumed. Sometimes they were called the Pisgah Rats, since they hung out up at Pisgah Mountain getting drunk every weekend.

"Uh, since I'm doing so shitty in history, I'm, uh . . . " I didn't want to tell her I couldn't go, because I was unofficially forbidden to go anywhere until my grade improved.

"I get it," she said, looking down, sadly. "Here are the notes. If you can get them back to me before the end of the day. I need to study, too."

I watched her turn the corner towards the lunchroom feeling like a loser, until I looked at the paper. She had scribbled her phone number in the top corner and the message, "Eight o'clock, Pisgah, bring a jacket."

End of the Hall

At home, Mom had pizza ready for dinner, and by the time Dad came home, I excused myself to my room explaining I had to study for my history quiz. Mom seemed rather surprised, and Dad seemed happy. I was sad to disappoint them when seven-thirty came around and I snuck out of the bedroom window and made for the George Washington trail, heading toward Pisgah Mountain.

With flashlight in-hand, and Kristen's notes, I was a bit anxious to see her. What would we talk about? *Uh, yeah, so there's this one-eyed woman stalking my house at night . . . or not!*

I followed the trail to a fork, and went left to another well-worn path, occasioned with dead branches and overgrown brush. The darkness took on a shape of its own, making it hard to see past the immediate trees. A fox whined in the distance. I felt the sensation that I was being followed, half expecting to turn around and see the woman with the one blue eye, especially with the frequency of strange sounds emanating from the darkness—footsteps, and lots of them.

"Davey Crockett's gonna lead us, boys!" Duff, one of the Pisgah Rats, rushed out of the woods, followed by a half dozen other high school seniors.

"What're you doing here?" I asked, even though I knew the answer.

"Hey, I think we scared him," said another kid.

Then I saw Tad's bushy mop of hair and his favorite green jersey poke through the group. "Ooh, someone's gonna be in trouble."

The group laughed and started walking ahead. Tad lingered behind, curious what I was doing. "Which girl you got a crush on? Beth? No, it's Kristen, isn't it?"

Hunter Ligoure

I tried to play it off, but he kept teasing, until I punched him in the arm.

When we finally reached Pisgah Mountain, I was sweaty and self-conscious about seeing Kristen. There was nothing I could do about it. We took a short cut to the top, which only made me even more drenched and disgusting. At the top, we heard voices and heavy metal music played on a portable radio. A group of girls, including Kristen, lounged around a bonfire that provided warmth and light. The smell of cedar filled up the air, reminding me of cold winters when my dad and I would make a fire to heat up the house. There were at least twenty-five kids sprawled out over different areas of the smooth purple and white rock. Some moved on to higher, more private spaces, while some danced or played hacky-sack in a circle.

Kristen saw me just as Tad and his friends disappeared toward the dark part of the outlook. "You came." Her cheeks were flushed and her hair curled. She wore a lavender hooded sweatshirt.

After we made small talk and I gave her back the history notes, Kristen led me to her favorite spot, a private area where tiny blue flowers grew along the edge. Some kids walked by, poking fun at us for being alone, assuming something more intimate was going to happen. Kristen shrugged them off. "This is how it all begins." I looked over at her, confused. "The rumors. I'm not sure why I come. Maybe because I can't stand to be at home." She sighed and I waited for her to continue. "My mother usually has a boyfriend over. Sometimes she drinks a little too much." She looked up at me quickly. "I'm not wild, Davey, regardless of what everyone says. I come up here to do my own thing, not get wasted. I could do that at home if I wanted to."

I thought that was kind of cool. "I don't listen to rumors," I said. She smiled.

We were quiet with one another. I walked to the edge and tried to glance over the side.

"It's bad luck to look over where someone died." Kristen pointed to a pile of rocks gathered to form a base that held up a cross, constructed from two sticks and string.

"Who was it?"

"Don't know. Some of the older kids might. It happened a long time ago. Whoever it was must've died instantly. It's a really long drop."

I sat next to her, wanting to take her hand, but didn't want to ruin the moment, plus I was too scared.

Kristen pointed. "In the daytime, you can see the center of town from here, the church steeple, and even the Dairy Serve. You can probably see your house, too." She glanced over at me and smiled. "So, what's keeping you from sleeping? You look so tired in class."

Her voice trailed off, as I laid back on the rock. It was peaceful. An occasional breeze filled the air with the smell of burnt embers. I wanted to answer and tell her about the window and the footsteps, but my eyes grew heavy. Kristen's voice faded as she encouraged me to rest.

Through the web and darkness of my dreams a young red-haired woman knelt at the edge of the cliff. She was singing a song, softly. A bottle of rum was beside her. A mixed crowd of teenagers called for her, "Daphne, come on, you're missing all the fun." Daphne joined the drunken dancing and laughter, and then one kid pushed another. Daphne lost her balance and in an instant her body disappeared over the side.

The teenagers disappeared. Time had passed. The night seeped along the edges of the cliff where the cross took the place where Daphne once stood. Then a scraping sound, like metal on stone, filled up the void. It was coming from the side of the mountain. A pale arm reached up out of the abyss and pulled its battered body onto the purple rock. The woman with the one-blue eye came at me, sneering, as worms and maggots spat out of her mouth as she tried to speak. One twisted leg dragged behind her, but she still came at me fast. She reached out and grabbed my arm, sending an electric current of images to my waking mind: *a full moon, a lavender shoe left behind, a newly erected cross, Kristen's tearstained face, my hand covered in blood, a bouquet of blue flowers, discarded, and rain.*

I screamed, waking myself, pulling free from an invisible grip. At first I thought I was alone, but behind me two grungy work-boots stepped closer. I tried scrambling to my feet.

"Where's Kristen?"

"Never mind about Kristen." Duff, who was all muscles under his jean jacket, glared at me. He was also Kristen's ex-boyfriend.

"Duff, leave him alone." Kristen's voice came from behind him.

"He needs to leave you alone," he said.

"We're not together anymore. You have no say."

"Really?" Duff stepped closer and hit me. I fell backward, touching my hand to my face. Blood. I was seeing my hand with blood, like I had seen moments earlier when the woman touched me.

End of the Hall

Duff grabbed a protesting Kristen and left me, as I used my shirt to wipe my face. I started to go after them, but lost my way, and ended up circling back to the cliff's edge, until I finally found the trail back to the bottom. It was two o'clock in the morning. Hardly anyone was left. The fire was out. I asked if anyone had seen Kristen or even Tad, but no one did. I was forced to head home, hoping my folks were still none the wiser that I'd gone out.

Shadows encroached from the forest around me, as I reached the bottom of the mountain, and picked the George Washington trail home. My flashlight gave me little advantage to see ahead. Then somewhere to my left, I heard a sound, like something was being dragged. My first thought—the one-eyed woman was close by.

I started to run, nearly wiping out as I leaped over a decaying log, and then almost into the water of a small brook. When I thought I was a safe distance away from her, I turned my flashlight back, but she was still there coming for me. Her boots made that horrible sound, echoing in the night air. I ran faster, trying to lose her, but it was as if we were glued together by an invisible cord, one I couldn't get free from.

The light from the porch became visible through the last stretch of woods, as I ran as fast as I could, fear taking over me. I didn't stop until I was safely up the steps. The woman coasted by me, toward the side of the house, and neared the second-story window.

"Davey!" My mother's voice made me jump. "Where have you been?" She was waiting for me by the kitchen sink, her angry face turned to worry as she glanced over my appearance. My shirt was covered in blood, and my boots were caked in clay and mud.

"I think someone's out there." I wanted to tell her about the woman. She looked concerned, and for a moment, I thought she'd skip grounding me, until Tad showed up, grinning. "Hey, Mom. Sorry I'm late." He looked at me, kicking his boots off on the porch. "Looks like you beat me home from Pisgah."

"Pisgah? I told you both to never go up there."

"It was my first time," I told her, but that only made her angrier.

"One too many!" She threw the sponge at me. "You're both grounded, and you can start with washing the dishes."

"But Mom," Tad started, giving the usual excuses, like that we were only there was a little while, like that mattered, or that we weren't doing anything bad, like drinking. But she stopped listening, and went to bed.

We did the dishes in silence, then slithered off to bed. I slept with one eye on the window, but it never opened. Not that night at least.

***

The next morning I slept in late and spent most of the day cleaning my room. Each time I thought I was done, Mom would inspect it and find something else for me to do. The last task to organize was the closet. Underneath my clothes, a deflated football, and board games, I found a box that wasn't mine. Inside were photo albums and books, like *Flowers in the Attic*. I flipped through the yellowing pages and a photograph of two teenagers fell out. It was Mom with Daphne, the woman from my dream.

End of the Hall

"Lunch is ready." Mom leaned in the doorway. "What did you find there?"

I hid the picture and pulled out the box. "I think it's yours."

"I was looking for this. I must've missed it."

Before I could see any more of the box, she closed it, and took it away, but I still had the photograph.

Later in the day, I tried to call Kristen, but the phone just rang and rang, not even an answering machine picked up. Oddly, when I went downstairs I saw Kristen's mom leaving from our back porch. Mom was sitting at the table where candles and incense were lit.

"What was Mrs. Avery doing here?"

"Not that it's any of your business, but she was calling on me for a little advice, that's all."

On the table were tarot cards spread out in a pattern. Mom was collecting them in her hand.

"I didn't know you still gave readings."

"Occasionally. Seems like I lost the gift."

"Grandma Issy could see things in the future, right?"

"Yes, and when she died, it passed on to me."

"Do you think I could have the gift, too?" I wanted to tell her about the vision and the woman, but didn't think she'd believe me. Besides, I didn't want to bring up Pisgah Mountain again.

"I don't know." Mom put the deck into a red velvet bag.

I sat in the chair at the table. "Why don't you do a reading for me?"

"Like I said, the cards are cold today." She blew out the candles and packed up her things. "Another time."

Hunter Ligoure

"Mom, do you know a woman named Daphne?" I could tell I caught her off-guard.

"No," she said flatly. "Why, where did you hear that name?"

"Nowhere."

"You had to hear it from somewhere." She tilted her head, curious.

"It was nothing. Forget it."

Later on, Tad and I had stayed up watching a rented movie. I went to bed around midnight. The house was quiet and I dosed off quickly. Around two a.m. I woke to the creaking sound of the window opening. I sat up in bed, just as the woman's footsteps rushed toward me—before I could move, she was there, hovering, grabbing me by the arm, her rotted face, swelled and bloated, was nearly pushed into mine, and the one blue eye stared at me. "The way the wind blows . . . " she howled. She covered my eyes, sending an electric current through me, along with a vision . . .

Pisgah Mountain. Daphne and my mom, and some other kids from school were out late, partying, when a gale of storm hit. No one seemed to care, drunk and dancing. Then one guy pushed another, causing everyone to buckle—Daphne lost her balance. The wind was so strong, and there was nothing to grab ahold to. She disappeared over the side. My mom screamed for her, trying to stop her, but it was too late . . . then the vision switched, and it was Kristen on the mountain, with Duff and the other Pisgah Rats—the moon was full, and a storm came from nowhere . . . then I saw a newly erected cross and a lavender shoe left behind, and Kristen's tearstained face, screaming, as she slipped over the side . . .

End of the Hall

I woke abruptly. I was alone, the window open, the house cold. The woman—Daphne—was gone.

Outside, a storm started. I was disorientated, unsure of what I'd seen, but once the rain started on the window, I knew I that the vision was a warning, and I had to do something.

I ran downstairs to my old room and woke Mom. "Mom, we have to get help. Something bad is going to happen to Kristen."

"What are you talking about?" She sat up groggy, startled even.

"Remember how you said I might also have the sight, well, I just know. We have to hurry."

Mom met me in the kitchen, dressed. I had two flashlights ready.

"Where are we going?"

"Pisgah," I said, watching the muscles in her face tighten.

"You know I don't like that place."

"But you never told me why. It's because of Daphne, isn't it? You couldn't save her."

Mom started to cry, her face sad. "I've been blaming myself all these years."

"But she showed me, Mom, that it was the wind, the wind that caused her to fall. You weren't to blame. It was just an accident."

"Daphne told you this?"

"I think she's been trying to tell you for years." I explained to her about Daphne's visits each night.

"I guess I shut her out, too unwilling to let go of the blame."

We embraced.

"I think she's here to stop another fall."

Hunter Ligoure

"Then let's hurry," Mom said, hurrying me out of the house. "That mountain's taken too many children."

We traversed the George Washington trail, to the base of the mountain. The rain and wind were already a torrent. Lightening flashed and thunder rang out overhead.

At the top, we found the remnants of a bonfire, beer bottles, and kids fleeing for shelter. I also found a bouquet of blue flowers, discarded.

"It's just like the vision. It's happening right now." I searched the area. "Where is she? Kristen," I called out.

"We'll find her, Davey. Let's go this way."

"How did you know that's the way to her special spot?"

"I know my way around this mountain; it was my special spot too."

I led the way, along the edge of the mountain. The rain got heavier, and when the lightening flashed, I spotted Kristen through the trees, in her special spot, struggling with Duff. She screamed.

"Kristen!" The rain made the rocky surface slippery, just as I rounded the corner toward her. The thunder exploded above us, forcing me back against the rocks.

"Davey," Mom called.

"She's over here."

"Davey, keep away from the edge!"

I reached the spot, but Kristen and Duff were gone. Then a figure appeared, moving toward me. I aimed my flashlight to see who it was, when someone came from behind, knocking it from my hand. I was pushed into the rocky wall, face to face with Duff.

End of the Hall

"What did you do to her?" I yelled.

"Go see for yourself." Duff disappeared through the rain. I followed, the climb slippery and more dangerous. Mom was right behind me.

"Kristen, where are you?"

The rain fell harder and the thunder continued to ripple loudly overhead.

"I know you're here."

Mom scanned the area with her flashlight. Abandoned at the edge of the cliff was one lavender shoe. "Over here!" I knelt to pick up the shoe and heard a faint cry.

"Kristen."

"Here, I'm here."

The voice came from the darkness, over the side. I panned the light and saw the top of her head. She was hanging onto a tree root.

"I can't hang on much longer. My hands are slipping."

Fear shot through me. "I've got you!" I leaned over, but couldn't reach her. "Mom, help me!"

"Try again. I'll hold your legs."

I laid flat and spread out over the cliff, while Mom held my legs. It was just enough to reach Kristen. Just as I grabbed her, the thunder crashed overhead with a loud BOOM! I jumped, our hands splitting apart. She slipped further away. I reached further, slipping against the rock and gravel.

"I can't hold you much longer," my mom yelled.

And then, as if an invisible hand came with the wind, my arm stretched out, grabbing Kristen's wrist, pulling her up, through the trees. Mom heave-hoed, until we were back on the cliff, and safe and sound.

Hunter Ligoure

Kristen hugged me; Mom hugged me. Then the lightening crashed, making everything bright, and I saw Daphne.

"Mom, she's here."

Mom turned and went to her. We watched, as the rain poured. Then she was gone.

I turned to Kristen. "Are you okay?"

"I am now." She kissed me.

Even though I was cold and wet, that kiss warmed me up inside.

Mom called us.

Back at home, Mom called Kristen's mother to have her picked up. They talked in the kitchen for a few moments, giving Kristen and me a few last moments together.

"See you in class Monday?" I asked.

"I was thinking we might see each other tomorrow." She kissed me on the cheek and left with her mother.

I joined my mom on the porch, where we drank hot chocolate together. Her face was sad, like she'd been crying.

"Tell me, Mom."

Mom said, "It was Daphne's eighteenth birthday, and it was tradition back then, like it still is, to go to Pisgah to celebrate. We had all been drinking pretty heavily, and when the guys started fooling around, the next thing I knew, Daphne had gone over the side. But it doesn't change things. Not really. When you see your sister fall to her death, and you were there to stop it. Plus, your Grandma Issy blamed me."

"What did she say to you up there?"

"She told me to remember the way the wind blew."

End of the Hall

Mom shook her head. "I'd forgotten about the storm until you'd said something. All these years she's been trying to tell someone it wasn't my fault. First, Grandma Issy, when she lived here. She could never get through to me. But when you showed up in the room, she found hope again, that someone would get the message."

"I got it loud and clear." I smiled, adding, "Do you think we could switch rooms again?"

Mom hugged me. "You can stay home from school tomorrow and we'll make the switch then."

The next night, we all went to the Dairy Serve for ice cream. A television crew came all the way from Hartford and interviewed Kristen and me about the storm, and my heroic rescue, as Kristen put it. We were stars for the whole week at school, but eventually life went on. A fence was put up across the path to Pisgah, but after a while, it was cut through and people climbed to the top, regardless of the danger.

Mom released Tad and me from being grounded, and I got my room back. It helped that I passed my history quiz. The best part of it all is that Kristen was not only my new study partner, but my new girlfriend too!

While I lie here in bed, I can see the clock nearing two o'clock. I wait for the sound of the window to open, and the footsteps on the floorboards above me. I can't help wondering if she'll ever visit me again.

Snowmen

DAVID DUNWOODY

Some people call suicide taking the easy way out, but there's nothing easy about it—neither doing it, nor coming to the decision in the first place. E. Woodrow understands that and that's what he tells the people. It's not an act of cowardice either. Fear is a primal thing, a cold, driven needle with no measure of subtlety. Despair, the engine of suicide, is a degenerative toxin that erodes the soul.

We're all made of stars, they say. Some of us remember.

***

E. Woodrow finishes his shift at nine P.M. and spritzes his headset with an antiseptic spray, then wipes it down for the night-shift user. He normally works graves himself, but Carol Mussman asked him to trade shifts because she needs the extra night differential pay for the holidays. Her son wants a Speak-and-Spell or something like that. Woodrow doesn't mind. He pats his hair until it settles flat in thin, waxy wheat-colored strands. He uses the same cloth to wipe his

Snowmen

glasses as he did the headset. His cubicle is bare, save for the Dark-Ages computer that dominates most of the tiny desk, and the phone. Some of the other employees keep half their lives in their cubicles, trucking family photos and joke-a-day calendars in and out every shift. Woodrow travels light. He whisks his jacket off the back of the chair and is off.

It's quite dark out, but it's that weird winter darkness where the cloud cover is slate-gray and almost seems to possess a faint luminescence. Beneath the clouds, the borough Woodrow calls home is cast in orangish-reddish hues by cheap streetlamps and security lights. The snow on the ground looks like Martian dust. The air is still and it doesn't even seem cold enough for even this smattering of precipitation. The world feels altogether alien, and Woodrow finds that he likes it. He strolls leisurely down the sidewalk through a light curtain of flakes.

There's a snowman on the corner of 49th and 5 North. It's a squat little fellow, only a few feet in height, made from three dingy, misshapen spheres and with only empty pits for eyes. Whoever made him must have shoved their gloved thumbs into his head to make the sockets, but lacked any rocks to place in them. A shallow slit drawn straight across the face is presumed to be a mouth. The snowman doesn't look happy. Woodrow has paused to study the work, and he notices that there are neither footprints nor any other tracks in the thin layer of snow at his feet. Where did the kids scrounge up the matter to make this pitiful thing? Maybe it had snowed harder in the early day, and this is all the evidence that remains. The snowman is already sagging slightly to the left and what stability it appears to have is probably an illusion. Woodrow imagines he could topple it with a gentle nudge and watch the head explode on the curb. He doesn't. Its eyeless eyes don't speak to him the way that others do.

He turns off onto 5 North, where there is less light and the stoic brick buildings give way to walls of chain-link fences guarding shadowy heaps. Junked cars, a failed garden space, a disused playground. Better to leave in the dark what won't grow.

Woodrow nearly plows right into the next snowman, but sees its outline at the last second. This one is a bit taller than the other, though as his eyes adjust Woodrow sees that it is similarly without detail, without sight. He runs his bare fingertips across the surface beneath the eye sockets and feels another thin, dispassionate mouth.

"Where they come from?"

Woodrow is startled and spins around, his right hand dipping into his jacket pocket. A scraggly man in three layers of threadbare clothing stands hunched there. The man's foul Tenafly Viper breath blasts Woodrow's face as the transient says, in a voice louder than necessary, "Who put 'em here? They all around."

"I don't follow. The snowmen?" Woodrow's hand is still in his pocket, closed tight around what is there. Though he can't make out much of the homeless man's features, he watches the man's outline for the slightest wrong movement.

"Yeah, the damn snowmen," the man coughs. "Ain't enough snow for snowmen. Ain't enough snow for snow. Hot as the devil to me. I'd shed this big coat if I had a place to put it."

"What do you mean, all around?" Woodrow

Snowmen

removes his right hand from his pocket. He fishes his left hand through his jeans for his keychain. It has a powerful little light on it, and he snaps it on. Immediately he sees them there, just on the fringe of that small but piercing halo of light, and he pans over the snowmen standing in the street.

Little ones, big ones. Fat ones and skinny ones. The observation reminds him of a jingle from his youth but he can't quite place it. Snowmen—snow*things,* really, sexless golems, and each missing its precious eyes of coal.

The old man had been right—it had felt unnaturally warm—but suddenly E. Woodrow feels chilled.

There are some foot tracks weaving amongst these snowmen, but no trails indicating where modest snowballs had been rolled into thick orbs. A prank, perhaps, or some modern art piece? Now Woodrow is reminded of a *Calvin and Hobbes* strip where the titular boy creates a snowman installation in his yard with the express purpose of watching them melt and contemplating mortality.

They ought to be melting already. It's really quite warm.

Warm outside, bones chilled within, Woodrow shivers and returns his attention, as well as his keychain light, to the transient.

The old man winces as the light strikes his watery eyes. "How 'bout it?" he asks.

Woodrow feels he understands the question. Studying the man's weary and pained countenance, he places his right hand back into the jacket pocket. This time, when he withdraws it, he has the object, and a light flick of the wrist brings the blade out and he cuts cleanly through the old man's windpipe.

David Dunwoody

The man's eyes widen. Woodrow is able to watch the misery flee from them, just as the last poisoned breath whistles and then sputters from the open throat. He helps the man to sit against the chain-link and tugs the collars of his many coats closed over the neck wound.

Woodrow turns to continue on his way, but keeps the light in his left hand trained on the snowmen. There are more ahead of him. He pauses by a particularly hefty specimen and slides the blade into its gut in order to clean it. Replacing the knife in his pocket, he quickens his pace.

***

The next time Woodrow looks at his watch he is startled to see that it's after midnight. He has been walking for hours in mobs of snowmen. And he has come to several forks in the road—intersections painted in ruddy light where snowmen continue on in this direction and that. But no cars, not driving anyway, not on the road, and few people to be seen. Those he has passed on the sidewalks seem to shrink away against the buildings, not from him but from the other things. Many of the windows in those apartment buildings are occupied by silhouettes. They must be watching the snowmen. They must be watching E. Woodrow, too, muttering their theories as to why he walks fearless amongst the frozen and sightless.

I always have.

So many blinded in their own inexplicable grief, by cosmic ennui deep within that cannot be expressed as visions or sounds or even ideas. Just despair. These snowmen, speechless, eyeless—Woodrow can't get a read on them, can't say with certainty that they feel

Snowmen

that despair. At first they struck him as static ghosts, more living dead, but maybe they're not imprisoned within their featureless forms. Maybe they're guarded. Immune. A lovely, lofty thought.

He's worked at the suicide hotline for eight years, far longer than anyone else has ever managed. He can hear the pain in those crackly electronic voices just as sure as he sees it in the eyes of the downtrodden. He wants to know what's inside the snowmen, because their blankness unnerves him in a way he can't articulate.

He looks upward, past the gawkers in the tenements, to the sky. There are no stars, only slate-gray clouds.

St. Michael's, in spite of its regal architecture, looks squat and sad between the apartment blocks. There is a dense cluster of snowmen at the base of the church's steps. At first it looks to Woodrow as if they are standing vigil, perhaps hoping to gain entry, but as he draws closer he sees that their blind eyes are facing every which way. Of course they don't know a church from a bodega. An odd thought, that they'd know *anything*—he's been thinking a lot of odd thoughts tonight—disturbed again, Woodrow squeezes through the mob and ascends the steps.

The doors are unlocked. He enters and finds empty pews lit by a few small electric lamps set against the walls beneath the indifferent stained-glass martyrs.

A shadow disengages itself from the darkness behind the pulpit. A priest waves gently.

"The doors were open," Woodrow says.

"I thought it might be a good idea." The priest has a clutch of blond hair atop his head, but his face and walk betray his advanced age. He comes to Woodrow and offers his hand.

"You've seen them?" Woodrow asks. The hand feels like bones wrapped in crepe paper.

"Oh, they're everywhere, son. I was watching them on the TV up until about an hour ago. That's when the feed cut out. I don't hear the news choppers anymore. Is there anyone else out there?"

"Just them," Woodrow says, and the priest nods.

"Well," he says, gesturing to a pew, "Why don't you have a seat? I'm going to make some more tea."

"Do you . . . " Woodrow shakes off the question and falls silent.

The priest leans into him and smiles a little. "I don't know, son. I'm trying to work it out myself. May not be brimstone coming down out there, but it ain't manna either."

The priest's eyes are kind. He has his faith, Woodrow muses, although it's clear that The Man Upstairs has yet to return any of the preacher's calls tonight.

He decides to leave before the man returns with the tea. He doesn't belong here.

***

It's three A.M. now and Woodrow is downtown. A five-way intersection sits quiet and dominated by snowmen. Woodrow looks from one to the next, from one nothing-face to another. His hands are trembling and he shoves them into his pockets. There his right hand finds the knife, and he stands toe-to-mound with a snowman precisely his own height. He looks directly into those empty pits.

"Say something."

Snowmen

Do something. Give me something.

He flicks open the knife and cuts deep into the belly of the snowman. His fingers follow the blade and plunge into ice. He rips the knife out and slashes the snowman's mouth. He swings his fist into the side of its head, but fails to knock it from its mooring. Woodrow growls and stabs at the eye sockets again and again until there are no discernable features left in the snowman's face. He carves through the frozen flesh and retraces his own lines and intersects them and cuts star shapes into the snow. He does this with the next one, and the next, running to each snowman with a terrible cry, as if hoping to rouse fear from them. They do not react and he obliterates their faces one after another, his arm aching, then numb. His voice grows hoarse and is reduced to a grating wheeze. Woodrow hacks at the snowmen until his knees give and he collapses atop a sewer grate.

The snow is red in the streetlamps. His skin is red and beaded with sweat. The knife is wet and clean and it gleams. Woodrow can't stop shivering. He draws himself into a ball and pinches his eyes shut.

***

The sun rises at 6:58 in the morning. Within the hour, the people begin to come out of their homes and gather on the sidewalks. Some wonder and laugh strange laughter while others weep. The night is over, but nothing is what it was.

The snowmen have melted. In their place, in stagnant pools, slouch oddly-shaped skeletons. They sag forward or to the side, uneven tangles of rib-like bone compressed against pelvic bowls which serve as their bases. Their big round skulls are cocked to and fro, all with the same false smile.

E. Woodrow is there, as well. He still lies atop the sewer grate. He is frozen solid.

Pieces of Me
T.G. ARSENAULT

Please reconsider your decision!
For someone to listen, please call . . .

I could just make out the words on the sign and only three of the numbers. The bottom of each letter bled like an orange tear. One corner of the sign was curled into a comma, its edge jagged and flaking with rust. Long strands of dead grass partially hid a number of bullet holes unworthy of a grouping. Tilted at a severe angle, the signpost looked exhausted and ready to topple.

I sucked in a breath until my chest felt capable of pulling in the clouds above. I let it hiss between my lips with a slow and forceful exhale. My index finger scraped at the side of my right thumb, peeling away a dried piece of skin—a nervous habit I never outgrew.

I read the sign again. And again.

My eyebrows merged themselves into a modicum of concern, but the sign did nothing in tempting me to comply with its instructions. Like any child told exactly what to do, I jutted my chin, squared my shoulders, and did *exactly* the opposite.

T. G. Arsenault

Pushing through the long grass, I stepped past the sign and almost tripped over a moss-covered log. I continued into a forest so dense even my footsteps were silenced. With every step, the forest closed behind me. I left chirping birds, a cloudless blue sky, and a breezy field. Soon, my hair stuck to my forehead with a thick sheen of sweat. Two more steps and I stopped, cast a wary glance over my shoulder, and then at my surroundings.

Silence covered me like a thick shawl, yet not nearly as comfortable. My chest seemed to constrict under its pressure.

Sprawling branches replaced blue sky; they weaved through each other, blocking out the sun to create a thick and shadowed ceiling. My nose filled with the scent of moist earth, almost cloying. Cold drops fell onto my arm. I imagined the twisted branches above salivating in response to a new visitor.

My heart pulsed inside my ears with thunderous beats. A profound feeling of desolation seeped into my bones. Emptiness. Belying the thick vegetation surrounding me, a sense that nothing lived within this forest permeated everything. Seeing the trees, brush, and vines drain of color, wither, and die before me would have produced the same feeling.

It's why I came.
It's why we all came.

***

I didn't have a direction in mind, only wanted to go as far and as deep into the forest as possible. Into the weave and folds of countless trees and branches and brush. Hidden amongst the flora, absorbed into its universe.

Pieces of Me

Unseen, unheard.
Alone.

The first steps were the easiest. I let go, giving myself up to the gods of this new world. I saw the first signs of previous inhabitants, no different than seeing litter left behind by careless hikers. Well . . . perhaps a wee bit different. Many, I imagined, had the same issues, thoughts, and desires I did, coming here for the same answer to everything.

A wallet covered by a few leaves and splayed open, had family photos perched around it, some leaning between branches or vines as though presented for proper viewing on a makeshift altar. Jewelry littered different spots. Wedding bands and necklaces, bracelets and rings, all looking gently placed on the ground and set into specific arrangements. Faces peered from stained and dirty lockets. These were the intimate items left behind by different people and they tugged at my heart. Slowed my pace. Had me considering turning around.

Almost.

I lifted a heavy foot and pushed forward with the other.

Soon, I saw the ingredients with which nightmares were prepared.

Needles, spoons, and syringes still filled with brown liquid. Full bullet casings—live rounds—littered the ground in ones and twos. Handguns, as well; some were rusted, others shiny. I thought about the Taurus 9mm I carried along with a box of new shells, presuming myself a terrible shot, I suppose. Most prevalent of all were small amber plastic containers, most with prescription labels torn away. I picked a couple up, shook them. They rattled.

T. G. Arsenault

When I scanned the canopy above, I noticed something else.

Knotted nooses hung from thick branches. Empty. No bloated bodies—eyes bulging, black tongues hanging loose—swung in gentle circles, nor did the ropes move at all in this vacuum-like world. Evidently, I had a slew of options—a smorgasbord of euthanasia lay before me, no different than cold cuts behind the deli counter. More of the same presented itself to me in varying combinations of utensils and mediums. I eventually lost interest and took note of the trees. Something peculiar kept nagging for my attention at my periphery, contours and shadows creeping up on me.

Such odd shapes they were, accentuated in this gloomy environment. Their branches twisted into odd angles, curled over each other, and even grown into knots in places. Wispy strands dangled from branches that looked so much like human hair I thought a head would rise from each. Their trunks were bulbous and seemed to swell with deformed pregnancies. Fluid oozed from deep, jagged scars. Random knots appeared to create abnormal, cycloptic eyes. Fossilized tears appeared to drip down thin, papery bark that assumed the guise of dried, dead skin.

My mind created weird faces in the bark with shadows angling this way and that. When I imagined one of the eyes blinked, I picked up my pace.

Tripped and fell.

Barely missed the trunk of a fallen—oak, pine, birch—I had no fucking idea. All I knew was that something was staring back at me with a glazed, lifeless eye. I didn't feel the severe sprain—broken for all I knew—in my ankle, until I tried to get away.

Pieces of Me

A scream pierced the distant gloom and I bolted upright, heart clinging to the sides of my throat. I scrambled to my knees, and then my feet, standing on two shaking stalks that felt ready to buckle. The scream didn't linger, sounding almost swallowed in one gulp. A thick silence pressed in from all sides. I strained to hear beyond the pounding in my ears, so hard my ears started to itch like mad. A gurgle shattered the eerie hush, somehow sounding worse than the scream itself. At least until a moist pop echoed alongside a series of choking gurgles.

I sucked at blood seeping from my thumb—I just couldn't stop digging into it. My skin rippled with waves of bumps, hairs along my arms standing erect when a small puff of air touched the nape of my neck. Not from a breeze; at least, I don't think so. More like . . . well, like a *breath*. You know, like when someone gets just a little too close?

I spun on my heels and dropped my bag, sending frantic slaps to my neck before staggering against a tree. I slid to the ground and my shirt crawled up my back, my skin not scraping against bark, but slipping against something akin to . . . sweating flesh, that's all I could picture. My insides curdled in disgust. I wanted to pry my body away from the tree, but could only slide farther down.

I braced my slow fall, hands cushioned by thick moss, fingers buried deep. One palm trapped a seedling, bending it beneath my weight. I felt it snap and the ground trembled, and then every limb, branch, and leaf. Drops fell like rain upon my exposed flesh, down the back of my neck, and beneath my sweaty collar. A shiver rattled my teeth. My nerves were frayed, heartbeat accelerated. I couldn't catch my breath. My chest seemed to shrink beneath a suffocating tightness. I dug deeper into my thumb and it started dripping instead of oozing, blood sliding from my flesh and into the moss.

In the short distance ahead, I spotted the first mound of what appeared to be branches at the base of a crooked tree, odd and seemingly out of place. Curious, I followed the trunks of other trees to the ground. Scattered around the forest, other small piles in varying states littered the bases of random trees. Some of these branches looked familiar. Off-white in color, many were splotched with dark stains while others had flaps of what looked like loose bark curling up like postage stamps losing their adhesion. Some looked moist to the touch, containing a glistening sheen that existed even in the gloom. And when I squinted hard to look even closer . . .

My blood turned cold.

I realized what I was looking at, what those flaps of bark actually were. A hot flash burned my cheeks as a cold sweat dotted my brow. My mouth filled with saliva. Confirming my theory and spawning an acidic dose of nausea, the tree closest to me recently must have invited someone to sit down beneath its many welcoming arms to ponder his or her immediate future. I could not tell which by the rib cage or the skull topping the pile, although a lengthy swath of dirty-blonde hair still clung to one temple with a blackened scrap of flesh.

I hissed when something sliced into one of my palms, sending a flaming bolt into my wrist and up my forearm. My muscles contracted, pulling my fingers

Pieces of Me

into clenched fists. I felt half-moon fingernail indentations soon became crimson smiles, feeding more blood into the moss. I tried to pull away, *hard*, but my hand was caught in a spreading web of roots and vines. With each attempt, my bonds grew tighter. The tips of my fingers went numb.

I arched my back and screamed, the invasion continuing, muscles releasing involuntary spasms with every poke and prod.

My legs kicked when ropes of razor-sharp barbs seemed to unfurl within my veins, shredding my insides and leaving not a single path unexplored. My entire body felt like a molten wave about to crash against my ribs. I feared my heart, once consumed, would be the end of me. Yet, somewhere in the recesses of my mind, I thought it really didn't matter. This was why I came, wasn't it? I mean, for all intents and purposes, all I *really* wanted to do was stop my heart and leave this world behind. But, I didn't want it to be so *painful*.

My feet were next, vines paving through the heels of my boots and plunging into the small space between my first few toes, the same place on a body some of the needles littering this forest would have gone. I thought about the syringes still full of liquid, never used, and only brought in hopes of saying good night to the world. Like the gun in my bowling bag.

As if a serpent had loosened its hold around my chest, my breaths became deeper, stronger, and cooler in comparison to the rest of my body, offering a short respite from the inferno now only smoldering. Maybe my insides were just numb, succumbing to this alien assault. For a moment, I was thankful, but a terrifying unease seeped into my bones. I waited in silent anticipation of . . . *something*. It felt like my body was being prepared for something more, something *worse*, and I merely an observer.

And then it came.

When the first bone snapped, not even a squeak spilled from my mouth. In utter shock, my eyes grew wide as my right foot was pushed into an impossible direction, breaking at the ankle. The top of my left foot lay flat against my shin, my Achilles tendon severed and recoiled somewhere inside. I felt nothing, though my jaw reflexively clamped shut and my teeth chirped as I ground them together. Either my brain was a few seconds behind or maybe just placing everything into slow motion, making it easier for me to adjust, but when the pain finally registered and I screamed, I did so until my throat felt lined with broken glass. Never had I felt such pain.

The periphery of my vision clouded, then grew dark. Darker. Another bone snapped and stars filled a near-black sky. Explosions in my ears sparked even more when my bones snapped in quick succession. The taste of chalk and copper sprinkled the back of my throat, the same flavors I had experienced at the dentist when I needed a tooth filled.

The pain crawled up to my hips with what felt like serrated claws. I chanced a glimpse between eyelids dotted with moisture. Blinked. My legs . . . my legs were nothing but ribbons in front of me, deflated with the absence of any structure contained within my flesh. My jeans looked like they were gently placed upon the ground in need of folding.

I dry-heaved. Felt something coming up, but this

Pieces of Me

was not vomit ready to spew. No acidic burn sat in the center of my chest and nausea didn't line my stomach. Instead, something solid was scraping its way up my esophagus and tearing tender muscle. I grimaced, eyes watering, gagged. My jaw stretched open wide, popping on both sides. Hollow echoes of my overextending jaw echoed in my ears.

I retched. And retched as it got stuck sideways in my throat. My eyes bulged and I gagged again, stomach muscles quivering and sore. I finally produced enough force to spit it out, anxious to see it, but not really. More like the propensity to keep plucking at a scab or turning to see the bloody aftermath of an accident. I just *had* to do it.

Between heavy tears, I saw part of my foot lying on the ground. Tendons and metatarsals gleamed white, stark between thin strands of moist red muscle. A string of bloody saliva was still attached to the big toe, the other end clinging to my lower lip like a long strand of a spider's web. I felt my gorge rise, but forced it down with a hard swallow and a touch of willpower.

Vines crawled in, up, down, and around me, and fast. I didn't have time to consider what had just happened before both hips sounded like a double barrel shotgun, both triggers pulled at once. The pain was immeasurable, existing as a blinding white flash behind my eyes. When the vines twisted and turned beneath my flesh, and then squeezed into vice-like knots, my pelvis shattered. Bones were pushed upward with pulsing contractions, some punching through skin, stripped of tendon and sinew. But most, most tumbled from my mouth in chunks and splintered fragments.

T. G. Arsenault

Weaving new paths throughout my body, the vines gained strength and size—growing, throbbing, becoming . . .

. . . part of me.

More vines sliced and curled into my feet, plunging both deep into the ground, rooting them in place. My skin stretched, catching the tips of spiny thorns, and then stretched some more. Parts of me were stretched to the point of almost tearing, burning. My arms were driven out to my sides and then up, up, up. I felt tied between two saddles as horses galloped away from each other.

My view changed as I grew longer, taller, the world below swimming on the blurred edge of consciousness. I could hear bones snapping and popping, their echoes reverberating inside a shell that barely contained any of me. Only numbness remained.

The last thing I remember was spitting out my teeth before the world faded completely.

***

When I awoke—if you'd call it that—my senses were in disarray, almost foreign. A thin film covered my eyes, the world itself out of focus, and everything a light shade of gray. An unquenchable thirst consumed me, yet I couldn't feel my tongue. Like I had a thousand fingers, each of them wiggling in the breeze, but I couldn't see any of them.

My ears picked up every vibration in the forest, felt more than heard. And the smell, so different than the thick and cloying scent I smelled when I first entered the forest. The fragrance had permeated my body's every cell and fiber, and felt more like an actual piece of me. When I breathed, my entire body seemed to expand and sway.

Pieces of Me

Through an almost intoxicated haze, memories resurfaced, the only hint of me that still remained.

My wife had found a younger man with a larger bank account, leaving me with a teenage daughter with issues. *Real* issues. Not the kind I thought typical of any teenage girl. I never saw the signs, but soon realized I wasn't even looking for any. I assumed the visits to the bathroom after every meal were normal; that her door closed and locked most hours of the day was only for privacy. The open sores on her face I thought were merely acne gone awry. And her teeth—disgusting. Looking back, the list seemed endless.

When she hadn't eaten breakfast, lunch, or dinner, I forced her bedroom door open. The earth crumbled below my feet when I found her hanging in the closet. I struggled to read the short letter barely sticking out of her shirt pocket, just enough to notice. Collapsed. If I only would have paid attention, or talked to her more, or just . . . *listened*.

I had failed as a husband, and then as a father.

Memories. They haunt me still, though for how long now, I have no idea. Time is irrelevant, belonging to another world altogether. The only certainty is that I was such an absolute failure I couldn't even kill myself.

And I am not alone.

I see their faces peering from the other trunks of flesh, almost camouflaged in the same gray, sickly color. Some of their faces—those here the longest—were high on the trunk, eyes glazed, long since given up as time passed, choosing to simply exist. Perhaps a penance accepted for ever having the desire to take their own lives in the first place. The shorter trees, my fellow brethren, still hold hope with clear, dripping eyes, and gleaming bones at the base of their trunks.

We scream most days, coming in high-pitched wails so similar to gusty winds when a storm blows through.

When another visitor appears, we tremble. Shake. Cry, tears falling from our leaves in a shower of despair.

We live. We LIVE!

And pray—oh, do we pray—that one day, *one day*, someone will be kind enough to bring an ax.

Neighborhood Watchers
MARIA ALEXANDER

The elderly woman stood in the street that morning in her wrinkled cargo pants and billowing pink top, staring at our house as if murderers lived inside.

"Why is she doing that?" I asked my husband Dan, yawning as I stirred my coffee. Among other things, the previous owners hadn't disclosed the 3:00 a.m. train horns or that the house was directly in the airport flight path. Dan could sleep through anything, but *my* sleep was suffering.

"Maybe she's curious about the new owners. Or maybe she's casing the joint." He slurped down the last of his coffee, patted his pockets for his cell phone and yanked his car keys from his pocket. "I've got to run. I'll try not to hit her on the way out."

"You're a hero," I teased as he swooped in for a goodbye kiss. Soured by annoyance at his long work hours, I kissed back half-heartedly.

By the time he was pulling out of the driveway, the woman had moved to the sidewalk but far to the side, gawking at the house through the gate. One hand rested on a metal bar as if she were about to slam the gate shut, a bulging leather purse hanging from the crook of her arm. The wind played with her wooly locks, blowing them from her ears as she shielded her eyes from the sun.

I needed to finish putting together the project plan for my client, not to mention continue to unpack, call the plumber to fix the broken bathroom faucet, replace the busted heating furnace, solve The Mystery of the Weird Smell in the Hallway that started last week, deal with the electricians, the warranty company, the insurance—it all fell to me since I was the home-based freelancer. I hated it, and was already resenting Dan's job even though it was a financial game changer. That said, I couldn't concentrate on anything knowing this woman was standing outside our home. Staring.

Sod it. I'm going to talk to her.

I pulled my hair back into a ponytail with a rainbow scrunchie so that I wouldn't look like a total wild woman. I opened the front door and flashed her a big smile in an attempt to convince her I wasn't going to eat her. It didn't seem to work. She stood there looking startled. Maybe she had Alzheimer's or plain old dementia. If that were the case, I wanted to be respectful. My own mother couldn't have been more than a couple of years older than this woman when she passed last year from heart failure. I missed her every day. As I walked toward the woman, her mouth opened.

"Hi," I said, extending my hand. "Can I help you? My name's Beth."

The woman trembled but took it nonetheless. Her skin was smooth and, despite the heat, ice cold. "Poor thing."

Neighborhood Watchers

"I beg your pardon?" I let go, heart skipping.

"Nothing, my dear. Welcome to the neighborhood. My name's Wilma. I live six houses down. The two-story with the copper gate."

"Thank you," I replied, not feeling thankful at all.

She reached into her purse and withdrew a dusky pink flyer that she promptly handed to me. "I wanted to invite you to the neighborhood meeting tomorrow."

Neighborhood Watchers Committee Meeting
October 1
2:00 p.m.
59627 Bellomy Way

Watchers? That sounded a bit weird. But then, so was Wilma.

"We look forward to seeing you there." As she walked away, she added, "Meanwhile, don't go under the house." By the time I'd registered what she'd said, she was gone.

That afternoon, the sickening smell in the hallway worsened, engulfing my head like a cloud of gnats as I searched for the source. Per my sister Lucy's suggestion, I checked the floors for stains and rechecked Winston's litter box in the hallway bathroom. It wasn't clean but it certainly wasn't the problem. Winston had been upset by the move. He'd hidden under the bed for the first three days. Lucy thought perhaps the fuzzy little jerk was still mad and showing his displeasure by doing a wee outside the box. After all, we'd made him leave his comfy townhouse in San Diego, where he could watch the birds in the trees from his window box in the master bedroom. The new house was one story with only a view of the slightly green pool that was hopefully going to get cleaned as soon as I hired a pool service. But if Winston was still upset about the move, he certainly didn't look it. He was splayed on the couch, belly up, white paws of his tuxedo suit curled as he snored. I was scooping his litter, wondering if something more serious was happening like a sewage line leak, when the doorbell rang.

Shit. I'd completely forgotten the electrician was coming to look at the wonky kitchen lights and give us an estimate for some other work. When he stepped inside, it wasn't two minutes before he wrinkled his nose and said, "Sorry to interrupt, but did something die under your house? This is how it smelled when a cat died under my uncle's house."

We rescheduled for Friday because he couldn't work with the smell. As soon as he left, I jumped on Angie's List and found an animal trapper named Johnny who came to the house two hours later. I led him around to the back of the house where the crawlspace door was located. I'd always imagined that door would resemble the storm cellar door that Dorothy kicks in *The Wizard of Oz*, but ours was just a small, rectangular piece of metal mesh that was wedged into a likewise-shaped hole on the bottom of the west stucco wall between two bushes. Without any bizarre neighborhood warnings, I was already scared to death of actually opening it and going inside.

Fortunately, Johnny wasn't. After he carefully removed the metal mesh from the wall, he tugged down hard on his Hooters baseball cap. Then, brandishing his cell phone flashlight in one hand while

Neighborhood Watchers

clutching a big plastic bag in the other, he stuck his head inside the space. I thought my heart would stop as he wiggled farther underneath, his muscular, tattooed calves and sneakers trailing until he disappeared.

"Oh, man. It really stinks in here!" he said. "I just hope it isn't wedged between your tub and the wall. I won't be able to get it out without cutting into something."

"Me, too," I replied, squatting near the opening.

More groans. "I found it. Holy smokes. Looks like a giant dead possum."

"A possum?"

"It must've been attracted to the water," Johnny gasped as he struggled back out of the hole. Filmy spider webs stuck to one ear as he emerged. "You've got a big leak under there. It's like a lake."

Leaks? Dead animals? My head started shrieking with panic about what was going on under my house and if the warranty would cover it. "But how did it *get* down there?"

Johnny slung the enormous bag of rotten possum to the ground by my feet. "I dunno. Let me put this in the truck first and we'll find out."

Together, we checked the house perimeter, especially the wire mesh-covered openings along the bottom. Johnny stuffed some small holes with wool and caulking, but we found nothing big enough to admit such a huge creature.

"Gimme a call if you find any other openings," he said before he left.

Don't go under the house.

Wilma must have known there were problems with

my place. She probably chatted with the previous owners before they'd passed away. We were told it was an estate sale, that the people who'd inherited the property lived on the other side of the country and were looking to make some money. As we'd toured the house, a disaffected real estate agent sat in a folding chair stationed in the breakfast nook, thumbing the screen of his cell phone. He didn't seem to care who bought the house. He knew it would sell, either to developers who'd tear it down, investors who'd rent it out, or a family who'd paint, plant and fix for years to come. Having fallen in love with the crumbling Craftsman, we came in with the highest bid—twenty-five grand over asking price—and that's all he cared about. It wasn't worth that much, but we wanted it nonetheless.

And now it was a low-level disaster.

When I called the home warranty customer service, they said they couldn't get a plumber to come out until Friday. "What?" I said. "There's a *lake* under my house! It's an emergency!"

They wouldn't budge. Desperate to take care of the problem, I texted my friend Beverly. She recommended a plumber named Oleg that she and her wife often used. "He's kind of quirky," she said, "but he's super dependable and affordable." I called Oleg, who sounded the opposite of quirky. In fact, he was very dour and Russian. We scheduled an appointment for him to come out late the next afternoon.

After the "Neighborhood Watchers" meeting.

At least the smell of the dead possum had abated. I never again wanted to hear the words "giant dead possum" in my life.

Neighborhood Watchers

I got up early the next day to write emails and pay bills. Dan stuck his head in the office before he went to work, locks damp from his shower curling on his forehead. I shrugged off the headphones so I could hear him.

"You sure you don't want me to come home early to go to that meeting with you? I totally can, you know. I'll just say I have a doctor's appointment."

I shook my head, resentment building. Maybe he should stay. "That's okay. I'll text you as it's happening. How's that?"

"I guess. I just have a weird feeling about these people. Did I tell you I saw three elderly women talking together down the street? They had a gaggle of little Yorkie dogs that barked at me like hell hounds."

"At least they aren't the knuckleheads," I said, referring to our neighbors down in San Diego. We shared a wall with a hotheaded family from Romania whose teen sons blared rap music whenever Mom and Dad weren't home. And when they were, their parents shouted at each other in both English and the mother tongue about their money and marital problems. When Dan got the job offer at Disney in Glendale, I danced and fist-pumped for days. "Thank the Mouse, we're lucky to be out of there."

Dan grinned and swooped into my office for a kiss. "I'm the lucky one. I love you so much."

"I know."

He laughed, and then I shooed him out the door.

I really was dreading that Neighborhood Stalkers meeting. I put off getting dressed until the last possible minute, managing only a pair of black baggy culottes and a soft, dark blue T-shirt with brown sandals.

Maria Alexander

Dropping my cell phone in a loose pocket, I scratched Winston's ears soundly before I left.

As I made my way down the sidewalk, I recalled how we'd loved all the rose bushes in the neighborhood when we were looking. The area was tranquil, unassuming, and full of white-haired folk. We had at least a quarter century to go before retirement, but we appreciated having neighbors who were always home, walking their dogs, waving to one another. When we checked the L.A.P.D. crime website, we were dismayed to see a number of car break-ins and assaults on the main road nearby. We chalked that up to the risks of living in L.A.

I opened the copper gate and stepped down the stone path to the gorgeous Mediterranean-style home where Wilma lived. White, pink, and magenta roses surrounded a sparse, drought-thirsty lawn. Wee dogs yapped and yowled at me from inside as I rang the doorbell. The door opened, revealing a spacious home decorated in swanky gold drapes with fat tassels, marble tile floors, and oversized leather furniture.

Another elderly woman in the background held back the Yorkies of Doom on their slim leashes as Wilma greeted me. She led me to the living room where sat at least twenty more white-and gray-haired women of all sizes and ethnicities. No men. They chatted amiably over tea and cookies.

That is, until they saw me.

Based on their odd expressions, I wasn't sure they wanted me at all. Finally, Wilma spoke. "This is Beth. She and her handsome husband bought Nina and Albert's house."

Some smiles and greetings. Perhaps looks of . . . pity?

Neighborhood Watchers

I really wanted to leave, but I needed to find out who our neighbors were. Surely I felt uncomfortable because I was the newcomer. One-on-one encounters with strangers were fine. And I had no problems conducting business in conference rooms with development teams and management, but social groups and parties made my skin crawl if I didn't know anyone.

Trying to relax, I held up a stiff hand in greeting. "Hi. I'm Beth."

Wilma ushered me to an empty seat and pressed a glass of red wine into my hand. It smelled glorious and tasted even better. Maybe this wasn't going to be so awful after all. The ladies sitting closest to me introduced themselves as Devanya and Cecily. Devanya's magnificent, earth goddess hips filled the accent chair she sat in while Cecily perched primly on the edge of what looked like a dining room chair. They offered me a platter of orgasm-inducing gourmet chocolates, all the while chatting about their kids, grandkids, vacations and so forth. No mention of spouses. They stole looks at me over the rims of their wine glasses as Wilma officially started the meeting.

"Ladies, thank you for coming to this month's meeting. It's an important one, as you know, with Hallow's Eve rapidly approaching. Since Nina's death, we've already experienced a number of unwelcome events. So, per the bylaws, we need to bring Beth up to speed on what's happening and her role in the community."

Everyone looked at me as I devoured another chocolate.

Was I supposed to speak? To offer an opinion? I

definitely had one. "Bylaws?" I swallowed the confection. "We weren't told this neighborhood had an HOA. If there is, I have a lawsuit to file."

Shrill laughter chopped the air. "An HOA?" More laughter. "Depends what the 'H' stands for," someone else interjected. And they laughed harder.

Just as I was going to stand up to leave, Cecily held up her hand. "I believe it might've been too early to invite Beth."

Wilma frowned, waving her hand. "Nonsense! If nothing else, we should've done it sooner." She addressed me directly. "My dear, I know this is sudden and unexpected, but the truth is that we need you to be aware of your duties as a Watcher. If you neglect them, there will be dire consequences."

Everyone nodded, drinking deeply.

Although profoundly uncomfortable and more than a little put on the spot, I decided to at least find out what they wanted. "So, what does a 'watcher' do exactly? I mean, obviously they watch. But what? Strangers? Suspicious cars cruising the streets? Because I really don't have time for that sort of thing."

Devanya held up her hand to Wilma's undisguised ire. "Can I? 'Cause I think y'all's messin' this up enough." Wilma rolled her eyes and Devanya turned to me. "Okay, a 'watcher' is like bein' grannie to the seven-year-old grandson who's stealin' cookies from the cookie jar. You just tell 'em, '*You* gotta wait until *after* dinner.' That's exactly what a Watcher does, but instead of grandsons it's boogeymen tryin' to wreck y'all's house. Y'all just gotta tell 'em no. With the right words, 'course. And that's it!" Devanya drained her wine glass.

Neighborhood Watchers

Boogeymen. I tried to comprehend this explanation. "Are you serious? You want me to 'backhand' bad guys?"

"'Course it don't make sense," Devanya said, wagging her chin. "*Death* don't make sense." She motioned to her neighbor. "Gimme that bottle, Ce-ce."

"The boogeymen Devanya refers to aren't necessarily human criminals, although they can certainly appear that way if they think it's more frightening," Wilma replied. "They're more of a . . . supernatural . . . origin. You do believe in the supernatural, don't you?"

What could I possibly say?

Wilma continued after an awkward silence, her hands shaking. "At any rate, we meet here every month to discuss the manifestations, resurrections, and demonic activity so that we can take precautions if necessary. But mostly everything is fine as long as we are all performing our Watcher duties." She smiled, but it seemed forced. "You don't have to do that much, really. We'll show you the ropes. They're in the garage with the knife and bottle of protection ash." The room was silent. "Any questions?"

As I shot past Cecily, I upset her wine glass, leaving in my wake a flurry of dismayed comments. I sent Dan a text as soon as my feet hit the sidewalk.

Great. We'd moved into a neighborhood full of winos and crazies. Dan called me to express his disbelief just as Oleg's plumbing truck pulled into the driveway. I told him we'd talk later.

As no-nonsense in person as he was on the phone, Oleg came around the side of the house and slipped on his protective yellow jumper. Short and bald, he seemed like a perfect fit for our crawlspace door, which he opened. I told him about the dead giant possum. "It was probably attracted to the water," I said.

"Perhaps. Sometimes things just crawl under house to die," he said. "I'll take quick look. If is sewage, it is necessary to call restoration first and turn off water for a couple of days. But perhaps not. Should know in a few minutes."

With that, he brandished his cell phone flashlight the way Johnny did and wormed into the darkness.

I heard nothing but the breeze blowing through the bushes flanking the opening, as well as the occasional car whooshing past on the main road, radio blaring.

"Oleg? You see the 'lake' the trapper mentioned?"

No answer.

Maybe he couldn't hear me. Johnny could hear me just fine. Was Oleg hard of hearing?

I waited. After ten more minutes I started to get impatient and more than a little scared. Dogs bayed mournfully in the distance. Maybe he couldn't hear me and he was examining something more serious.

I dialed his cell phone.

It rang on my end, but I heard nothing from beneath the house.

Of course, he must have turned off the ringer. He wouldn't want anyone bothering him while he was working.

As the minutes ticked on, I melted down into a puddle of panic. Wilma's sinister admonition shrieked savagely in my head. After an hour, heart pounding, sick with worry, I called the police.

Oleg never came out. And, over the next week, multiple police searches yielded nothing.

Neighborhood Watchers

For two weeks, I couldn't work, couldn't sleep, every thought shackled to guilt over Oleg's disappearance. Useless, I huddled on the couch with Winston, watching movies on Netflix about miserable British people in historical costumes. A police officer took pity on me and babysat another plumber as he fixed the leak under the house. I sat by the pool, frozen with anxiety until it was over.

My sensitive geek husband went raving mad. One night, he woke up multiple times, wondering if he'd heard Oleg.

"It's not Oleg, honey. He's dead."

"Oleg *can't* be dead," Dan whispered as he crept back in bed. "He'd smell worse than the possum."

The hollowness in my chest told me we wouldn't find Oleg under the house. Ever.

Even Winston would disappear for hours on end. I'd search for him frantically to no avail. Then, just as I'd conclude with anguish that he'd somehow gotten outside, I'd find him sleeping on the bed or strolling down the hallway, chittering with excitement, head bumping my leg for a pet.

And whenever I looked outside, three or more elderly ladies would be staring at the house from the street. Despite the bizarre nature of what had happened, I couldn't for a moment accept that Oleg's disappearance had anything but a natural explanation. *Just because you don't know the answer doesn't mean something impossible has happened.*

This was crazy and needed to stop.

I'd been avoiding calls, texts, and emails from Lucy for the last two weeks. I'd call and leave her a voice mail when I knew damned well she couldn't answer.

Maria Alexander

She was a teacher at an adult learning center during the day and a folk guitarist/Mom/cat rescuer at night. Desperate to find a solution to the madness, I decided to tell her what was going on and get her advice. I hated burdening her with anything because she was the one living closest to Dad and spent the most time visiting him.

This time I called when I knew she'd be home and she answered.

"Give me one good reason I shouldn't smack you for avoiding me," she said upon answering.

"Okay, how's this: We had a plumber disappear under our house."

"*What?*"

I told her about the whole incident, from the difficulty with the warranty company to calling Beverly for a reference, and the unbelievable results. The police investigation was ongoing, with Oleg listed as a missing person. "They had to tow his truck from our driveway," I explained. "And just before this all occurred I had the weirdest neighborhood meeting you can imagine!"

Lucy was even more interested to hear about the whacko wine club. But when I told her how I'd bolted out, she let me have it.

"Oh, Lizzie, you're so *boring*!"

"What do you mean? I couldn't sit there and listen to that rubbish."

"You *know* what I mean. You have no imagination."

"Look, I didn't call—"

"HUSH! You wanted my input. I'm giving it."

I gritted my teeth. "Right. Continue."

Neighborhood Watchers

"Some of these retired women are probably widows. Their kids don't come around much, and they feel empty. So, they've made up this whimsical cabal where they protect their neighborhood from monsters. Why couldn't you just humor them and enjoy the wine? And when they brought up that watcher business, you could have just said, 'Oh, okay.' I swear, I thought you'd become more fun after you married Dan, and then after you moved to California. But apparently not. You've got a terminal case of the dulls."

"Are you quite finished?"

"No. In fact, here's what I think you should do. You should ring up this Wilma person and tell her that you've reconsidered the little job they want you to take on. You don't have to mean it. Just play along. Be neighborly. You were so combative with everyone in San Diego."

"I hate people. You know this. Especially when they're loud and obnoxious."

"And you hated your HOA, too, remember?"

How could I forget? They were a toxic bunch of bastards who never answered emails or fixed anything. I considered getting on the board, but I couldn't stand dealing with them. We were on the verge of taking them to court when Dan's headhunter called him.

"This isn't the horrible, evil HOA. They're sweet old ladies who can't make you do anything you don't want to do. So just have some fun, won't you?"

Lucy was right. I'm not a joiner and this advice made me bristle. But when Dan came home that night with Halloween decorations, singing "This Is Halloween" from *The Nightmare Before Christmas*, something shifted.

Maria Alexander

"*We* are going to celebrate Halloween as actual homeowners. We're going to dress up, hand out candy to children, and crank up spooky music. It's going to be awesome!"

"What are you so cheerful about?"

He dropped two massive Halloween Store bags on the dining table and started pulling out all kinds of ridiculous decorations. Strings of yellow plastic skulls with lights inside. Bags of fake spider webs. A giant plastic jangly, glow-in-the-dark skeleton. Even a black cauldron, ostensibly for holding candy. "I got some very interesting news today."

"Oh?" I dug into the bag and found six bags of small candy bars. I was going to protest, but then I realized I'm supposed to be fun now and candy bars were surely fun. Look—they even said "Fun Size" on the bag.

"Well, I didn't tell you because I thought you might flip out over the expense, but I had a private investigator do some poking into Oleg's life and he found some things."

"Really? Like what?"

"It seems Oleg had a very unhappy marriage and that his wife of fifteen years had filed for divorce. If granted, he would've had to pay a significant chunk of his business earnings to spousal and child support."

"So you think he devised some kind of disappearing act."

"Hell yeah."

"But why our house? And how?"

"Plumbers know all the tricks and traps of old houses."

"But even the police couldn't find an exit."

Neighborhood Watchers

"Remember that news article I sent you? About how they have an I.Q. cap on the people they recruit?"

He got me there.

"Besides," he continued, "this house is identical in layout to many in this neighborhood and no doubt countless others in Los Angeles. He probably chose this one because he knew how to get out without anyone knowing."

"I suppose . . . "

"There's probably a way in up into the house that we're not aware of. He might have been planning it for a while, and when he got your call, he decided this was his golden opportunity."

This explained so much. I took Dan in my arms. "God, I love you."

"I know," he replied.

The next day, I got up early and flew through a surprising amount of work thanks to my renewed sense of—hope? Clarity? After I enjoyed a cup of coffee and gave Winston some undivided attention, I decided to follow Lucy's advice.

Wilma looked positively alarmed when she opened her front door.

"I'm so sorry for how I behaved," I started. "I hope you'll forgive me."

She welcomed me inside with open arms. This time as I entered, I noticed her living room décor included crosses with incense holders mounted to the walls: north, south, east, and west. It felt decidedly Hammer-esque, especially with the dramatic standing candelabra. I then noticed a large circle had been drawn on the floor in the living room on the tile. There were words around the circle, but I couldn't make them out and it felt rude to stare.

Wilma lifted two wine glasses and a bottle of wine from a latticework wooden cupboard. It appeared to be an antique. "I'm sorry if things look strange. We've been preparing for Samhain, especially since it seemed you weren't amenable to being a Watcher."

"On the contrary, I'd be happy to do whatever the neighborhood needs me to do." I felt a tingle of excitement. Maybe my sister was right. I *needed* a shot of community, to feel like I was part of something bigger, even if it was ridiculous.

"Really?" Wilma nearly dropped the glasses as she sat down in one of the accent chairs. "What changed your mind?" She seemed to realize that she'd not actually offered the alcohol she was pouring. She lifted a glass and I indicated my approval.

"Well, I realized that I'd been selfish because I'd not even let you fully explain what this task entailed before assuming I wasn't interested. It sounded like something you really needed me to do."

Wilma nodded emphatically. "Absolutely. We wouldn't have asked if it weren't necessary. In fact, I was hoping I could speak to you again and impress on you the dire urgency of the matter. Living at The Crossroads is dangerous, especially at Samhain, when the veil is thinnest between the living and the dead. You had a workman disappear, I hear."

"Yes, unfortunately," I said, quietly admiring Oleg's cunning escape.

"I wondered if that might change your mind. Anyway, we don't have a moment to waste. Follow me."

Neighborhood Watchers

The interior of her garage made my skin crawl. It was painted entirely black and crammed full of creepy vintage trunks and cracked leather chests blanketed in spider webs. "I recovered this from Nina's just before she died, thank goodness. I don't think her son would have understood." Yanking hard, she dislodged a large red wicker picnic basket from between the chests. She handed it to me. "You'll find everything you need in there. Now, because you're the newest Watcher, you must light all of the candles in the sconces on the house gates by sundown. And then you must draw the *vévé* of Papa Legba on your deck in a circle ten feet in diameter before repeating the incantation in the book where it's bookmarked."

I pretended to take notes on my iPhone. "Papa . . . Legba," I repeated.

"Don't worry. I'll email you the instructions. The candles are very important because they represent the bonfires."

"Um . . . okay. Everyone has a bonfire? I mean, a sconce?"

"Yes."

"Even me?"

"Oh, yes. You didn't notice? It's on your gate. Don't worry, I'll place the candles at dawn that morning, including yours." She went on to instruct me to keep watch that night by the *vévé* until sunrise the next morning, burning the incense at my side. If anything strange appeared, and it shouldn't but you never know, I was to stab it with the knife. If that didn't work, I was to use the ropes. "You don't really need to tie up anything. Just throw the ropes over the creature. It'll remain until the sunlight burns it up."

Maria Alexander

I stifled a laugh. These ladies had really created quite a Halloween ritual. She handed me the basket, which was much heavier than it looked, and gave me a smile that wasn't remotely reassuring.

"Thank you, Beth. I didn't want to scare you with stories about the terrible things that have befallen our neighborhood in the past when a Watcher didn't fulfill her duties. Suffice it to say, you're quite literally a lifesaver."

With a few more purchases from the Halloween store, Dan turned the front of our house into a graveyard full of Styrofoam headstones and hung the skeleton from the eaves over our garage. For the first time since childhood, I fell under the spell of Halloween, delighting in the ghosts and ghouls pasted in windows and popping out of hedges. The spectacle pleased Dan beyond words. I had no idea he loved Halloween this much. Maybe he didn't, either, until now.

The ladies of the neighborhood smiled and waved to me as they walked the Yorkies of Doom. And I waved back. The morning of Halloween, just as she'd promised, Wilma placed a candle in the sconce attached to our gate. I found it when I went to get the mail that afternoon. As the sun dipped into the horizon, I began the ritual Wilma had outlined in her email by walking through the neighborhood and lighting the candles. The major boulevards formed boundaries to the area, which turned out to be quite a lot of territory. However, I was able to finish by twilight.

That's where I stopped. The rest of the directions seemed daunting and pointless, especially if no one

Neighborhood Watchers

would be wiser. Our fences were high. No one would know if I just hung out on the deck and drank.

Dan cranked up the Halloween "mixed tape" he made on a CD to play out of our garage window for the children approaching our house. Wearing an elaborate Captain Jack outfit complete with heavy eyeliner, which looked kind of sexy, he handed out candy to the adorable little comic book characters, rainbow unicorns, and Disney princesses who wandered up to the house and uttered the time-honored phrase to get their treats.

Meanwhile, I lay out on the lawn chair by the pool in the darkness, smoking a rare cigarette and drinking spicy pumpkin ale, which I kept at hand in a cooler. The Great Candle Lighting had worn me out. Still, I'd offered to help hand out candy and Dan refused. He had a whole patter worked out. "Arrrrrrr! Who knocks on Davy Jones' locker!" he'd bellow as he opened the door. Winston was stashed in the master bedroom with a mountain of his own treats so he wouldn't zip outside at the first chance.

I laughed as I watched Dan's antics. I'd pulled back the drapes for a clear view through the sliding glass door. At that moment, I realized how much I loved him. It hit me with an aching wooziness that flowed through me so powerfully I couldn't have spoken at that moment if I had to. He was my everything.

By nine o'clock, the trick-or-treaters had petered out, as had Dan's energy. He stomped out onto the deck, hands on hips. "Ale wench, serve me some brew!"

I handed him a beer and he sat next to me. We shared a yeasty kiss and rested in silence for several minutes. "Any candy left?" I asked.

"A little," he said, drinking. "But I think they're done for the night. I should turn off the front porch light."

"Mmmm."

I followed Dan inside, wandering into the kitchen to get something to eat. Just as he flicked off the porch light, someone knocked. I looked up from the refrigerator because I heard something else entirely in the distance.

A blood-curdling scream.

Halloween. Gotta love it.

Dan opened the door. His arm flew over his nose. "Goddam—"

The smell of decay flooded the foyer and the adjoining kitchen. I recognized it from the possum incident, but this was *much* worse. A short man stepped forward and slid back his black hood, the gray skin of his bald head wrinkled and reptilian. His preternaturally large bloodshot eyes glistened as he laughed and shoved a gun barrel into Dan's chest.

"Trick!" he hissed and pulled the trigger.

Dan crumpled to the floor as the smell of gunpowder singed the air.

The creature pointed the pistol at me and laughed. "The Watcher not watching. Is too bad."

He pulled the trigger. I dove behind the refrigerator door and the bullet ricocheted off. Throwing the door aside, I dodged into the dining room.

That voice. Like Oleg's.

The world blurred into a white-hot streak of terror. Another bullet shattered the sliding glass door. I fled back outside to the deck. Reaching in the basket, I grasped the hilt of the one thing that might stop the

Neighborhood Watchers

nightmare. I then threw myself against the stucco wall in the shadows.

The black-robed man burst through the glass door opening. Just as he did, I drove the blade into him with a backhand motion as hard as I possibly could.

He collapsed in a molten heap that seeped into the concrete. A huge murder of crows flew overhead, shrieking, cawing, flapping.

And then they vanished.

***

The grief rips through me afresh every day. Somehow I survived dealing with police. Family. Funeral. My wonderful, sweet, funny man who I love more than anything isn't here anymore, and it's killing me. My family worries I'll do something rash. Maybe I will. The pain is overwhelming. I often don't even have Winston to comfort me. He disappears for days at a time and returns with dead . . . *things* . . . in his mouth that he drops on the kitchen floor.

What hurts almost as much are the looks from the old women as they stand in the street. And stare.

They know I lied. I can't face them because I know that some of them must have suffered because of my negligence.

No one will buy my house. Or rent it. It's mine, the bank says. The previous owners have gifted it to us. Even when I move out, I wake up back on the deck, where I should have drawn the *vévé*. All of my furniture returns. I'm paralyzed in this evil place. The Crossroads.

One night a year, I have my revenge and drive every one of those fuckers back to Hell. Or wherever they come from.

I'll do it until Dan returns from the dead.

And when he does, maybe he'll take me back with him.

The Story of Jessie and Me

TIMOTHY JOHNSON

The world as we knew it was over. It doesn't matter how it happened, whether by fire or disease or natural disaster. In truth, it was a little of all those things.

We always thought there would be some kind of sign, a flash of light maybe, the voice of God, something to tell us things would never go back to the way they were. But we had to figure it out for ourselves. Things got bad, and one day, one way or another, we all realized there had been a time when the world was more or less kind. And then it wasn't.

Jessie and me were together since the high school gymnasium in Joshua. Every day, we got up off our part of the floor, folded our blankets if we were lucky enough to have them, got our rations of boiled water and whatever was coming out of the community pantry that day, and then we waited. We waited for someone to come and make everything all right. The state of the world still seemed temporary. We didn't know any better.

The Story of Jessie and Me

Months passed. Spring turned to summer. The jets screaming toward Dallas had stopped. At one time, eight different voices on eight different radio stations broadcast reports from all over, and then the last guy on the air, on 1100 AM, was asking if there was even anyone still listening.

In all that time, Jessie and me stuck together, but we didn't get to know each other too well. We were guarded, and hell, we thought it would all be over soon, and we'd all go back to our lives.

Then, the military came. We had this fence we'd stripped from the baseball fields and put up around the parking lot, and they just plowed right through it in their armored Humvees. We should have known right then and there.

They spread out from their trucks and rounded everyone up, got everyone together beneath the flag pole. The Lone Star was still up, but the Stars and Stripes had been taken down even before the school had turned into a refuge.

The soldiers said they had a camp outside Fort Worth. They had food, water, shelter. We said we already had those things. Those soldiers, most of them no more than boys and girls, gripped their rifles tight. We could see it in their stiff postures, the fear. They weren't afraid that we might try to hurt them. They were afraid of what they might have to do.

They said they could protect us. Jessie was the one who said we should go because, she knew, our food and water were going with them whether we were or weren't.

She was good, Jessie. In all the suffering that came on, she was a good thing. She straightened me out and kept me straight. She kept me going. But more than that, she kept me smiling and laughing at times I probably shouldn't have. And I missed it, how lucky I was.

We went with the soldiers to that camp. And, of course, it fell. I was so stupid. Even then, we were still looking for that thing, the feeling of safety, of civilization. We were still convinced it existed somewhere and that, if we could find it, we could hold onto it.

Thing is, we don't want to hold onto it. We don't want to do the work. That's the whole point. We want a place like that so we don't have to worry about holding it together, but we didn't know things didn't work like that anymore. We thought we were safe with those high sand bag walls. But we didn't think, when the food, water, and medicine ran out, the outside world wouldn't have to come in and end what we had. We did it ourselves just fine.

The world's patient. Sometimes, it'll chew you up and spit you out; sometimes, it'll swallow. Sometimes, it'll just sit and wait for you to rot. In the end, it always gets its due, always takes everything it can.

Jessie and me had something, though, something most of the others didn't. Mind, it wouldn't have stopped us from killing each other if that's what we had to do, but it kept us fighting and holding on just a little longer. And that made all the difference.

When the camp went crazy, soldiers shooting people like animals, Jessie and me hid until nightfall, and then we just up and left. Of course, it was dangerous getting out of there. Some of the people had gotten guns from the soldiers, and at a certain point, everybody was just shooting everybody.

The Story of Jessie and Me

That coping we had to do with the world, it didn't sit right with most people. In a way, if you had to point to one thing that ended it all, it was madness.

The dirt roads turned to mud, but I couldn't remember the last time it had rained. So much blood was spilled that night. I remember falling and catching myself in something warm and wet. Fumbling in the dark, I gripped the cold steel of a revolver. Jessie told me I better come on. I showed her what I'd found. Even though it was soaked and caked with dirt, Jessie knew then and there that gun would be useful. She told me I better hide it and come on.

We got out of there with nothing but the clothes we were wearing and each a backpack of rations we'd saved up or stolen just in case we had to leave like that. No water, though. That was more valuable a commodity than food, and harder to hide, too. We suspected the soldiers had rationed it so tightly so that no one could leave.

My father was a hunter and a survivalist. He told me, he said, you go out there in the wilderness, you need but two things: your wits and water. Ain't nothing more important than those two things. You got those two things and you got time, time to figure out what to do.

Smart man, my father. He never did tell me what to do if I didn't have those things.

We walked as far as we could. We didn't know where we were going, just that east into Dallas wasn't a good idea.

So we followed a highway south. We could have gone back to Joshua, back to the school, but there was nothing left for us there. Figured we would try Fort

Timothy Johnson

Hood. And if nothing else, we knew we'd eventually hit the coast, and then we'd figure something out.

That day, the Texas sun baked us to our bones. We got far enough that I didn't know where we were anymore. The road signs didn't make sense. I'd never heard of any of those places.

And that night, we found a house in the middle of nowhere and started a fire. I remember I was real proud of it. My first fire. We heated up a can of sausages, and then we turned in.

His name was Jake, and he carried a hammer.

While we were asleep, he and three other men came in through the busted front door. They surrounded us, and I imagine they waited there for a time, just watching us sleep, before Jake somewhat politely nudged me with the toe of his boot.

It was the first time Jessie and me embraced. We came together beside the dying fire, backs against a beat-up, moldy couch. The moonlight poured through the window and made their skin pale. The fire glow reflected in their eyes.

Jake bounced the hammer in his hand, testing its weight. No, demonstrating its weight. He introduced himself and his crew, though I can't remember their names. They didn't matter. Jake's the one who had our attention. There was something in his eyes. Some might think it was psychopathic. But I think it was a sort of kindness. He didn't want to do what he was doing, took no enjoyment from it, but he believed he had to.

The others took our bags, zipped them open, dug through what we had. Some of our cans clattered on the wooden floor, and they paid no mind.

The Story of Jessie and Me

Jake scratched his head with the claw of his hammer. He told me I was stupid, said Texas is a real flat, open state, said they could see the fire from a mile away. He asked me what I thought was going to happen. He shook his head, closed his eyes, and called me stupid again.

I remember Jake kneeled to meet me at my level, and we just listened to the pop of the fire for a while. He explained they were going to take everything we had. Then, he said, they were going to take Jessie. He asked if I preferred to watch or if I'd rather them kill me before. Said it made no difference to him. Said we would both be dead by the end anyway.

I was quiet, just stared at him, and the man actually smiled, rubbed his chin like he was thinking some real deep thoughts. Then he patted my boot as if it were an encouragement and told me I would watch.

Jake stood and held out a hand. One of his men passed over our bags. Jake nodded, and they bore down on us.

Jessie, bless her, she fought back. But she was not strong, not physically anyway. One of them, he had long, dark, curly hair, grabbed her arm and yanked her up. She clawed him right under an eye. I wanted to go to her, protect her from what was coming, but the others held me down. The curly-haired man snatched her by her throat and dragged her outside. Then he shoved her into the dirt. The other two yanked me up and kicked me off the front porch. They stood near me to keep me from getting away, as if I was going to leave her. I may have been stupid, but I wasn't no coward.

They didn't restrain me, and that was their mistake, because as the man with long, curly hair kneeled, unzipped his pants, backhanded Jessie, and as the others watched, I eased my way to the revolver in my back waistband under my shirt.

The man took Jessie. I'm ashamed to say I hesitated. It took a long moment to summon the courage, and when I pressed the gun barrel to the side of the first one's head, he stopped moving, breathing, thinking. His eyes shifted to me; I could see every bit of his blue irises, the red cracks on the whites.

I could feel the other one moving. Even if I shot his friend, he was going to disarm me. I'd messed it up before it even began.

Jessie was crying. The man was grunting. I pulled the trigger.

It felt like creating a void.

The other man grabbed me, one powerful arm around my throat, the other reaching for my gun. There was a moment where we were locked and his fingers reached and clutched as if he was trying to stretch them like rubber.

Jessie was screaming. The curly-haired man hit her again, and she got quiet.

I rolled on the ground with the man, and somehow, the gun ended up pointed at his chest. I pulled the trigger three times, and he let me go.

As I got to my feet, Jake stepped toward me with his hammer. I leveled the revolver at him. He stopped and gazed at me with a cocked head, as if he were trying to figure out a bothersome riddle.

The curly-haired man let Jessie go, and she scurried away, covering herself as best she could. He stood, zipped his pants, dusted himself off, and sighed like he was annoyed or content or both.

The Story of Jessie and Me

Jake said bullets were in short supply. He said I had at most two more and that he didn't think I could kill them both from where I stood. He said it was a Mexican standoff.

Jessie told me to kill them.

Jake's sneer grew, and then he jerked like he was going to lunge at me. So I shot the curly-haired man in the throat. He went down quick. We all watched him kicking in the dirt for a time, and then he stopped. I didn't think much of it, but I don't think he was in pain. He just sort of drifted off peaceful.

I returned the revolver to Jake, and he froze in place. He told me I had one more and that I better make it count. Or, he suggested, I could put the gun down, and he'd walk away. He said that last bullet was my only sure-fire ticket out of this. He said if I missed or if I didn't kill him, he was going to kill me and then Jessie.

At the mention of her name, I shot him in the gut.

For a moment, Jake didn't move. A rose bloomed on his shirt. He looked down disappointed, as if he'd spilled something on it, and then, with his hammer in hand, he took a step toward me.

He fell to a knee and struggled there a moment. He groaned as if he were merely frustrated. He got back to his feet and shuffled over to his truck, stumbled as he opened the door, started the engine, and sped off.

Jessie and me embraced for the second time, and I felt like I wanted to never let go. That night, I think we both learned we didn't have nothing without each other. The world was changing us, changing what we meant to each other, and in all of it, Jessie and me, we were a good thing.

Timothy Johnson

We stood there awhile in the front yard of that home, the color draining from the dead men, and all the world was a bluish gray.

The dust in the pickup truck's wake lifted into the sky like the spirits of those men, and then everything was quiet.

It occurred to me that I'd become a murderer, and right then and there, I knew the old world was gone forever. Even if we reached some kind of return, I could never go back. I was ruined. And it was Jessie who took hold of my face and looked me square in the eye and told me, "No." She said that's what life would be now. She said we'd be fighting but that we'd always be fighting together. She said we had to move on. So that's what we did. We moved on.

We didn't bother putting out the fire. As we walked into the night, I turned every once in a while, the house an orange beacon in a dark world. And then I turned around the last time, and it had winked out, not even a faint glimmer on the horizon. I set my head down and just kept moving.

In the morning, we found some ripe prickly pears. I took my shirt off, and Jessie got this confused look on her face. She wasn't a Texan. Mind, she lived there before, but she'd grown up in the Northeast. When she looked at cactus, she saw a monster of a plant. She didn't know we could eat their fruit.

I used my shirt to protect my hands, and I told her we could burn the spines off and peel the skin, and underneath all that horror was good eating. She didn't question me. She just started a fire. This time, though, even with the sun rising, we built up the sides with rocks.

The Story of Jessie and Me

I got about a dozen of them, and when they were prepared, we devoured them. It was the first time for either of us that we'd been so desperate. We'd both lived in a time when food and water was always just in the next room. We didn't understand hunger and thirst like that. We didn't understand what it does to you inside. Having that fruit was like being a dry, hard sponge thrown into a bucket of cold water.

We looked at each other over the fire, red juice all over our faces, knowing it wouldn't be the last time we'd be so close to the brink, and we fell into laughter that we couldn't stop. She and I looked so ridiculous, like bloodthirsty animals, with the red juice dripping off our chins, dirt and dust caked on our skin, disheveled and ratty hair. She had this mischievous smile, and she told me I didn't scare her. I told her that, in a time when everybody was afraid of everybody, that was a good thing. I told her maybe we should get married, and she said that would be just fine.

We toasted each other with another pear over the fire. I held onto her gaze, and I'll never forget it was the moment I realized her eyes were a soft hazel. There in the firelight and the dawn, her irises glimmered like gems. She was precious, Jessie. Did I know then that I loved her? That's a stupid question.

We got moving again so we could put some miles under our feet before it got too hot. We walked along the highway, still south, until late morning. Then we got in some shade under a tree and intended to rest until it cooled down a bit.

We dozed. We let the day wear on because, especially with nothing to drink, we would do more

Timothy Johnson

harm than good walking in that heat. So we stayed put.

I was exhausted. That kind of tired, it's more than a feeling like weights attached to your arms and legs. Your insides feel heavy, your mind like a vacuum. I fell asleep before I knew it, like someone had come and turned the lights out on me mid-thought.

Then Jessie was screaming, and I heard the rattle. She was shuffling away in the dirt and put her back against the trunk of the tree we were under. I was up, and the snake was holding its ground, shaking its tail like an ornery old man's fist. I grabbed a rock about the size of a baseball and threw it at the thing. I missed, but it got the idea and slithered off into some fluffgrass.

Jessie was gasping and crying, clutching her thigh. A small tear flapped away from her jeans, and the denim was darkening with blood. She looked at me and told me to suck the poison out. I shook my head, told her that's not the way it works. She told me to cut her open and suck at the wound. I said we had to find antivenom.

A defeated look came over her face. She said she was going to die. I said she wasn't.

Trouble was, earlier that morning, I'd seen signs along the highway and knew where we were. It was over forty miles to the nearest hospital. I didn't tell Jessie that. I just got our things together and got her moving.

It was slow going. She said her leg already felt stiff, like it was on fire and dead at the same time. I offered to carry her, but she looked at me like I was some kind of idiot.

When we got back to the highway, I prayed a

The Story of Jessie and Me

vehicle would come and that whoever was inside would be friendly. We'd survived heartache after heartache, and we just needed a win. We needed a break.

If we didn't get one, I'd do what I had to do.

After thirty minutes on that highway, we got one.

Jake's truck was parked off the road in the dirt. The straight lines of his tire tracks looked like the vehicle had just coasted off the asphalt and come to a stop kissing an embankment. The engine was still running. Though I couldn't see anything through the back window, I already knew I'd find him inside.

I helped Jessie to the truck and leaned her against the bed. She winced, but we were quiet. With a cautionary stare, she told me to be careful. I pulled the revolver from my waistband. It was empty, but Jake couldn't be sure of that.

I yanked the door open, and there he was, slumped over toward the passenger side, only the seat belt holding him up. The blood from his wound had pooled in his lap and run onto the floorboard.

Jessie asked me if he was dead, and I nodded. I reached in to pull him out of there, and when I pressed the button on his seatbelt, he groaned.

Jessie wanted me to leave him there by the road to die, but I couldn't. I reached in and took his hammer. Then, I went around to the passenger side, got my hands under his armpits, and pulled.

Jake screamed. It was the first time I'd heard a genuine scream of pain. When someone screams because they're in so much pain that they can't bare it, it's a sound of defeat. It's more of a moan, the sound of giving in, of choosing death over this.

Timothy Johnson

I got Jake over on the passenger side, and he slipped back into unconsciousness. As I helped Jessie into the cab, she looked at me with something like disappointment, but she didn't fight me. I followed her in, and I handed her the hammer. She placed it on her lap, and we both gazed at it a moment.

I backed the truck onto the highway, and we continued south.

It wasn't long before Jessie's fever set in and she fell asleep, and then all I had to keep me company was the rattle of the truck and the roll of the road.

Before everything, I found drives like that peaceful. But riding on that empty highway, Jessie beside me and Jake on the other side of her, both of them dying, my heart thumped loud in my ears and measured the passage of time. I reflexively clicked on the radio to drown it out or get my mind on other things. I tuned it to 1100 AM, but there was just static.

Jessie took my hand in hers. She woke long enough to comfort me. She said whatever was going to happen was going to happen, and if I could save her, I would.

I told her that was the biggest pile of shit she'd ever said. I told her to get rest and I'd find a hospital or pharmacy or something. I told her there was no if. I said I would.

She smiled, patted my hand, and dozed off again.

It took me a long time to understand what happened in that truck. What Jessie had done and what she'd said had been two different things. She'd said what I'd needed to hear. She'd said it so I'd refuse it, so I'd understand on my own, so I'd believe it.

Even then, that woman knew me better than I knew myself.

The Story of Jessie and Me

We didn't hit a roadblock of dead cars. The truck's transmission didn't blow. No militarized men ambushed us with road spikes. For forty miles, the way was clear for us.

But the hospital looked dead. Bullet holes marred the brick facade, and red smears painted the parking lot. The automatic doors to the ER were locked wide open, and it was dark inside. A column of smoke out back rose into the sky. Something had caught fire not too long ago, but the blaze wasn't out of control yet. I had to hurry.

Blind and stupid with worry, I shook Jessie. She wouldn't wake. I told her I'd be right back, and then I took the hammer, left her with Jake in the truck, and went through the emergency room doors. In the dark, I didn't know what I was looking for or where I'd find it. I tripped on an overturned wheelchair. I shoved papers off of desks. I sent equipment clattering to the tile floor. Like some big, dumb idiot.

That's when I met Anna. She stepped into the daylight that was coming through a window and blinked at me for a moment like I might have been a mirage. She was dressed in nurse scrubs. She had blood all over her arms and shirt, but I didn't pay mind to that. I just knew she could help me. I knew she could help Jessie.

But she asked me for help. Her voice was small like she wasn't used to it. She sounded thick, strong, but there was a break in her. Someone had torn her up good.

I eased my way across the floor, and she began to weep. She collapsed, and I caught her. With her face buried in my chest, she said she was sorry but they were in trouble and some people needed my help.

Timothy Johnson

I asked her to show me.

She led me down a dark hallway. Sunlight leaked in through office windows, but it wasn't enough. It was never enough.

Anna scurried to a door with a cutout window. She crouched and peered through the glass. She told me to look, and I did. Out behind the hospital, some men were burning bodies. Some of those bodies were still moving.

She told me, when it all ended, people left the hospital one by one. She said, when it was all said and done, it was just her, a Doctor Norcross, and the patients who were too sick or hurt to leave. As things got worse, more people showed up for help, and Anna and Doctor Norcross took care of them as best they could.

Then, these men came. They said they could keep the place safe and secure. They said they could contribute. But, Anna said, she knew what those men were.

There had been a sickness in the hospital. Those men decided to burn everyone they thought had it. She said she and Doctor Norcross protested, said not everyone was ill. That was when those men slit the doctor's throat.

I counted five men out back, and I asked Anna if that was all of them. She nodded.

I gripped the empty revolver in my left hand, Jake's hammer in my right. I told Anna about Jessie in the truck out front, said what had happened. She said she thought they had antivenom. I told her to see to Jessie, to take what she would need to make her well, and to drive away and never come back.

The Story of Jessie and Me

She looked at me like she was simultaneously grateful and horrified, and then she snuck off.

I remember the sound that door made when I opened it, like rusty nails pulling from rotten wood. The rest is a blur. I know I leveled the revolver. I know those men didn't look surprised for a minute. And I know one of them said I had a nice hammer, said they had a friend who had one just like it.

I told them I knew Jake. I told them I knew Jake but that he was dead. I said I'd killed him.

At that, they spread out and surrounded me. I told them to count the bullets in my gun and how many they were. I said they could just leave. But I guess they had more on their minds than living.

Before everything, I hadn't been good at much. After the end, it took me a while to understand, but I learned that I was pretty good at killing.

They called my bluff, and I flipped the revolver around in my hand. One of them lunged at me from the side, and I cracked his eye socket with the butt of the gun. Another came at me from the front, and I kicked him in the testicles and then brained him with the hammer.

It was the first time I felt blood on my face. It wasn't much different than warm motor oil.

That's when things went dark. I got hit from behind, and it was like the shadows jumped at me from the corners. I almost went out, but I held on as they dragged me toward the fire. I came to when they got one of my legs in, and feeling the hammer's weight still in my fingers, I put its claw in one of their throats. It stuck there, bobbing like a new, useless appendage.

Timothy Johnson

The others let me go, and I rolled off the flames. My leg smoldering, denim caked to my shin, I got up.

The man still had my hammer buried in his neck, and he was kicking on the ground. One of his friends was trying to help. Then arterial spray shot into the air like a geyser, and I realized he wasn't trying to help at all. He just wanted that hammer.

The other man picked up a flaming board from the fire, and they came at me together. I caught the hammer before it hit me, but the board broke two of my ribs. They took me down, but I didn't let go of the hammer, and they came down with me.

None of us were letting it go, so we wrestled on the ground like awkward children fighting over a toy. It didn't take long for one of them to snatch the hammer from my grasp and the other to mount me with his hands around my throat.

The man with the hammer sneered. He could have put me out right then and there. But these men, they weren't made for this world.

I went for the eyes. My thumbs buried all the way back and scraped bone. He fell off me and rolled onto the fire, stood with his hands cradling his face and ran off trailing flames.

The last one came at me as I struggled to breathe. I got to my knees, and as he brought the hammer down, I launched into him like a linebacker. He lost the hammer, and its head buried into the ash and dirt.

He gasped when I pressed my knee down on his chest. Then I took the revolver and smashed it into his skull until he stopped thrashing. It was the most horrible thing I'd ever seen.

Then I kept going. I hit him with everything I had

The Story of Jessie and Me

left. I hit him until my arm went numb. I hit him until it became hard to pull the gun away because the blood and the brains were creating a wet suction.

Someone said my name. Jessie, she was at the door, looking pale as death, but she gazed at me with something like affirmation. It wasn't pride. It was more like acknowledgement.

I had done what I'd had to do, and Jessie said it was okay. She said it was over.

That was when the shakes took over my body, and Anna was rushing to catch me before I hit the ground.

***

I woke in a hospital bed. It had clean sheets. The blood and grime had been washed from my body. A thick gauze was wrapped around my leg. An IV was sticking in my arm. I had a window, and the light was beautiful.

Voices trickled in from the hallway.

I tried to sit up, but my chest rattled the broken glass inside. I couldn't get nowhere by myself.

I called out for Jessie. And in a moment, she came. Like a miracle, she looked like her old self. Anna had saved her. Anna had given me back my Jessie.

She told me about my wounds. She said I would live but that Anna was being careful about my leg. She said she was worried about infection. She told me Anna had said amputation might be necessary, but Jessie said she wouldn't allow it. I told her it was okay, that I knew where there was a good wheelchair.

She said I'd killed four of the men outright. The fifth, the one I'd clubbed in the eye, his brain had swollen, and he died hours later. Anna couldn't have done anything for him. I supposed whether she could or couldn't, that was true.

Timothy Johnson

Jessie told me Jake was alive. She said Anna didn't expect him to last much longer, but she was trying to keep him comfortable. Even so, he was in a lot of pain. Anna had said gunshot wounds to the gut were one of the most painful ways to go. I said that was just fine, and I told Jessie I wanted to see him. She didn't fight me. She just nodded and helped me up, like she always did.

Jake was a few doors down. In between our rooms were some other patients, ones I'd saved from the fire. Jessie said most of them would probably never even know what I'd done for them. I said that was fine. She said that some of them did know, though, and I said nothing.

I expected Jake to hate me for shooting him. Maybe he did, but he didn't ask why I'd done it. He did ask why I saved him, though. I told him it would have been harder not to, harder to pull him out of that truck, and he nodded.

I don't think he actually understood.

**

For a time, I was with Jessie. We lived in that hospital. I took care of her as best I could. We lived together the best we could. I'd even call those times happy.

When she went into labor, we knew something was wrong. Anna said Jessie's blood pressure had skyrocketed and she was bleeding too much. She told us she didn't know what to do. Jessie said she knew exactly what to do. She told Anna to deliver her baby.

Jessie fought for hours, and I watched her fade. I could do nothing for her this time, and admitting that was unbearable. We'd been through so much together, and we'd beaten all the odds. I had begun to feel

The Story of Jessie and Me

something like hope again, and it terrified me to know that I had this good thing but was powerless to hold onto it.

I watched as Jessie and Anna battled, and then there you were, covered in blood and gore, born with hair that was dark and thick and curly. Anna gave you to me, and she went to work on Jessie. I looked down at you, and I didn't know what I was going to do.

I looked at your mom, but she was already gone. Jessie, she was a good thing in a world of wrong, and she'd given me you.

You're grown now, so I won't hold back from telling you that it occurred to me to snuff you out right then and there. Mind, it would've been out of love. Your whole life, everyone and everything would be trying to do the same, and I thought maybe I ought to be the one to do it, rather than some strange man who'd do God knew what first.

But I didn't. Maybe it was because you didn't know that old world. I thought, maybe one day, if there was a chance, you could find happiness like I did with Jessie, even if it was only for a time.

Or maybe it was because I was weak.

Gaping at your face, hazel eyes already open and looking at the world in awe, I thought it was a little of all those things.

I Will be the Reflection Until the End

MICHAEL BAILEY

"Don't judge each day by the harvest you reap but by the seeds that you plant."—Robert Louis Stevenson, *Admiral Guinea*

"Life will find a way."—Michael Crichton, *Jurassic Park*

My sister used to collect cherry plum pits in her napkin, secretly, under the kitchen table. A strainer full of mixed yellow and red and deep-purple fruits would separate us each spring, with a small bowl next to it to collect the pits—although mine were typically the only ones in there—and a plate beneath the strainer to collect any drips from the rinsed fruit. My sister was coy like that. *Her* lie had become *our* lie, and every once in a while she'd throw a pit in the bowl to make it look like we were being honest. She knew I wouldn't bring it up to Mom, because that meant I could have more if I kept my mouth shut. It was one of the few secrets we kept from Mom in our youth. Call it a sibling bonding moment.

I Will Be the Reflection Until the End

We sat one morning—the day Tari entrusted me with another of her secrets—eyeing each other, neither saying a word as we ate as many of the cherry plums as the years we'd lived up until that point, and then some. Mom's rule. "Any more than your age and you'll find yourself sick," she used to say, her polite way of not saying *diarrhea*, a word she despised. We of course both knew what she was talking about because we'd been there, and *she'd* been there, although neither of us had ever seen our mother eat her age in cherry plums. And of course we ate more than our summed ages, because of the napkin Tari kept under the table. Mom probably knew, but it was a fun thing for kids our age to do, a part of growing up.

Tari was ten, then, and I had recently turned eight, which meant I got an extra one this year. We'd both leaned forward, counting as I tossed in another of my pits. Twenty, and then eighteen again as Tari moved the two extras into her napkin before Mom could count them herself and pretend to be upset. "I won't tell if you won't tell, Cubby," her expression told me.

She'd call me that most times instead of Chicago—the city from which I was named—because that's where Dad was from and he'd always try to watch a Cubs game whenever one was on, which wasn't often because they typically "sucked," as Mom would say, since she was a San Francisco Giants fan. My sister and I had these nicknames for each other, because neither of us much liked our given names. Tari was short for Ontario, the street in The Windy City on which Dad used to work before he moved to California. Sometimes she'd call me Chicago, but only if she were mad; the name sometimes sounding like a swear.

Michael Bailey

Another pit disappeared under the table. How many Tari had tucked away was a mystery. How many *Mom* had had was a mystery as well, since she was thirty-eight and was entitled to thirty-eight. By the time the strainer was half empty and Mom said, "Okay, that's probably enough," Tari had discretely wadded the napkin into her pocket. We'd had our fill by this point. I knew *I* had. Then Mom smiled and said, "Well maybe a few more each," taking one from the bowl herself and tossing another to each of us. And we *had* to eat them, despite what our stomachs told us. These things were candy. And what child ever denied just *one* more cherry plum?

I never saw Mom throw any of her pits into the bowl; I half-expected her cheeks to be full of them, tucking them away, like a chipmunk collecting acorns for winter.

"Want to pick more after the two of you eat some *real* breakfast?" she'd asked, meaning something with protein, probably eggs again, or yogurt. We'd picked a strainer's worth of cherry plums the previous night, but now those were half-gone from the three of us annihilating them one-by-one. Dad would have helped in the cause, but he worked a lot of weekends around this time and was gone before any of us had woken up.

"I'll need about twice what you picked yesterday to make jam. How about each of you fill a gallon-size Ziploc: one of you pick yellow, the other red."

Kay, we'd said in unison, and the next thing we knew, we were running through the yard out back with empty plastic bags billowing behind us.

There were cherry plum trees scattered around the property; you just had to find them. The two biggest

I Will Be the Reflection Until the End

trees with the always-bigger cherries were on the outskirts of the driveway in the front yard, up by the well, but those were about done because they were always in what Mom called "direct light," and most of the other trees—although their fruits smaller—were by the creek out back, because water ran most the year; those fruits had turned from green to a varied spectrum of yellows and reds, and were prime for picking, their branches sagging from both sweet and sour marble-sized balls that helped define our childhood springtime.

When we had first moved to the property, the trees were nonexistent to us, hiding amongst the bay trees and birch and California oaks; not until our first early spring there had they made their presence known, the trees exploding seemingly overnight with either white or pink popcorn-like flower bursts.

I remember one time picking what resembled a cherry from one of the gingko biloba trees—this was late summer, so I should have known—and sinking my teeth into the hard flesh of what I can only describe tasted the way Dad's socks sometimes smelled. Dad harvested them each year—the gingko fruits, not the socks—and always intended to do something with them. He'd collect them after they'd fall to the ground, and would let nature shrivel them up until they looked like orangey-brown prunes, and then would peel away the rotting flesh to reveal the seeds beneath. They smelled *awful*. He could never find the time to roast them, as intended, although he always told us how the seeds would split apart like pistachios to the good part—the part you'd panfry in oil and spices. They were supposed to be good for you, for your memory or something, but we never had the chance to try them while living there. Dad *did* manage to make tea from dried gingko leaves and lemon mint collected from the property, and that was delicious, and we always had a generous supply of bay leaves to put in spaghetti sauces he and Mom made from scratch, but besides what we'd pick from our garden, Tari and I loved collecting fruit that grew naturally around the yard: blackberries, figs—only Mom liked figs—and cherry plums.

In total, there were probably a dozen or so cherry plum trees throughout the property, all wild, native, and that fascinated me. We'd always had a vegetable garden growing up, from as far back as I can remember, but we had done everything by hand, sometimes starting the plants from seedling, sometimes from seed, pulling weeds, trimming them back, endless watering. A lot of hard work went into keeping those plants from simply shriveling up and dying, as they would've without any help. Yet these cherry plum trees yielded some of the most delicious fruits we'd harvested, and it took absolutely *zero* effort on our part, besides collecting them. Every year we looked forward to cherry plum season. The trees were planted there from birds dropping seeds or whatnot, according to Mom, and then, by design, the trees would drop their spoiled fruits to the ground each year to create new life, new trees, their roots pulling water from the ground from rain and the always-running creek. Unlike our ever-dependent garden, the trees took care of themselves.

"You ever feel sad," Tari said that day, stopping halfway to the cherry plum trees, "taking them?" She'd reached into her pocket to pull out the crumpled

I Will Be the Reflection Until the End

napkin. She dumped the used pits into her other hand, twenty or more.

"What do you mean?"

"Taking the plums. You ever feel sad taking them?"

"Do you?"

"Sometimes. I know they're just plants, and don't have feelings, but sometimes I wonder if they do; have feelings, I mean."

Where we stood, when she revealed this to me, there was a dip, a small valley of sorts, which ran from one side of the property to the other. Grass grew greenest there for two reasons: because heavy rainfall in the winter sometimes created a shallow pathway for the water to run so it wouldn't collect against the house, and because this was where the leach line ran from the house. The ground was softest there compared to all other parts of the yard.

"I don't feel bad," I told her. "If we don't eat them, the birds will, or the bugs. We later learned there were deer and fox and bobcat and skunk and bear, all of which ate the fruits, or so their scat told us. We even had a river otter one year when the February rain—it always seemed to rain the hardest then—was nonstop for a solid week and rose the creek a good three feet, so that it roared to life the following month. "You shouldn't feel bad," I told her.

They're here for *us*, I'd always thought.

"I know. Sometimes my mind just works that way, though." She tossed a few pits at her feet and buried them into the ground with her toe, threw some toward me, and threw some as far as she could along the "greenline," as we'd sometimes called it—all one word. "Someday maybe these can be trees," she said.

Michael Bailey

My stomach had ached then, and at first I thought it was from eating twice my age in cherry plums, but later, much later, I realized the pit in my stomach was in fact a feeling of empathy for the pits in the bowl, the ones I'd thrown in the trash.

And then Tari reached into her other pocket and pulled out another handful.

"How many did you *eat*?" I'd asked.

Instead of answering, she smiled, knowingly, held out her hand to me, and dumped them into the cup I'd reflexively made with my hands beneath hers. One at a time, I threw the pits along the *greenline*—the amount adding to our combined age, and then some.

She'd taken them out of the trash; she must have.

From that point onward, pits from the cherry plums I'd eat were never thrown out. We'd collect them each day and made a routine of tossing them along the *greenline*.

The next spring, we walked the property to look for seedlings, and after not finding any, we changed from *tossing* to *planting*, burying them a few inches into the ground with trowels. Over the years there must have been thousands upon thousands planted there, but none had ever sprouted from our efforts. The trees along the creek multiplied plenty, though, on their own.

There were perhaps thirty cherry plum trees spread along the creek banks by the time we'd moved closer to the high school where Tari was accepted. I was in seventh grade at the time and didn't want to change middle schools, but I wasn't old enough yet for my opinion to matter. Our new place was closer to Dad's work, closer to the fields where we'd play soccer

I Will Be the Reflection Until the End

and baseball during the sports seasons, closer to just about everything; one of the benefits, I guess, of moving into the city. Sometimes we'd go back to pick blackberries or cherry plums from what we'd always refer to as "the property," but it was never the same as when we'd lived there.

Every year was the same: more trees along the creek, popping up like matchsticks, and the same treeless *greenline* between the creek and the house. I went there again after Tari had gone to college, me and Mom and Dad, the three of us trying to pick final memories from the place.

We rarely saw Tari outside of holidays and birthdays when she'd come home for a few days. Her junior college was an hour away, but she might as well have been out of state, or out of country, for that matter. She'd blossomed into a woman over the years, but unlike the intensely-colored cherry plum trees each spring, she'd not exploded into something wonderful in her early adulthood, but something not so wonderful. She'd somehow imploded, collapsing into herself like a dying star . . . into a black soul, perhaps. She wasn't gothic, by any means, but *dark*, and something about her wasn't right.

Mom and Dad always said Ontario was an old spirit, linked to the world in ways none of us would ever understand. She reacted differently to certain things, felt more deeply than the rest of us. *Connected.* She'd learned to avoid the news because all it ever was, was bad. "Media is a reflection of our wrongdoings in this world," she'd said once, maybe when she was thirteen. Wars crushed her. Poverty and famine kept her rail-thin. When the buildings in New York fell, she

Michael Bailey

fell with them, both metaphorically and literally; we'd watched the plane fly into that second building when both our ages were single digits and she had cried like I'd never seen a person cry before, and she crumbled to the ground in tandem with the buildings. I was too young to understand, but her crying led me to crying.

Years later I'd reflect on the little things about her: the way she'd look after plucking a flower, as if she'd killed something beautiful; the careful way she'd walk, always looking down to make sure she avoided stepping on anything alive; the way she'd thank the plants when we'd take from them; the way she'd always eat *every*thing on her plate, nothing ever going to waste. "We're taking their unborn children," she'd say sometimes, about the plants, "so we better make the best of everything they're giving us." I watched her turn from carnivore to herbivore, from vegetarian to various stages of vegan. Tari was a minimalist, even in childhood. She never had a lot of toys, never asked for—nor desired—anything on birthdays or around Christmastime, and her room was always spotless. Whereas I was the exact opposite.

She said something that morning we'd first thrown cherry plum pits together, something that's stuck with me my entire life, a phrase that defined my sister in both its simplicity *and* its complexity: "I will be the reflection until the end."

I'm as old now as my parents were then, and I'm still trying to figure out my reflection in this world. She'd figured it out at ten. I'm not even sure Tari knew I'd heard her say those words, because she'd whispered them as cherry plum pits rained over us.

We saw less and less of her while I finished out

I Will Be the Reflection Until the End

high school in the country and she moved on to college in the city, while Mom and Dad's attempts at us seeing her grew more and more prevalent, almost to the point of desperation. *Come home we miss you*, was a common phrase to hear Mom say over the phone—as if those five words were instead five syllables to a much longer single word—although she only ever talked to Tari's voicemail. "Why does she even have a cell phone if she never uses it," Dad would say sometimes, as a statement, not a question.

It took Tari those first few years of community college to figure out what she wanted to pursue, and she eventually chose art, which wasn't too surprising. Growing up, she was always into coloring and sculpturing and for the most part creating somethings out of nothings. What *was* surprising was that she came home at all. We hadn't seen her for most of the year, although as soon as she'd walked through the door, it was as if she'd never left.

"You should be happy, Dad," she'd said before anything else, "I'm moving closer to Chicago," meaning The Windy City, not me. "Back to your roots. Oh, hey, Cubby!" she added, giving me a fragile hug. She felt thinner, if that were possible, and her eyes bore dark circles. She had looked so tired, then. "Man, you've gotten tall," she'd said, and it was true; I'd grown a good four or five inches those final years in high school.

I had once looked up to Tari, but now she would forever look up to me, a sentiment that is, yes, now both literal *and* metaphorical.

"What's in Chicago?" I think it was Dad who'd said that, which was funny, since he of all people should've known.

Michael Bailey

"The Art Institute of Chicago," Tari said, and by the enthusiasm behind her voice, I instantly knew it would be good for her. She needed a drastic change in her life, a change country life couldn't offer.

Mom had thought the opposite: "How are you going to survive in the city? Oh, and hi, by the way. Haven't seen you in a while. Your birthday present's in the living room."

"You know I'm not big on presents," Tari said, and that was the last of the softer-spoken words that afternoon.

Her birthday was September 13th and this return home of hers was for Thanksgiving. She'd left her present, still wrapped, on the living room coffee table after the fight that had quickly ensued. There were a lot of words spoken between her and Mom, and a few supportive words by Dad, but apparently none of these words were important enough to remember now. Tari calmly gathered the rest of her things from the house, walked out the front door, and after some goodbyes, she simply drove off—not in the typical angry storm-off one would expect after such a fight, by any means, but that was Tari; she was never one to raise her voice, not even in argument.

I followed her to her car—a beat-up hatchback of some kind—and hugged her again, longer this time, and a part of me thought she'd break. I didn't know when I'd see her next: a month, a year, ever again? Her car was already packed, every inch of it. She was apparently on her way to Illinois and this was simply one of her pit stops before going. She started the long drive that same afternoon. Three days later she texted to let me know she got there safely. She'd texted Mom,

I Will Be the Reflection Until the End

too, I later found out. Ontario was on her way to become a city girl.

She'd send me some of her photography every once in a while—her primary area of study—and it was good. The images, sent primarily through text, focused on life taking back what it could from the city, or so I soon put together. The first was a picture of an old Presbyterian church, a gothic-looking castle of sorts with thick green Ivy covering nearly the entire stone building. Others included zoomed-in shots of the tops of smaller skyscrapers that she'd apparently taken from taller skyscrapers, roofs adorned with greenery: trees, shrubbery, flower gardens, vegetable gardens. Some of the images were both sad and beautiful: a close-up shot of a pane of glass with the white imprint from a bird that had flown into it; a crack in some section of sidewalk from which a single purple wildflower started to bloom.

Along with her art, she'd randomly send long facts about the city through texts, some in the form of questions: *Did you know there are over 6000 homeless in Chicago? But it's going down, so I guess that's good. 50 people were shot in the city this weekend, but not me, yearly average of 3 per day. Did you know nearly every sidewalk down the Magnificent Mile is adorned in the fall with beautiful displays of cabbages and kales? There are signs in each box warning the homeless that the plants are sprayed to look nice, so they're not edible. Wonder what they'll plant in spring. Probably enough to not feed 6000 homeless. Maybe the decreasing homeless population is from death. The Buckingham Fountain holds 1.5M gallons of undrinkable water. There are*

Michael Bailey

so many skyscrapers in Chicago and so tall they create wind. You'd think we'd harvest that energy. There are metal-looking statues of people in a small section of Millennial Park and no one seems to go there. I sat next to a metal man sitting on one of the park benches, for nearly an hour. They look so lonely, these fake people. Did you know the Chicago River used to run the opposite direction? Used to run into Lake Michigan. Civil engineering reversed the flow. Pollution is so bad you can't eat the fish. Did you know the John Hancock building is made from 5M pounds of aluminum? Remember recycling Dad's beer cans when we were little. Imagine recycling that building. LOL. The buildings in Chicago are like teeth, cutting the sky, devouring the heavens. The city's taken the stars and will never give them back. When are you coming to visit? Come see the metal people.

Eventually I did. For high school graduation Mom and Dad got me a roundtrip ticket to Chicago, and enough cash to pay for a taxi to and from the airport, and for food during my stay. They didn't tell Tari I was going, wanted it to be a surprise. They put me up in a slanted-looking hotel called Sofitel Chicago Water Tower, because it was in "the safe part of the city"—the heart—which apparently surrounds a stretch of Michigan Avenue known as the Magnificent Mile. I spent some of the money to go to the top of the John Hancock building, where on the 94th floor you can walk around the perimeter of the building for a 360° view of the city, and part of Lake Michigan, which looks like an ocean. According to the information displays, when I was looking south, I was looking at not only Illinois, but Indiana, Michigan, and Wisconsin. This was where

I Will Be the Reflection Until the End

Tari had taken that first rooftop photo she'd sent me. She was curious, like me, and had leaned against the glass, in the exact spot I had first leaned against the glass, and nearly straight down was the green rooftop of the smaller skyscraper she'd shot, adorned with grass and trees and potted flowers—a defiance of nature, perhaps from someone who'd moved in from the country, like Tari.

I spent that first day walking Michigan Avenue, both during the day and then again at night, and it was like two different worlds. Tari was right, you can't see stars from the city—not like back at home where you could sometimes see the white stripe of the Milky Way—but the buildings create their own starlight at night and it's somewhat magical. It's a beautiful city. "Chicago's your name," Dad had said, "you may as well see what it's all about." Beautiful, sure, but I could never live there.

Show me the metal people, I texted Tari the next day.

Cubby! she'd texted back, and then a time and an address to something called The Bean. She knew I was in the city because I had sent her my own from-above photo of the rooftop. I later found out The Bean was exactly that—a giant chrome jellybean-looking thing, which was close to the Art Institute. I'd seen it in a movie once, but didn't know it was in Chicago. It was fall, so the maple trees in Millennial Park were in the middle of turning from yellow to red, like the cherry plums we used to harvest. Against the reflection of The Bean was an obfuscated, bendy reflection of the city at my back, with the trees in the foreground impossibly bending inward. You could walk underneath the thing as well, and see an endless circular reflection of yourself staring up. I couldn't help but wonder if this is how Tari saw the world. She found me there, staring up into the swirl . . . the two of us staring up.

"I can't believe you're here," she'd said.

"I can't believe it, either."

We walked around the park for hours, admiring what she probably saw on a daily basis on her way to and from school: fountains hiding within canopies of trees, odd over-sized statues, a pair of green-copper lions, the creepy and mostly empty park of lonely metal people. It was this part of the park that intrigued me most. The statues were life-size, some alone, some staring up into the sky, others just standing there, one holding the hand of a child, and of course I recognized the one sitting on the bench from the photo she'd sent me. I took a selfie with this one, both our heads tilted back, eyes closed.

She showed me the Art Institute and her studio, and then we walked to an exhibition of her work in one of the old churches close to my hotel, the one with the ivy overtaking the stonework. One of her displays included a dozen or so pictures—"Reflections of the City"—taken from placid pools of rainwater collected on the streets. Another of her pieces was a blown-up digitally-enhanced shot I recognized as part of the Magnificent Mile, taken from the center of the street late at night; the city was captured in vibrant color with the tops of the skyscrapers glowing purples and reds and greens, the shops and surrounding buildings exploding in neon and seemingly violent light, headlights and taillights streaking white and crimson along either side, with the plant life in each modified

I Will Be the Reflection Until the End

to dull black-and-white, which I guess was the entire point.

Car horns must have been blasting around her when she'd taken the shot. And another was a simple picture of the Chicago River taken at dusk; the river runs through the middle of the city, yet she had somehow captured some sort of wide-angle view of only the water, the city reflected off of its wavy surface like the broad strokes in a Monet painting. She had an eye for capturing light, and I knew she'd spent hours on some, waiting for that perfect moment when the sun peeked between buildings, or fell behind false horizons of the cityscape.

"There's a lot hiding in this city," she'd told me while I was there, but at first I thought she meant *beauty* and *life*. She'd seemed as happy as I'd ever seen her, but there was still that darkness behind her eyes, as if she could see things in this world the rest of us couldn't, like some sort of tear had opened, exposing another layer onto our existence, and she could see everything ugly that had leaked through.

She eventually moved back home, to country-life, but not by choice.

Her last text to me read: *I can no longer reflect. Is this the end?*

I hadn't put it together then, but those words scared me, and later scarred me. I had tried texting, calling—this was about a year after I'd visited her—but she'd never replied. I'd thought of calling the Art Institute of Chicago to track her down, but only ever *thought* of doing it; instead, I'd figured those thoughts on reflection and the end were more of Tari's typical anti-normality. It wasn't until a few days later when

Michael Bailey

Mom took the call from Mercy Medical that we'd discovered she'd cut herself, both arms, lengthwise, from palms to elbows. The student she lived with had come home to find her naked in the bathtub, no note or anything, and thought she was dead; campus police determined she wasn't and called the ambulance.

She'd tried killing herself, what she'd meant by *the end*.

What if I had stayed with her in Chicago? What if I had continued to call? These questions haunt my mind, even today. There were countless things I could have done, that anyone could have done, but we didn't.

And this is how we got her back, not by action, but by reaction.

Tari moved home that same week, but as Mom and Dad both knew—and I knew as well—home was a place other than this. Home was not Ontario or Chicago; home was Tari and Cubby and where we grew up, what we always called "the property."

Somehow the following spring we moved back there, all of us. Mom and Dad didn't mortgage the place—couldn't afford it, really—but the owner had owned multiple properties by this point and let us rent the house for as long as we'd need, which turned out to be seven years. It seemed the same as we had left it, the California oaks stretching their limbs to the ground, the smell of bay trees down the driveway, the gentle flow of the creek, which we all knew must have roared the month prior, and the cherry plum trees and their spectacular blossoming.

Tari would never be the same after what she'd done to herself, what she knew she had done to all of us, but something in her expression changed as we were

I Will Be the Reflection Until the End

pulling into the driveway. She'd seen something we hadn't. Tari was first out of the car and yanked on my arm so that I'd go with her, and she seemed so fragile to me, her arms like matchsticks ready to ignite, as skinny as they'd been when she was ten and I was eight, only bandaged now, and I couldn't help but stare at them. She held my hand, smiling as she led me to the backyard, nearly at a run under the dusk sun, to the *greenline*, to the hundreds of cherry plum trees that ran along its course.

The Honeymoon's Over
E.E. KING

My brother Chris and his new bride Margaret were as happy, good looking and nice a couple as you could hope to see. Chris was tall and slenderly muscled. He had long, laughing hazel eyes and a wicked lopsided grin. His mop of dark hair was usually unruly, in a cute way. Maggie was a red head, creamy skin and wide blue eyes that seemed to reflect the whole sky right back at you.

They weren't altogether practical, but you couldn't really hold them responsible. Fortune had smiled on them and they smiled back. Who cared if they lacked money or jobs?

Chris was a musician and Margaret a writer. They eked together a living, he, by playing bar-mitzvahs and weddings, she, by writing articles for Good Housekeeping and Better Homes and Gardens THAN yours.

Together they were irresistible, a combo of charm, brains, enthusiasm and cheerfulness, that would be right at home in a Disney movie. Oh, they had their

The Honeymoon's Over

moments, like anyone else, I guess. Chris could be a little lazy and Maggie liked to buy things she couldn't afford, but who could blame them? We all knew they'd work it out.

They had a cute little apartment off Hill Street. It was a quiet neighborhood. Chris could bike to his part time bar job at Frankie's. Maggie stayed up nights writing.

They adopted a puppy, a spaniel/retriever mix, with curly golden hair, long ears and huge, liquid, soft brown eyes. He was irresistible! They named him Mr. Baggins . . . Mr. B for short.

Now they had their troubles . . . sometimes they'd fight a bit, all kids will, and I always thought of Chris and Maggie as kids . . . I mean he was my baby brother.

Well, one day Chris comes home from Frankie's a bit late . . . He always came home late, it was a bar after all, but this time it was later than usual, and he was a tad lit. To make a long fight short, they quarreled. Maggie didn't like him drinking and biking home and Chris, bless his heart was not at his most reasonable when drunk. Still, it was nothing, really. I know it. One of those little squabbles you don't even remember in the course of a year. Chris woke up late and hung over. Maggie and Mr. Baggins were gone. Now I don't mean they'd left or anything, they were just out for a walk. Chris felt grumpy and ashamed. But, he was still angry with Maggie for not leaving a note. By 4:00pm, he was worried. She'd never been gone this long.

He was leaving the house, when a neighbor came up, dragging behind him a whimpering, dirty Mr. Baggins. She'd found the dog running, hysterically crying through the streets. Somehow, she'd manage to catch hold of his leash and bring Mr. B home.

E. E. King

It didn't take long to find out what had happened. They found her near the dog park, broken and crumpled in the street. It had been a hit and run, not much to go on.

It's still hard to talk about that time. Seems like we just froze while things moved around us. There was the body . . . God! To call Maggie "the body," but that's what she was now. We had her cremated and kept her ashes. Chris wanted to take them to Italy with him. He and Maggie had always dreamed of going there.

Chris and Mr. Baggins moved in with me. I knew he shouldn't be alone, and frankly, I was glad to have him by me. I'd hear him weeping in the night, with Mr. Baggins making little sounds of comfort. I think that dog comforted him more than I could . . . and he comforted Mr. B, too.

Maybe it sounds strange, but that dog was nearly as heartbroken as Chris was. For a week, I couldn't get him to eat. But slowly, slowly they both began to mend.

The weather was lovely. That warm caress in the air that spring brings. Every morning like clockwork, Mr. Baggins and Chris would jog off to the dog park.

That summer Chris went off to Italy. I got emails daily and two calls. It's a good thing I wasn't the jealous type, 'cause I swear he missed Mr. Baggins more than me.

I took Mr. B on his walks, watched him race around the park like a wild thing. When we'd get home he'd fall asleep at my feet. When I came home from work, it was as though he hadn't seen me for a year. He'd jump up and down, wagging his tail and looking at me with eyes full of love. Yet, I swear, since Maggie's death they always held a deep touch of sorrow. I began

The Honeymoon's Over

looping Mr. B's leash around my wrist. I said it was because Chris—and I—would have been heartbroken to lose him. I pretended it was to keep him safe. But, really, it comforted me to feel the leather wrapping me like a bracelet. It was like having a friend hold your hand, feeling Mr. B so close.

Chris only stayed away two weeks. Just couldn't stand imagining Maggie there with him. After a month or so, he got his own apartment. I sure did miss him and Mr. Baggins, but I was glad, too. I wanted him to get his life back. I had loved Maggie, probably as much as two sisters can love each other . . . but I didn't want Chris to live in the past.

I still saw him and Mr. Baggins often. Every Saturday we'd meet at the dog park to watch Mr. B have a morning frolic, then spend the day together. Go to a movie. Go for a walk. Or sometimes just have a big long meal and usually end up drunk.

It was the sweet time of sorrow. The time when the wound has healed enough, so that you can remember, talk, and even laugh about the past.

Then one Saturday, God I'll never forget it, I headed over to the park as usual. About a block away, I heard a noise I'll never forget. If I could sleep, I'm sure it'd be in my dreams. It was a kind of heavy thud, and then a wail. A horrible cry, a howl that was more than animal, but surely not human.

I ran, but I wasn't even aware I was moving. I don't know what I thought I'd see, but as soon as I got close, I knew. Knew that somewhere inside I had known what I'd see.

There was Chris, my beautiful, beautiful, sweet baby brother, my only family, my best friend. And there he lay, in the street. His bloody body arched at an unnatural angle. Mr. B was by his side. I swear to you, that animal was weeping as hard as I was.

We went through the motions. Got a police report. People at the park had heard the squeal of brakes, but no one had seen anything.

I don't know how I got through the next few weeks. If Mr. Baggins hadn't been there, I swear I would have just dried up and died. His big, sad puppy eyes reflected the pain and hurt I felt.

They say time heals all wounds, and I can't say I think that's true. Some wounds never heal, but life goes on, no matter how you feel.

One day, Mr. B, who was watching me bathe, stood up to sniff the water and tumbled in. I laughed. For the first time in forever, I laughed. Mr. Baggins looked embarrassed, but I swear he chuckled a bit, too. There are few things as faithful and accepting as a dog.

The next day we went out for our morning walk. The sky was blue and clear, birds were singing. I looped Mr. B.'s leash around my wrist. I know it was silly, but somehow I felt closer to him that way. It connected us—like those braided friendship bracelets children swap. I felt better than I had since Chris died.

Suddenly Mr. Baggins took off, running as hard and fast as he could. I pulled on his leash.

"No, Mr. Baggins, sit." But Mr. B did not sit or stop or even slow.

"Mr. B! Heel!" I screamed. But, he raced, full on, heading at a dead run toward the street that edged the park in a blind corner. Although I couldn't see round the bend, under the twitter of bird song I could hear the growl of a motor.

The Honeymoon's Over

You know how they say, that right before the end your whole life flashes before your eyes? Well that wasn't true for me—though time did slow down. Instead, I saw Maggie—Maggie, beautiful alive and laughing . . . then Maggie, just a crumbled corpse. I saw Chris, my beautiful brother, from burbling baby through carefree boy, handsome man and loving husband, my Chris.

I dropped the leash, but it was looped round my wrist, not a bracelet, but a noose. It held me fast, cutting into my flesh, dragging me into the street.

The last thing I saw was Mr. B turning to look at me, with detached curiosity, out of those big, big, brown eyes before leaping onto the sidewalk—just clearing the wheels of the oncoming car.

There was blackness, the grind of breaks, a car door slam and a high shrill scream.

Mr. B gave a little yelp, like he was crying.

The last sound I heard was an unknown voice saying, "Oh you poor, poor sweet dog, don't worry I'll take care of you."

Song In A Sundress
DARREN SPEEGLE

"**Nana?** **I said**, gazing out over the vegetable garden from my seat by the kitchen window as I enjoyed my grandmother's famous biscuits and gravy for the first time in two years.

"Hmm?" she said without looking back from the counter where she was preparing her equally famous apple pie.

"Can you tell me that story again? The one you used to tell me when I was boy? About what happened to Viv?"

She turned, glazed spoon in hand, looking at me oddly as she said, "Viv? Do you mean your great-uncle Elbert's girl?" She shifted uncomfortably. "Your father's cousin? Why would you be asking about her now, Dennis? You're a grown man in college."

I smiled. "Humor me, will you, Nana? That story has haunted me for years."

"You sound like you did back then, liking the thought of ghosts. Like I told you then, if she was going to wander anywhere, it definitely wouldn't be our backyard."

Song in a Sundress

"Yeah, I remember. But that's just it. You never explained that to me. When I asked, you said that part was not for a boy's ears. Can you kindly give me the full version now?"

"Why?" Spoon still hanging there, almost dripping now.

"Set a young un's mind to rest."

She'd called me that when my parents would bring me up to visit for a week in the summers, as I was doing now, clearing my head for my last semester at State.

She put her spoon aside, came over and sat down across the kitchen table from me. "Dennis, you haven't changed a bit, have you? You were always such a persistent boy. Making me talk about dead people like that."

"That's how it was?" I chuckled. "I thought you were giving me a lesson on how to keep my rambunctious ass out of trouble."

"Hmph. Like there was any hope of that." She shook her head. "All right. I'll give you the short of it while you finish up your biscuits, but then I have to get back to my pie. But there's really no story to it. Your mind might remember it like that, but there was no drama. She was here, then she was gone."

"Still."

She sighed. Always that prerequisite, as I remembered it, in her storytelling. "Well, she would come in the summers like you did. Stay a couple weeks then go back home, leaving me and grandpa lonely as hell until the next un came. We never had to wait long before we'd have another of the young folk around. But she was special, Viv. Pretty as a button, smart like you wouldn't believe, helpful as all get-out, a little adventurous like you but a real darling and delight. We really loved her. *I* really loved her.

"It was one of those dark rainy summer days. She was washing berries for me, as I recall, doing her normal sweet-hearted job of it, I'm sure. But on that particular day, unlike most times, she didn't bring me her work when she was finished. Instead, she got that itch of hers. A girl of twelve, mind. Blossoming into a young woman already. But she still had that urge to go to the brook to look for turtles. She loved turtles, was fascinated by them I guess, being from the city."

She paused, reflecting.

"I went out to check on her at some point, found she'd left the berries in the bowl by the back door and was nowhere in sight. I glanced across the garden, which looked about the same as it does right now through that window beside you. But she wasn't looking for rabbits in there among the lettuces and carrots, so she must have gone to the brook. I didn't like her going there. It can be dangerous, especially after the heavy rains we'd been having. But I knew that's where she'd gone.

"So I called for your grandpa, then realized he was up at Nance's for some fresh milk—or might have been a bottle of whiskey, knowing him. So I went myself, feeling awfully anxious as I did. Feeling a kind of premonition, you know? Normally, I wouldn't take those extra instincts of mine much into account. Always had 'em, just not always to any kind of use. But this time was different. I knew the girl was in trouble." She shivered. "Felt cold in my bones. The water in that little brook was high. Even if I hadn't noticed the day

Song in a Sundress

before, I would have known. And after a hard night's rain, it had to be worse today. I dreaded what I was going to find, which as you know was her summer dress, caught on the jagged end of a log downstream. Now that you're older, I can tell you that was the single most horrible thing I've ever seen in my life, after that drunken accident with your grandpa. No, worse than that. Because I'd always believed something of that sort was going to happen to your grandpa one day, but not Viv. She was immortal to me. A song that nothing could take from the world."

I waited for more. When it didn't come, I said, "And?"

"And what, Dennis? The child was dead, drowned."

"But there's more. More you wouldn't tell me when I was a boy."

As she looked at me, I thought I saw a tear threaten to form in her eye—which I couldn't remember ever having seen before. I was about to tell her forget it, I hadn't meant to upset her, when she said, "They didn't find her body around here. The current took her down to where the brook meets the river. She was found three miles downstream from there, at Cranston Fork, on the bank. The animals had got to her. Sherriff Lolly told us it was pretty bad. It would have been hard identifying her, he said, if they hadn't known she was missing. Nearly killed Elbert, the shape she was in. He started drinking not long after, went out shooting whatever beasts he could find—wild dogs, bobcats, pigs, vultures, coons, anything he could get his eyes on. Loading that shotgun again and again, by the way Fran told it, after anything that might have been involved, including . . . oh never mind. Suffice it to say he cracked."

Darren Speegle

"Wait a minute, Nana," I said. "Cranston Fork . . . do you mean the supposed prowling grounds of that local legend thing, the Cranston Animal?"

She looked away, the tears evident now. "Oh, shush with that superstitious nonsense."

I shushed, but I could see it in her face. If she'd allow for Viv's spirit wandering somewhere—wasn't that the implication in "that's not where she would be wandering"?—she'd allow for other strange possibilities. And what, exactly, was the "oh, never mind" Elbert might also have been loading shells for?

***

I had to go. I wasn't about to tell Nana my intentions, but I had to drive to Cranston Fork, find an access into the wilds that surrounded the place, and just be there, in the company of this lost relative, a relative who'd died before I was born but I felt I nonetheless knew somehow. Perhaps because of Nana's convincing skills at painting verbal pictures. Nana had never meant to do any harm. It wasn't she who brought up the subject in the first place.

I drove down the county road, lights piercing the early dusk, thinking *you are one foolish, silly, imaginatively adventurous boy again, aren't you, Dennis? What can you gain from this? What indeed do you expect to find? How old were you during your summer visits to Nana's place? Nine the first time, twelve or thirteen the last, right? About Viv's age when she'd met with her tragedy?*

Maybe that was it. You were of a similar age, and related, even suffered with her. So much so that you imagined you saw the ghost of her moving in a glowing halo out there around the garden, roaming

Song in a Sundress

aimlessly, with no way back and no way out. And maybe in fact that's why you decided to further explore the thing nearly a decade later by night rather than the more advisable light of day. Maybe a lot of things. Maybe you've been so troubled ever since, that this visit to Nana's after the years is less to do with the intervention in your early adolescence of your parents' divorce, a change that left you firmly in the care of your mother, wherever she decided to go, which was far from these parts and her drunken ex-husband and his poisonous family.
Maybe.

But I did have sense enough to be prepared tonight. I'd rummaged through the jumbled contents of Nana's back rooms while she was out weeding, perhaps not specifically looking for the old single-load Ithaca shotgun the old man had left her and which she'd allowed me to use *only* for scaring away or killing the crows that got into her corn, but which I'd uncovered in any case. That along with a case of shells. God only knew how old they were, the shells as well as a pair of flares I'd found in an old chest in the shed out back. The likelihood of either packed tube working after the years was pretty damned slim, but I took them. I took a flashlight, too, which worked when I tried it, after knocking its butt against my palm a couple of times. But again, the extra batteries I found were practically frothing with dried-up flaky acid. I felt better believing myself equipped, though.

I shivered at the thought of the mission before me.

But who wouldn't be, chasing phantoms from childhood into a forest that as far as I knew still frightened locals. Where had I even heard those stories? Might have been Nana but was more likely the farm boys that lived around my grandmother's house, with whom I'd often played at the brook, though their names and faces were far less distinct in my mind than Viv's.

Her *face*? Really? I thought as I neared the turn I wanted to take. I was focused on accessing the place now. I remembered a lot about the area, but in this case had seen the sign coming in—*Down Fork Falls picnic area*. What kind of name was that? Down Fork Falls? There was no Down Fork that I knew of. Did they mean downriver, below the Fork, and if so, why point out the fact?

The turn led me down a dark forest road, pavement turning to gravel along the way, for about a half mile before it split. A sign pointed left; I took the markerless dirt affair to the right, which clearly led in an upriver direction. The narrow road grew rugged, increasingly so as I struggled to negotiate its deep wounds, my brights penetrating basically nothing in this hole through the trees. The profuse foliage of overreaching limbs seemed to appear spontaneously in front of me, bugs swirling all around in the stunted headlight beams. I was entering another world. I'd have liked it as a seventeen-year-old with my junior high school date in the seat beside me, so much promise in front of me. But there was no one sharing the cab with me in my college kid's used pickup; there would be no getting any tonight that didn't involve fluids of a different color.

I felt this, and very strongly, but only when I reached a dead end, came to a stop at a sign that outright blared, in the headlights, KEEP OUT, did I begin to fully

Song in a Sundress

appreciate the foreboding that had been crawling in me. I'd known the sensation before, but never in this sort of context, these strange circumstances, never to this degree. Who said keep out? Who was doing the commanding? Why not just NO TRESPASSING, which by definition indicated private ownership. All the uncultivated land surrounding the river belonged to the Black Forest Wilderness Area as far as I knew. Government didn't put up crude wooden signs with red spray-painted messages.

I let the engine idle for a moment before I made my final decision. When I did, the thing was done, I was going in there, all the way. Flashlight in hand, loaded shotgun slung on a crumbling leather strap over my shoulder, flares, batteries, extra ammo in my backpack—a pack I used for books, no less—I proceeded by foot along the trail. Pray I'd found the access I was looking for and wouldn't have to do this all over again at a different location. Pray, indeed, I got past *any* trail's lurking dangers in these black fucking woods, regardless of where I was geographically, or of the question of access to whatever it was I was looking for. Alone at night, even with a cloudless sky's half moon overhead, the business stank of the carcass you could potentially leave behind.

Really, Dennis? Wild dogs? Boars? Bobcats? Nana had missed, I thought, the black bears that could come down from the hills in search of food. But weren't they just as harmless, just as shy, just as frightened of humans as these other examples of the local wildlife? Wild dogs being the possible one exception. But what wild dogs had Nana been talking about? What had she really been saying?

Darren Speegle

She hadn't been saying anything about animals attacking a living somebody, Dennis, that's for sure. You're forgetting yourself. This is about a mutilated corpse, not a walking intruder in these depths. Don't want to be here, brother, then don't. But don't make up fantasies.

Which it had been easy to do before, was much easier now as I pushed farther and farther into this forest realm as if on some schizoid mission the sane part of me knew was folly.

***

I saw her first.

Over a cacophony of crickets and whizzing clouds of flying insects, I'd heard, then smelled the river. It was flowing smoothly through the dark. This the main body of water, not the Cranston tributary. But the latter would come into the picture soon enough as I followed the river trail to the left, downstream. In minutes I was in an open place that had apparently once, long ago, served as a rec area, judging by the half-dissolved piles of wooden picnic tables and benches. It was a ruins for all intents and purposes, and more than that, a message that rang louder than the sign I'd encountered at the end of the road. *Get the fuck out of here*, it said. *This is your last warning.*

I switched off my flashlight. It had no place here as I let my eyes adjust to this cavern of silhouettes and passageways beneath a moon whose light managed to get through the whole concoction with little resistance.

As I stood there listening to the promise of dire consequences, I heard a change in the rhythm of the river. I let my senses gingerly guide me to the bank and in the vacancy immediately saw the other dark stream

Song in a Sundress

coming in at an almost right angle from the opposite side. The other tine of the Fork. The Cranston Fork. This was the place they'd actually given a designation? You could have casually lobbed a rock across the one stream and waded across the other. It seemed awfully uninspired to me.

But what did get me—it took a moment but then set in—was the tangle of river debris, limbs and whatnot in a backwash formed by the odd geometry of the confluence, aided by a boulder, just in the crook. Something told me that was the place. The place Viv had been deposited in the flood. Dead, alive, maybe in the balance. The terrifying balance.

I closed my eyes, imagining Nana's description of her to go along with mine. Slowly, out of nothingness, I heard what might have been the song she'd been to Nana. It was so soft, so tempting, it almost resisted its own reality for me . . .

Then I saw her, on the bank beneath a tree whose gnarled claws seemed to hold the bank together. She was looking to her left along the tributary's path through the trees, which I could not see. She didn't illume, not like I remembered. There was no halo around her. She was rather a shadow, though ever slightly tinted, catching the moonlight in the merest whisper of her summer dress.

I wanted to call to her, to let her know a loved one was here, not just any loved one but me, Dennis, who'd watched her in her nightly ballet. But her eyes were only for the depths of that tunnel along which she looked. I wanted to know it, but then I did not. What could it be to her? Her journey had begun in a brook, where turtles lived, not in any sort of place like this.

Darren Speegle

If it were only the beginning of a journey that mattered.

I moved along the bank, careful of my step but always intent on her, my sole reason for being here. It wasn't particularly difficult going, not physically, but on other planes it was hell, the foreknowledge having assumed magnificent proportions. I literally ached imagining what she was seeing. Her widened features told it all.

Oh Viv, I wanted to call as I reached the point where I was in position to look, which I violently resisted, staying concentrated on her.

Slowly, sundress whispering, she turned her head and looked at me. I imagined I heard words in the night—why did you come—but it might have been the insects.

I couldn't stand it. I had to know—

Do then, her eyes seemed to say. *It's going to happen again!*

As gradually as she had turned to me, I turned to look up the Cranston River, and there it was, monstrously large and creeping through the water on multiple sets of legs, two long clawed appendages stretching across the space in her direction. Its eyes . . . though black, they shone against the night, seeming to see everything.

I would not die trembling like a coward, I thought. This was Viv. I unslung my gramp's Ithaca, aimed and pulled the trigger.

The force threw me backward. I hadn't remembered how powerful a shotgun was.

Recovering immediately, I snatched off my pack, fumbled with the shells then found something else. Something better to the fingers' appetite. I glanced up

Song in a Sundress

at the last, the decision in hand, to find the Cranston Animal bearing down on me like a spider on its prey. I watched the flame of my lighter magically go up and ignite, despite my crazy seizure hands. Caught the knowing and fascinated eye of my song in a whispery sundress. Nana there, too, a tear in her eye, as I waited until the beast was almost upon me, claws high, mouth open and expanding, foul-smelling throat exposed. And then . . .

***

Coming alert again in a strange place, a man in a brown costume with a badge looking down on me.

"Welcome back, son."

"Where's Nana? Viv . . . "

"I'm sorry, Dennis, but your grandmother died eight years ago. Vivienne's been gone a lot longer than that. I'm Sheriff Lolly. Maybe your grandma told you about me?"

"What the fuck is going on?"

"Only what's been accomplished, Dennis. Some of us, we know what you did. It won't be printed in any papers, but we know. Rest yourself, okay? Just wanted to check in."

"But why am I here? Is this a hospital? I don't feel anything."

"It's because you were poisoned. You got lucky. Just a graze of the claw before you killed it. You mention Viv. She would be proud of you, can rest because of you. Your grandma too."

***

Then I woke. In a forest, dawn coming. Nothing remained. Just rivers meeting, the echo of a song in a sundress twinkling out there a moment, then gone.

Weighing In
CYNTHIA WARD

After her boyfriend's outburst, Brandi Miller jumped in her Jaguar and drove. It wasn't fair. She *tried* to control her weight! She worked out with Arykka, her personal trainer, every day. She ate protein for every meal. But she still weighed eighty-nine pounds.

Brandi brushed at her tears, careful not to rub her eyes and make them red. Couldn't Harold see her weight problem upset her as much as it did him? Couldn't he be a little more supportive? Especially since all those three-martini lunches with actors and agents had porked him up past 350 pounds.

When Brandi finally looked around, her stomach tightened, like it did whenever her agent was about to tell her if she'd gotten the part (so far, she hadn't). There wasn't a house or mall in sight. Where was she? It was getting dark, even though the dashboard clock said 2:30. She flipped on her headlights with a shaking hand.

She was in a narrow canyon with high, wooded sides. She'd been driving for hours. Was she still in L.A, or way out in the San Gabriel Mountains?

Weighing In

Her headlights caught an ESTATE SALE sign. In the darkness, the sign and open gate were as inviting as the lights of Citywalk. Brandi turned her XJ6 onto a private drive, overhung with dead ivy that made her shiver, like that bony old producer who stuck his tongue in her ear when she was auditioning for that reality-TV show about starlets trying to land their first role.

The blacktop turned to rutted dirt as it twisted up and up. When Brandi finally got a view, she swallowed. She was driving along the edge of a cliff, and there wasn't even a guardrail.

Finally, she spotted a Spanish-style villa through the eucalyptus. It was huge, but totally neglected for years, judging by the dead weeds jutting from all the cracks in the buckled patio tiles. The ESTATE SALE sign looked new. Was this some reality-show trick that would make her look like an idiot to millions of TV viewers?

Brandi jumped out of her XJ6 and almost *ran* into the villa.

Dust lay thick on heavy furniture and out-of-style clothing that wasn't even retro. Brandi couldn't afford anything (Harold could, but he didn't like her spending too much of his money). She wondered how the sellers could ask so much for such hideous old crap, until she overheard two other browsers discussing the recently deceased owner, a famous actor.

"He became a recluse when he got old and ugly," one beautiful young man said to the other. "But he had a gorgeous young starlet living with him."

"I heard they looked like concentration camp

victims when the bodies were found," said the other. "At least *he* had the excuse of old age."

"Anorexia's always been a problem for vain little starlets."

And for beautiful young men, Brandi thought, enviously.

She slipped into a master bath bigger than a Cineplex. Nothing on sale here, she thought, until she noticed a tag on the old-fashioned dial scale in the corner. The price was almost reasonable, five bucks.

She stepped aboard. The dial spun and settled. She blinked. Eighty-four? She weighed five pounds less than she thought! Okay, so the thing wasn't, like, totally accurate. But why argue with a reading like that? And it wasn't every day you got a chance to buy the bathroom scale that told a former "Hottest Hunk in Hollywood" how much he weighed.

In the morning, her new purchase indicated Brandi weighed four pounds less than yesterday's reading. She laughed. Worrying about Harold's outburst had totally burned some calories!

***

Sophie Greenbaum followed the ESTATE SALE signs up Laurel Canyon Boulevard to a hideous contemporary mansion, one of those cantilevered glass-and-concrete slabs that jutted from every hillside like enormous toxic crystals from outer space. But this one had a view to die for, and Sophie enjoyed the smoggy vista of the San Gabriels as she winced over the ridiculous prices and eavesdropped on the nosy neighbors checking out the house.

"Can you believe it?" said one model-slender shiksa to another. "They both wasted away to nothing!"

Weighing In

Sophie shook her head. Who knew a girl that skinny would think anyone could lose too much weight?

Sophie found herself in a chrome and black marble bathroom bigger than her one-bedroom apartment. Nothing for sale here except an old-fashioned bathroom scale. Priced right, though: five dollars. Sophie's ex-roommate had stolen her scale when she threw the meshuggenah Vanna-wannabe out.

Sophie reached for the scale. What the hell. She could stand to lose a few pounds.

Reliving the Past
MICHAEL HAYNES

Eric wandered off the trail in the state park, hoping the tree he remembered was still there. Thirty years since he'd last been in these woods. The old tree could've died and fallen over in a stiff breeze or been struck by lightning and incinerated. If it was gone, then any hope he had was lost.

Lots of other things had changed in those thirty years. Friends and family moved on, died. Fashions, technology, politics—all changed. And it was one thing to see these changes on television or hear the newer inmates at Black River Prison talking about what the world of the 21st century was like. It was quite another to live in it every day.

The sun was low to the horizon when Eric spotted the tree; it had four distinctive gnarls near its base, shaped so they looked like a smiling face. The tree had been their favorite hangout spot when they were young teenagers. It was only when they got older, during their senior year, that another place took precedence.

Eric unfolded the pocket shovel he carried and dug

Reliving the Past

straight down from the central gnarl, the "nose." Metal clinked on metal and soon he was pulling out the old Six Million Dollar Man lunch box. He remembered frantically pulling it from a shelf in his parents' garage the last time he ever set foot on their property. Getting back in his car and driving away as fast as he dared.

The lunch box was dirty and rusty but with a little muscle he pried the latch open. Inside everything looked remarkably like the day he had put it in there, a half-assed time capsule, full of memories of the worst day of his life. John's class ring. Alicia's sunglasses. His own pocket knife. And the key.

The pocket knife came up over and over at the trial. It clearly couldn't have been the murder weapon which the prosecution failed to ever present but since it had been something everyone knew Eric carried and he claimed to have lost it on the very morning of "the day in question" . . . Well. It did, as the jury was told repeatedly, seem a very odd coincidence. Did it not?

The first time John had led Eric and Alicia to the Rankin house he told them, "You've got to leave a token of your good will."

"Like an offering?" Alicia asked.

"Nah, you take it back when you leave. But it shows that you're not just some bozo stumbling around. That you're . . . " He hesitated a moment, then snapped his fingers. "Respectful. Like kissing the godfather's ring."

They each left the same thing behind every time they went inside. Every time, of course, but the last. Class ring, sunglasses, pocket knife. John first, then Alicia, and Eric, tagging behind. Always tagging behind.

"You were jealous of John, weren't you?"

Michael Haynes

Eric had lied when the prosecutor asked that question, lied even though he had sworn to tell the truth, so help him God. Back when he held on to fragments of belief that such a thing still mattered.

He had been jealous of John. Had always been jealous of him. But John didn't deserve the fate he'd suffered. No one did.

***

Eric waited until the morning after unearthing his time capsule to drive to the Rankin house. He'd considered that it, too, could have been a victim of time, caught in a forest fire or rotted and fallen in on itself. But unlike the tree, Eric didn't believe the Rankin house could die so easily.

He climbed the porch steps, key in hand. A cool wind ruffled his hair. In a pocket of his jacket he carried each of their special "tokens" for the house. But just as the three teenagers had done on their final visit, he didn't set them on the porch.

The door looked the same as before and the lock was dull metal. Of course, it could have been changed twenty-nine years ago and look dull on this day.

Eric realized he was stalling and before another breath passed slid the key home—a perfect fit—and turned the doorknob.

Rank air coursed over him as the door swung open. The smell almost gagged Eric but he collected himself, crossed the threshold, and shut the door behind him.

"I'm back," he said to the empty foyer.

Eric walked through the room and into the main hallway. The floorboards creaked with every step. In the hall there were no windows and only pools of light which spilled in from other rooms illuminated his

Reliving the Past

path. But he didn't need any light; he could have walked through the house blindfolded and not stubbed a toe.

Hanging out at the smiling tree wasn't cool enough for the three seniors. "Kid stuff," they'd declared it. So dozens of lazy afternoons and evenings had been spent here in the Rankin house just hanging out, talking about whether The Bomb would fall, listening to cassettes on a portable tape deck, and thinking about anything other than school. Though classes and studies were off-limits, the three did talk about their futures. Alicia wanted to be a veterinarian. John still thought he had a future as a football player. Eric didn't know what he wanted to do. At the time, it had made him feel unambitious. Now it just meant that he didn't hold on to a specific dream unfulfilled. There hadn't been a future for any of them.

Eric's skin prickled as he went deeper into the house, a feeling he remembered all too well.

"Something's wrong," he had told John and Alicia on that last visit. "I've got a bad feeling about this."

John had laughed. "Thanks, Han."

"No, I mean it. Don't you guys feel it?"

They both shook their heads but Eric was sure he saw Alicia hesitate long enough to see John's reaction before giving her own. He'd relived that moment over and over during the weeks after his arrest and even into the first years of his imprisonment. Had she been lying? What if he'd pushed her harder?

Now, as then, the uncomfortable feeling intensified when Eric entered the house's library. The shelves were bare of books, bare too of birds' nests or any other signs of encroaching life. All they bore was dust.

Michael Haynes

A sound, like an echoing voice, made him flinch.

"Two for flinching!" He remembered the glee on John's face every time he delivered that particular punishment, wondered how many of those punches he'd taken from John over the years.

Eric slowly turned, scanning the library, but there was no one, and nothing, there. He pulled out his knife and held it in the palm of his hand, displaying it to the room before returning it to his pocket. Next he brought out Alicia's sunglasses and slid them onto the top of his head, the way she always used to do.

More sounds. Scratching and something that sounded almost like a scream. This time Eric didn't flinch.

Last of the tokens was John's class ring, the one Alicia had always said she didn't want to wear. "The first ring you give me, Jonathan Wilcox, had better have a big ass diamond on it!" Eric had no such reservations. He slid the ring onto his finger.

The room fell into greater darkness and the air, already oppressive, closed in more tightly around Eric. He had seen the empty bookshelves with ease when he walked into the library, but now they were completely obscured.

"Eric."

Of course it would be her, talking to him with a want in her voice that she'd never used with him when they were kids. He hesitated, knowing what he would see when he turned to look, knowing it would be gruesome. But this is what he had come for.

He licked his lips, took in a shallow breath of the awful air, and turned to face Alicia, less than a dozen feet away from him. She stood there and he could see

Reliving the Past

her, blue jeans and green top and bright red blood, though there was no light.

"Eric," she said again. "You've changed."

Alicia smiled. He had changed but she hadn't. Eric's gaze narrowed to that smile, to her undamaged face, and it was as if the past thirty years had all been a nightmare from which she had just awoken him. She tilted her head just slightly and Eric felt a surge of something more than just adrenaline, more than just fear.

She moved closer to Eric and hungers denied for decades coursed through him. He took a step and then another, lips parting to form her name or prepare for a kiss.

They were almost close enough to touch. Eric reached out a hand and his eyes caught sight of the red gem on his ring. John's ring. And seeing red there he saw it also on Alicia—no, on the thing which wore Alicia's face—and he remembered that those thirty years were not a bad dream and neither was this.

He spun away from the Alicia-thing just as its own hungry mouth opened. As he turned away, it unleashed a terrible scream, louder by far than the one that Alicia had let loose when she first saw an apparition on that day.

John and Eric both had asked her what was wrong in the silence that followed that scream.

"Don't you see her?" she'd asked the pair of boys—young men, now, each of them having turned eighteen the month before.

"See who?" John had asked. Eric didn't ask because by then he had seen her, too. A little girl, maybe five years old, naked and covered in blood, a giant hole in her chest where her heart should be. And walking, slowly, step by step toward Alicia.

And then there was chaos. All three of them were shouting and Alicia crumpled to the floor, her sunglasses clattering beside her. The girl was there on top of Alicia, a feral hunger in her eyes.

John tried to help but his hands passed through the vision of the young child. Even though he'd been a lineman on the football team, he couldn't lift Alicia from where she had fallen.

Eric had only been able to watch, sickened, until a thought struck him. He pulled out his knife and snatched up the fallen sunglasses.

"John! Give me your ring!"

His friend didn't answer and Eric stepped closer, yelling in John's ear.

"What the—"

"Just do it! Now!"

John's eyes fell on the knife and sunglasses and he must have understood. He tugged his ring off and placed it in Eric's hand.

"Run!" John said.

Eric had done just that, reaching the porch in seconds. He'd placed the three tokens down as they always had. Class ring. Sunglasses. Pocket knife. He knew he needed to go back inside but fear clutched at him. He was free. It was his car they had driven in, his car they had always driven in so Alicia and John could neck in the back seat on the way to and from wherever they went. He joked about being their chauffeur. Joked because it was easier than admitting how much it hurt.

The air that day had been split by another scream, this one deeper. John's. And despite his fear Eric had

Reliving the Past

plunged back into the house. But when he got to the library, he saw he was too late. Human bodies don't function with their heart removed, like the little girl's, or their throat torn out like Alicia's or their spine snapped, their body contorted into a V-shape like John's was. He ran out of the house as quickly as he had re-entered.

Eric's defense had used the state of John's and Alicia's bodies as their prime evidence. They had experts who said that Eric simply wasn't tall enough or strong enough to have the leverage to break John's body that way. But the prosecutors talked darkly of what people could do when hopped up on PCP and reminded the jury that it wouldn't have taken much strength at all to do what had been done to Alicia.

Alicia.

The gouge in her neck, thirty years later, reached more than halfway across her throat but this vision or spirit or whatever it was showed no signs of discomfort. The only emotion he saw in its eyes as it closed in on him again was hunger. It was the same as what he'd seen in the eyes of the girl-thing.

And this wasn't Alicia. It was an Alicia-thing.

Behind her he saw a John-thing, wobbling forward with a broken back. And the heartless girl. And farther back there were others which he couldn't see yet and hoped never to see.

A compulsion washed over him, a desire to fall to the floor, to submit to the ministrations of the Alicia-thing. He could hear her voice now, in his mind, telling him all of the things she could do for him, all the things he had fantasized about on those hot high school nights as he lay in bed.

Michael Haynes

Eric pulled the container of lighter fluid from his other pocket and splashed its contents on the ground between him and the thing that looked like Alicia. He pulled the matchbook out but she kept coming and her suggestions grew cruder, things that Eric hadn't ever imagined doing or having done to himself.

His legs weakened and then he was kneeling on the floor, looking up into her face, looming over him from just feet away. Unable to turn away from her, he fought for control and blindly tore out a match. He struck it once, twice, and only the sound of ignition and the smell of the flame let him know that he'd succeeded.

Alicia joined him on the floor, her face close to his, her words drowning his thoughts. She reached for him, slowly, slowly, and he was just about to fall into her embrace when behind her blonde hair he saw John looming over them.

His mind broke free at the sight of his rival, his friend, and he took the lit match which had almost burned down to his fingers and used it to light the rest of the book of matches. He threw the matchbook onto the soaked floor and rolled away as he did so. The floor erupted with a *fwoomp* and a gout of flame.

And then, like he had thirty years before, Eric ran. He ran to the porch and this time he waited there, hoping that the house that had been too evil to die on its own wasn't too evil to be killed.

There were screams from inside and Eric stood his ground. Smoke billowed out the front door, finally forcing him to retreat to his car.

He stayed there until the flames burst through the roof of the house and then, satisfied, put his car into gear and drove away.

Reliving the Past

"You're a free man," the guard had said when Eric had been let out through the gate. "Now don't fuck it up."

The guard had been wrong. Eric hadn't been free knowing that he had spent thirty years paying for a crime he didn't commit, knowing that the true killer still lived and could kill again.

But now, as Eric pulled onto the interstate, ready to find a new city to live in and a new life, he felt like he was starting to be free.

The Long Haul
LEIGH M. LANE

Peter brushed himself off with a gloved hand. These older buildings were a cinch to get into, the rooftop access hatches always leading to some kind of ceiling entry, be it through the air ducts or past a layer or two of insulation. This one had challenged their skills, the layout and security cages calling for blueprints and a careful cut to recently-installed motion sensors, but the pay-out had been worth the effort: several bottles each of Diazepam and Oxy's, and a box of morphine patches. They never took longer than five minutes, in and out, once they broke in, and the practice had kept Peter out of prison all but once. The hard time had afforded him some new connections, and despite promising Wendy long ago his criminal days were over, he couldn't help himself.

They hadn't needed the money, although now they could use every pound they could get their hands on. The thrill of getting away clear and free had always held just as much allure, and not only from eluding the bobbies. He hated to admit it, but getting one past

The Long Haul

Wendy only compounded the excitement, as guilty as she had made him feel when she'd caught him coming home with traces of insulation in his hair or sheetrock dust on his jumper. He'd learned years ago to wear an extra layer, covering his head and every other possible centimetre with materials that were easy to remove, then leaving the evidence locked in his work toolbox. Either the approach worked ridiculously well or Wendy had simply given up on the issue.

Not that it would matter much anymore soon.

Peter and Andrews hopped in the idling car, and Cory hit the gas before the doors could close. He turned down a side street, lights off, and parked long enough for Peter to take the stash to his van, where the men parted ways—an added measure. If anyone saw anything in front of the drug store, they'd be reporting a blue sedan, not a white van. Wendy never looked in the drug safe anymore, so it didn't matter that he'd need to sit on the payload for a few days while Andrews arranged the drop.

Peter opened the mudroom door to a wave of warm air, sweat trickling beneath his shirt despite the shed layers. He went to the kitchen first, locked away the loot, then steeled himself before moving to the living room to smells of Vicks and decay.

Wendy lay on the sofa propped up against two pillows, her sunken eyes fixed on an advert. She shifted her attention to him as he made his way to the sofa's edge.

"Hey," he said.
"Hey."
"Did you eat?"
She shrugged. "A little." She sat up, limbs shaking

with the effort, and adjusted the cap that covered her bald head. "I need to use the bathroom."

He helped her up. "When did the nurse leave?"

"When you were *supposed* to be getting home from work."

"Yeah . . . sorry about that. Got a little side-tracked and lost track of the time."

They reached the lavatory, which had been transformed into an ugly mass of support bars and hospital equipment. He helped her sit. "Where were you?" she asked.

"I told you, I went to the pub with Cory and Andrews."

"Sure that's the story you wanna stick with?"

He sat on the edge of the bathtub, the room feeling a little warmer. He unbuttoned his collar. "What do you mean?"

Wendy blinked hard, paused for a moment, then shook her head. "Nothing." She finished, letting Peter help her back up in lieu of wasting any strength on the assistance bars.

She leaned heavily on him, even more than yesterday. Would he be carrying her tomorrow?

"Bed or sofa?" he asked.

She sighed. "Sofa."

They returned to the living room, and he fluffed up her pillows as she returned to her spot in front of the television.

"Can I get you anything?" he asked.

She shook her head, covered her mouth with the back of her hand as she went a paler shade of grey and began to sniffle. Finally, "Who is she?"

"Who is who?"

The Long Haul

"Whoever it is you're stuffing, Pete." Her lips trembled when he didn't immediately respond. "I called the pub an hour ago. You weren't there."

"Did you ever consider the possibility that we went to a different pub tonight? Maybe because The Den was crazy busy—"

She fell into fits of tears, almost delirious. "Bullshit!" Her cries transformed into violent coughs, and soon she was retching into her hand.

Peter rushed to give her a tissue then turned away at the bloody mucus, fighting tears of his own.

"If you're going to cheat on me, could you at least have the decency to wait until I'm dead? Could you do just that much for me?"

He held his breath. If he tried to speak now, he'd lose it himself. He forced down the emotions, managing to say, "You're the love of my life. I'd never cheat on you."

"Then where were you?"

"I just had some pints with the guys, I promise." He moved to sit directly at her side, taking one of her hands in his. "My god, Wendy, how could you think I'd hurt you like that?"

She wiped her face dry with her free hand, a futile effort. "Because I'm disgusting." She held up a skeletal arm. "Look at me!"

His own tears finally came. He kissed her hand. "You're beautiful. You'll always be beautiful."

Her features hardened even more, a hint of anger, another wave of grief. She shook her head, turning back to the television. She scoffed, "Look, you too can lose two stone in one month!"

"Wendy—"

"Best. Weight. Loss. Regimen. Ever."

"Come on, don't be like this." He turned off the television.

Silence took the room. Peter searched for something to say, anything that might diffuse the moment, but his mind had gone blank.

Finally Wendy said, "A new nurse from hospice came by today. Nice lady. Left out two morphine ice lollies, just in case you stayed out late—which you did. Not that I had the energy to get the second."

"Do you want it now?"

She nodded.

He disappeared back into the kitchen long enough to fetch the medicated treat, unwrapped it for her, and licked his fingers. "I'm sorry. I'll come home directly after work for the rest of the week, okay? We'll do whatever you want to do."

She glared at him, sucking on the cherry ice. "Nothing left to do but die."

His gut wrenched with the thought, because he knew it was true, and his mind fell back into that terrible place . . . the one in which he laboured to fathom how he'd survive that first lonely night without her. The one where he priced plots and coffins and picked out her final dress and decided on Enya for the funeral track. The one where he learned what true emptiness felt like. He turned away, his words catching in his throat. "Jesus, Wendy . . . "

"I'm sorry, I didn't . . . " She took a shaky breath. "I'm not thinking clearly. My mind's a jumble today. I'm just so tired."

He nodded as though he understood.

"A bit confused, too. This new nurse, she wanted

The Long Haul

to know how I got such a rare cancer. Said there's only one way to get it."

"Oh?"

Wendy nodded with a grimace. "Asbestos."

"Asbestos? When were you ever exposed to asbestos?"

"That's the thing. I don't remember ever being exposed."

"Well, the nurse must've been mistaken."

"No..." She held up her mobile. "I looked it up. You see it mostly in construction workers, people who worked on old buildings before they changed all the insulation."

Insulation...

His heart sped up. "But you don't see asbestos anywhere nowadays."

"Could've been exposed forty years ago. Takes decades to develop." She let him take the phone for a closer look.

He skimmed over the page, confirming the information.

"All it takes is one fibre to trigger the cancer," said Wendy.

The words threatened to catch in his throat: "One fibre, you say?"

She nodded, coughed again, worked up another mass of phlegm. "I just don't know where I could've come in contact with the stuff. I don't think I've ever even been to a construction site."

"Hmm." He stopped to paraphrase a short passage out loud: "Could've come from anywhere, really. It was in buildings all over the place up until the '80s or so, albeit tucked tightly in the walls and ceilings. All the builders used it, didn't know how dangerous it was."

"Yeah, I saw that."

He scrolled lower, found another link at the bottom and followed it to a new page. He read silently, *Mesothelioma has also been found in family and friends of workers exposed to asbestos, the fibres hitchhiking on clothing and hair and transferred through close proximity* . . . . Mental images flooded in of the powdery insulation falling down over the crew like snow all those years ago, coming down with the bits of ceiling they'd busted through. Had this been the same lung cancer that had killed one of his former crewmates a few years ago? He'd never given it a name, nor had he ever mentioned a specific cause. He'd just said the cancer was exceptionally rare and impossible to treat.

A pang of nausea hit Peter, and the rest of the world fell away as he pulled her to him, into his arms, and fell into heavy sobs. "I'm so sorry . . . God, I'm so sorry."

A bony arm hugged him back. Loving. Needful. Empty. "Me, too," she cried. "I hate that you have to go through this. I wish my life had begun right when I met you . . . then maybe things could've been different."

"Yeah," he said, struggling to mask his horror. *But instead, that's where it ended.* Even now, she suffered because of him, and yet she forgave him at every turn. How could she still love him after everything he'd put her though these past thirty-eight-in-December years? How couldn't she see that he was her malignancy?

"It's just not fair, Pete."

He hugged her a little tighter. "No, it's not . . . not fair at all."

Dust Devils

MARK CASSELL

I **engaged the** handbrake, switched off the engine and leaned back against the head restraint. Spot on 7 p.m. I'd always been one of those guys who were somehow in tune with time, bang on the diary slot. One more pupil, then home.

Rain still pelted the windscreen and within moments the country lane vanished in a grey blur.

I yawned.

A tightness lingered in my lower back—I'd been slumping too much lately. I guessed that's what happens when you have to cram more driving lessons into the day. Fuel prices, car issues, household bills. The usual shit, all resulting in longer hours. I also craved a cigarette having cut back to a couple a day. A habit that didn't help with weekly expenditure, but I was trying; I'd been smoking since my teens. So, what was that, thirty years?

Usually about now, and equally as prompt, this last pupil of the day, a man in his 50s called Jim, would shimmy between the ragstone wall and his wife's Ford. An attentive learner and a good driver, he'd never before needed a car until they'd moved to the countryside.

I released my seat belt and opened the door. It swung towards the hedge that separated Jim's garden from the road. Cold rain speared me as I leapt out. I slammed the door behind me and rounded the bonnet. My shoe slid in mud and I laughed. That'd top my day right off should I end up on my arse covered in mud. The rain trickled down my collar and I shrank into my jacket as I got back in the car, this time in the passenger seat. I clawed fingers through my hair and wiped my face with a sleeve, and squinted through the windscreen. As always, I marvelled at his house: a six-bedroom detached surrounded by God-only-knew how much of a garden. It squatted between an impressive copse of looming oaks and a row of well-trimmed conifers.

Archaeology clearly paid well.

I'd still not seen the usual curtain twitch, but maybe I'd missed it. The rain obscured my vision after all.

As an archaeologist, he often shared fascinating stories. He was one of the good guys, and I enjoyed our lessons because I'd learn historical stuff while I taught him to drive. It was always a pleasure to see his name in the diary. Honestly, there were some names that would be impossible to look forward to.

It was now five-past the hour. Where was he? I really hoped he hadn't forgotten.

I checked my phone to see if I'd missed a text. Nope.

Another minute trickled past while I watched the rain on the windows. Finally, I got out of the car,

Dust Devils

pulled up my collar, and headed for the front door. I'd not noticed earlier but his wife's car wasn't there. A faint smell of oil lingered on the air. Jim once told me the village was so remote, even British Gas hadn't connected to it, and so most houses had an oil container in their garden. I couldn't see theirs, and I guessed it hid beyond a ship-lapped gate which was currently wedged open by a large red bag.

The 'Beware of the Dog' sign was a lie; they had a rabbit called Dennis.

Still no curtain movement.

I got to the front door that stood proud beneath a tiled portico supported by white pillars. It always reminded me of something Roman. Now sheltered from the rain, I went to press the doorbell.

Thump-thump.

Something overhead.

From inside the house.

My finger hovered in front of the button. What was it I'd heard? It sounded like something fell. I pressed the button, and it buzzed into the silence. My ears strained beyond the hammering rain and the water pouring down drainpipes. No doors opening. No footsteps, nor rattling keys. I looked up the side of the house. No curtains twitched.

I again rang the bell. Still no answer.

This was unlike him. Slipping a hand in my pocket, I found only a cigarette lighter—my phone was still in the car. I stepped back into the rain and again glanced up. Just beneath the guttering, where the telephone line connected to the house, scorch marks blackened the masonry. Whatever happened there looked serious.

I turned to head for the car. If he had forgotten—after all, their car wasn't on the driveway—I'd get home earlier.

From behind me, near the gate, I heard a shout. A man's voice. Jim?

Out of sight, a door crashed against a wall, followed by rapid footsteps. Then the gate swung wide and rattled against the brickwork. The red bag shifted sideways.

Jim.

Absurdly, he wore his PJs. They flapped around his small frame.

My voice snatched in my throat.

His bare feet tangled with the bag, and he flew towards me, arms outstretched. White and brown envelopes scattered, and several parcels tumbled across the paving. The bag gaped, the Royal Mail emblem facing upwards. He sprawled at my feet.

Lightning thoughts flashed through my mind. Why was he wearing PJs? What the hell was he doing with the postman's bag? Why was blood pouring from his nose even before he'd tripped over? Where was the postman?

"Jim . . . " I finally managed to say, and lifted him to his knees.

He moaned, a nasally whine through nostrils clogged with black blood. It streaked his face and caked what little hair he had. His palms were a mess of shredded skin and grit.

"Charlie," he shouted, "help me!"

"What is it?" My stomach churned. What the hell was going on?

"Can't find Ronda," he sputtered, eyes bulging. "She's gone."

"Her car's not here."

"She . . . "

"What's going on? Why are you—?"

"They took her." He clamped bloody fingers around my forearm, pinching. He coughed.

"Who?"

"They!" he shouted up at me. Spit peppered my cheek. "Them! I don't know. Whatever the fuck they were!"

"Jim—"

"They came through the fucking walls."

"What are you talking about?" I hefted him up, and his legs folded. "Come on!" I shifted position and grabbed him under the armpits. He was heavier than he looked.

"She was there one moment, then gone the next."

"We have to get you cleaned up."

"You'll think I'm crazy," he yelled, "if I tell you what I saw."

The state he was in, I already thought that.

"She . . . " he began, then lowered his voice. "She vanished."

Having been teaching him for several months, I'd never known him like this. Even in the most heated of situations, frustrated at his coordination while trying to balance clutch and accelerator, with the impatient bastard behind honking a horn, still he remained calm. But this . . . this was entirely different.

He glared at his feet as though willing them for support. Again, he coughed. "We have to find her."

"You're not making any sense." I hooked his arm up and wrapped it round my neck, and together we stumbled for the gate. "Tell me what happened when we're indoors."

Mark Cassell

He muttered something as I nudged the gate with my shoe, enough for us to stagger into the garden. The back door hung wide, and I lugged him towards it. Our feet scuffed and shuffled, and finally we lurched up two steps and over the threshold. The smell of coffee filled my lungs as we paused on the welcome mat. Two stools sat either side of a breakfast table, adjacent to the sideboard. An overturned box of Shreddies, crushed beneath one of the stools, lay with its contents spewed over the tiles.

Across the kitchen, his legs proving to be even more useless, I dropped him onto the stool. His head lolled as I released him.

In any other circumstances, I would've been embarrassed at my ragged breathing. I scanned the sideboard. My hands were slick with his blood. It also smeared my jacket. Kitchen roll, that'd do. I snatched it up and unravelled several sheets, tore them off and shoved them into his limp fingers.

"Tell me what's going on!" I really needed a cigarette.

His eyes darted around the room.

At the sink, I grabbed a dishcloth. It wasn't too dirty and I gave him that, too. I knew it wasn't the best thing to use but it was better than nothing. I ran a tap and used washing-up liquid to clean my hands. My rapid breath swallowed the fresh scent of lemon.

Jim's voice was soft. "I'm usually more careful."

I found a towel and dried my hands. I glanced around the kitchen. Was there a phone in here? Maybe I needed to call the police. "Who's taken Ronda?"

"I breathed in that stuff." He'd not bothered to clean himself. Fresh blood trickled from his fingers.

Dust Devils

"What stuff?" I approached him, not having any idea what to do let alone what he was talking about. I gently turned his hands over and he dropped the now-red tissues. For the first time, I wondered if the blood that covered him was actually his own.

"I'm so stupid," he whispered.

"Tell me."

"Ronda!" His eyes bulged. His face caked in several red shades, he truly looked like a madman.

"What happened?" I hoped to hell he hadn't killed her. I had no idea what I'd do if I found her body. "Where is she?"

"They took her!"

"Who?" I demanded, unable to help but raise my voice. He wasn't making any sense.

"They fucking took her!"

"We need to call the police." I released his hands and stepped back. Would I be safe here? Would he kill me, too?

"We can't."

"Why the fuck not?"

"Line's dead."

"What?" I thought of the black marks I'd seen beneath the guttering.

"Mobiles don't work out here, either." His lips twitched. "Reception's terrible . . . We need to find her."

"Where did she go? Who took her?" This was insane. "Help me out here, Jim. What can I do?"

His mouth parted, about to say something when a thump sounded from upstairs. Same as earlier.

We both jerked upright and stared at the ceiling.

And again, *thump-thump-thump*.

"They're coming through again."

"Who?"

He pushed himself against the wall and muttered something.

"What the hell are you talking about?" I stepped back farther. Cereal crunched beneath my shoes.

"Ronda!" he yelled.

I went to the doorway, craning my neck to listen. I steadied my breath—which was incredibly difficult. Was his wife upstairs?

Voices. Though I couldn't make out what was being said.

A glance at Jim and he just stared at the floor, brow furrowed.

I turned back and headed down the hallway, walking softly, not really wanting to find out what was going on. The woman may be in trouble, injured. Bloody hell she may be dying.

I ran.

"Don't!" Jim yelled after me. "Charlie, don't!"

Bounding up the staircase, my footfalls echoed as loud as my heartbeat. I reached the top step and paused on the landing. The curtains beside me allowed the thinnest strip of twilight to push along the hall. A gloom pressed down, revealing little of the patterned wallpaper. My fingers curled around the banister.

And I let go.

My hand came away sticky.

Blood? No. No, it wasn't. It was dark and gritty and felt like brick dust, but . . . but sweaty. Clumpy and moist. A faint earthy, damp smell wafted up as I rubbed the crap down my jacket.

Dust Devils

Four closed doors lined the hall, and past those an archway led into a darker area of the first floor.

"Ronda?"

No answer.

It took a moment for my feet to move. I had no idea what I was doing, nor had I any clue as to what I'd find. My shoes pressed into the soft carpet, one step after another. Suddenly I was not in a hurry. I nearly grabbed the banister again.

I didn't.

Perhaps I should've taken a knife or something from the kitchen. Defenceless and useless, I headed for the first door. What was I even doing? I should be in my car right now, calling the police. Or at least driving far enough to get reception should I need to.

At the door, I realised I held my breath. I breathed out and tried to relax.

No sounds came from behind the wooden panels. My grip slid on the door knob—more of that filth. The metal itself was cold. That's when I saw my breath cloud in front of me, subtle in the gloom. I'd not noticed the temperature drop, though I guessed I was sweating like hell.

I twisted the knob and gently nudged open the door.

Split cardboard boxes filled the room, surrounded by stacks of magazines and books. A threadbare sofa sat askew near the far wall, its cushions covered in electric appliances with cables snaking onto the carpet. Only a junk room. Although it surprised me given that Jim had always come across as a neat and tidy kind of guy.

Leaving the door open, I went along to the next

room. The door knob was like a ball of ice, and also coated in filth. Before I managed to open it, a sharp crack sounded. I jerked away with that sticky shit coming with me.

The wood splintered downward from top to bottom, jagged like a lightning strike.

"What the—?"

***

From beyond the archway a series of thumps shook the floorboards. I staggered and gripped the banister. It was soft like clay, as though that black goo had eaten into it.

I frantically wiped my hand on my jacket.

The floor shuddered again. A layer of dirt covered the carpet, although it was tricky to see in the poor light. There were even a few footprints—bare footprints that I assumed belonged to Jim.

"Charlie?" Jim's voice seemed close, perhaps at the bottom of the stairs.

The cracked door hung askew, threatening to fall. Splinters stuck from the panel like needles all the way down it, from top to bottom. The black stuff had sprouted from the grain like mould spores.

Was that it? Was that what Jim had inhaled?

The floor no longer shook. I looked up and down the hall; I'd somehow backed up to the archway, facing a door that had opened after the last rumble. Silence pressed in, as dark as the surrounding gloom.

I had to get out of there. Whatever the hell was going on, it wasn't natural.

Between the narrow slit of door and frame, something flitted in the shadows, like someone darting across the room. Ronda? I squinted, stepped forward

Dust Devils

and pushed the door. It swung inward and the darkness somehow shrank back. Shadows recoiled as though my perception shifted to allow horizontal strips of fading daylight to stream through the blinds above a large desk.

"Ronda?"

Regardless of those twilight rays, I reached round the door frame and slapped the wall until I found the light switch. I winced as brightness flooded the room.

My fingers came away gritty.

This was evidently Jim's study, somewhere to bring his work home with him. A swivel chair lay overturned amid discarded paperwork and beside a laptop with its screen cracked. Black sand coated everything, kicked about by the same footprints as in the hallway. The desk was littered with notebooks and scraps of paper. An overturned mug had spilt dregs to stain some notes brown.

No Ronda.

Adjacent to the desk, one wall was covered floor to ceiling in pinned diagrams, and also photos of what my lack of knowledge saw as hieroglyphs. There were several newspaper clippings, too. A small table was in the opposite corner of the room, upon which was a metal tray beneath two spotlights. Cradled in that was a chunk of stone, grey like slate. It looked heavy. More black sand heaped the tray, appearing as though the stone had half crumbled.

A hand gripped my shoulder.

I cried out, my stomach crashing into my heart, and I spun round.

"Bloody hell!" I shouted into Jim's blood-smeared face.

"Charlie—" he began and his gaze flew past my head, his eyes widening.

Beside the overturned chair, the black sand hovered a few inches above the papers and laptop. It kind of shivered in the air, agitated. Began to rotate, picking up more sand. Round and round, snatching up paper. Those black grains spun, forming a miniature tornado, pulling in the mug, the notebooks, more papers.

I backed up and bumped into Jim.

The laptop next, round and round. Growing, rising, that tiny cyclone stripped the wall of photos, building girth, swaying left and right. Drawing pins fired across the room, pinging and ricocheting, and—

The laptop hurtled towards us.

I ducked and it smashed into the hallway wall.

Thump-thump. Thump.

"They're coming!" Jim's voice blasted into my ear.

I squinted, the cold wind strengthening.

He tugged my jacket, then turned and ran. I stumbled after him. As I reached the top of the stairs I grabbed the banister.

The wood disintegrated as though it was rotten.

I yelled, my hand clutching nothing but dust.

And gravity shot me sideways. I slipped down several steps, agony tearing up my spine. I scrambled to my feet and took the rest two at a time. Jim had already disappeared. More thumps shook the house, and the wind shrieked amid smashes and what I guessed to be cracking doors and walls. Downstairs, I raced along the hall and out into the kitchen, into the garden, splashing through puddles that soaked my trousers and froze my skin. I sucked on the cold air. It

Dust Devils

had stopped raining. The skin on my back felt like it was on fire.

The security light had come on, reaching its white glare into the garden. Jim clutched his stomach, doubled over, coughing and spitting blood. Beyond him . . .

***

My throat tightened.

Something I'd not noticed earlier. Something . . . someone I'd not seen as I'd concentrated on carrying Jim indoors. But now . . . now I saw . . .

It wasn't Ronda. It was the postman.

His body split in two, separated by a deep trench as though the grass had been ploughed, cleaved wide from the direction of the house out towards the tree line at the rear of the garden. The man's trousers and shirt were fused in a glistening mess of fabric and bone and mangled flesh. Cauterised it seemed by whatever had scooped up the earth. His mouth was set in a scream, blond hair covering one eye that stared up at the nearby bird feeder. Blood peppered his cheek. Blistered skin, red and black like burnt pizza, mingled with the upturned soil and clumps of grass.

I fought hard not to vomit. This was insane.

A howl raged above. I could only guess it had been one of those black tornadoes that killed the postman.

Jim was still coughing.

The mortar below a window had crumbled, and what looked like burn marks streaked the brickwork down to the ground. The rabbit hutch lay in pieces among splintered wood and twists of wire mesh. Shards of a food bowl sat among scattered food pellets, and the water bottle had rolled away to rest against a cracked plant pot. More scorch marks traced the uneven patio slabs, following the path of the deepening trench and through the postman's mutilated body.

I could imagine seeing your first dead body was weird enough, but to see it spliced in two and cauterised was a horror I'd not wish on anyone. The half that was closest seemed to move, something black near the knee. There was no way the man was still alive, so what was it? Was it another freak tornado?

A pair of eyes caught the security light, twin orbs glowing. The rabbit, Dennis.

I laughed—my immediate response. Their pet had survived its hutch being demolished. Poor thing was hungry. It nibbled the grass near the dead postman's leg, nose twitching.

I laughed again, that's all I could do.

Jim's cough became a hacking violent choke and he spat again. It wasn't blood that was coming up, it was the black stuff. It coated his chin and dribbled down his neck. He'd said he breathed it in. It must've happened in his study when examining the stone fragment. I guessed it was the sand, or the dust he brushed from it. I had no idea. What I did know is that I had to get him to the hospital.

"Jim." I stepped towards him. "Let's go!"

The overhead roar intensified, screaming almost. More thumps, too—rapid and shaking the ground. Whatever that cyclone was doing inside the house, it wouldn't be long until the whole place collapsed.

I gripped Jim's shoulders and tried to straighten him up.

An upstairs window cracked and shattered. A white mist of glass rained down on us, and I shrank into my jacket. I shook my head to rid my hair of the tiny glass beads. They tinkled across the patio.

"Come on!" I yelled. He was unrecognisable, like he wore a mask. I couldn't tell apart blood from the black stuff.

Someone screamed, piercing and louder than the escalating wind in the house. It was a woman and came from the driveway.

Black spit bubbled at Jim's lips as he said, "Ronda." His eyes rolled as though drunk.

His wife stood at the gate, shopping bags in either hand. Although the security light reflected off her spectacles, I knew she stared at the postman's body. One bag slipped from her fingers and clattered on the paving. A tin of baked beans rolled away.

I looked at Jim. Ronda hadn't been taken by whoever he thought were—what did he say?—coming through the walls. The man had clearly lost his mind, not even realising she'd gone shopping.

***

The house had quietened. A silence descending, deeper and darker than the night that now pressed in. A glance up to the broken window revealed nothing, just a busted frame without glass. Not that I knew what to expect. The silence was unnerving. No thumps, no crashing. I hoped the whirlwind had stopped.

Ronda's lips moved but nothing came out.

I grabbed Jim and hoisted him up. His head wobbled.

"Let's go," I told him. I staggered, almost tripping over my own feet let alone his unresponsive ones. Glass crunched beneath every step as I headed towards his wife.

She still stared at the postman's remains.

I shuffled closer. "Ronda?"

Still she didn't move. Her chin quivered, forehead wrinkled above tiny eyes.

"We need to get Jim to a hospital," I said.

The other bag slipped from her fingers and rustled to the ground. I pushed past her and she staggered. For a moment I thought she'd fall over, and I really did not want to carry her as well.

Everything in the house remained quiet, nothing at the window. Whatever the freak occurrence was, perhaps it had ended. We were safe.

"Come on." I grunted and heaved Jim upright. "Almost there."

That black stuff bubbled on his lips as he mumbled.

Footsteps from behind told me at least Ronda followed.

"Jim!" she shouted and pulled his other arm around her neck. It helped. Her voice was shrill. "What happened?"

"I . . . " What could I say? "Don't know. Really have no idea."

Another glance up to a window and I saw nothing. I thought of the black stuff everywhere.

"The postman." Her cheeks were red. "Tell me."

"Something to do with that black stone," I told her. "The one in his study."

"The stone?"

"He said he inhaled the dust, the sand."

We bustled down the driveway. Even with Ronda's assistance, my strength felt sapped.

Ronda blurted, "I touched it!"

"What?" I asked as we took slower steps. Jim's legs dragged behind us.

Dust Devils

"He was still in bed ... when I heard voices in the study." Tears glistened on her puffy cheeks.

I stopped to adjust my grip on his slumping body. I wondered if he was unconscious.

"I went in," she added. "Those voices had stopped but I wanted to touch the stone. It was like a work of art. Those markings were so ... so intricate."

I thought of when I'd seen it, how it had been just a broken mess in a pile of black sand.

I said, "Let's talk about this more in the car."

"I didn't mean to break it. It just ... "

"What?"

"It just broke, crumbled to dust."

Together, we managed to get past her car and to the end of the driveway.

"Open the back door," I said as we propped Jim against the bodywork. The car remained unlocked, having assumed I wouldn't leave it unattended for long. How wrong I had been.

Still the house remained quiet.

Jim murmured something.

Ronda shrieked, "Jim!"

"More than ... " His eyelids flickered. "More than a gravestone."

Ronda glared at me. "What's he saying?"

"Imprisoned ... " he said.

"What?" I asked.

"Blood and breath." His eyes rolled back.

Ronda held his head, stroking his face. "Jimmy ... "

He muttered, "We're fucked."

***

We soon had him slumped on the back seat, unconscious. Blood and filth unavoidably streaked the upholstery. There was a towel in the boot—one part of my survival kit that included spare bulbs, a fuel can, emergency warning triangle and the like—but I knew it wouldn't have helped. With Ronda beside me and fumbling with her seat belt, I started the engine and sped off. Mud and stones kicked out behind us as the wheels lost traction, the back end fishtailing. I hadn't even checked my blind spots.

This wasn't the time to be the perfect driver.

The headlights speared into the evening.

"It's all my fault," Ronda said.

A red van was parked on the edge of the lane, and as I manoeuvred past I saw the Royal Mail emblem. I thought of the postman's mutilated body.

"My fault," Ronda repeated.

I didn't know what to say.

Thump-thump.

I scanned my mirrors but saw nothing.

Thump.

The steering wheel vibrated.

A darkness rushed at us, as though night had completely fallen. From the direction of the house, a vortex of shadow and debris tore through the garden, straight towards the car. *Thump.* It came up alongside us and I saw . . . I had no idea what I saw. It made no sense. It was like a ghost or phantom—a flickering image of something with too many limbs whirling around inside the black storm, raging and hitting the rounded sides, punching and kicking the inner wall. *Thump, thump-thump.* Round and round, huge pale fists. Shimmering, haunting, it thrashed against the confines of that whirlwind. It was like the thing wanted to get out, to be released. I guessed that was what it wanted, but somehow couldn't.

The wind howled as deafening as those continued thumps.

I floored the accelerator and hurtled down the lane, still in sight of their house. But . . .

Metal shrieked as the darkness battered the car. The steering went light, the tyres—the whole car—lifted off the tarmac. The engine roared and Ronda screamed. Gravity pressed me into my seat as the bonnet pointed towards the dark blue expanse of night. Moonlight pushed through streaks of cloud.

The car bucked, tilted sideways, forwards. And the ground rushed up. The house, the trees, the garden . . .

Our screams blocked the sound of the roaring wind and engine.

Airbags exploded. I gulped the acrid stink of fireworks as white fabric filled my vision. The windscreen shattered and branches scraped the bodywork. Metal wrenched and groaned.

Finally, we stopped and the car rocked once amid a series of creaks. The engine sputtered and died.

And silence, save for my heartbeat.

My hands were still curled around the steering wheel and it took such effort to peel away my fingers. The car angled towards the driver's side. The only exit was through Ronda's door where a bright light from somewhere flooded the wreck. Glass tinkled.

"You okay?" I asked her.

She pushed her spectacles back along the bridge of her nose and nodded.

We released our seat belts, and at the same time twisted round to look on the backseat, at Jim who, I knew, hadn't been wearing a seat belt. Not that it would've mattered.

The back of the car was missing.

From the central pillar behind our seats the metalwork and upholstery had been cut clean as though by an angle grinder, leaving only heaved earth and grass and a tangle of brambles. The metal still glowed in places. The smell of burnt fabric and hot metal, and the aroma of the triggered airbags lined my throat.

No Jim.

Only his bare foot. *Just* a severed foot cradled in thorny brambles and leaves. A piece of pyjama fabric had fused with the cauterised flesh. No blood, only blistered skin and black bone. Faint wisps of smoke curled from the blackened stump of ankle.

Ronda's scream tore through my brain.

She leaned into the door, kicked it, and yelled. It juddered open and she scrambled out. I clambered after her. The cold air washed away the burnt smell.

We'd landed in the middle of their back garden, not far from the remains of the postman and the other half of my car. The security light spotlighted everything. Evidently that whirlwind did not want us to get far. Which was absurd. My head pounded. Ronda was running towards Jim's body which lay like a discarded mannequin a short distance from the trench. Scanning the shadows where the light failed to reach, I couldn't see anything move. No whirlwinds, no *things* trying to escape. All was silent.

I lurched after her, every movement firing knives through my body, and passed the rear of my car. The

Dust Devils

bodywork was dented, the windows broken. Everything from the boot—my survival kit—littered the grass.

I took a large stride over the chasm that divided the garden. It was like a digger had scooped up the ground. Buckled pipes poked up through the churned earth, and I could just about see the panel of what I assumed was their oil tank. Oil trickled from a crack in the corner, filling the trench.

I knew I should be running in the opposite direction and not towards the gore that was both the postman and Jim. I wanted to escape this madness, get the hell out of there. By now I should've been sprinting to their neighbours' house. There I could get help, call for an ambulance, the police.

Ronda knelt beside her husband, shoulders quivering. As I slowed alongside the cleaved ground to stand behind her, I stared at the blackened stump where Jim's foot once was. With my back to the house I felt as though I'd miss the approach of another whirlwind, but a swift glance over a shoulder revealed nothing. Still silent.

Ronda cradled Jim's bloody arm.

I said, "We've gotta get out of here!"

She ignored me.

"Get up!" I yelled.

Her tears glinted on cheeks below glasses that were slightly fogged.

"Let's go!" I gripped her shoulder.

"But—"

"We can't do anything for him." I yanked her up and she released his arm. It flopped to the ground and splashed mud. As I steadied her, I saw her hand. Her fingers and palm were red and silvery as though she'd been burnt.

"It's . . . " she began and snatched her hand out of sight. "It's nothing."

I thought of Jim's last words and said, "Blood and breath."

"What does that mean?"

"When you touched it and Jim inhaled the dust, you started something."

She went to crouch again and I caught her. Perhaps my fingers dug into her shoulder too tightly and she winced. "Leave me!"

Another glance back at the house. I was just waiting for the cyclone to tear through the garden, to slice us both into pieces.

Jim's chest rose, and we both gasped.

It was though he breathed, but . . . but something wasn't quite right. I pulled Ronda away. A little lower than the triangle of exposed chest, the pyjamas rippled like something was trapped underneath. A crimson blotch spread, staining the fabric. Something snapped—a loud crack, sharp on the night air—and his chest cavity burst open in a red spray. Jagged white bone and shredded skin flapped as a corkscrew of solid darkness shot out. Its movements were familiar, twisting like a cyclone.

We staggered back, Ronda's hands clutching mine. Blood peppered her face. She screamed, I yelled, and we both scrambled away.

The tiny black hurricane danced across Jim's twitching body and tore into it. Chunks of flesh and strips of pyjama fabric churned with muscle and bone, grass and mud, spinning, swaying left and right.

Dust Devils

Having gained considerable girth, it stretched and headed for the nearest half of the postman's body.

I'd forgotten about the trench and went sprawling into it, Ronda colliding into me. Wet mud chilled my skin and the bitter taste of earth crunched in my mouth. I tasted oil.

Ronda slapped the mud, screaming. The wind howled as it stripped bare the postman's clothes and skin. Blood flew and bones broke. In a chaotic twist of crimson gore, that insane storm sucked up the other half of the man's body.

We were out of the trench, and started running alongside the conifers towards the gate. With my back to the whirlwind, I waited to be snatched up into its devastating embrace.

From the house, that too-familiar *thump-thump* made me stumble to a halt.

The masonry cracked, creeping down the wall from top to bottom. Dust drifted in a haze.

Again, *thump-thump*.

From inside to out and as tall as the house itself, a darkness passed through the wall, somehow without breaking it—a twist of shadow that formed into another ferocious cyclone, larger, faster. It left the wall intact, with only black filth dribbling from the crack. The cyclone spun towards us, devouring paving slabs and soil. Stone shards flew around us. As earlier, the thing with too many limbs raged inside those spiralling confines.

Only one way to run, Ronda and I darted away from the conifers, away from the smaller whirlwind of gore behind us.

Darkness rushed in, to obscure both moon and

security light, and in a wave of freezing wind that swept my legs from under me those two cyclones collided.

It was like a thunder crack.

Agony hammered my body as I slid and tumbled across the grass. A kaleidoscope of colours blinded me. I lay on my back, every inch of me screaming bruises. My breath came in sharp, short gasps as a shrieking wind battered me. I had no idea where Ronda was; all I saw was a seething darkness.

And the jittery image of that grotesque *thing*.

Although still behind the now-thinning veil of shadow, it no longer thrashed around. Its flesh was pale and sickly, almost luminous against the black winds. The surrounding vortex now looked more like a whirlpool of diesel and blood, chunks of gore circling, closing in towards the thing at its centre. That featureless entity sat there, squat and obese. I couldn't even tell where its arms and legs were. It shimmered, crackling as though I watched a dodgy VHS copy of an 80s movie. The image faded in and out of focus, patiently awaiting the wash of blood, of flesh and bone. As the hurricane winds dwindled, the closer the churning red mess got to its doughy torso.

Slowly, I pushed myself up, kneeling. My head throbbed.

Clumps of meat and strands of tendons began to slap the thing's pale flesh, and jagged splinters of bone stabbed it. What looked like tiny threads of darkness seemed to stitch the thing's flesh with human skin and muscle. More gristle and bone and sinew—was that the postman's hair?—covered its mass, weaved to create a gory patchwork, bulking out the entity's already-obese body.

Dust Devils

The surrounding darkness shrank in a final puff of black dust, joining the natural shadows of the garden. A silence closed in. My fists were pressed into cold mud. I had to get up. Where was Ronda?

The entity shifted—a wet, sloppy movement. Perhaps it was an arm that rose. I still couldn't make sense of its anatomy. No longer did its body shimmer. It was solid, complete. *Released.* Every inch of its hulk was a wet mélange of yellow and red and purple with bone shards glinting between black threads. From underneath its stitched folds, a tiny whirlwind fluttered. A puddle of oil rose with it and splashed across the thing's body. The globules reflected moonlight as they traced the contours of lumpy flesh, zigzagging down between sections of skin.

That spiral of black wind swayed left and right . . . and shot towards me.

I ducked as it raced past, tearing up mud and grass.

It headed for Ronda's motionless body. I'd not realised she lay amid a pile of concrete slabs and fence posts.

I stood up on unsteady legs.

The dark wind circled Ronda's outstretched arm, seeming to caress the skin. It lingered at the palm she'd burnt when first touching the stone in Jim's study. With a jerk, the miniature hurricane tore into her skin. Blood sprayed. It burrowed into her arm, shredding flesh. Veins snaked as though energised, and knotted together with thin coils of darkness. Pulled by her veins, hooked with those black tendrils, her body emerged from the rubble, and was dragged towards the grotesque creature.

Maybe I saw terror flash across her face.

Mark Cassell

A dozen yawning holes had appeared in the entity's stitched flesh. Tiny black whirlwinds belched, and as though vacuumed, her clothes and skin tore, bones snapped and cracked in a black and purple blur. A moment later, she was little more than churning meat vanishing into the creature's stomach. The mouths closed, blending with the rest of its patchwork bulk.

The thing visibly bloated, dripping sweat and blood. Dark veins wriggled beneath every fleshy segment as its muscles flexed, then slumped as though satiated.

All I heard was my heartbeat and my ragged breath.

Underneath that monstrosity oil leaked, snaking dark rivers that reflected the security light, pooling outward. As the thing moved, oil and muck flicked up.

I needed to end this.

On legs that wanted to buckle, I sprinted to the back end of my car; the twisted half-wreck that had landed beyond the trench. The boot was open, busted wide, and had vomited my survival kit. Among the bedlam of spare bulbs and heaped grass, and the warning triangle and broken fence posts, and a towel and jagged paving slabs ... somewhere was my—

There it was: the petrol can.

And a rag.

I grabbed them and twisted off the cap, and stuffed the rag in the hole, careful not to get any fuel on my fingers. The harsh stink burned my nostrils. A quick glance at the quaking monster and I saw the lethargic raising of a floppy limb.

I rummaged in my pocket. The cigarette lighter ...

Where the hell was it?

Dust Devils

Mouths opened and closed, dark clouds pluming, forming an all-too-familiar twisting wind . . .

Which pocket was my fucking lighter in?

Slithering in mud and filth, the stumpy appendage punched the oil tank. The panel rattled, issuing a hollow echo.

"That's right," I shouted, "do that again!"

My lighter.

Finally.

A few clicks. Only sparks.

"Come on!"

More clicks . . .

It ignited, and at arm's length I held it to the rag. The flame curled around the fabric, so . . . damn . . . slowly.

Those black clouds spun faster.

"Hurry!" I shouted at the rag. "Burn!"

A miniature tornado broke free from the patchwork flesh that was once Jim, Ronda, the postman.

"Burn!"

Hoping to hell the flame didn't die, I hurled the can towards the quivering hulk of filth and flesh. Arcing overhead, the can trailed fire like a meteor to land with a *whump!* in the centre of that faceless thing. Blinding yellow flames spread like a blanket. The holes, those *mouths*, burst open spitting blood and gulping fire. A rending scream drilled into my skull. Fire raced across the ground, licking the oil tank, flowing into the trench.

I backed up, hands pressed to my ears.

An explosion threw a ball of fire upwards, and bellowing smoke blocked out the moon. I reeled backwards. My foot slid in mud yet I remained upright. Clumps of meat pounded the garden around me. Amid the orange glare, wobbly limbs flailed and whipped fire in all directions. Grass and bushes and trees burned. Tall flames hurtled along the trench.

Still the scream filled my head.

The heat made my scalp and face itch. I backed off, careful not to slip again, reluctant to look away. The fire raged while the scream diminished, while that foul body sank into itself, thrashing fat limbs. The scream dwindled. The body slumped. Silence now, save for the hiss and pop of burning wood. A smouldering stink clouded the garden, drifting on a wind . . . a natural wind. I choked.

From somewhere in the distance, far away in a world I thought once sane, sirens approached.

At the heart of the blinding flames, eventually nothing moved. No foul limbs twitched. Nor were there any spiralling winds. The fire continued to roar, framed by thick black smoke that burned my throat. I coughed and wondered where the pet rabbit was.

I coughed again, this time into my hand. My palm came away wet. I did not want to see the colour.

Liminality

DEL HOWISON

It is a fearful thing to fall into the hands of the living God—Hebrews 10:31

They were looking at me in panic as they stood pressed against the side of the split rail fence. The eyes are always the tell. The emotion was palpable, a stench of fear in the air, the sweat, the sexuality, the sensual desire for raw that comes with the terror.

She kept her daughter pressed against her side, ready to shove her behind herself for protection. It was instinct, like many of my own actions. She darted a look over to the man on the ground, I presumed her husband, and then back to me. His guts, some of which dripped from the long sides of my muzzle, were torn from his body. He had groaned only once after the initial shouting and was now unmoving on the ground. His body was covered in dirt and dust from where I'd been slinging him about the ground with my mouth as I ripped open the fleshy seal of his skin to get to the soft delicacies inside. The dirt yard looked as if a giant broom had smoothed the surface and one could truly imagine that were the case, if it weren't for the bits and pieces of body parts that had fallen out during the struggle and now lay scattered.

The mother's eyes were large as poker chips, and although she clutched her daughter to her with one arm she tried to cover the young one's eyes with the other hand in an attempt to protect her from the sight of the carnage, the man torn asunder and me. I am something to see, I am sure. Spotty gray fur covers most of my body and parts of my mouth, caught in the nether regions between man and wolf, is misshapen and grotesque with dripping intestinal matter leaking onto my arm. That is correct, I said *my arm*. The appendage on my left is still human while a fully formed wolf leg protrudes from my right shoulder.

My face, even in the presence of her vivisected husband, must present an alarming visage—eyes, heavily veined and yellowed, nose shoved up and back onto the base of what has apparently elongated into a snout-like protrusion that was of no use except to hold my upper jaw and extra teeth in place.

She continued to move backward, slowly away from me, and was now backed flat against the split rail fence. She had quickly spun her daughter from her left side, around her, and then to her right side, putting her closer to the gap in the structure and a possible run for the house that stands about 25 yards behind her. She could dash for the wagon to her other side, but that is almost the same distance and offers no real protection upon arrival. I can tell that she understands she will only have one chance. She is a smart woman.

Even as I sit on my twisted haunches and make that horrible guttural noise in my throat that I have no

Liminality

control over, I want to reason with her. I want to tell her that there are things over which I have no control. My looks, my instincts are now there, deep inside of me and they control me more than a twelve-year-old boy is controlled when he discovers his sexual drive in the palm of his hand. My mind can reason but not control my actions, just as my vocal cords can sound without my being able to speak.

I have no plans to attack her or her daughter. Her husband should satiate my lust for food and then I will leave and she will be safe to carry on with the lives I have spared. He was a sinewy farmer, but held enough fat for flavor and I am sure that my hunger will be slaked after I lay down to digest. She looks sad but I have no particular emotions for her or her offspring.

I am only sad for me, for my condition, for the spot I have found myself in.

***

You would not recognize me had you known me prior. Young and full of all the elixirs of life, I had traveled from the East, out to this godforsaken dirt pile, to take on the position of schoolmaster for a town of silver miners and their families. The church and the schoolhouse was one structure, interchangeable, being built in such a rush and with the school not in session on the Sabbath. There were few single females, outside of saloon fodder, but I, with my quirks and personal proclivities, did not find the lack of the opposite gender a problem. I also assumed that as more of the ore was brought up from the earth the town would grow in a symbiotic relationship with the silver. In turn more miners would come in and the town would continue to grow and provide a larger and more . . . varied population.

Del Howison

When I stepped off the stage onto the dirt street for the first time I thought, *What have I done*? But I was here and there was work to be accomplished so I found my rented lodgings and proceeded to make a home and profession for myself. Life was fairly uneventful save an occasional drunken brawl in the street below my room or the moronic parent who felt their child was above learning and needed to be on the farm instead of sitting in a school desk. I never taught the children to swear but used that terminology in my own mind many times regarding the parents.

As I had predicted, the town grew parallel with the silver vein and that growth, though in spurts, was inevitable. I did not socialize much save the parental talks about their offspring, church, and the occasional foray to the local eatery which was neat, clean and served an adequate enough breakfast. I preferred my time alone.

Eventually the town gave birth to a crudely written but mildly interesting weekly newspaper that reported all the gossip along with town hall information and the sheriff's arrest tally for the past week. This last was more for the titillation of the locals who all knew each other than for any journalistic purpose. The people were simple and stupid but gaining knowledge on a daily basis due to my direct and superior methods of teaching. I believed that my technique was totally novel and intended to write a book about it during the next summer break. However, prior to my being able to gather that time period for myself, I was approached one day by the local constable and summoned to attend a meeting of the heads of the town. Although wondering why they needed to speak with me

Liminality

(probably some problem beyond their limited comprehension), I gracefully accepted and that evening I headed over to the meeting hall.

***

The woman acts as if she is looking about for a weapon for protection from my attack. I have seen that crazed look in a person's eyes before and quite frankly they can be dangerous when their minds tell them that they are on the brink of extinction. Actually any animal can be. You should be careful of the little ones, like rats and prairie dogs as they can get quite snippy. With her hip she pushes her daughter slowly sideways along the fence line while scuffing her feet in the direction of the opening. If she thinks she can fetch to the house faster than I can run her down, she is sorely mistaken. Another growl sounds out, emanating from somewhere deep in my chest, and her eyes shoot up to meet mine. She stops where the two of them stand and I can see her breathing from here and only imagine the sound of her own heartbeats in her ears. The stare down between us begins. She should not play games with me but remain still and let me finish my task at hand.

***

I attended this town meeting and was surprised to hear that some of the outlying ranches and homesteads had been devastated by the indigenous people of our fair territory. Families had been slaughtered with some members being killed only after the most deplorable sexual acts one could possibly imagine were perpetrated upon them, while other family members were forced to watch. Then their houses were ransacked and burnt to the ground. The crops were trampled and any livestock that existed was either taken back to where these savages lived, or set free. To hear it told made it all sound revolting and extremely unpleasant. It was no wonder the white man needed to eradicate these barbaric people. The soldiers at Fort Squander could not be spared to just hang about the town hoping to catch these vicious rabid criminals in the act. There was no help coming for us even though it had been requested. It made me wonder what it was possible for anybody to do.

The mayor and his council had an idea. They said they had requested my presence at this meeting because I was the most learned person in town. This was true. They wanted me to write up a treaty or something more akin to a local plea to get these heathens to stop hurting us. In return they promised them some trinkets and a cow or two. There was even a backward, simple girl who lived in some abandoned mine shafts out the west end of town, and ate off the charity of the locals whom they said they would toss into the bargain as a mate for one of the uglier, irreligious fellows. They wanted me to write this all up for them and then go out to where they knew the encampment to be located to present the proposal. In exchange for this extreme act of bravery I was to be given a house of my own and a promise from the town fathers to work quicker to construct my school building.

Not being a stupid man (as you have probably noted) I thought it over for a moment and then asked whom they would send accompanying me out there as I am not a gun-toting type of individual, though heroic and warrior-like as the next man. I would need a show

Liminality

of strength to let these Indians understand I meant business. They said that one of the deputies and one of the mine guards would escort me. I agreed, somebody said, "Done," and we all shook hands on it as a pledge of our word. I was to write up the treaty this week, let the fathers look it over and approve the paper before heading out.

***

I hear a crack as the woman manages to push her opulent posterior hard enough against the fence to force loose one of the crossbars from its post mooring. I, being lost in my thoughts the way I do after a satisfying meal, haven't noticed her subtle but constant movement backward, applying pressure against the weathered wood. The loud snap of the timber brought me around and now we stare into each other's eyes, trying to precipitate the next move. There is a slight shifting on her part so I take a step closer and snap at her, best I could with only half of a wolf's muzzle, and she stops perfectly still as if portraying Lot's wife in the church play. I run my tongue out from under my top teeth and it lies on its side, flapping with my breathing and dripping saliva along with the fluids that come from the man on the ground. I don't believe she's even blinked.

***

Approvals had been made, the day had arrived, and I (in the lead, of course) and my two companions were off to sooth the angry beasts. This would be my opportunity to show them how diplomacy is more effective than might. I was sure they had never been exposed to an opportunity like this, that is to attend a bargaining meeting with someone of knowledge, and

Del Howison

I was convinced it would be an eye-opening experience for them. The breeze was pleasant, the air was warm, and the day could not have been any more agreeable.

As we got closer to where they had made their smelly camp from animal skins and sticks, the deputy pointed out half naked men hiding in trees and atop of some of the cliff faces. I supposed they were watching us in fear of what we might do and must have been frightened enough not to interfere with our passage. As we rounded a final clump of trees the camp spread out awkwardly before us with no real geometric design or placement to it. The denizens stood on either side of the entry trail as we passed by and I felt somewhat like Christ must have felt as they placed palm leaves in the path for his donkey to walk upon.

I had expected to be met by a grey-haired chieftain who would be dressed in some sort of ceremonial garb, offering me a pipe of peace. But when he stepped from his bark and hide covered abode he was small and brown. I would say almost shriveled and I was a bit disappointed that I would have to waste my time with this shrunken rucksack of a man. We pulled up a few feet in front of him and I stared down at the gnome. His eyes were intense. I remember that, and he never took them off me to glance at the other two riders. Not once.

I put my right hand up to show that not only was I not carrying a weapon but that I was also pledging or swearing that what I was about to say was the truth. He spit once near the front hooves of my mount, causing it to snort and take a step back. He seemed unimpressed, obviously not aware of my keen insight and education. I turned to my right, figuring that

Liminality

maybe by introducing the deputy it might make the reason for our visit a bit more poignant. As I pointed, palm up and open handed toward the badge on his chest, a spear caught the deputy just below his head in the hollow of his neck and took him completely out of the saddle. I heard the wooden shaft of the lance snap on the ground. I could not see him as he'd fallen on the far side of his horse. But I did see the rabble swarm him with rocks and clubs and never heard a single sound from him.

I was stunned, frozen in place, but the miner jerked his horse's head about and scrambled back in the direction from which we'd come. The sheer number of arrows sticking out of his back, within what seemed an instant, resembled nothing less than a porcupine. He tumbled to the ground in a raggedy heap, twitching like a rattler with its head pinned to the dirt. I sat as stone still as if I had just seen Medusa, for my entire body had gone numb and the mechanism that connected my brain to my muscles had ceased to exist. I could not move. I could not run. I could barely reason.

***

Another snap and the wooden rail breaks free and drops to the ground at her feet. Maybe she is going to reach for that as a distraction while she gives her daughter a shove toward the front door. It might work for an instant, but not long enough. If she would just stop moving and let me finish with the man, I truly intend to go away. Some people are just too foolhardy for their own good. I take another step toward her and she holds her ground as we try to stare inside each other's brain.

Del Howison

***

Bound with my hands trussed behind my back, laying on the ground inside one of their teepees, the only light that came in was from around the flap, the fire, and the hole at the top where all the poles came together and the smoke streamed out. I could hear chanting and singing while drums beat a consistent rhythm. Soon the flap opened and a garishly dressed savage approached me, beads clacking around his neck, while he shook some beaded rattle thing in his hand at me. He was followed by a couple of younger braves who stood to the side while he danced about, waving and shouting and making me dizzy.

Suddenly he stopped and bent down to where I lay on the ground. He spoke some gibberish which one of his sidekicks translated.

He said, "I think I am a big man."

"No," I countered. "No, just a humble school teacher."

I tried to keep my speech from sounding shaky.

He said, "I think I am a great hunter who can lie to them with cheap trinkets and items to change their ways."

The medicine man had read the paper I'd authored and was not happy.

"Oh that," I said, "was just nothing. The mayor and sheriff of the town forced me to write that"

He said he would make me a great hunter since that seemed to be what I desired, a devious hunter who slinks in shame during the moonlit nights. He would turn me into a wolf. But I would not be *just* a wolf. Since he was to work his shamanism upon me, I would be an enchanted wolf, an especially sinister beast,

Liminality

hated by all who came in contact with me. I would exhibit the mark of Cain. This guy was crazy as a hoot owl.

I knew I had to get out of there. They untied me and the two strong fellows held me down while mad Geronimo chanted and sang. They stripped my shirt from me and began to rub me with some balm. It stunk but he hadn't even finished when I began to feel the tingle move past the top layer of skin and deep into the frame of my body. My limbs twitched and throbbed while the nerves in my face jumped about like they were being stuck with hot needles. The pain was incredible. I would have done anything within my power to escape. He pulled a knife out, for God knows what, but accidentally dropped it, and as one of the strong boys turned to pick it up for him I seized my chance.

I reached over with my suddenly free arm and grabbed a burning wood faggot from the fire. Knife boy turned back just as I swung the flaming weapon. It caught him on the side of the head and sent a shower of embers across the tent. My other side was suddenly free and people were screaming. The sage's hair was on fire and he was rolling about on the ground. I pulled up the bottom of the teepee and ran faster than I'd ever run before. I felt different, awkward, and mean at the same time. I didn't stop for quite a while. When I did it was dark and I collapsed from exhaustion.

When next I awoke it was still dark and I was burning up. I needed to drink and I thought I could smell water on the breeze. I sat up and started off in that direction when I fell in on myself. My legs weren't working correctly and when I reached down to them I found they were misshapen and covered with a thick layer of hair. I fearfully brought my hand up, and in the moonlight it looked fine. My other arm moved discomfited from the shoulder and bent precariously wrong. The control of my muscles was spastic at best and I felt as if I had to learn to use my muscles and tendons differently just to get my arm to move. As I brought it into sight I saw that it too was lupine in shape and covered in fur. I let out a scream of those swear words I saved for the parents, but the sound was muddled, guttural gibberish. More groaning than human speech, I could hear the canine in me. I put my good hand up to my mouth and realized it had also transformed. My bottom jaw was the same and shaped as it always had been, but my upper lip hurt and was stretched out, bleeding across what can only be described as a mutated wolf's muzzle.

I forced myself up on my haunches and tried to walk or drag myself toward the water I smelled. I was parched and would die without some liquid. As I became acquainted with my newly malformed body the muscle movement became a bit more fluid and, although not perfect by any means as I had to practically remain on all fours, it was soon requiring less effort from me both mentally and physically to move about in the direction my mind was telling my body to go. With some effort and a keen sense of smell, I managed my way to a stream that moved slowly and calm out along a pathway it had carved through the forest and onto a widened flood plain.

There, in the moonlight, reflection mirrored in the water, I saw myself for the first time. It was hideous. I was an appalling amalgamation of two beings—part

Liminality

wolf and part man, ultimately neither. As a beast I was neither here nor there. While the realization set in, I discovered that my tear ducts still worked in the same manner they always had. I drank and cried, my voice reaching new heights of volume and echoed in the clearing as I raised my head and screamed. I was a beast in agony, an abomination of God. The moon mocked me by lighting my reflection and I knew I had been hexed. But why hadn't I been transformed completely into this lobo creature, or remained a man? How did I get stuck betwixt and between two worlds? Neither animal nor man, I would be forced to roam as a legend and creature to be spoken of when telling campfire fables.

It was many months before I finally realized what had happened. The witch doctor must have died that night. I saw him on fire, rolling and screaming as the others tried to help. He had only partially completed the transitional ceremony when I had made my move. I had literally cursed myself and become stuck on this threshold, never to be allowed all the way inside or back the way I'd come.

***

Now I am old, and the grey threads that weave themselves throughout my fur feel physically heavy. Incomplete, I stand in the hot sun. I desire to carry this burden of life no longer, but at the moment I am looking into the face of a very scared human being. She is complete. She will never know the agony that courses daily through my veins. She neither knows nor cares about the decades of pain that drive me along daily with the animal instinct to survive. She flinches and I know she is going to make her move very soon.

Del Howison

There's that telling twitch near her eye. I've seen it before in poker games. There is always a tell.

I intended to leave and let her be. But the man at my feet has grown cold and dirty. My interior beast is now stronger than ever. I am not full and she is not yet inside the house.

The Gardener
GENE O'NEILL

1.

Ann and Amy were identical twins, with two noticeable differences. Ann, the older, was a strawberry blonde, whereas her sister had flaming orange hair. But their important difference was in temperament. Amy, the redhead, was quiet, soft-spoken, kindly, and reserved; Ann was outgoing, opinionated, aggressive, and impulsive. She was very protective of her younger twin. In fact, one might say Ann was an avenging angel whenever Amy was embarrassed or hurt by someone.

In the past, Joey Carlito, the star running back, had grabbed Amy's ass at a high school dance in their junior year, and said, "I'd like a piece of this, you stuck-up, red-headed bitch." Sobbing, Amy ran home from the dance. A bit later, when Ann arrived home, Amy explained why she'd bolted so suddenly from the dance.

Ann ground her teeth as Amy finished the story, planned revenge, and whispered under her breath, "I'll kill the asshole."

Gene O'Neill

Two weeks later she was waiting in the shadows of the trees lining the high school gym's parking lot. Joey Carlito was one of the last football players to leave the locker room, finally waving goodbye to two other lollygaggers. Night was settling in as he stepped into the well-lighted parking lot.

"Hello, you handsome devil," Ann said in a sexy voice, remaining hidden in the tree shadows.

Of course Joey stopped, grinned, and peered into the darkness. "Who is that?"

"It's me, lover boy," Ann said in her disguised voice, "and I have something very special waiting here for you. Come and get it."

Joey hurried out of the well-lighted lot and into the shadows.

Ann, wearing all black including a ski mask, surprised him. Stepping in close to meet Joey while he was vulnerable, his eyes still adjusting to the dark, she swung a Louisville Slugger with the force and precision of a clean-up hitter on the high school softball team.

Crunch.

Joey's right leg buckled as the bat crashed into the side of his knee. He went down in a heap, clutching his badly damaged knee in both hands, and screaming in agony.

Ann stared coldly down at the boy writhing in pain on the ground. "You need to learn some manners big shot, how to properly treat women. And while you're at it, keep your hands to yourself." She lifted the bat onto her shoulder and casually strode off into the darkness, never looking back.

Joey Carlito had a bad meniscal tear and serious anterior cruciate ligament damage to his right knee. He would never play another game of football.

The Gardener

After correctly guessing what Ann had done to Joey, Amy made her sister swear to *no* more physical revenge on her behalf—a promise Ann regretted and had difficulty keeping in the future.

2.

Almost four years ago, Logan Jones began planting his secret garden, out beyond his Napa Valley neighbor's vast vineyard, on a sliver of land isolated from view by a string of tall black oaks lining the Napa River bank. He planted mostly rhododendrons and azaleas, adding a few camellias closer to the trees—all young plants that loved the shade. The plants immediately did well, thriving in the rich river loam. By early fall, Logan was enjoying a multi-colored carpet of bright reds, pinks, purples, whites, and variegated blossoms.

Whenever he felt stressed out by his new job or about life in general, he knew he could always decompress in his secret place—a four or five-minute walk from his house through the vineyard and trees. As dusk settled, he would stretch out against his favorite oak trunk, enjoying the bright array of colors and the pleasing sound of the rushing river. The cooling fog blowing upriver from the Bay Area, helped deflate the built up pressure of the day. The relaxing nature of the place also helped him control his recently recurring stammer.

Logan's stammering had returned just before he decided on making his first plantings in the shade. His Kaiser doctor didn't believe it was brought on by anything physical. He thought it was probably psychosomatic related to new job stress. He

Gene O'Neill

recommended Logan see a speech pathologist, and also make an appointment with a psychologist or psychiatrist. Even though Logan did indeed feel some initial pressure during his first few weeks at the Napa branch of the San Francisco accounting firm, *Jackson, O'Donnell & Associates*, the stress had ramped up after two months on the job, at the early onset of his busy first tax season. Nevertheless, he hadn't completely taken Dr. Patterson's advice.

Logan didn't like the idea of seeing a *head* doctor for any reason, not after his bad childhood experiences during foster care with therapists of all kinds. When he was twelve he was referred to a clinical psychologist by one of the ineffective speech therapists for his terrible stammer. After a brief interview and some tests, the psychologist recommended *nothing* to relieve Logan's stammer, but warned, "You live too much in a fantasy world; the danger being that someday you may lose the ability to differentiate between what is real and what is not." Insulted because young Logan believed the man was suggesting he was crazy, he never voluntarily spoke to another psychologist again.

But, like in the past, Logan did reluctantly make an appointment to see a speech pathologist, who'd recommended several specific stress reducing practices like deep-breathing, daily meditation, visualization while speaking, and even singing a phrase that he'd recently stammered on—he always sang the repeated lines perfectly. The techniques all helped to some degree, but he'd only made significant improvement after discovering the isolated stretch of riverbank, where he'd planted his secret garden. Even after only

The Gardener

one garden visit his stammering made a dramatic improvement—almost completely disappearing overnight.

Tonight at home, Logan was feeling lonely. Whenever he felt this way he climbed up on a stool and dug out his box of keepsake treasures. The box was located in an attic crawlspace only accessed from a square in the back corner of his bedroom closet ceiling—he didn't want to share his treasures with anyone, including his part time housekeeper. He set the small box down on the foot of his bed, reached underneath his stack of diaries, and took Jody's tiny teddy bear up into his hands. Rubbed it against his face. He closed his eyes and smiled. Jody had been Logan's first real love.

They'd met at the Napa branch office four years ago, during his first few months on the job. He'd graduated with his BS in Accounting after finishing his last class in summer school at State at the end of July. He was hired immediately as an accountant at *Jackson, O'Donnell, & Associates* after having successfully served a year as a part time intern at the main office in San Francisco.

Jody was the sole heir of her Uncle Noah's very minor estate. As the most junior accountant in the Napa branch of the firm, Logan had been assigned Noah Hendrickson's tax file just days before the old man died. Jody lived in L.A., but she flew up several times to go over tax matters on her small inheritance.

Although strictly against company policy, on Jody's third visit to Napa, Logan finally built up enough nerve to ask her out on a date.

"W-W-W—"

Gene O'Neill

He'd stamped his foot to break the embarrassing stammer, which had recently reappeared. Then, he closed his eyes, took several deep breaths, visualized speaking perfectly, before slowly restarting, "W-Would you like to go to the Rutherford Grill for dinner tomorrow, S-Saturday night." Logan spoke almost perfectly in a controlled, slow manner.

He'd been stammering off and on for as long as he could remember. It probably started after his parents died suddenly in an automobile crash on Highway 101 near Candlestick Park. As a four-year-old stammering bed-wetter, he began a series of multiple placements in the State's Foster Care system—seven different homes in those early painful years. But then, after years of ineffective help from three or four different speech therapists, the stammer had finally improved in the eighth grade. Still, Logan had remained a social isolate through the next four years of high school. Other kids called him *The Brain* or *The Numbers Guy* in a dismissive, derogatory manner. But what really hurt were the jocks constant bullying and calling him *Repeat*.

Logan had continued being kind of a loner through college at San Francisco State, having only two casual male friends, but never going out on a real date with a young woman. Even though by then he'd gotten a really good handle on the stammering. His *modus operandi* was to always carefully pause, close his eyes, and take a few deep breaths before slowly beginning a measured sentence. But despite all the little tricks, the stammering had re-appeared again suddenly on the first days of the new job, getting worse after the stress had increased in intensity during the beginning of tax season.

The Gardener

Jody, a petit brunette, had waited patiently without interrupting him, smiled, and, then said, "I'd love to have dinner with you, Logan. I've returned twice in person hoping you'd ask me out."

He glowed.

They had a wonderful time at The Rutherford Grill, and later he'd taken her out to see his new home in the vineyard country north of Napa—a rambling three-bedroom ranch-style house with almost an acre of land.

But Jody was gone now, disappearing abruptly from his life much too soon, after he'd known her for less than six months. She'd left her bear behind for him. He treasured the tiny bear, a childhood keepsake that Jody adored. She called it "Pooh." She'd clutched and handled it so much growing up that she'd worn off most of the brown hair. The bear only retained a few spots of rough fuzz.

Whenever Logan picked up Pooh, it immediately reminded him of Jody, and her memory made his eyes moisten. He loved and missed her terribly. The young woman would always have a special place reserved in his heart.

Logan sighed and put the bear back in the box under the banded diaries, and returned it to the attic crawlspace.

Several evenings later, Logan returned slightly refreshed after a short visit to his secret garden on the riverbank. But his mood soon soured, turning melancholy and lonely in the big house. He climbed the stool and took down his box of keepsakes. He reached in and withdrew the beautiful origami replica of a three-inch high red stork. It reminded him of his second love.

Gene O'Neill

He'd met Keiko at the Visitor's Center in Japan Town, after stopping and inquiring about a good Japanese restaurant.

Once every week on late Friday afternoons for his first year or so on the job in Napa, he had to go into the main office of *Jackson, O'Donnell & Associates* on Montgomery Street in the heart of San Francisco's financial district. A training seminar for all junior accountants, which during the late Fall was an updating and discussion of new or proposed tax laws, especially how they related to corporations, big and small—like the many Napa Valley wineries that employed the Napa branch of the firm.

Keiko was a young, attractive woman of sleight build, rosy checks, dark brown hair and the brightest dark eyes—childlike, shining with intense curiosity.

She pointed at the book Logan carried. "That is a favorite of mine," she said in perfect English.

He smiled, holding up the hardback of *To Kill a Mocking Bird*. "I just picked this up at a bookstore near here to replace a worn paperback in my library at home. Love the book, too."

The young woman smiled. "Where is your home?"

"The Napa Valley," he said, smiling inwardly, proud of his complete lack of a stammer.

"Oh, I hope to visit that famed valley someday soon. See a winery or two."

They chatted on briefly, introducing themselves formally. Eventually, Keiko recommended three restaurants right there in Japan Town.

Surprising himself with his sudden boldness, Logan said, "Why don't you eat dinner with me tonight, Keiko? You can pick the place."

The Gardener

She hesitated only a brief moment before nodding, smiling broadly, and saying, "Yes, what fun to go out with such a handsome American who also appreciates Harper Lee's masterpiece. I suspect we are going to have much in common to talk about."

They had a lovely sushi dinner in Japan Town. Afterward before saying goodbye, Logan invited Keiko to come up to the Valley and see his modest library the following weekend. "Of course, you will have your own private bedroom and bath," he said. "It's a large house and stresses my budget, but I couldn't resist the location and the beautiful but empty book shelves in the den. They were begging to be filled, although at first all I've had were mostly my boxes of paperbacks from college."

"I'd love to come for a visit," the young woman said, her dark eyes shining brightly.

"I'll pick you up Friday evening after you get off at the Visitor's Center."

Saturday morning after an early breakfast at *Jax Mule* in Napa, Logan drove Keiko up-valley, first taking the ski lift up to Sterling Winery perched on a little knoll, a small facility that offered an informative self-guided tour on making and storing wine. They leisurely explored the quaint up-valley towns of Calistoga and St. Helena, neither having any chain restaurants, department stores, or hotels. On the way home to Napa, they ate barbecued ribs and key lime pie for dessert at The Rutherford Grill, lingering over drinks at an outside table on the patio.

And of course Keiko was delighted, perusing his library of mixed old paperbacks and new hardbound books arranged alphabetically in the oak-stained floor-to-ceiling bookcases occupying two walls in the den. She was especially delighted when she spotted the several English translated books by the Japanese surrealist, Haruki Murakami. She clapped her hands together saying, "I have only read a couple of his books in Japanese. But I think he is an exceptional writer. I'm surprised that you even know his work. Most of your books are classics, written by Americans like Hemingway, Steinbeck, Mailer, Faulkner, Algren, and such . . . although I did notice you have several books here by Joseph Conrad and Somerset Maugham."

"Yes, you're right, my library so far is very deficient in good work by any of the great Brits, or Russians, or the French, or other Japanese, or for that matter dozens of other good foreign writers. I will be adding some selections of that work soon. But Murakami is so well known and respected here in literary circles that I had to recently get some hardbacks of his best work. I definitely enjoy his stuff. This is my favorite. Have you read it?" He selected a book from the shelf and handed it to her, *The Wind-Up Bird Chronicle*.

She looked at the title in English and slowly nodded. She gave the book back and said, "The relationship between the narrator and the weird, young neighbor girl is very interesting, quite sensual, without anything sexual actually ever occurring. But the non-described sexual tension is still always keen between them. I liked his solitary meditations and speculations when he's down in the dry well."

Logan agreed with her take on the book.

After spending the day with her, he realized she was indeed quite well read. Keiko had been a joint

The Gardener

English-Literature major at Tokyo University, aware of most of the best American writers. She could discuss intelligently Logan's favorites, even Nelson Algren's, *Man With the Golden Arm* or, *A Walk on the Wild Side*, novels he knew were now under the radar of the majority of the American reading public, perhaps some older people remembering the two excellent movies made of the books.

It had been a grand weekend.

But Keiko was gone now.

Logan glanced down at the elegant piece of origami in his hand. He missed the lovely, bright, and talented young woman so much, reserving a special place in his heart for her.

He sighed and carefully put the crane back in the container, and hoisted the box back to its storage spot.

Sunday evening, feeling lonely, Logan had gone to the North Beach section of The City. He'd recently read an intriguing article about *The Body Shop* in the Chronicle, the piece mentioning the unusual opportunities offered *amateur* exotic dancers at the once-a-month Sunday night specials.

Procrastinating until almost midnight, Logan finally forced himself to enter the bar, which was located in an alley off Broadway, well lighted with a blinking, gaudy neon caricature of a naked, buxom redhead over the entry.

Self-consciously, he took a table distant from the ringside stools around a tiny stage with a center pole. He sipped his watered-down gin and tonic, at first fascinated as the tuxedo-adorned MC announced another *amateur* dancer. "And now the lovely Ms Roxy, who is a full-time kindergarten teacher from the peninsula. Give her a nice hand." The modest crowd responded with mild enthusiasm.

The spotlight focused on a middle-aged woman, who moved out awkwardly onto the stage in the shortest, sequined, white dress, her pale breasts pushed up, more than half exposed. She spun around the pole to the music from the three-piece band, barely visible in the dimness of backstage. Ms Roxy made a series of crude bumps and grinds against the pole, badly timed to the loud music. When she clumsily discarded her short dress, her bared breasts sagged, nothing hiding her flabby body. She finished her performance to a short and minor round of applause, and collected tips from only two very drunken men sitting ringside. Logan didn't believe she was a kindergarten teacher at all.

The last so-called *amateur* performer was a single-mom bartender, her face adorned in garish purple and green eye make-up. She too was a clumsy performer. But in addition to her much firmer breasts, for the briefest moment as the spotlight died, she bared her unshaved pudendum. This generated a boisterous round of clapping and whistling from those remaining along the bar front and even a loud shout of, "Big bush!" After slipping back into her g-string, she moved around the bar circling the stage, momentarily squatting in front of a tipper long enough to allow a bill to be slipped into the waist band of her skimpy apparel.

Logan decided the whole thing was disappointing and disgusting. He was glad when the shoddy, sleazy strip show finally concluded, and he could leave without causing a stir. He drained his drink and stood

The Gardener

up to go . . . But the middle-aged kindergarten teacher appeared suddenly at his side, blocking his path, as she pushed a breast against his arm, saying, "How 'bout buying me a drink, sport, then I'll give you a lap dance? Half rate cuz you're so cute." Up close, her heavy perfume didn't quite mask the locker room sweaty, musky smell. And her gaudy make-up didn't quite mask the deep wrinkles and the crow's feet etched into the corners of her eyes; the purple mascara doing little to disguise the ancient nature of those dead eyes.

Stiffly, Logan eased around her, and stammered, "N-N-N-No t-thank y-y-y—" With a clear shot at the door finally, he broke away from the woman, his jaw clenched tightly.

At the door he heard her shout at his back, "Hey fuck you, you faggot asshole."

He burst out into the chill of the foggy night, which was ice for his bruised psyche. Catching his breath, Logan glanced back over his shoulder. Thankfully, no one had followed him out of *The Body Shop*. He breathed a deep sigh of relief, and then hurried to his car. The evening had been a terrible mistake in judgment, a total disaster, and he headed for Napa, ashamed, sad, and even lonelier.

At home, Logan made a beeline to his bedroom closet, and removed his box from its secret spot. He took out his most recent memento from *Irish*, a small, spiral sketchbook. They'd met five months ago on-line at a literary books chat room. But even after they finally got together several times for coffee at Starbucks, she still kept her real name a secret, preferring he call her, *Irish*. She eventually told Logan her real name after he'd taken her on a date for dinner and a book signing by Michael Chabon in Berkeley. But, by then, the name, *Irish*, was so ingrained in his mind, that's how he thought of her, only occasionally remembering and using her given name. Shy and timid but always lady-like, *Irish* was the youngest but the favorite of his three loves. Although, just like the other two, she was gone now; and he was again alone.

Logan sat on the corner of his bed and slowly flipped through the twenty or so penciled sketches. They were mostly animals or birds or outdoor landscapes, except for the last one. It was a dark sketch of the downstairs basement, a soundproofed room, where all three young women had been restrained after they refused to voluntarily move in with him. He'd kept them down there, and tried his best to persuade them to change their minds. But, alas, they had all been very *stubborn* young women.

Unlike Logan's first two loves, *Irish* had local relatives who'd immediately made a big fuss to local authorities over her sudden disappearance. Unfortunately, Logan had texted the young woman a number of times after meeting her in the chat room. Apparently, from those texts, the police had been able to trace him to his home.

Detective Sergeant McKinney of the Napa PD had showed up one night with a search warrant. Fortunately for Logan, he'd disposed of the restraints, mattress, and thoroughly cleaned the basement before the detective's first visit. There were no clues that Jody or Keiko or *Irish* had ever been locked in the basement. Sergeant McKinney came back two more times, the last visit with dogs and their handlers. The

The Gardener

cadaver dogs unsuccessfully sniffed all over Logan's outside acre.

Finally, after that last visit, the detective admitted to Logan that he was no longer *a person of interest* in the disappearance of the young girl. Sgt. McKinney had even suggested that Logan may have been a victim of *ghosting,* when *Irish* disappeared so suddenly.

After the detective left, Logan googled the slang term, which he'd never heard. He read the definition and smiled wryly. Of course he hadn't been a victim of *ghosting* by *any* of the three young women. He hadn't *allowed* any of them to leave.

Tonight, after *Irish* had been gone almost four months, Logan decided it would be safe to visit his garden on the riverbank. He was sure he was no longer under surveillance by the police.

3.

It was after dark before Logan reached his secret spot under his favorite oak and stretched out. He glanced over the colorful plants, and enjoyed the early winter evening. The air was crisp as fog crept up the river, spilling up over the riverbank and blanketing Logan.

He shivered, wishing he'd brought more than a windbreaker.

Then, a nearby movement startled him.

Logan blinked and gasped!

An apparition was just visible in the swirling mist, standing about twenty-five yards from where Logan had lounged against the oak. And it was slowly gliding through the shaded plants toward him. As it grew closer and took shape, Logan recognized the familiar orange hair, the facial features. But it couldn't be *Irish* . . . That was impossible!

The figure moved even closer, only ten yards away now.

It was definitely her!

Logan jumped to his feet, held up his hands in the maneuver of fending someone off. And in a loud hoarse voice, he stammered, "N-N-N—"

He stamped his foot, sucked in a deep breath, and said, "N-No, No, Amy.

Y-Y-You aren't real . . . "

He paused and pointed at two spots covered by pink azaleas and red rhododendrons. "I-I-I permanently planted you in my garden four months ago . . . right *there*, between Keiko Watanabe and Jody Hendrickson."

The figure stopped drifting closer, stood in place, and smiled. She reached up, pulled off the orange wig, and shook out her strawberry blonde hair. Still smiling wryly, she said, "My name isn't Amy. I'm Ann, her twin sister. And mister, you are so fucked."

Sgt. McKinney stepped out of the shadows next to the young woman, as Logan's knees weakened, and he slowly slumped to the ground.

4.

Two weeks after Logan Jones confessed to killing and burying the three young women in his garden on the Napa riverbank, Detective Sergeant McKinney visited and made a startling revelation to Ann.

"There was only one real gravesite in that garden, your sister, Amy's."

"Are you sure?" Ann said, puzzled.

The Gardener

Sgt. McKinney nodded. "We dug up the whole flower garden area, went up and down the riverbank as far as possible. Logan Jones only planted *one* body up there in his garden."

"Then, where are the other two young women?"

The detective lifted his eyebrows, slowly shook his head, and made a shrugging gesture. "That's just it, Ann, we don't think there were two other victims. Jody and Keiko, as Jones called them, don't exist outside of his imagination."

"Whoa," Ann said, frowning. "Back up, and explain all that, please."

"Well, after digging up a good part of Napa County unsuccessfully, we went back to where Jones lived on the other side of the vineyard. We found a secret cache in a crawl space we'd previously overlooked, accessed from the corner of a closet in his bedroom. He kept a box up there, with a series of dated journals and his keepsakes. In the most recent journal, he talks in detail about Jody and Keiko, as if they were both real girlfriends in the past four years. Jody was an heir of a client, Noah Hendrickson. He met Keiko where she worked in San Francisco at the Visitor's Center in Japan Town. A teddy bear in that box belonged to Jody. An origami crane belonged to Keiko. But in his earlier journals, which go back to junior high school, there are references that the teddy bear was actually *his*, a beloved object he clung to through all his foster home placements."

"And the crane?"

"We think he made that himself. He was taking an origami class in Japan Town after his employer's seminars on Friday afternoons . . ."

Gene O'Neill

The detective paused a moment, ordering his thoughts.

"So, we checked thoroughly on the two women. Jones *was* indeed the accountant for a Noah Hendrickson, but the old man died intestate. He had no heirs. And we can find no California Driver's License or any record of a Jody Hendrickson, the correct age and description, from the L.A. area. The woman carefully described in the later journal just doesn't exist."

"And the other woman, Keiko Watanabe?"

"There is no record of a visa for her from Japan, or of her working at the Japanese Visitor's Center in San Francisco. We believe both women were products of Jones' loneliness, an elaborate fantasy he created, kind of like detailed imaginary friends. And in the end, he was unable to separate fantasy from reality."

"But my sister wasn't imaginary," Ann said, frowning.

"No she wasn't . . . And Logan Jones will pay dearly for what he did to Amy."

Ann dabbed her eyes, nodded, and said in a harsh voice, "I hope he gets what he deserves."

"He will, the courts will see to that," Detective Sgt. McKinney said, concluding his visit.

Condo by the Lake
JEFF CERCONE

The spoon stirred, metal scraping the bottom of the pot as whatever was for dinner thickened on the stovetop.

Mira used to be able to tell what Mama was cooking from the smell, but not lately. Last night it was oatmeal, bland and pasty. No butter, no milk, no sugar. What they had set aside, they choked down today for breakfast.

She took her seat at the table, and Vivian sat on the floor next to her. Even the dog seemed uninterested in the meal to come, but Mira would make her eat. She reached down to pet her, and the dog's ribs under its harness jarred her fingers. Mira would slip the dog some of her meal as well, when Mama got distracted trying to find something on the radio.

The spoon clanked three times on the side of the pot, and Mama clicked the gas off. Turn right to turn it off, Mira thought, left to turn it on until you hear the clicking stop and the flame light up. She had tried it a few times herself with Mama around, just to be safe, but the thought of cooking on her own still frightened her. She could handle the microwave with the braille numbers.

"Give me your plate, sweetie, it's ready," Mama said.

Ugh, sweetie, Mira thought. Mama still talked to her like she was a child instead of a teenager. Maybe if you did more for yourself, it'd be different, she thought, then forced a smile.

She held her plate up and "it" landed with a wet slap. She waited for the second slap before putting her plate down.

Mama filled her own plate, then scooped some into Vivian's dish. They ran out of regular dog food a week ago, so Vivian ate what they ate. And it didn't always agree with her, judging from the smell coming from the balcony, where Mama let Vivian do her business. Mama forgot to dump it over the side sometimes.

Mira fished out a spoonful of her meal and held it to her crinkled nose but still couldn't tell what it was.

"It's mashed potatoes," Mama said, a bit annoyed. "You like mashed potatoes. I added a can of the mixed vegetables. There's some Ritz crackers near your plate if you want to scoop it on them."

"I like potatoes," Mira replied. "I just couldn't tell is all. They don't smell like anything."

"I'm doing the best I can with what we have left, honey," Mama said.

Mama always used sweet words like honey, sweetie and dear, even when she was angry with her. Or had her feelings hurt.

"No, it's good, honest," Mira said, trying to close the wound before Mama started weeping again. Vivian slowly slurped at the bowl beside her. "Viv thinks so, too, listen."

Condo by the Lake

The older woman laughed, but it didn't sound happy and ended abruptly. Mira could hear Mama's hands fiddling with the silverware and knew there was something she was afraid to talk about.

"What is it, Mama? What's wrong?"

"What's wrong? What's wrooooong?" she replied, her voice rising, before another sharp laugh.

"Be quiet, Mama, they'll hear," Mira pleaded, her grip on her spoon tightening.

"I'm sorry, sweetie," the older woman whispered, her voice now choking the way it does when she's about to cry.

There was a long pause. "The food is almost gone. We've only got two days' worth, maybe three if we stretch it out. I've got to go down there."

Mira slammed her hands on the table, forgetting her admonition about noise a moment earlier.

"No, Mama, no . . . ! You can't," she shouted, then lowered her voice. "Mama, please," Mira said. "After what they did to Frank?"

Frank was the building super mama had been sleeping with. She hid it from Mira for the longest time. Mama thought she was real smart, but Mira could smell his cologne on Mama's sheets when it was laundry day and in the bathroom some mornings. And she could hear Mama trying to stifle a snicker when he said he was here to lay some new pipes in the kitchen.

It bothered Mira that Mama thought she was still a child, but she let them have their secret because Daddy had been gone for years and she liked Frank, with his booming voice and thick Midwestern accent. Or aaaaccent, as Frank would pronounce it. She liked him mostly because of how happy he made Mama.

Jeff Cercone

But Mama and Frank dropped all pretense a while back when he moved in with them, after those things started coming out of the lake.

Those things. They looked like giant, translucent slugs, Frank said, like clear sacs of jelly just lying there on the Lake Michigan beaches.

Frank said his nephew, Tommy, had seen them up close when it started. He was at North Avenue beach to play volleyball with his friends when they started washing up on the shore. He was taking a break and people-watching when a cluster of five or six of them hit the sand.

He thought they were jellyfish. They moved, slowly, away from the water. There was something inside them. Not organs, Tommy said, but strands of long, flowing strings, like spaghetti.

Tommy said a little boy and his older sister approached one, and the boy reached out with a stick and poked the thing, which had stopped moving at their approach. Its body seemed to vibrate, then the sac began to expand. The boy took a step back just before the creature burst with a loud pop.

And those white strands flew out of it and onto the little boy. And . . . into the boy, Tommy told his uncle.

"They just chewed their way inside," Frank told them.

Tommy picked up the screaming boy and ran to the lifeguard stand. He laid the boy down on the boardwalk as the lifeguard radioed for help, when all of a sudden the boy grew quiet, then stood up, staring straight ahead toward the lake, his eyes open but lifeless.

He turned away from his sister and the lifeguard

Condo by the Lake

and made a beeline to a woman sunbathing nearby. She had her iPod on and was sleeping on her stomach and missed all the commotion.

Tommy followed to see if the boy was OK and he saw a long, pink, writhing thing protruding from the boy's left eye socket. It poked and prodded at the woman on the blanket, who opened her eyes in time to get out one scream before the boy's entire body burst open, showering her with long, white worms that burrowed into her. The boy's body, his skin really, collapsed to the ground as if he had just discarded a coat.

Tommy heard screams from all over the beach and saw hundreds of people heading in his direction toward the city, to safety, as the scene replayed itself up and down the shoreline.

That was two months ago. Tommy made it to safety that day, but Frank hadn't heard from him or the boy's mother since.

There was news coverage for a while. It wasn't just happening in Chicago but near every body of freshwater across the country. They could hear helicopters hovering sometimes and sporadic gunfire. Then the news just stopped. The only channel they could get on their TV was the security channel that showed the front lobby of their building.

The channel came in handy three days ago. Frank had gone down to the little overpriced convenience store just off the lobby to grab what he could when their supplies began to run low.

Mama was watching the lobby on their TV screen, her phone out, ready to warn Frank if she saw anyone near the lobby. He made it to the store and back to the stairwell safely with a large garbage bag stuffed with whatever he could find in one hand and his cell phone in the other. An old, wooden softball bat was tucked under one arm.

They lived on the 14th floor, and Frank made it up the first 10 flights safely, whispering to Mama "It's OK, nothing here" as he reached each level. But then he heard someone crying for help on the 11th floor.

Mira listened on speaker phone as Mama begged Frank to let it be and keep moving, but they both knew Frank better than that.

"It's Mrs. McGarry," he told Mama. "I gotta see if I can get her upstairs. If something happens, the food is in the stairwell."

Mira hoped he didn't bring her up here. She was a nasty old woman who always clucked her tongue at Vivian in the elevator and reminded Mira to clean up after the dog, even though she knew Mira couldn't very well see where the dog was going to the bathroom outside.

They could hear the woman pleading, "They're in me! Oh, they burn. Get them out! Oh no, no Frank, we can't leave him here."

Mama was yelling at Frank to run, but it was too late. Soon, there was a loud pop, like a balloon bursting, and Frank began to shriek, an unexpected high-pitched yell that Mira remembered being surprised to hear.

They listened for a while longer and could still hear Frank moaning softly and some rustling noises. Finally Mira couldn't bear to listen anymore and pried the phone from Mama's hand.

Mama hasn't been the same since, mostly keeping

Condo by the Lake

to herself and weeping. But now she had it in her mind to go down there and get that bag of food.

"Mama, I can't watch your back for you," Mira told her.

"I know," she said, then paused. "But she can."

Mira gasped and instinctively reached down and touched Vivian.

"Oh no, Mama, no. I need her. Please."

"She'll see them before I will. She'll protect me."

Right, Mira thought, and you'll throw her to them as a sacrifice so there's one less mouth to feed. She hated herself for thinking that, but she knew Mama never liked dogs. She always urged Mira not to rely so much on Vivian and to learn to get around without her.

But she knew Mama was right. They had to get that food, and she couldn't go out there alone.

"It's only three flights of stairs. Frank made it up and down easily. The stairway was clear. They only got him because he opened the door for that old bat," Mama said bitterly. "We've got nothing left to eat."

"But that was three days ago. You don't know that it's clear now. And the hallways aren't clear. We hear them all the time."

"I know but it's quiet now. They might all be in the stairwell for all I know. But we do know we're out of food and low on bottled water. Do you want to drink out of the tap? Do you think that's safe?"

Mira said nothing, then nodded. She dropped to the floor to hug Vivian, who licked her face in return, oblivious to what may be waiting outside.

"Come help me move this, honey," Mama said, no longer across the table but across the room.

Mira grabbed Vivian's harness.

Jeff Cercone

"Leave the dog, Mira. You know where the front door is. You best learn to get around alone. We've lived here 10 years now."

Mira dropped the harness and slowly made her way to the door, her hands stretching out in front and beside her to avoid bumping into furniture. When she got there, Mama led her to one end of the dresser they had pushed in front of the door.

"I checked the peephole, it looks clear," Mama said.

They lived in the middle of the floor near the elevators, and the stairway Frank went down was on the far end of the hallway on the right. Mira figured Mama could at least peek her head outside and make sure the hallway was clear. If it wasn't, she would have time to get back in and shut the door.

They slid the dresser back, and Mama undid the door chain, slowly. She took a last look through the peephole, then opened the door.

"Hallway's clear. Give me her leash. I've got to go fast." Mama's voice was shaking, but firm. Mira sensed she was seeing something she didn't want to share.

Mama decided against trying to find a weapon, since avoidance was the best one, and they only had one phone left, so Mira would be in the dark as to how it was going.

"You don't open this door unless I sound like myself, all right?" Mama whispered. "Promise me."

"I promise. Please be careful."

Mira heard their footsteps fade away down the hall and wished she had taken Vivian's collar off. She could hear the tags jangling. And if she could hear them, so could they.

She shut the door behind her, locked the doorknob,

Condo by the Lake

then the deadbolt, and fumbled for the chain, sliding it into place.

She felt the locks now with her fingers, judging the distance from the handle to each. She did this several times so she would be sure.

She decided against pushing the dresser back in front, even though she promised Mama she would. If seconds counted for them, she couldn't waste them moving that out of the way.

The locks would have to do for now. No one had come to the door for a while now. At first it was just neighbors, looking to see if they needed help or wanted to join them as they tried to get out of the city.

But Mama wouldn't open the door for any of them, except Frank. After a while, no one came, except them. They could hear them shuffling about in the hallways sometimes, and once in a while one would pound on the door, but they usually stopped if they were real quiet.

Mira pressed her ear against the door until she heard the stairwell door down the hall close, then leaned back against the dresser and waited. She tried to calculate how long it would take. It was only three flights up and down, but Mama was pushing 60 and not in great shape. The plan was under 10 minutes, but Mira had her doubts.

Mira's mind began to wander, going through all the possible scenarios if Mama didn't make it back.

She would have enough to eat for a few days, maybe a week since it would be just her. Then she would have to go outside herself, without Vivian, only her cane to guide her. That wouldn't do.

She didn't tell Mama this, but she thought if they

didn't come back, maybe she was going to end it. There was no sense waiting for help. Nobody was coming.

The only question was how to do it. She could swallow Mama's sleeping pills, she thought, but that was too risky. What if she grabbed the wrong bottle or didn't take enough. She could cut her wrists, but that seemed too painful. She decided she would find her way to the balcony and jump over the railing.

Mira checked the time, her fingers moving over the braille watch Mama had gotten her last Christmas. It had been about six minutes. She pressed her ear against the door again, listening for any sign that Mama was on her way back.

A door opened down the hall. It closed with a heavy thud. She had made it! She could hear Vivian's collar jangle and their footsteps on the wood floor as they hurried down the hall, and that's when Mira heard a second door open, this one closer to her own.

Mama screamed. "Frank!"

There was only a loud moan in response, then a loud popping sound. Mama screamed again, much higher this time, like she was on fire.

Mira opened the door a crack, the chain still attached.

Vivian barked and yipped and the sound of her got closer. Mama was still hollering down the hall, but she managed to say "Mira . . . don't" before the only sound that came from her was that awful moaning.

The moaning got closer and louder as Mama moved down the hall toward Mira. Vivian barked louder, running back toward Mama with sharp, warning barks, then back toward the door.

Mira had only seconds to decide. She unlatched the chain.

Condo by the Lake

"Vivian, come! Come!"

The dog didn't hesitate, hurtling inside, almost knocking Mira down. She slammed the door shut and her fingers found the deadbolt and the chain locks swiftly. Mira's practice while she waited had paid off.

It took all her strength to push the dresser back in front of the door and all her will not to scream when she heard Mama outside the door moaning.

Where had Frank come from? It sounded like he came from an apartment a few doors down. But how did he get in? They hadn't heard any doors being broken down.

But he had keys. Keys to every door. Did he still know how to use them? Was there some sort of memory left inside?

Had Mama brought her keys?

BAM!

Mama pounded on the door. Just once at first. Then 10 seconds later, another. Then with both hands, a flurry of fists began raining down on the door. Vivian barked and whined behind Mira.

Mira backed away, tripping over Vivian's water dish, but managed to regain her balance on the dining room table to keep upright. She kneeled down and called Vivian to her.

The pounding on the door stopped. The only sound now was her breathing and Vivian's whining.

She heard the door handle begin to move now, a loud creak as it slowly turned. It moved back and forth as Mama tried in vain to open it, then pounded again on the door with her other hand.

"Go away!" Mira shouted, hoping some part of Mama could hear her . . . Could still understand.

Jeff Cercone

That's when she heard the key rattling around in the top lock and then the deadbolt click open. She froze. The same key would work on the doorknob, as well.

All that would be between her and Mama was that flimsy chain and that dresser, which she had managed to move by herself with only a little strain.

The bathroom, she thought. That door would lock and Mama had no key, at least not on her key ring.

"Vivian, bathroom," she commanded the dog, then grabbed onto its harness as it led her to the master bedroom, which Mama had let her have because it had a private bathroom.

She closed the bedroom door and found her rocking chair a few feet away and pushed it in front of the door. She took a moment to reorient herself, then counted the 20 steps she knew it took from the door to the bathroom.

She called the dog in with her, locked the door behind them, and pressed her ear to it to check on Mama's progress. The chain didn't hold because Mama was now slamming the door against the dresser.

Mira backed up and felt for the toilet seat, closed the lid and sat down, snapping her fingers for Vivian to come.

She went through her options. She could wrap the shower curtain around her and just run out the door past Mama. Maybe the thick, plastic curtain would stop those things from getting inside her. But where would she go from there?

If she could make it to the balcony maybe she could grab Mama and try to push her over the railing.

Maybe she should just go there now and jump

Condo by the Lake

before Mama got in. But what about Vivian? Should she take her along? She didn't want her to starve to death alone in here.

She got up and reached for the curtain and began unfastening it from the rings. Vivian let out a little whine and Mira stopped, kneeled down and hugged the dog tightly. Vivian's tongue licked her face in return.

"We're gonna be OK, baby, don't worry."

Mira held her still against her body as the dog licked at her right arm. She rubbed her left hand down across its ribs, checking for injuries but finding no wounds, then began to scratch that spot on her bottom that Vivian loved.

She stopped when she felt a tongue lick that hand. She moved her hand up slowly and found Vivian's ears and snout, while whatever was on her other end still licked at her right arm.

The last thing she heard after Mama burst through the bedroom door was a loud pop, like a balloon bursting.

The end?

Not quite . . .

Have you read the other three volumes yet?

Tales from The Lake Vol.1—Remember those dark and scary nights spent telling ghost stories and other campfire stories? With the *Tales from The Lake* horror anthologies, you can relive some of those memories by reading the best Dark Fiction stories around. Includes Dark Fiction stories and poems by horror greats such as Graham Masterton, Bev Vincent, Tim Curran, Tim Waggoner, Elizabeth Massie, and many more. Be sure to check out our website for future *Tales from The Lake* volumes.

Tales from The Lake Vol.2—Beneath this lake you'll find nothing but mystery and suspense, horror and dread. Not to mention death and misery—tales to share around the campfire or living room floor from the likes of Ramsey Campbell, Jack Ketchum, and Edward Lee.

Tales from The Lake Vol.3—Dive into the deep end of the lake with 19 tales of terror, selected by Monique Snyman. Including short stories by Mark Allan Gunnells, Kate Jonez, Kenneth W. Cain, and many more.

If you enjoyed this book, I'm sure you'll also like the following Crystal Lake titles:

Quiet Places: A Novella of Cosmic Folk Horror by Jasper Bark—The people of Dunballan, harbour a dark secret. A secret more terrible than the Beast that stalks the dense forests of Dunballan. A secret that holds David McCavendish, last in a long line of Lairds, in its unbreakable grip.

The eleven stories in *Ugly Little Things* by Todd Keisling explore the depths of **human suffering and ugliness**, charting a course to the dark, horrific heart of the human condition. The **terrors of everyday existence** are laid bare in this eerie collection of short fiction from the twisted mind of Todd Keisling, author of the critically-acclaimed novels *A Life Transparent* and *The Liminal Man*.

Behold! Oddities, Curiosities and Undefinable Wonders—Want to see something weird? Embrace the odd. Satisfy your curiosity. Surrender to wonder. Includes short stories by Neil Gaiman, Clive Barker, Lisa Morton, Ramsey Campbell, John Langan, Kristi DeMeester and many more.

Whispered Echoes by Paul F. Olson—Journey through the Heart of Terror in this eerie short story collection. Listen. They are calling to you. Do you hear them? They are the whispered echoes of your darkest fears.

Twice Upon an Apocalypse—Lovecraftian Fairy Tales—From the darkest depths of Grimm and

Anderson come the immortal mash-ups with the creations of HP Lovecraft. These aren't your mother's fairy tales.

The Third Twin—A Dark Psychological Thriller by Darren Speegle—Some things should never be bred . . . Amid tribulation, death, madness, and institutionalization, a father fights against a scientist's bloody bid to breed a theoretical third twin.

Embers: A Collection of Dark Fiction by Kenneth W. Cain—These short speculative stories are the smoldering remains of a fire, the fiery bits meant to ignite the mind with slow-burning imagery and haunting details. These are the slow burning embers of Cain's soul.

Aletheia: A Supernatural Thriller by J.S. Breukelaar—A tale of that most human of monsters—memory—Aletheia is part ghost story, part love story, a novel about the damage done, and the damage yet to come. About terror itself. Not only for what lies ahead, but also for what we think we have left behind.

Beatrice Beecham's Cryptic Crypt by Dave Jeffery—The fate of the world rests in the hands of four dysfunctional teenagers and a bunch of oddball adults. What could possibly go wrong?

Visions of the Mutant Rain Forest—the solo and collaborative stories and poems of Robert Frazier and Bruce Boston's exploration of the Mutant Rain Forest.

Where the Dead Go to Die by Mark Allan Gunnells and Aaron Dries—Post-infection Chicago. Christmas. There are monsters in this world. And they used to be us. Now it's time to euthanize to survive in a hospice where Emily, a woman haunted by her past, only wants to do her job and be the best mother possible. But it won't be long before that snow-speckled ground will be salted by blood.

Brief Encounters with My Third Eye by Bruce Boston—over one hundred of Boston's best short poems (under fifty lines) from more than forty years of publishing, including fifteen award-winning poems.

Biographies

Maria Alexander is a multiple Bram Stoker Award-winning author of both YA and adult fiction, and a long-time student of Japanese swordsmanship (don't ask her which is mightier. You might regret it). She lives in Los Angeles with two ungrateful cats, a Jewish Christmas caroler, and a purse called Trog. Want more? Visit www.mariaalexander.net.

Originally from Maine, **T.G. Arsenault** retired from the U.S. Air Force after 22 years. He is the author of *Forgotten Souls* and *Bleeding the Vein*, and recently finished his latest novel, *Fall of an Empire*. His short fiction has appeared in multiple online venues and print anthologies and received an honorable mention in the *Year's Best Fantasy and Horror, Sixteenth Edition*. Visit T.G. Arsenault at www.tgarsenault.com.

Michael Bailey is the multi-award-winning author of *Palindrome Hannah*, *Phoenix Rose*, and *Psychotropic Dragon* (novels), *Scales and Petals*, and *Inkblots and Blood Spots* (short story / poetry collections), *Enso* (a children's book), and editor of *Pellucid Lunacy*, *Qualia Nous*, *The Library of the Dead*, and the Chiral Mad anthologies published by Written Backwards. He is also an editor for Dark Regions Press, where he has created dark science fiction projects like *You, Human*. He is currently at work on a science fiction thriller, *Seen in Distant Stars*, and a new fiction collection, *The Impossible Weight of Life*.

Max Booth III was raised in Northern Indiana and now lives in the forgotten basement of a hotel somewhere in the surreal void of Texas. He's the Editor-in-Chief of Perpetual Motion Machine and the Managing Editor of Dark Moon Digest. His latest novel is *The Nightly Disease*. Follow him on Twitter @GiveMeYourTeeth or visit him at www.TalesFromTheBooth.com.

Kealan Patrick Burke is the Bram Stoker Award-winning author of *The Turtle Boy*, *King*, and *Sour Candy*. Visit him on the web at www.kealanpatrickburke.com

Mark Cassell lives in a rural part of the UK with his wife and a number of animals. He often dreams of dystopian futures, peculiar creatures, and flitting shadows. Primarily a horror writer, his steampunk, dark fantasy, and SF stories have featured in numerous anthologies and e-zines. His best-selling debut novel, *The Shadow Fabric*, is closely followed by the popular short story collection, *Sinister Stitches*, and are both only a fraction of an expanding mythos.

Jeff Cercone is a journalist living in Chicago. His fiction has appeared in *The Best of Horror Library, Vol. 1-5*.

Born in Texas and currently wandering somewhere in Utah, **David Dunwoody** writes subversive horror fiction including the Strange Dead series, *Hell Walks*, *The 3 Egos* and the collection *Dark Entities*. His fiction has been published by outfits such as Gallery, Shroud, Dark Regions, Permuted and Chaosium.

Ben Eads is a writer, author, and editor of horror fiction. A true horror writer by heart, he wrote his first story at the tender age of six. The look on the teacher's face when she read it was priceless. Since then, his fiction has been published by *Shroud Magazine*, numerous anthologies, and his first novella *Cracked Sky* was published by the Bram Stoker Award-wining press Omnium Gatherum. He loves martial arts and is a student of the Japanese sword.

A life-long resident of New York's haunted Hudson Valley, **JG Faherty** has been a finalist for both the Bram Stoker Award® (*The Cure*, *Ghosts of Coronado Bay*) and ITW Thriller Award (*The Burning Time*), and he is the author of 5 novels, 9 novellas, and more than 50 short stories. He writes adult and YA dark fiction/sci-fi/fantasy, and his works range from quiet suspense to over-the-top comic gruesomeness. As a child, his favorite playground was a 17th-century cemetery, which many people feel explains a lot. You can follow him at www.twitter.com/jgfaherty, www.facebook.com/jgfaherty, www.jgfaherty.com, and http://jgfaherty-blog.blogspot.com/

Bruce Golden's short stories have been published in more than 30 anthologies and across a score of countries. Asimov's Science Fiction described his second novel, "If Mickey Spillane had collaborated with both Frederik Pohl and Philip K. Dick, he might have produced Bruce Golden's *Better Than Chocolate*"—and about his novel *Evergreen*, "If you can imagine Ursula Le Guin channeling H. Rider Haggard, you'll have the barest conception of this stirring book, which centers around a mysterious artifact and the people in its thrall." Golden's upcoming novel, *Monster Town*, is a satirical take on the world of the hardboiled detective, one populated by the monsters of old black and white horror movies. http://goldentales.tripod.com

T.E. Grau is the author of dozens of stories and other written works, including the books *The Mission*, *Triptych: Three Cosmic Tales*, *The Lost Aklo Stories*, and *The Nameless Dark*, which was nominated for a 2015 Shirley Jackson Award for Single-Author Collection, and ranks as the bestselling book published by Lethe Press in both 2015 and 2016. His most recent work is the Dark Muse Award-winning novella *They Don't Come Home Anymore*, which was published in late 2016 through UK press This Is Horror. Grau lives in Los Angeles with his wife and daughter, and is currently working on his third novella, second collection, and first novel.

Michael Haynes lives in Central Ohio. An ardent short story reader and writer, Michael has had stories appear in venues such as Ellery Queen Mystery Magazine, Beneath Ceaseless Skies, and Nature. His website is http://michaelhaynes.info/

Sheldon Higdon has had numerous publications in various magazines and anthologies such as Rue Morgue Magazine, *Writers on Writing, Vol. 4*, Portland Magazine, Shroud Magazine, *Shock Totem 4.5: Holiday Tales of the Macabre and Twisted*, *Madhouse* anthology, and *Death, Be Not Proud* anthology, to name a few. He is also an award-winning screenwriter.
www.sheldonhigdon.com @sheldonhigdon.

Del Howison is a four-time nominee and a winner of the Bram Stoker Award. He has also been nominated for the Shirley Jackson and the Black Quill awards. For over two decades along with his wife Susan, he has owned Dark Delicacies "The Home of Horror" in Burbank California.

Timothy Johnson is a writer and editor living in Washington, D.C. He is the author of the sci-fi/horror novel *Carrier*. Nothing frightens him more than the future, so he writes about it in hopes that he is wrong. Find him at www.timothyjohnsonfiction.com.

E.E. King is a performer, writer, biologist and painter. Ray Bradbury says King's stories " . . . are marvelously inventive, wildly funny and deeply thought provoking. I cannot recommend them highly enough." Her books include *Dirk Quigby's Guide to the Afterlife* and *Another Happy Ending*, available on-line, in print and audio. The New Short Fiction Series, Los Angeles' longest running spoken word series, launched her first anthology, *Real Conversations with*

Imaginary Friends sponsored by Barnes & Noble. King has won numerous awards and is published widely. She's worked with children in Bosnia, crocodiles in Mexico, frogs in Puerto Rico, egrets in Bali, Mushrooms in Montana, archaeologists in Spain and butterflies in South Central Los Angeles. Check out her stories, paintings and publications at: http://www.elizabetheveking.com

In addition to over twenty-five years of speculative fiction writing, **Leigh M. Lane** has a third-degree black belt in karate, performed the National Anthem for the opening of a Dodger's game, and sung lead and backup vocals in bands ranging from classic rock to the blues. She currently lives in the dusty outskirts of Sin City with her husband, an editor and educator, and the recently departed spirit of one very spoiled, very missed cat.

Joe R. Lansdale is the author of over fifty novels, among them *The Bottoms*, The Hap and Leaonard series, *Freezer Burn*, *Sunset and Sawdust*, *A Fine Dark Line*, and others. Lansdale has written approximately four hundred short pieces, stories, essays, introductions, articles, and is the author of numerous comic book scripts, and TV scripts for Batman the Animated Series, as well as Superman the Animated Series. He wrote the screenplay for the animated movie, *Son of Batman*. His works have been turned into the films *Bubba Hotep* and *Cold in July*, the TV episode for *Masters of Horror*, "Incident On and Off a Mountain Road," as well as the hit TV series, *Hap and Leonard* on Sundance Channel, for which he wrote the fifty episodes of the second season. His tenth Hap and Leonard novel, *Rusty Puppy*, and a short story collection of their adventures, *Hap and Leonard, Blood and Lemonade*, have recently been published.

Hunter Liguore holds degrees in history and writing. A three-time Pushcart-Prize nominee (including 2017), her work has appeared in over a hundred publications worldwide, including: Orion Magazine, Bellevue Literary Review, Irish Times, The Mindfulness Bell, Great Plains Quarterly, Strange Horizon, and many more. Her eco-fiction novel, *Silent Winter*, is forthcoming from Harvard Square Editions. www.hunterliguore.org

Jennifer Loring has been, among other things, a DJ, an insurance claims assistant, and an editor. Her short fiction has been published widely both online and in print; she has worked with Crystal Lake Publishing, DarkFuse, and Crowded Quarantine, among many others. Longer work most notably includes the contemporary/sports romance series The Firebird Trilogy and the psychological horror novella *Conduits*. She lives in Philadelphia, PA with her husband, their turtle, and two basset hounds.

Gene O'Neill has seen 160 of his stories, novellas, and novelettes published. Some of these have been collected into seven collections. In addition, he's had seven novels published. He's been a Stoker finalist eleven times, winning once for *Taste of Tenderloin*, a collection, and once for *The Blue Heron*, a novella. Upcoming in 2017 are the last volume in The Cal Wild

Chronicles, six short stories, a novelette, and a novella. He has hopes that his long book, *The White Plague Chronicles* has found a publisher.

Darren Speegle's short fiction has appeared in various venues, including Clarkesworld, Subterranean, Subterranean: Tales of Dark Fantasy, Cemetery Dance, The Third Alternative, and Crimewave. His latest collection, *A Haunting in Germany and Other Stories*, was published in 2016 by PS Publishing. He's several books coming in 2017-18, including the novels *The Third Twin* from Crystal Lake and *Artifacts* from Dark Regions. Dark Regions will also be publishing his co-edited (with Michael Bailey) anthology, *Adam's Ladder*. Collections are forthcoming from Raw Dog Screaming Press and Crystal Lake Publishing.

Damien Angelica Walters is the author of *Sing Me Your Scars* (Apex Publications, 2015), Paper Tigers (Dark House Press, 2016), and the forthcoming *Cry Your Way Home* (Apex Publications, 2017). Her short fiction has been nominated twice for a Bram Stoker Award, reprinted in The Year's Best Dark Fantasy & Horror and The Year's Best Weird Fiction, and published in various anthologies and magazines, including the 2016 World Fantasy Award Finalist *Cassilda's Song*, Cemetery Dance, Nightmare Magazine, and Black Static. She lives in Maryland with her husband and two rescued pit bulls. Find her on Twitter @DamienAWalters or on the web at http://damienangelicawalters.com.

Cynthia Ward has published stories in Asimov's Science Fiction, Shattered Prism, Weird Tales, Athena's Daughters, and other anthologies and magazines. She edited the anthologies Lost Trails: Forgotten Tales of the Weird West Volumes One and Two for WolfSinger Publications. With Nisi Shawl, Cynthia co-created the groundbreaking Writing the Other fiction writers workshop and coauthored the diversity fiction-writing handbook *Writing the Other: A Practical Approach* (Aqueduct Press). Her short novel, *The Adventure of the Incognita Countess*, is available from Aqueduct Press.

Connect with Crystal Lake Publishing:

Website:
www.crystallakepub.com

Be sure to sign up for our newsletter and receive a free eBook: http://eepurl.com/xfuKP

Books:
http://www.crystallakepub.com/books.php

Twitter:
https://twitter.com/crystallakepub

Facebook:
https://www.facebook.com/Crystallakepublishing/
https://www.facebook.com/Talesfromthelake/
https://www.facebook.com/WritersOnWritingSeries/

Google+:
https://plus.google.com/u/1/107478350897139952572

Pinterest:
https://za.pinterest.com/crystallakepub/

Instagram:
https://www.instagram.com/crystal_lake_publishing/

Tumblr:
https://www.tumblr.com/blog/crystal-lake-publishing

Patreon:
https://www.patreon.com/CLP

With unmatched success since 2012, Crystal Lake Publishing has quickly become one of the world's leading indie publishers of Mystery, Thriller, and Suspense books with a Dark Fiction edge.

Crystal Lake Publishing puts integrity, honor and respect at the forefront of our operations.

We strive for each book and outreach program that's launched to not only entertain and touch or comment on issues that affect our readers, but also to strengthen and support the Dark Fiction field and its authors.

Not only do we publish authors who are legends in the field and as hardworking as us, but we look for men and women who care about their readers and fellow human beings. We only publish the very best Dark Fiction, and look forward to launching many new careers.

We strive to know each and every one of our readers, while building personal relationships with our authors, reviewers, bloggers, pod-casters, bookstores and libraries.

Crystal Lake Publishing is and will always be a beacon of what passion and dedication, combined with overwhelming teamwork and respect, can accomplish: Unique fiction you can't find anywhere else.

We do not just publish books, we present you worlds within your world, doors within your mind, from talented authors who sacrifice so much for a moment of your time.

This is what we believe in. What we stand for. This will be our legacy.

Welcome to Crystal Lake Publishing.

We hope you enjoyed this title. If so, we'd be grateful if you could leave a review on your blog or any of the other websites and outlets open to book reviews. Reviews are like gold to writers and publishers, since word-of-mouth is and will always be the best way to market a great book. And remember to keep an eye out for more of our books.

THANK YOU FOR PURCHASING THIS BOOK

Lightning Source UK Ltd.
Milton Keynes UK
UKHW02f1008081117
312356UK00005B/196/P